CM Elliott was born in the UK, educated in Australia and has worked in the safari industry in Zimbabwe for many years. She took up writing in 2010. *Sibanda and the Death's Head Moth* is her second novel.

First published by Jacana Media (Pty) Ltd in 2015

10 Orange Street
Sunnyside
Auckland Park 2092
South Africa
+2711 628 3200
www.jacana.co.za

ISBN 978-1-4314-2148-0

Cover design by publicide
Set in Berkeley 11/15pt
Printed and bound by Creda Communications
Job no. 002458

Also available as an e-book:
d-PDF 978-1-4314-2242-5
ePUB 978-1-4314-2243-2
mobi file 978-1-4314-2244-9

See a complete list of Jacana titles at www.jacana.co.za

Sibanda and the Death's Head Moth

CM Elliott

For Alan

CHAPTER 1

Detective Inspector Jabulani Sibanda sat bolt upright in bed as though zapped by a scorpion. Something was wrong. He didn't believe in superstition or omens, but he'd had this feeling before, gut-wrenching gloom in the pit of his stomach and an elephant sitting on his chest, squeezing the oxygen from his lungs. It always spelled trouble for someone. He threw back the covers and drew back the curtains to a thick puddle of blue-black ink that spilled smoothly from the north-eastern sky, blotting out the Gubu township dawn and staining the first sunlit page of the day. It threatened to bring heavy rain. Whatever had dragged him from a deep sleep was out there beyond the houses and shacks. He grabbed a swig of water and, with the crust of sleep still clinging to his lashes, he pushed through his front door and loped gently for some metres. Nothing was stirring; most of the village was still asleep.

The air was moist and sticky with promise. It didn't deliver the fresh jolt Sibanda was hoping for, but he would settle for tepid fug if it meant the rains would come. This year, they had been erratic. Gubu district and Matabeleland North in general had been overlooked by the gods of falling water. Officer-in-Charge, Gubu police, Stalin Mfumu, and his congregation, The Brethren of the Lord's Blood, were exhorting everyone to pray for rain on Fridays at noon; as a result, the police station came to a halt.

He stepped up his pace to a steady jog and headed like a homing pigeon for the railway line, crossing over and working his way westwards toward the very limit of the village where it met bushland

and the edge of the National Park. He was driven on by instinct or intuition or just plain madness. He didn't know which. The bonus to his detective's hunch was that, this early in the morning, he might catch sight of a few nocturnal species, lingering, knocked out of habit by the darkening sky. Leopards in particular loved an overcast day. They languished like liquid kings in the soft light, draping their bodies over branches. Sibanda looked for hanging tails, the unnatural straightness a giveaway among the gnarled and twisted limbs.

Sibanda was running effortlessly now with the lazy grace of the leopard he hoped to glimpse, scanning the track for the trouble he expected. He headed to Buffalo Avenue, the last road in the village. To the right lay bushland unsullied by human habitation until it nudged the Botswana border. To the left, a row of dilapidated railway houses looking out across the rolling Kalahari sandveld of grassland and teak forest. There weren't many; the railway network had diminished in recent times. Gubu was no longer a great rail hub. It only hosted an occasional goods train or a collier when the drag line at the Hwange pit was working. The houses lay empty. The drivers and stokers, the conductors and station masters had been shunted into a forgotten spur on a track going nowhere.

Sibanda, still driven by the certainty of crime, was scanning the road for a clue, any hint of what might have happened. He noted fresh, wet, elephant signs on the potholed road. The elephants had started to graze on the summer grasses; gone were the dry, stringy, bark-filled droppings of winter. Slightly older, darker coils of buffalo pats dotted the lacy tarmac that had been excavated by previous rains and filigreed with neglect. The Park herds didn't understand boundaries; the villagers didn't understand their taking of territorial liberties. This very road marked the conflict between man and beast. Baboons had raided the mango trees, plucking the fruit indiscriminately and discarding anything unripe, leaving behind a trail of half-eaten fruit, fibrous pips, crushed leaves and very human-like excrement. No, not a road for the fainthearted; he wished he lived there.

A flash of lightning stripped across the morning sky followed on its heels by a crash of thunder. Maybe nothing had gone on, maybe it was just the heavy weather that was messing with his mood, flooding his gut with karmic antibodies that were hounding him. An even louder, closer clap of thunder caused him to flinch. It was pointless. His reaction would be too late. If lightning struck, he would never hear the thunder, never know what hit him. He put on a spurt. He was wasting his time and perhaps there would be rain sooner than he thought. He didn't want to get caught in a torrent to satisfy some ridiculous whim.

His thoughts strayed, as he sprinted, to the last storm he had been caught up in – literally and figuratively. His chase through the bush after the viscous, twisted *muthi* murderer had taken place on a stormy night with lashing rain and fierce lightning. The administrative thunderstorm that followed was an even bigger squall. An influential governor had been questioned as part of the investigation. Sibanda had been hauled well and truly over the coals for breaking protocol without authority. He had narrowly missed demotion. None of that worried the detective though. He had crossed swords with the powerful before, and nothing would stop him from doing his job. It was the personal turmoil of meeting up with Berry again and losing her for a second time that was causing him sleepless nights. Not that she had ever been his in the first place.

He came to an abrupt halt near the last house in the road as if the grapple hooks of the gods had reined him in. It was a solitary and abandoned relic of the colonial railway service with a shabby veranda, cracked windows and a front door that hung listlessly from its hinges. He sensed he was near to whatever was causing the unease. The racing wind, sucked to areas already cooled off by rain, was bristling the leaves of a couple of teak trees. Sibanda jogged on the spot, deciding whether to go in, but his instinct told him otherwise.

Pity, he thought, he would like to move to a house like this, but now was not the time to explore. The dwelling was surrounded by bush on two sides and, being on a bend, faced away from the distant neighbours. The nearest inhabited house was probably two hundred metres away. He would need time, money, influence and reams of bureaucracy to secure the unwanted lodging, none of which he had access to, or patience for.

His reverie probably saved his life.

The detective left the width of Buffalo Avenue, loping like a wild dog on fresh blood spoor and took a narrow path through the bush. It led back in a loop to the centre of the village and his house in the vibrant eastern township of Soweto, named, almost as a joke, for a much more famous, but equally crowded conurbation on the western boundary of a much larger city. So far there was nothing out of place. Was he mistaken? Was his mind playing tricks? But the churning hadn't gone away, his disaster-meter was still on red alert. Sibanda kept his wits about him in the high grass. He could run full tilt into an old buffalo bull, a cantankerous old dagga boy who wouldn't think twice about charging at anything that irritated. Or worse, a puff adder curled on the path, diamond markings blending with the shadowed sand, too indolent to get out of the way. Cytotoxic fangs in the ankle were the most common bite in this part of the world.

Sibanda was unwittingly focusing his hazard alert wide of the mark, and he was wrong about the lightning. He heard the ear-splitting explosion moments before he was slammed to the ground with such violence that his running vest shredded like cheese through a grater. Winded, deafened and dazed, he lay prone in the high elephant grass a metre from the path and about fifteen metres from a large mopani tree in front of him – or rather, that had been in front of him. It was now reduced to a smouldering bonfire of logs, splinters and shrivelling leaves. The pungent smell of sulphur revived him with the jolt of smelling salts. His understanding was immediate, arriving in a wave of awareness along with the pain – he had just missed being fried by lightning, his thigh was in agony and this was the rendezvous he had been led to. He touched his leg. The exploration produced a handful of blood. He had been stabbed by a large shard of wood, sharpened and hurled like a dagger by the powerful blast. It was still embedded in his flesh.

Once his lungs reinflated, he stood up, the wooden wedge still sticking out of his thigh. It had missed the major arteries, a small consolation for the pain he was in. He couldn't walk even though he had to go forward. The impulse was strong.

He had no choice. He grasped the wooden stiletto and wrenched it from his thigh with one great heave, collapsing in a groaning heap. He cursed every bad word he knew in every language and dialect he could remember. When he had recovered enough to move again, he bound the wound as best he could with strips of his running shirt. It was several minutes before he levered himself up with the aid of a branch, intact despite the explosion. Using this makeshift crutch he limped along the path with some urgency until he came level with the site of the strike.

Around the stricken mopani, the grass for a wide radius was flattened and burnt, and several small fires were smouldering at the periphery. The wind that had earlier blown up was gusting and encouraging the flames to grow. Sibanda groaned. He had no option but to try to extinguish them before they flared up and became a bush fire. The tall grass was tinder dry and leaf litter lay in small hillocks, gathered by the wind. There was plenty of fuel lingering from winter to start a fire big enough to threaten Gubu village.

He hobbled around the circumference of the burn, hopping and stamping out the licking flames with his good foot until he was satisfied the site was safe. And then Sibanda's internal radar was suddenly beeping with the frequency of a scud missile honed onto a target. He leaned heavily on his branch. The breeze that chased away the bubbling, magenta clouds had stirred up ashes and unearthed a distinctive smell hiding behind the sulphurous vapours – burning flesh, and if Sibanda wasn't mistaken, burning human flesh. He had only smelled it once before, but it assaulted his nostrils now as it had that day in Nottingham, where he was on secondment. A little terrace had gone up aided by an accelerant, incinerating a young mother and her toddler triplets. He had been sent along with others on the first response team. The fire fighters in attendance took one look at his youth and wished him a strong stomach.

'You'll not see worse than this,' one of them said, as they left the burnt-out building, rolling up hoses, tipping back visors and checking equipment in a sort of mechanical routine designed to minimise the impact of viewing burnt babies.

Sibanda had no routine or distracting behaviour to fall back on. The horror and suffering of the scene seeped into his psyche, raw and not yet numbed by experience. He hoped he would never see the like again. He returned to the station white faced.

'If you can tolerate that, lad, then we'll make a copper of you yet. We might even make an Englishman of you if you continue to turn pale,' commented the grizzled duty sergeant with a chuckle.

Sibanda did not take offence. He knew none was meant. 'I'm not sure I want to be a policeman if I'm going to be dealing with people who can do this.' He kept his thoughts on becoming an Englishman to himself.

'You'll get over it. Those black, contorted crisps huddled together in a corner will fade from your memory and you'll be the better cop for it. We see sights every day in this job, sights the general public can only guess at, depravity not yet invented, even by the tabloids. Put your disgust to good use. Get the bastard that did this. It's a rum old world, son, full of more deadly sins than you can shake a biblical fist at. Welcome to it.'

He had taken the advice to heart, although he didn't sleep that night for the visions that came when he closed his eyes. He had several tormented nights over the next couple of weeks, but they did catch the arsonist, the mother's boyfriend; he had wanted the children gone. They cried and complained and kept their mother occupied when her attention should have been focused solely on him. Sibanda remembered thinking how close to animals the human species was. Lions did that, killed and ate cubs so that the mother would come into season again – lust, the deadliest of the sins in any species.

The old sergeant had been right. The tableau of twisted, charred corpses had faded, but the memory of the stench had remained. It had clung to his clothes and crawled up his nostrils with long claws like a bat finding its roost. It was unfurling its wings again now.

Sibanda hopped across the burnt ground, stirring up the black snow of carbonised grass with his makeshift crutch. He used it, balancing on one leg like a marabou stalk, to dig around in the smouldering branches and fragmented wreckage of the tree. The mopani had been in full leaf and the fallen canopy made a good fist of concealing anything beneath it. It took a while to push aside the debris, but Sibanda rummaged harder as the stink of the sizzled flesh became overpowering. It brought back long-buried images.

He unearthed an arm first. The fingers were clawed. The heat had shrivelled and contracted the tendons. A few fingers were missing and some flesh torn from the bones. Squatting on his one good leg, he gently lowered himself into a sitting position. The pulse was gone. He hadn't expected one. No one could have survived lightning at the heart of the strike. Could he have saved this man if he'd run faster, told him not to shelter under a tree? Was this what all his early morning angst was about?

He glanced at the display on his phone. It was already 6:14am. He hit the button for Gubu station and was grateful when Police Constable Khumalo answered. She was the most switched on of all the constables at Gubu.

'Zanele, who's on duty?' he cut off the niceties of station telephone etiquette.

'Is that you, sir?'

'Yes, it's me, Zee. Is Sergeant Ncube there?'

'No, he came in at six, but he's already on his way to roadblock duty on the Vic Falls road at Gwaai.'

Sibanda clicked his teeth in frustration. Ncube had been with him on the previous case, a murder for body parts and *muthi,* involving political untouchables. The sergeant had come in for censure by association. The whole station knew he hated roadblock duty. They knew he objected to the mindless checking of licences and the unloading of overstuffed buses full of travellers who had passed through several similar stops on the way from Bulawayo. Each roadblock delayed the journey by at least fifteen minutes and exacted a toll to line the pockets of the underpaid police. Ncube didn't have the stomach for corruption, bribery or terrorising weary travellers, although he did have a stomach ... Sibanda smiled wryly at the girth of the jovial sergeant and wished he was here now.

'I need someone at the path leading from Buffalo Avenue to Giraffe Way. There's a body, a lightning victim. The corpse has to be guarded until an ambulance can get here.'

'That'll make it four this month. We had three deaths a couple of weeks ago near Cross Gubu,' she said, referring to the small group of shops and houses that had grown up at the point where the Gubu road intersected the main road. 'Why do people shelter under trees during a rain storm? It's crazy; don't they know it's a death wish?'

'So, who have you got for me, Zee?'

'Constable Tshuma, sir, he's new, just been posted here.'

'Does he know the village yet? Can he get here without getting lost?'

'I'll give him directions, but he'll have to walk. The only vehicle we have running is on its way to drop the roadblock detail off at Gwaai. It'll be at least an hour.'

'Right, get Tshuma on his way then.'

Sibanda pocketed his phone and lamented the demise of the station's other vehicle, an antique Land Rover, Miss Daisy. She was the most cantankerous, unreliable, steam-snorting vehicle he had ever come across, but she had four wheels and consented to move on a good day. She had been languishing in the station car park for some weeks and the only trip she was likely to take was to the wrecker's yard.

Something Constable Khumalo had said struck home. There had been no rain worth sheltering from so what was this person doing under a tree this early in the morning? He dug further with his stick, uncovering more of the body. A lightning strike usually left a hideous exit wound. A standing victim might have his feet blown off or a severe leg wound. By the time the electrical charge exited the body in a blow hole of energy, it had cooked most of the internal organs. So far this victim was only displaying injuries associated with a blast and some burning from the pyre of logs. It was difficult working from a sitting position and with one leg throbbing, but he managed to move a large branch that had been covering most of the body, revealing a face untouched by flame, but obliterated by fury. This man looked as though he had been shot through the head.

The detective studied the wound. It was massive and gruesome. A large section of the forehead was missing, exposing the brain. The back of the head was blown away. Could this have been caused by the electrical blast or a shard of wood like his personal mopani dagger? He stroked his chin as he thought. Violent death was rarely a clean-cut affair.

He hauled himself in closer. His instincts were not wrong. The injury had the distinctive hallmarks of a bullet wound. The damaged skull bone showed the tell-tale signs of inward bevelling left by a round. It was difficult to get a better look at the bullet channel because he couldn't squat over the body. He bent forward from his sitting position and got as near to the opening as he could. It was not a pretty sight. Fragments from the skull had been carried into the brain. The back of the head had been blown away, dwarfing the damage at the front. What weapon could have caused so much damage? It had to be something low velocity, relying on destruction over energy and speed. This wasn't the sort of damage that came from a high-calibre rifle – a shotgun maybe? But there were no signs of dispersed pellets. Sibanda's brain began to tick over, flicking through references to previous gun crimes he had investigated. Nothing fitted the bill.

Sibanda was about to straighten his back, beginning to ache and cramp from the strange posture he was forced to adopt, when he spotted something out of place in the bloody crater. It wasn't bone or a bullet fragment. It had a frayed edge. Carefully, and against all police crime-scene protocol, he teased the foreign body from the cerebral cortex of the victim. A piece of fabric had been carried into the brain. Had the victim been wearing a hat or a cap? If so, there was no sign of it now. He should have left it up to Forensics to decide, but they were notoriously slow in getting results.

Sibanda straightened and hoisted himself upright using his crutch. The renewed blood flow to his thigh sent fresh waves of pain to his own wound. He took a moment to recover.

The detective heard the pounding of size tens on the sandy track before he saw the accompanying body. Around the bend in full trot swung a young police officer.

'Hello, sir, I am Police Constable Tshuma, here to guard the body.' The young man was breathing hard from exertion. It was a fair run from the station, but he had done it in good time.

Sibanda took in the impressive constable. He was smartly dressed, fit looking and had an intelligent glint in his eye. Perhaps things were looking up if this was the calibre coming to Gubu these days.

'Constable, the victim is no longer simply a lightning casualty. He has a bullet wound. I'm returning to the station. I'll send more support and alert Forensics. This site will have to be scrutinised with a fine-tooth comb to find anything that survived the blast. Don't touch a thing.'

'Yes, sir, do you think it's a suicide or a suspicious death?'

'Impossible to tell with all the destruction to the site and the body,' but even as he answered he knew without doubt this was a murder. His sixth sense had been right. He had done well not to ignore it. Unseen, he slipped the bloodied square of cloth between the screen and cover of his phone and began to stumble away down the path leaning heavily on his branch, aware he made a pathetic sight.

'Are you alright, sir? You are limping. Can I run back to the station for help?' the young constable was both eager and concerned.

Sibanda turned, 'No, thanks Tshuma. Look after the evidence. I can manage.' In turning, he caught sight of a movement from one of the logs that hadn't fully burnt. A swarm of bees was exiting a knot hole in the fallen limb, frantically buzzing around what was now a destroyed hive. From their confusion and panic emerged a moth, much larger than the bees, but striped in similar fashion. On its thorax was a perfectly formed skull and crossbones, like the Jolly Roger on a pirate galleon. Nature didn't normally mimic such a distinctive human design. It was always the other way around. The detective registered the unusual markings and thought he would look it up. These things interested him.

CHAPTER 2

'Tomorrow, I'm on roadblock duty,' Sergeant Ncube had announced at dinner the previous evening, once the little ones had been put to bed. He shared his disappointment with his wives not only out of frustration, but because he knew they would lavish sympathy on him. There would be something special in his breakfast and lunch boxes. He was not wrong and he needed the extra attention at the moment. He had a lot on his mind.

'I will prepare my *amaqanda esidlekeni* for you,' Suko the youngest of his wives chirped in, 'it will cheer you as the day opens and give you heart and strength to deal with the drivers.'

'That will be *mnandi*, delicious, Sukoluhle. I am honoured.'

He had watched Suko as she had taken two fresh, brown speckled eggs collected from her hens that morning, and boiled them gently. She mashed some baked beans, added a little fried onion and chopped chilli and plastered it to the roughed-up outside of the peeled egg. Carefully, she lowered the delicacy into the empty bean tin oiled with cooking fat and lined with a thick paste of leftover mealie meal. Once the egg was sealed in its white nest, the tin was placed at the edge of the fire and turned until the outside coating became crisp and golden. He barely restrained himself from eating it there and then.

'I thank you, my stomach thanks you, and the drivers, who might otherwise be plagued by my irritability, thank you. Suko, you are a queen in the kitchen.' Ncube said this while glancing across to Nomatter, wife number two. She was already busy preparing his lunch. He could smell simmering bones and the pungency of chopped herbs. It would be his favourite: herbed mealie dumplings in a sea of rich gravy. A little competition between his wives was not a bad thing. Sometimes he thought they got on too well. He never favoured one above the other. A leopard, after all, licked all its spots, both black and white.

Blessing, his senior wife, was washing the evening pots. One glance and he knew her sympathy would be dispensed in the sleeping hut.

He reported early for duty the next morning with a sinking feeling in the pit of his stomach, although he hoped the culinary offerings from his wives might allay this shortly. He even snapped at the comely constable Zanele Khumalo. Life recently had become difficult and confusing.

'Check car licences and driving licences,' instructed Stalin Mfumu, Officer-in-Charge, Gubu, seated comfortably behind his desk, 'and there has been a report from Bulawayo of a number of robberies, small electrical stuff, and a stolen car … licence plate …' he hesitated in the interests of accuracy, carefully leafing through some papers. 'ADN 468 – a silver Toyota Hilux. '

'Right, sir,' said a glum Ncube when he received his instructions. He didn't want anything to do with Toyotas of any colour or model after the trouble the last case had got him into.

Constable Khumalo came into the office. Ncube's spirits lifted a little. There was nothing like a well-padded woman to brighten his day, particularly Zanele Khumalo. She oozed the best of Matabele womanhood with plentiful curves, full lips, and eyes that promised something he knew he would like to be on the receiving end of.

'Sir, you should read this before Sergeant Ncube is deployed,' she passed the Officer-in-Charge a report. He read it carefully, two or three times, his lips mouthing the words, nodding his head and murmuring understanding with a bi-tonal 'hmm umm' at the end of each sentence. Stalin Mfumu was a considered man, careful and measured in all his dealings. He was not about to rush an important communication from the Zambian Police.

Sergeant Ncube waited patiently. In fact, he didn't mind the delay at all. Each moment was a reprieve from a day of sorting through bags of blankets and clothing, and intimidating drivers.

Finally Mfumu spoke. 'Sergeant, we have received this report from our Zambian colleagues. They suspect ivory is being smuggled across the border, either through the Livingstone–Victoria Falls border post or, more likely, being ferried across the Zambezi River at night. Zambian game scouts shot a poacher in Livingstone Game Park last week. He gave them some information before he died. Ivory is being funnelled into Zimbabwe and shipped out to unknown destinations.' He placed the report carefully on his desk, ironing out a curled corner with the flat of his hand before transferring it to his in-tray. Mfumu liked order.

'Isn't that National Park's responsibility?' suggested Ncube, suspecting that this extra burden might cause more trouble that it was worth.

'Not if it is on our roads, Sergeant.'

'We will keep our eyes out for it. Rest assured, sir,' said the sergeant, although Ncube didn't believe for one moment that they would discover a shipment of ivory on the main road. Smugglers would be foolish to risk it. Tusks were very big things. Hadn't he been close to them personally, when they were still attached to a live elephant? Much too close, in fact, almost underneath them. He had nearly died of fright. Those massive white teeth, curving in front of tonnes of grey flesh, could easily have pierced the vehicle he was in. He would never have approached so closely, but he was with that mad detective, Jabulani Sibanda. The man might be a gifted detective and a genius in the bush, but he was as dangerous as a stirred-up hornet's nest when it came to wild animals.

'Check every single bus thoroughly and every bag of reasonable size. The smugglers could have sawn the tusks to manageable pieces. They will be cunning and desperate men. One of their gang has been killed.'

Ncube's face fell. His jowls sank onto his collar like a collapsed tent. Even the sight of Constable Khumalo's imperious rear end disappearing through the office door failed to lift them again. Having to sort through every bus would be the bitter end. His calabash of already soured milk had just smashed. It was going to be a doubly long day. He clomped out of Mfumu's office and proceeded to growl like a mangy dog at PC Khumalo over a triviality, a missing pen from the roadblock clipboard. Why was he was being mean to a valued colleague? It was wrong. He had to forget his problems and get back to normal as soon as possible.

Having reached the roadblock, Sergeant Ncube settled his weighty frame onto a convenient log that had been dragged to the site by a previous incumbent. He had donned his vest of shame, a fluorescent yellow affair that slid over his head. It cut into his armpits and only reached as far as his third shirt button like a child who had outgrown his bib. His stomach protruded beneath it – a mountain of consequence. His colleagues had already given him the temporary nickname, *Ibungayezi*, bumble bee. He didn't know it, but he wouldn't have minded if he did. Ncube wasn't a man to bear a grudge and he would see the funny side of the accurate description, fat, black and round with yellow stripes. Roadblock duty was the penance he was paying for tangling with the governor of the province in the previous case he had been involved in. He accepted it. Spilt water cannot be regathered.

A few metres to the north, barely concealed behind a bush, sat an armed officer. Currently, he was leaning against a tree and sucking on a stem of grass. His rifle, an AK assault weapon, leant peacefully against the same tree. Ncube was not at all sure what his role was, or who he was supposed to fire at. He was probably just there to reinforce the menace of the roadblock.

Two female officers in their dark turquoise uniforms and side-pinned trilbies were chatting in the middle of the road, protected by a few misshapen traffic cones and a chipped and faded sign wedged upright by a rock that announced the police roadblock ahead. They had donned fluorescent sleeves which buttoned onto their epaulettes and covered most of their hands. The women were currently idle, chatting, probably exchanging recipes, thought Ncube. Behind the sergeant, a group of reservists in their navy drill fatigues and forage caps stood boasting about the latest football scores. Mandebele Giants had beaten Caps United in an upset that pleased everyone. The local boys were finally showing promise.

Seated on the roadblock log, he opened the plastic container and there lay two nests waiting only for one bite to reveal the eggs within. Perhaps this would be a better day than he imagined. The thought was short lived.

'Sir,' chimed up one of the reservists, 'here come the first of the vehicles. It's a line of taxis followed by a bus and there's a bus coming the other way.'

Ncube snapped the lid back on his tantalising breakfast and stood up, 'Right, this will take all of you. Pull those buses over and go through every bag. Remember we are looking for electrical items and ivory. Check the operating licences as well. I'll handle the *tshovas*.' Gubu was now awake and on its way to work. In the distance Ncube spotted the three local mini buses weaving a plait down the road, stopping to pick up customers and then speeding to get in front of the one ahead. He recognised them and knew some of the drivers. Allah is Great would arrive at the roadblock first, followed by Waiting for Jehovah with Fifth Egg of Life bringing up the rear, in a rare and harmonious meeting of faiths.

Within minutes, the long-distance buses were pulled over and the passengers had alighted. The northbound bus was loaded with a bed and mattress, streaming a bunting of unravelling clear plastic behind it. Twenty or so taxi bags bulging with possessions were wedged and cobbled on the roof along with a plough that had seen better days and a donkey cart without wheels. No wonder the bus leaned precariously on the road shoulder as though any minute it would tip over.

The second bus heading south crabbed to a halt in a belch of black smoke. Ncube knew instantly that the chassis was accident damaged, hence its crippled gait, and the injectors needed seeing to. It should never have been allowed on the road, but roadworthiness was not his concern today. On the roof rack among the assorted baggage were two goats and several cages full of chickens. They seemed happy enough. Animal welfare was not his responsibility either. He had enough on his plate.

There were at least eight roadblocks within four hundred kilometres and that didn't take into account the speed traps and official toll booths. Travel these days was for the long suffering only. He felt remorse for the inconvenience, but could only watch as the blue-headed reservists swarmed over the buses like ants on spilled sugar before turning his attention to Allah is Great.

'*Salibonani*, Banda,' he greeted the driver. It was the nephew of his fishing buddy, Phiri.

'Yebo, Baba Ncube,' said Banda, turning to face the sergeant.

'Licences all in order? No overloading?' A pointless question, he realised. Overloading was the very definition of an African taxi.

The young man passed over his papers, keeping his head turned to the window.

Ncube flicked through them with a cursory glance before circling the vehicle, kicking the back left tyre and checking the disc on the passenger side window. He realised then why Banda was turning his head so sharply, 'Have you been in a fight, young man?'

Banda's hand went up to the large plaster on his right cheek. The swelling around the plaster had almost closed his right eye. The bruising was so bad it coloured the whole side of his face.

'Er, yes, sir. I had, er, too much to um drink … yes, beer at the Blue Gnu and …' Banda was stumbling over his words.

Ncube understood his embarrassment and tension. His uncle was a good Muslim. 'It's okay, Banda, Baba Phiri won't hear of it from me. What does the other man look like?'

Banda looked confused for a moment, 'Oh, er, he's a mess too.'

'On your way, and stay out of the bars in future,' the sergeant waved him back onto the road.

'Yes, sir,' he said with relief.

Allah is Great sped off towards Gubu. Ncube should have checked Banda for alcohol levels, but then drunken driving was not on his list either and, besides which, young Banda hadn't breathed beery breath on him. He'd probably slept it off by now.

The exchange had taken longer than the sergeant had bargained for. A line of cars was banking up behind the remaining two taxis. He waived the mini buses through. They were local, and not likely to be ivory smugglers, although he would have liked to chat to The Fifth Egg of Life to find out how he came by such an interesting name. This reminded him of the *amaqanda esidlekeni,* his own eggs still waiting for him next to his log. He sighed.

He sighed more deeply when he saw a silver Toyota Hilux join the queue. It was driven by a white man. Sergeant Ncube straightened up and tried to pull the fluorescent bib over his large girth. *Mukiwa* drivers at roadblocks were fawning, arrogant or angry, and all three types were judgemental. Normally he waived white people through. It was easier on everyone, but this was an accursed, silver Toyota. The number plates were not ADN 468, but it was easy to buy false ones.

He put on a smile, not a difficult thing to do with a face of practised muscles accustomed to such regular exercise.

'Good morning, how is your journey?' he enquired politely.

'So far, so good,' came a clipped reply full of flat vowels and ugly sounds. There was no music or rhythm in this accented voice.

'Your driving licence and log book, please,' Ncube recognised he was dealing with the arrogant version of the white driver. Minimal contact was prescribed. This man was part of the reason he hated this particular duty.

While the driver rummaged around in an expensive-looking wallet, Ncube had a chance to assess him. Long strands of dung-coloured, curly hair hung down either side of his plate face. It was unusual to see such hair on a *Mukiwa* already an adult of many years. Thin lips stuck out like a duck's bill with barely any flesh between the lips and nose. A narrow forehead overshadowed small, beady eyes like those of the *ingulube*, the bush pig, leaving not enough room for a brain, mused Ncube, and he certainly wouldn't like to be on the other end of them. Even though small they radiated darts of evil like the devil's arrows. Ncube shuddered, grateful he didn't wake up each morning next to them. Poor woman, he sympathised with a likely wife. The duck was short and barely able to peer over the steering wheel. There was not enough room for a heart either, not one that beat with generosity and joy at least. He happily drew his gaze to the passenger, but there was no relief there. The man looked like an albino white man. Ncube didn't know they existed. He had never seen anyone so ugly in all his life. His hair was the colour of a ripe mango, which clashed with the blood red of his lips. His skin was the white of the finest milled mealie meal, peppered with orange weevils.

The pale man spoke as the duck continued to rummage. 'Sorry, Sergeant, my friend here is from overseas. He doesn't have his papers to hand. It will take a couple of minutes.' Brilliant blue eyes radiated warmth and goodwill.

'Not a problem, sir,' Ncube smiled in response and recognised a fawner.

The documents all appeared to be in order. The engine and chassis number matched the log book. Duck Face's driving licence indicated he was from Nottingham in the UK. He recognised the city name. Detective Inspector Jabulani Sibanda had told him about his work there. As Ncube was examining the photograph and wrestling with the unfamiliar details, Pale Face spoke again.

'My friend is here on business. He is a tour operator and lodge representative – Spots and Stripes Safaris. He's bringing tourists back to Zimbabwe. We have come from Victoria Falls and we're heading into the Park now.'

'Then I won't delay you any longer, thank you. You may proceed.' The sergeant dredged up his most formal English words learned from *The Roadblock Manual*. It was important to be correct with foreigners. They expected it somehow. Pale Face waved as they drove off. There was no hand on the end of the arm he saluted with, just a glinting metal hook. Ncube's official face dissolved into surprise and shock. That had been the intention. He was delighted to see the back end of the vehicle disappearing down the road.

'Sir, I will take over now.' He turned, his mouth still agape to see one of the police woman at his shoulder. 'Detective Inspector Sibanda has come to collect you.'

Ncube didn't know what was worse, a one-armed white man with a lethal-looking metal hand at the roadblock, or Jabulani Sibanda standing there like firewood with a scorpion on it. Neither was a comfortable prospect, and both were probably dangerous.

Ncube was beset with turmoil as he walked toward the detective. Jabulani Sibanda was a strange mixture of the irritability of a one-horned cow and the soothing words of a brother. He muddled the sergeant with his clever talk and his intimidating bush knowledge, but he was a dunce around vehicles, and that was a fact.

The very sight of the detective filled Ncube with a jumble of delight and fearful apprehension. They hadn't spoken much since the last case, what was he doing here now?

'Sergeant, it's good to see you again.'

'And you too, sir,' responded Ncube although he could not make up his mind if it was a good thing or not.

'Get your stuff together, we have a suspicious death to investigate, probably a village man. I'm going to need your help.'

'I can't leave this post, sir. The Officer-in-Charge gave me this specific duty. He won't allow me to desert it.'

'Well, he has. You have his permission to accompany me back to Gubu. We need to get this death wrapped up as soon as we can.'

'Are you sure you have authority, sir? I thought you and the Officer-in-Charge were not …' he thought for a moment how to express the hostility that sparked between the two men like a badly connected car battery, '… not on the same side of the river.'

'We are now, Ncube, at least when it comes to you coming with me.'

'How is that, sir? The last time I checked the current was too tricky and much too fierce to cross.'

'Don't ask, Ncube. Just get your stuff. I'll fill you in on the victim, in the vehicle,' he didn't know if the sergeant would fully appreciate the extent of his sacrifice in trading attendance at the next four Friday prayer meetings for Ncube's leaving the roadblock. It had been a delicate negotiation.

'You are limping, sir, are you alright? What happened? Can I support you?'

'It's okay, I just had a run in with a piece of wood. You could drive though. It might be better. That way I can concentrate on the case.'

Of course it would be better, thought Ncube, the detective was a leaden-footed driver, who pumped the accelerator like one of his beloved elephants stamping on an ant. He ignored bumps and potholes and sped like a village dog chasing a hare. Miss Daisy had been on the wrong end of his wild driving. Even though together they had caught the murderous culprit, she had barely escaped with her life. It had taken many hours, a trip to the Central Mechanical Equipment Department in Bulawayo and bribing with multiple strings of smoked fish to get her running smoothly again. Not that anyone at Gubu station knew that. He was not going to reveal that she was a runner. He had simply removed the solenoid until he was ready to forgive the doubters, including the man sitting next to him, and until he was reinstated to patrol duties.

'How did you get the use of this vehicle, sir?' asked Ncube knowing the Santana was rarely released from the sticky grip of Assistant Detective Inspector Chanza, the Officer-in-Charge's favourite nephew. There was no love lost between Chanza and Sibanda.

'When a lion gets hungry it will eat grass, Ncube; I agreed to catch up on my paperwork.'

Ncube laughed for the first time in weeks, 'Ah sir, you are as clever as a locust in winter, but at what cost?' The whole station knew that Sibanda detested paperwork and that Stalin Mfumu thrived on it. It was a constant thorn in the fleshy side of each.

'I'll think about that later. Chanza has had to walk for a change. He's on his way to Barghees General Dealers to investigate a break-in.'

'Anything serious?' Ncube asked. He liked old man Barghee. They fished together sometimes.

'Just petty theft, electrical stuff, a lot of fans.'

The pair settled back into comfortable familiarity as Sibanda began his tale of the lightning strike.

CHAPTER 3

A ndries Nyathi took a last swig of the fiery liquid that would see him through the night, hoisted the ancient rifle and slung it over his shoulder. Its noble lineage went back to the earliest hunters and explorers. The stock patted his back with the familiarity of a congratulatory old friend. Soft leather caressed him as he walked. A faint smell of blood, death and weathered hide reached him with each rub of the sling against his shirt. The weapon had seen many battles and great hunts. It bore the scars. In his belt he carried an axe.

Nyathi's neighbours, who lived close to him on the Mpindo line, on the western boundary of the National Park, took him for an accomplished farmer, but that was his day-time occupation. Sometimes he hired out his farming skills. It allowed him freedom of movement and associations with men best left unnoticed, like Thomas Siziba, men whose status in the district could bring unwanted attention and alert jealous others. Andries did nothing to mark himself out as a man above men other than achieve success on the land. The agricultural sages in his community came to admire the fertility of his goats and the prosperity of his cattle. They fingered the neat and martialled rows of his maize crop or marvelled at the leafy plumpness of the drumhead cabbages that sprang from the furrowed sand on which he lived. They questioned the lack of disease in his cattle and the unblemished leaves of his crops that failed to entice the voracious jaws of the beetle or to attract the black mould that spread in a relentless fungal blanket with the arrival of one whimsical, airborne spore. His neighbours berated their continued, pestilential luck while envying Nyathi his bounty. He recalled previous conversations with the village headman, Moyo, and smiled wryly to himself as he strode out into the moonlight.

'Ayi, ayi, ayi, Nyathi,' said Headman Moyo, his nearest neighbour, 'I am counting *amathole,* the calves, that you have gained this year. Everyone of your *inkomokazi* has milk and is fattening her offspring with rich juices. Have you lost no beasts to the hyena or lions this year?'

'Ah, Moyo,' Nyathi replied, with a twinkle in his eye, 'they have learned well not to bother my herd.'

'You are a lucky man, *amhlope*, my friend,' sighed Moyo, 'I have been cursed by a leopard that has carried off three of my calves and mauled two others so that I had to slit their throats. It is a big loss. I wish I could move away from this place, maybe change my luck and find somewhere for my beasts to thrive without threat.'

'Luck is a talent and a lot of hard work, old friend,' he said, glancing sideways at the sturdy impenetrable scherm he had built with thick teak logs to keep his animals safe at night. Moyo had merely looked askance.

Andries shook off the conversation. He was glad he had something to report back to his contacts. They thrived on all the leopard movements he was able to tell them about. Was Moyo's calf killer collared and part of their study? He would tell them it was, keep them sweet with titbits. He needed them on his side and not only for the money they paid for information, although the extra dollars were proving useful in a year of inconsistent rain and failing crops. Even his admired cattle were suffering. Their feed was running out. He needed to find money to supplement their diet if they were to survive this season with their bones still inside their skins.

Andries walked comfortably in the dark. He was used to it. He passed the familiar local pump, a still and silent sentinel against the night sky. As ever it brought back vivid memories of his time as a herd boy and the year of the duck hunt.

At seven years old, Andries had not minded taking care of his father's herd, but it was hard for a boy his size and drained his reserves of strength. As soon as he was considered tall enough to reach the pump handle at its highest arc, even though he had to jump to catch it, the herding duties were his. His mind drifted back as he walked through the moonlight to the young carefree boy he had been …

Young Andries sat for a moment, lying back against an ant heap, his child's body exhausted from the man's exertion. He did not know that he had done a man's job; he just did as he was told and assumed that since his father had directed him to the task, he was physically capable of it.

Overhead a pair of lizard buzzards skirled in the bright sunlight. The boy lifted an imaginary rifle to his shoulder, braced himself against the ant heap and took aim with two quick-fire, phantom shots, nailing the birds with the ease of the fictionally practised. Satisfied with his accuracy, he lay for a few moments more, allowing the baked heat of the clay hill to soak into his wiry body. This would probably be one of his last herding duties. The rains were gathering, soon the cattle would be able to drink from the many pans that formed in the area, and in a few months he would be sent to school every day.

The boy was unaware of the activity behind his back. The ant heap concealed millions of masticating termites that had cemented his resting spot in place with their own excreta, taking decades, perhaps even hundreds of years, to build the mound he lay against. These very ancient insects had situated their fortress home with such climatic perfection it absorbed and regulated enough heat and moisture to cultivate areas of sponge-like fungus that fed the constant and gargantuan production of the queen's offspring.

Termites are the supreme architects of the insect world. Even the boy's sleeping hut, built of similar materials, could not rival the mound's ingenuity. This ant heap, like all others, was a masterpiece of futuristic, air-conditioned eco-friendliness. It was, proportionally, a building of such size that it dwarfed any of man's engineering mega marvels. It even housed a nest of thief ants, a colony of tiny yellow robbers that only live in termite mounds. The minute worker ants smuggle themselves along claustrophobic tunnels in the mound just large enough to admit their tiny selves. Once in the termite nurseries they kidnap the eggs and the young and drag them back down their shafts safe in the knowledge that termite soldiers are too large to pursue them. They feast on the babies and unborn at leisure. To Andries the boy, the mound behind him was just a lump on the landscape. Andries the man had no reason to change that view.

With spring well on its way, great activity was afoot in the hill.

The highly disciplined, eunuch termites were preparing for the most important event of the year, the grooming of the next generation. They were the dispatchers of the marriage flight. This year's crop of princelings and princesses, with their fragile wings attached, would soon be bullied out of their clay castle with the first heavy rainfall. The royal progeny were overwhelmed by an instinctive urge to fly as far as they could from their birth mound to seek a mate and to found their own dynasty. If they wavered, the eunuchs would be there to 'persuade' them to fly off.

Most of the desperate teenagers were picked off by squadrons of insectivores before they even uncreased their wings. Birds knew exactly when to station themselves at the mound's chimney exits, pecking at the endless conveyor belt of protein served up. Despite their slim survival chances, the termite virgins headed blindly for the tunnel exit only to be devoured by the beady-eyed gauntlet. Sheer weight of numbers meant that some would make it beyond the mound's exit, but other hazards were plenty. Many might drown in a shallow puddle, weighed down by their wedding wings, or become a reptilian lunch or a spider's snack. Statistics were bleak and yet termites rival cockroaches in historical longevity.

The boy knew none of this, he did not realise he was resting against an entire tunnelled citadel of frantic activity, totalitarian rule and high social organisation. In ironic contrast, he only knew calm and contentment.

Andries remembered a conversation that had taken place with his father around that time. It had heralded excitement, change and a new growth ring in his child's bones.

'Andries,' summoned his father, 'come and sit next to me here on the bench, *umtanami*.' The boy did as he was told. Theirs was a large family. His father did not often single him out unless to chide him for neglect of the cattle. His father's tone was encouraging. The boy scraped his morning porridge bowl, loosening the crusted remains, and placed it in the water bucket. He hastened to his father's side, allowing a momentary puff of importance to reach his cheeks.

'What is it, Baba?' he asked.

'How are the cattle, my son?' his father enquired.

'They are healthy, Baba,' he replied, 'I take them to the best grazing every day. I find them good shade when they wish to rest. I pump plenty of water, and I still my catapult and do not bother the birds that come to clean the ticks from their ears and under their tails. The cows know my whistle. They come when I call. Ubessie is our best *inkomokazi* and will surely give us another fat calf this year,' the boy finished his report. He looked into his father's face for approval.

'You are a good son, Andries, you will become a fine cattleman one day. It is in your blood.'

Andries remembered his pride and how his back straightened with importance. 'Thank you, Baba.'

'Next year, 1965, will be the year that you start school. You have grown, Andries, I have seen that your hand can now reach over your head and touch your ear. The time has come for you to learn to read and write. Even a cattleman must be able to count his herd and use his money wisely. Rodwell will take your place with the *inkomo,* he is old enough. He will be able to reach the pump by the time the summer rains have disappeared.'

The boy had absorbed this news with the excitement of change easily embraced by the young. He would begin to learn from books. He would mix with the other boys who ran, each morning, along the dusty path to the schoolhouse. His older siblings had told of the beatings he would receive from the strict teachers, and of the boredom and sometimes toilsome nature of the work, but it could not dampen his enthusiasm. He grinned wildly, 'I am very happy, Baba, and I will work very hard to make you proud.'

'I am sure you will, Andries,' confirmed his father. 'Now, there is another task that you must attend to before you can take your place among the scholars ...'

'Anything, Baba,' he interrupted, bubbling over with the joy of the recent news, 'give me anything to do and I will do it.'

His father smiled at his young son's energy and eagerness. 'This year you will be the umbrella boy at the bird shoot in the Park.'

Andries wriggled on the bench like a young puppy wagging its tail in the presence of bigger teeth. He could not believe his luck. His turn had come at last to join the fabled hunt, to join the white *Indunas,* the white chiefs, as they shot the ducks that flocked in their thousands to the summer lakes and pans of his home. How would he sleep until the big day came?

A flutter of wings and a gentle cooing stirred the boy. He sensed that enough time had lapsed to send the sweet smell of fresh water through the clear spring air, along undulating currents, and across sudden updrafts to entice his prey to the drinking trough. He had deliberately spilled enough of the precious liquid to form small puddles around the deep trough, making access to the water easy for the birds.

The doves had arrived to drink from his makeshift lure. The laughing dove was the only dove that needed to drink every day and the most pleasing on the eye. The boy moved stealthily now, raising his catapult and squinting against the target. He aimed at a plump bird, taking time to admire the dusty-pink head that darkened to cinnamon on the breast, and the subtle grey wing feathers that supported a sprinkling of rust splashes, but his lunchtime hunger had no truck with beauty. He loosed the missile with deadly accuracy. The flock launched itself upwards with the sound of a squeaking hinge as though the rust on the wings had bled into their joints, stiffening them. They wheeled in ragged formation over the muddied water and the placid cattle, confused, but knowing only that danger lurked. They darted for cover in a nearby thorn bush, wary, scanning the sky for sparrow hawks. One limp body remained.

Andries remembered scurrying from his hill to collect his booty. He picked up the bird and glanced at its clouding eye without regret. One dove was hardly a feast, but Andries had leftover mealie porridge from breakfast with him and a twist of salt. The three together would satisfy his hunger. He took his quarry to the ant heap and used a sharp stick to dislodge some of the termite's intestinal render, chipping away at it until he had enough to moisten and cover the dove, feathers and all, in a thick clay paste.

He walked away with his oven-ready bird to find kindling for a fire, oblivious to the chaos he had left behind. Already the robotic, termite soldiers were at the breach with their swollen heads swinging from side to side, massive jaws wide open, mouths filled with a noxious fluid ready to spew out at the first scent of an invasion. It was not the boy who was their perceived enemy, but the march of ant colonies whose roving spies would find the fissure. In no time, marauding armies of black ants could gather in hordes to swamp their cousins in a cannibalistic wave.

As the boy got his fire underway, so the sightless workers were vomiting up gobbets of slimy glue at the site of the damage. They were sealing up the hole. Any brave soldiers or frantic workers cemented out of their home in the panic were doomed. Termites cannot exist in isolation, without their colonial support network they perish, their death seen as a necessary sacrifice for the common good.

It was some weeks before the rains arrived and more weeks before enough had fallen to drown the landscape in a sea of waterholes, encouraging the wild, verdant grasses and reeds that attracted the ducks. The termites were already mated and starting the long road to a viable colony.

Frederick Courtney Selous, the great naturalist and adventurer, who trod the area a century before the boy was born, called the area The Land of a Thousand Lakes. He hunted and explored the territory for many years. He was a gallant and generous man who earned the reputation as a distinguished Nimrod of Africa. Andries didn't know he had several august connections in his family tree. He would come to know of Selous's existence from a book he was given, but he never knew his family was related to the legend; Selous was not a celibate saint.

The name Mzilikazi, the paramount king of the Matabele who preceded Selous and his travels by some considerable time, would find its way into Andries' lexicon by way of the local school, but that was still some years hence.

Mzilikazi gave the area, Tjolotjo, its name. He trekked to this lush summer land in search of new pastures for his people. He and his tribe had fled from the Transvaal Boers who themselves had flown the yoke of the British Cape Colonists in a serial, Archimedean displacement of human tide, all set in motion by a diminutive queen called Victoria.

Despite breeding nine children, Victoria wasn't nearly as prolific as her termite counterparts, but her colonies nevertheless expanded with similar tenacity, spreading vast pink, empirical swathes on nineteenth-century maps as opposed to dusty mud mountains on the landscape.

Tjolotjo is a San bushman word meaning the head of an elephant, and it was the summer elephants and their rich gleaming ivory that originally lured the white hunters. On 23 January 1965, it was the waterbirds that drew the current hunters.

As he walked towards the Park boundary, Andries recalled his first encounter with the white hunters and his childish naivety.

'I say, H.H., look at that,' said Sir Bingham Russell as he stepped down from the train and scanned the surrounds.

'Looks like we'll bag a bumper crop this year, Sir Bingham,' said Harry Haggard, as he too took in the vast swathes of silver water that had settled on the plains with the metallic glint of a highly polished drinks tray.

Sir Bingham Russell put up his binoculars and tracked a flock of red-billed teal as it circled a distant pan and glided to a silent landing on the mirage sheen. 'Can't wait to get started, H.H., let's get ourselves organised,' he barked, and they headed back into the carriage to check on their weaponry and the assorted paraphernalia of slaughter.

The shooting party had arrived by train on a line that ran directly from Bulawayo to Victoria Falls and bisected this Land of Lakes arbitrarily. To the west lay Tjolotjo and the boy's home, to the east lay the western edge of the National Park. The waterbirds knew no boundary lines, and neither did the shooters. They had been given the unrestrained access of the privileged. Poaching was not the word used, but for all the permissions that is exactly what it was – sanctioned poaching.

The party had journeyed in a convoy of three carriages supplied by the National Railways for their directors and friends: a travelling coach, a dining car and a sleeping carriage. The three cars had been expertly shunted into a shady siding and uncoupled. The steam engine departed in a cloud of wet, white fumes and pumping steel to labour elsewhere. It would only return at the end of the hunt to restore the gentlemen to Bulawayo, their wives and their clubs.

There were five guns in all, plus an entourage of cooks, butlers and cleaners. They had been joined by the local District Commissioner, who would serve as their guide to the area, and several of his staff, who would serve as bearers. Andries's father was well practised in the art of toting a weapon, having fulfilled the role for several years. His eldest son, Davidson, had been promoted to gun bearer for the first time, but he knew the ropes from previous expeditions as the umbrella boy. Andries had been less sure in the presence of such luminaries and chose to remain firmly in the shadow of his father, observing the bustle.

Andries had rarely seen a white man and certainly not up close, but as the staff unloaded boxes, carefully unpacked and polished weapons, and set up the starched table linen for lunch, he had plenty of time to observe and question.

'Davidson,' he had whispered discreetly to his older brother, 'look at the *umkiwas*, their skin is like the flower of the *umvalsangwani*, all white and waxy.' He was thinking of the blossom of the sweet-scented wild gardenia bush that the giraffe favoured. 'Do they keep it like that with wax from a candle?'

'No, stupid, that is how they are born, but wait, soon that skin will turn red as the sun cooks them. Watch their pinched noses. They are thin and straight but they burn like chicken skin on hot coals. The skin goes crisp, and in a few days you will see it peel and flake like the bark of the *umkwazakwaza* that grows near the waterhole. *Kwaza, kwaza, kwaza*,' Davidson hissed, imitating the sound of the brittle, paper-thin exfoliation of the *Commiphora* tree as it rustled in the wind. Andries had winced in distaste.

'And the fur on their skin ...?' asked Andries. Davidson could see his young brother staring at the exposed knees of one of the hunters. His meticulously ironed and creased khaki shorts stopped just above his knees and his thick woollen socks were pulled up and gartered just below them. On the small exposed space that remained grew a thick mat of black hairs. Davidson laughed, 'watch and learn, *umnawami, my brother*,' he said, 'and you will see that they are just like us except their hair is straight and comes in many colours, and their skin is sometimes pink and sometimes the colour of weak, milky *mahehu*,' he said, referring to the refreshing drink that their mother fermented for them in the summer months.

Andries continued to stare at the different shapes and varieties of these strange men that had invaded his land. One of them was excessively fat, shiny and greasy. Another had the legs of a stork that summered on the lakes, impossibly long, thin and knobbly and already turning red from the midday sun. He hoped that he would not be assigned to carry his umbrella. His arm, even though used to stretching for the pump handle, could never reach high enough to cover this man's head.

'Andries, *buya lapa*,' called his father, and the obedient son scuttled rapidly to his father's side as requested. 'Come and meet young master Garfield, he is the son of Colonel Murphy,' and he pointed to the tall, lugubrious man who had stalked past a few moments earlier. Andries glanced shyly at the boy in front of him. Where the father was tall and thin, the son was short and stocky, Andries judged him to be about his own age. He was an extraordinary-looking boy, even on this day of new sights and curious people. His face was flat and round, his skin a blinding white that not even the purest of Ubessie's milk could match. Dull, blood-orange hair clashed violently with his full lips that were the startling crimson of the *bilibomvu's* breast, but it was his eyes that held Andries' gaze for they were lashless and unblinking like those of the spitting cobra.

'Say hello, Andries, you must greet young Mr Murphy,' said his father.

Andries struggled with the unfamiliar word, but managed a guttural *haro*, and hoped it would do. The boy standing before him remained silent, raised his pale cream eyebrows, spun on his heels and walked away.

'Ah,' exhaled his father, 'The English do not understand the grace of a greeting.' It was all he said before he too strode away to continue helping with the preparations.

Once the shoot was underway, Andries was surprised to find that the only person who required an umbrella was the fat man whose name was Haggard. 'Stay close, boy,' were his instructions, 'and make sure that not a single ray hits my head.' Andries, who only spoke Ndebele, had not understood a word, but his father had coached him in the importance of his duty and he assumed that Boss Haggard was merely repeating his father's instructions.

Throughout that first afternoon as Boss Haggard struggled to keep up with the rest of the guns, he would mutter, 'Haggard by name, but not by nature, hey boy?' and he would chuckle to himself. Andries understood not a word, but he enjoyed the cadence and the balance of the phrase so that after several repetitions, he began to mouth it to himself, and by the end of the hunt he had it off pat. It was the start of his gathering of the English language. It would be years before the saying had any meaning and years again before he fully understood the wry humour involved, by then Haggard would be dead and much in Andries life would have changed.

It was not only an English phrase that Andries learned that day, but the vital life lesson that sufficient is never enough. His father had a saying that farmers only owned as many hoes as they needed, the number being adequate for the purpose, but as he watched the hunters blast the skies clean of the flocks, accumulating more birds that they could eat in a lifetime, he began to believe that power and wealth must come from excess.

Andries was an observer. He understood character as if by psychic osmosis. He defined everyone instinctively by their heart. He knew, for instance, that he liked Boss Haggard whom he followed all day. He was a jovial man; his heart was on the outside for all to see. He couldn't resist food. Colonel Murphy, on the other hand, despite his size, had a small heart and was impatient, he shouted frequently at his gun bearer, blaming him for missed birds or for moving as he took aim. Everyone knew this was not true. He was just a lousy shot. Child Murphy was both *nhliziyobomvu* and *ulenhliziyo embi*; he had the red heart of anger and the bad heart of cruelty. Andries steered clear of him.

Over the next two days, he followed the shoot, shading Boss Haggard with his umbrella. Haggard addressed him occasionally. He smiled as a reply. He only attempted to speak to Haggard once, to warn him. The boy had spotted a blacksmith plover, her wing hanging as if injured, fluttering pathetically in extremis. He knew it was her ruse to lead them away from her eggs lying exposed in a shallow scrape on the ground. But Haggard couldn't understand the boy's language. He strode on, his size-ten boots crushing the three palely, perfect eggs that would never hatch.

Andries's arm burned with fatigue, but he never wavered. Occasionally, he discreetly changed arms when the ache became intolerable, but it was with such sleight of hand that Haggard was never aware of the move.

As the days progressed, several thousand duck, knob-billed, white-backed and -faced, fulvous and teal, found themselves stashed, un-plucked, into freezers and loaded on board the carriages for transport to Bulawayo. Tens, perhaps hundreds more, were wounded and maimed, their mutilated bodies left to paddle in one-legged, endless circles on pans or to drag themselves desperately through the bush, grounded by dismembered wings, dying of thirst or their wounds. For days afterwards the District Commissioner's staff would patrol the area, dispatching the casualties with a quick wring of the neck. They were dismayed at the slaughter, but dissent in the Native Department was unacceptable, and criticism of the old-boy-hierarchy a dismissible offence.

The excitement of the hunt, anticipated for so many weeks, quickly wore off for Andries. He saw little expertise in pointing a shotgun into the sky, and firing a hail of pellets that could hardly miss the thick, black clouds of ducks that circled overhead. Where was the thrill of the lure, the skill, precision and careful placement of the missile, and what of the joy of preparing and eating the quarry? It perplexed Andries greatly. He began to feel the moral superiority of the great hunter he would become. Andries was not the only person lacking enthusiasm. Garfield Murphy had trailed after his father, deemed old enough to absorb shooting etiquette. His father was neither a good teacher nor a good shot.

'Garfield, come here, look alive, boy, and see how this is done,' he snapped, holding a loaded shotgun for his son to take charge of. The boy went to his father. Andries didn't witness the accident, but he heard the report of a discharged gun and the screaming that went on and on until it turned his stomach to water and he vomited behind a bush.

A screech penetrated Andries's childhood reverie and for a moment he thought he was genuinely among the white bird shooters. It brought him back to reality, to the dark path he was travelling. A barn owl hunting a mouse had let out a triumphal scream, that's all it was. Andries had crossed the Park boundary. It was time to concentrate. He moved stealthily, avoiding obvious paths, leaving no tracks. It would be a long night.

CHAPTER 4

S ergeant Ncube pushed his head around Sibanda's door. 'I have a name, sir.'

'Come in Ncube.'

The sergeant walked into the office. He could not keep the expression of amazement from his face. The detective's desk, normally a confusion of papers and files, pencil stubs, coiled sharpenings, discarded ball points and wire baskets stacked haphazardly like a hamerkop's nest was now a picture of neatness. Even the abandoned cobwebs that anchored the desk to the floor and trapped little more than a disturbance of Kalahari dust had disappeared.

'Ah, sir, the spittle dries in my mouth when I look at this office.'

'You're surprised, Sergeant, I know, but this is not my doing. Constable Tshuma, the new guy, offered to clean up for me, and since I had promised Cold War the turning of a new leaf in terms of documentation, it seemed a good idea.'

'Very smart, sir, he has done an excellent job,' commented Ncube, although he noticed that, as usual, the detective had managed to put trees and greenery in general into his conversation. It was an unhealthy obsession. He wasn't sure either why Stalin Mfumu had earned the nickname Cold War. There was certainly a war between the men, but if anything, he'd label it as a hot one.

'Yes, I could get used to this. Tshuma's a good man. Sit, Sergeant, and tell me what you know about the victim.'

Ncube eased himself into an upright wooden chair he had never seen before, previously camouflaged by cardboard boxes, paper stacks and a grey, threadbare towel of dubious origin. He liked the informality of an across-the-desk chat.

'We think his name is Mkandhla. A widow in the village is saying that her lodger hasn't been home for two nights. She said he has never been away before.'

'Not a local man with family here then?'

'No, he arrived about six months ago and rented a room from Mandlovu at number 1375. We are trying to find out if he had a job and who his friends were.'

'Did he pay his rent on time?'

'She said so, said he was quite flash with cash too. Insisted on a room to himself, didn't share with anyone. Bit of a drinker apparently. Glassy eyed at times, like a sick goat.'

'Mbanje?'

'I doubt it, sir. You will remember last year we had a big blitz on the weed. That bull's horns have been well and truly cut. There's no marijuana around these days.'

'So, no Binga gold?'

Ncube looked at the detective as though he had cooked a chicken with its beak on, 'Sir, we have no evidence he was a miner, and I have never heard of any gold finds in Binga.'

Sibanda raised his brows, Ncube had obviously not heard of the high-quality marijuana grown in the Zambezi valley. He changed the conversation. 'Where did he work? Any friends or colleagues?'

'Mandlovu never met anyone. She didn't think he had a job. Bit of a loner. He kept odd hours. Slept late in the mornings, out all hours of the night and not a security guard as far as she could tell.'

'What about the Blue Gnu? Does the barman know him? The patrons?'

The sergeant shook his head and with it the pendulous rolls that hung about his chins. 'That's the really strange thing; no one at the Blue Gnu has ever seen him there. A few of them have noticed him around. A couple of them shifted their eye balls as though they had seen a snake. Mkandhla, if he is our victim, has been up to no good.'

'Where has he been drinking? A shebeen?'

'I have, um … checked those as well. They were all as tight with information as the collar of a choking dog.' Ncube was hesitant. There weren't supposed to be any illegal drinking houses in Gubu but there were, and the police knew it. Ncube hoped CID knew it too.

'Covering up?'

'Maybe, but they aren't … er … licenced so perhaps they were just feeling nervous in case we were there to shut them down.'

'Right, Ncube, let's go and check his room out.'

'We aren't certain yet it's him and we don't have a warrant. Are you sure we should?' the sergeant sensed trouble. Officer-in-Charge, Stalin Mfumu, liked his crime investigation done by the book. The war, hot or cold, was probably going to escalate.

It was the detective's turn to look at Ncube bemused. He grabbed his jacket and strode out of the room dragging his game leg like a recalcitrant child. Ncube prised himself out of the chair and waddled behind.

'I still have the keys to the Santana, we'll drive.'

In the car park they walked past the sorry sight of Miss Daisy, the station's second vehicle, hugging the cyclone fencing, her wheels sheltering a colony of weeds from the midday sun and her candy-striped upholstery fading gently. Sibanda felt some remorse. He had probably bludgeoned the nails in her coffin.

'I suppose she'll be towed away soon,' he commented, 'a pity really, she performed quite well when she wasn't boiling or choking or breathing fire,' he glanced across at the sergeant. He was pleased to see he was unmoved. Perhaps the man was becoming rational about vehicles after all.

'You can drive again, Ncube,' he offered. He wasn't going to admit his leg was throbbing. Perhaps he needed to visit the clinic and get it seen to. But it would have to wait.

They pulled up outside a neat township house, mud walled and thatched. Inside the milk-hedged yard were the beginnings of a mealie crop, each plant growing at its own pace in the poor soil, stealing nutrients from its neighbour; the strong starving the weak, dwarfing them into poverty; Africa just doing what it did best. The widow would get few cobs for her efforts. The rest of the yard was swept bare and hard.

'*Qoki, qoki*, mama,' Ncube called from the gate, 'anyone home?'

'I am around the back. *Ngena*, come in.'

Sibanda and Ncube walked past the mealie patch and a sad-looking lemon tree, to the back of the house. Mandlovu was doing the weekly wash. She stood with her feet set apart and her legs straight, bending from the waist, hands expertly rubbing a bar of green soap over pummelled clothes and an old tin bath of sudsy water.

'The police again,' she muttered, barely disturbing her ergonomic action, if anything she brutalised her wash with more vigour, 'I've told you all there is to know. I don't know much about Mkandhla. He was so quiet flies settled on his mouth. He told me nothing and had no ear for chatter. Paid his rent and never quibbled.'

'Can we look in his room, Gogo?' asked Sibanda.

'Yes, but I don't have a key and it's locked,' she dropped the item of tortured clothing back into the water and shook the suds from her hands. 'Follow me.'

They walked into a small, enamel-painted room, home to an impossible squash of sofas and a coffee table covered with a starched lace cloth and a vase of plastic flowers. They scuttled sideways past the chairs and squeezed down a dark, narrow hallway with two doors leading off it.

'That's his.' She pointed out a padlocked door. 'I'll leave you to it, but don't use force, the whole place might come down.'

Sibanda tried his shoulder against the tongue-and-groove door, but Mandlovu was right and a few clods of mud render dislodged from the jamb.

'Please, sir,' admonished Ncube in a whisper, as he bent to retrieve the incriminating evidence and hide it in his pocket, 'remember we don't have a warrant. We don't want any complaints.'

'Are there bolt cutters or a screwdriver in the Santana?' The detective asked.

'I don't think so. Maybe I could borrow a hacksaw from old man Barghee.'

'That'll take hours. What have you got in your pockets?'

'What do you mean, sir?'

'Well, have you got any wire or anything you can pick this lock with?'

'I am not a criminal. I do not carry around the tools of illegal entry on my person. I have no skills for opening locks,' the sergeant huffed with indignation.

'Ncube,' the detective hissed in exasperation, 'just empty your pockets.' The cramped confines of the corridor were beginning to irritate him.

'I only have my keys …' he had barely removed them from his trousers, a manoeuvre of some difficulty given their tight fit, when Sibanda grabbed them and began to try each one in the lock. The padlock clicked open on the third attempt. Ncube looked shocked.

'Where did you buy the locks for your house Ncube?'

'At Barghees.'

'As does everyone in the village. He only sells one make and there are only so many keys, which is lucky for us.'

They walked into the tiny room. There was barely enough space for both of them to fit. Sibanda wanted a few moments alone. He needed to absorb Mkandhla's life and understand what might have led to his death. Ncube's rotund presence would be a hindrance.

'Sergeant, go back and question Mandlovu. The ladies warm to you. She might open up and remember some detail that has been overlooked.'

'Right, sir,' replied Ncube readily. He sensed the detective's patience was being tried and he knew the consequences. He had been on the receiving end of his short fuse before. He stepped back into the corridor and took a last look at the lock that was identical to the one on his front door. What would his wives think of this? They could all have been murdered in their beds.

The detective sat down on the narrow bed and immediately recognised an old friend. It sank in the middle like a hammock and trapped the sleeper in a hug of sagging springs. A brightly coloured, hand-knotted rag rug on the floor lay ready to cushion the footfall of sleepy feet. The window was curtained with a calendar tea towel from 2009 advertising a chemical company. A more recent paper version with a picture of the company's office in Bulawayo hung from a rusty nail whose very presence had started an ominous-looking, upward-thrusting crack. He stared across the meanly proportioned room to a wardrobe that probably held the entire contents of Mkandhla's life. It was locked. With his overcautious sergeant out of the way, he wedged his good foot against the wood and prised his fingers into the warped and gaping door. The lock splintered open with little effort. He heard Sergeant Ncube start a camouflage of coughing.

Inside the wardrobe there was little of value, nothing that spoke of a criminal life, at least. He rifled through some decent clothes, a suit that looked quite new, and a pair of trainers. Were they the Chinese, zhing zhong, seven-mile tackies pedalled from market stalls, or the real deal? Fakes were becoming better and better these days. On the floor of the wardrobe lay a pair of pliers, bits of wire, some empty cans and a dozen or so bottles of various alcoholic drinks, all empty.

Sibanda sat back down on the hard metal rim of the bed and rubbed his chin. It helped the thought process. He would have liked to lean back and take the weight off his leg which was beginning to ache again, but he might struggle to get out of the deep mattress hole. Mkandhla had been missing for two nights, murdered on the first; already dead a day when he found him. The clues to his death were in this room, but they weren't obvious. What was he missing?

He stood up and balanced against the wardrobe while he readjusted to the pain and then, as an afterthought, bent awkwardly to look under the bed. He didn't see it at first because the mattress depression almost touched the floor. At the very back of the personal space of night-time secrets and grey fluff balls lay an elephant tusk. The wound in his leg made it impossible for him to reach it.

'Sergeant Ncube,' Sibanda called through the window, 'here! Now!'

The sergeant crammed his bulk back into the room. There followed a comic tangle of limbs and bodies as Ncube tried to look under the bed while Sibanda flattened himself against the wardrobe. The bent sergeant displaced more space than the upright one.

'Back out, you idiot,' snapped Sibanda, fearful of Ncube's large rear end and infamous, leaky gut, 'let me get out of here before you suffocate me.' Ncube's face crumpled as he wedged himself back through the door and into the narrow corridor. He sucked in as much breath as he could to allow the detective to escape past him.

When order was restored, Ncube emerged with the tusk. Sibanda examined the creamy ivory curve. It was thin, probably from a young female. The cavity end was stuffed with dry grass to prevent it from cracking. Blood smears bore testament to a violent death. Grass stains indicated it was probably a recent kill. This young cow had fed on summer's growth.

'Is this what Mkandhla died for, sir?' asked Ncube shouldering the ivory out through the garden gate.

'It's a possibility. He was also a secret drinker. I saw about a dozen empties in his room, beer and hard stuff, maybe he was a loner, got aggressive when he drank.'

'A strange thing to die for, an elephant's tooth.'

'Not a tooth at all, Ncube, a tusk, white gold.'

'Is that like Binga gold?' asked Ncube, pandering to Sibanda's new obsession with mining.

Sibanda's patience was waning. 'No, Ncube, they couldn't be further apart. White gold is the name the early Victorian explorers gave to ivory because of its exotic rarity. They made it into billiard balls and piano keys for the idle rich who had little more to do than play music and parlour games. These days it's been hijacked by the Far East. Hong Kong is the clearing house. The Chinese and Japanese churn out tourist trinkets, skilfully carved, but trinkets none the less.'

'Sort of art then, sir. I have a cousin who carves soapstone. Some of his heads are so real, I swear they blink their eyes.'

'Not art in any sense of the word,' he snapped, 'you can't have art's good name sullied by animal death and extinction. The ivory trade thrives on greed and big business. More and more it's becoming a commercial trade to arm wars and rebellions, particularly to the north of us.'

Ncube shuddered, he was a gentle man. 'You don't think …?' He asked as he manipulated the tusk into the back of the vehicle.

'No, relax Ncube, no wars here for the moment.'

'I have just remembered, sir, that there is a recent Zambian police report, asking us to look out for ivory coming across the Zambezi and being shipped on. That's why we were being extra vigilant at the roadblock.'

'We could have our link, Ncube. Maybe this guy Mkandhla is an ivory mule. Maybe Zimbabwe is becoming an entrepot.'

'What sort of a … pot, sir?' Ncube's interest in food meant he was familiar with most cooking utensils.

'Not a pot, sergeant,' Sibanda's irritation was beginning to surface, 'an unofficial clearing house, you know, import/export, only undercover.'

Ncube hauled himself into the driving seat and decided to change the subject. He couldn't get his head around gold that wasn't gold or pots that didn't cook. 'Mandlovu didn't have much to report, she was very touchy. The police knocked down some of her rooms during operation *Clean up the Filth*.'

'Hardly surprising,' Sibanda remembered the horror of the politically motivated exercise to clean up larger towns and villages by knocking down informal shacks and driving the populace back to the rural areas where their vote could be controlled. 'We didn't earn many friends.'

'She did mention that Mkandhla is a very intelligent man. Her words were – he's as sharp as the spears of Mzilikazi's bodyguard.'

'Well, that's something to go on,' Sibanda commented, as the Santana drove along the dusty village roads avoiding dogs, groups of sauntering pedestrians, reckless children and a pecking of traffic-wise chickens.

They arrived back at the station to a commotion of cattle-dip-day proportions. Constable Zanele Khumalo had emerged from behind the desk and was trying to keep young Patel Barghee from attacking assistant detective Chanza. The shouting was getting heated. Patel Barghee was waiving his fists. Chanza's head was shrinking into his collar like a parrot trying to sleep. He had his hands on Constable Khumalo's shoulders and was using her as a shield.

'I want to see my father now and if you don't let me see him there'll be trouble,' said the young man.

'There'll be trouble if you come any closer,' Chanza's voice waivered, as he continued to dodge possible violence behind the barrier of Constable Khumalo.

Sibanda stepped forward into the melee. An immediate aura of calm descended on the warring factions. Ncube had witnessed the effect before. It was as if the detective cast a spell on those around him. His imposing stature, sinuous movement and compelling face mesmerised like a cobra swaying before the strike.

'What's going on here?' the detective spoke with authority.

'That man has arrested my father,' fumed the young Barghee.

'Mr Barghee senior was in illegal possession of a firearm. I have brought him in for questioning,' spluttered Chanza.

'He has done absolutely nothing wrong. That old thing was merely ornamental, brought from India by my great grandfather.' The young man was becoming further agitated.

'Sergeant, take everything through to my office. Let's see if we can sort this out amicably.'

The cavalcade of discontent grumbled angrily down the corridor to the office. Sergeant Ncube ushered them along.

'Are you alright, Zee?' Sibanda asked before he followed them.

'Yes, sir, it'll take more than a puny boy and that weakling Chanza to ruffle my feathers. I could take them both on any day.'

Sibanda laughed; he wouldn't like to tangle with Constable Khumalo either. She was a formidable woman.

'By the way, there was a phone call for you when you were out.' She returned to the counter and examined her notebook. 'From Mr Barton at Kestrel Vale School.'

'Anything from Forensics on the lightning victim?' he asked, deflecting attention from Buff Barton's call.

'Yes, but you aren't going to like it.'

'What have they found?'

'That's just it, nothing. They are saying he is a victim of the lightning.'

'What! He'd been missing at least twenty-four hours before I found him, certainly already dead, and I witnessed the strike. They are like a bunch of baboons picking over a rubbish dump. They couldn't find their arse from their elbow.'

Constable Khumalo flinched at the choice of the detective's language. She chose to ignore it. 'They do have the identity card, but it's burnt. They are working on getting the number off it.'

'Some consolation, I suppose,' he said, as he strode down the corridor to join the argument in his office. He would think later about the phone call from Berry's father. It had taken him by surprise.

'Is everything sorted?' he asked, as he entered his office.'

'Not quite, sir. A weapon was stolen during the robbery at Barghee's store last night. It was unlicensed.' Ncube had taken the role of judge in the dispute.

'A disabled relic,' interjected young Barghee, 'and this man,' he said, pointing a finger at Chanza, 'has put my father behind bars.'

Sibanda looked at Chanza, encouraging a reply.

'In terms of the act, all weapons need to be licenced. This firearm is now in the hands of criminals thanks to the careless behaviour of Mr Barghee,' Chanza's self-righteousness shone thin and yellow like an angry boil.

'Disabled?' Sibanda addressed the young Indian man.

'The frizzen was removed when my great-grandfather came here in 1912. The authorities saw to that. He had carried it as a gamekeeper for the Maharajah of Jaipur. It was just a souvenir.'

'What sort of weapon was it?'

'Maybe a muzzle loader. I don't know much about firearms.'

'A muzzle loader ...' The words dripped with sarcasm. He looked across at Chanza with a withering look. Behind that look his brain was ticking over. A disabled muzzle loader was stolen the night *after* Mkandhla was murdered. The weapon used to kill him had certainly been low velocity, something old and very low tech, a muzzle loader would fit the bill. Surely there was a coincidence of sorts, but what was the link?

'Sergeant, take young Mr Barghee to the front desk. A small deposit fine for a misdemeanour is in order here. Release Mr Barghee senior from the cells, he can go home now. Detective Chanza, a word please.'

CHAPTER 5

Sibanda emptied his office of Chanza, having given him a lecture on priorities.

'Old Mr Barghee isn't a criminal, a bit forgetful maybe, but not about to embark on a crime spree with a weapon over a hundred years old and not even able to fire. Catch the robber, that's your focus.' He had gone easy on the detective. If he had given him the tongue-lashing he deserved, the little weasel would have gone running like a whipped puppy to his uncle. The keys to the Santana would have been withdrawn. He suspected he might need them.

The phone call to Forensics had not gone well, there had been a few heated words, but in the end, given Sibanda's information, they agreed to review the time of death and the hole in the skull.

'Probably wooden shrapnel from the tree,' the pathologist had said, 'unlikely to be a bullet given the level of destruction. A lightning blast can cause devastating damage, you know. There's more explosive power in all that electricity than a tonne of TNT.'

'I do know, trust me,' said Sibanda, 'but look again.'

The second phone call had been to Buff Barton.

'Thanks for returning my call,' Barton had said warmly, 'I'm off to Thunduluka Lodge for a few days. It's still school holidays and I have well and truly earned a break from Kestrel Vale. You aren't far away. Come and join me for a drink if you have a moment.'

Why on earth would Buff Barton want to meet up with him? They barely knew each other. He'd only met the legendary Thandanyoni once, chasing up the blue paint that had been so important in the last crime he'd investigated. They both had a passionate interest in birds and wildlife, but Sibanda was certain he hadn't been invited to discuss the finer points of zebra shadow stripes and their north/south definition. This was Berry's father. Had he sensed something? Was he going to warn him off?

'I'm heading that way this afternoon. I could be there about 4:00.'

'Perfect sundowner time. See you then.'

Sibanda put down the phone and his hand went instinctively to his chin. He didn't enjoy being in the dark. He liked to lead the investigation, not be on the other end of a grilling. The truth was he did have to go to National Parks and advise them he had found ivory. The blood and any fingerprints would have to be analysed first before he handed it in. Thunduluka Lodge was not much further on, and a drive through the Park might distract him from the nagging ache in his leg, plus he was intrigued by Barton's invitation.

He would have liked to have set off early, and dawdle at a leisurely pace past the waterholes, seeing what was there of interest. Young warthogs would certainly be cavorting in the open air. Always the first born, they needed to be mobile and out of their burrows before the rains soaked the ground. Once rainwater began to linger in puddles, it didn't take much excess to form streams to drown the nursery and the helpless piglets. It occurred to him that bee-eaters were like that too. They nested in riverbanks and also produced their young early in the season. The multi-coloured flyers couldn't risk their eggs and hatchlings being washed away by rising waters. Besides which there were rich pickings to be had with the arrival of the rains. Fledglings were quickly taught to hawk flying ants on the wing. He had recently watched the Europeans and their brood-swooping and banking in a display of feeding resembling a balletic dogfight. How they avoided mid-air collisions was a mystery. Termite protein would build them up for their long migration back to northern climes.

He should have been clearing up paperwork. He should have been filling in his report on the victim and the ivory find, but his brain was visually re-searching Mkandhla's room for clues. This would be a murder investigation by tomorrow, spiced by the discovery of ivory. Forensics, given time and some encouragement, usually came up with the right conclusion.

Sibanda took another look at the official forms he had been filling in. He would never complete them, so why start? The forms, two carbon sheets and a starving ballpoint, instantly began the new mess that would once again threaten to swamp his office.

'Excuse me, sir,' Ncube's smiling face appeared around the office door, 'is this a good time?'

Sibanda swept the mistreated bureaucracy to the side of his desk and nodded to the chair, 'Take a seat, Sergeant.'

'Do you still have the keys to the Santana, sir?'

'As we speak, I do, but we both missed the obligatory prayer for rain while we were searching Mkandhla's room.'

'Flies don't ignore rotten meat and neither could we turn up the opportunity to find out about the man. Does that mean I have to return to the roadblock?' Ncube's face crumpled like an unwanted bill.

'It's more likely I will pay for our absence with the loss of the keys.'

'Has the Officer-in-Charge said anything yet?'

'Not yet, but I'm expecting him any minute. My clean office might cheer him at least.'

Ncube glanced around at the rapidly deteriorating desk space and the grey over-washed towel that had found its way back to the chair. 'You'll have to cry with one eye when he comes in if you are to convince him you have turned over new grass.'

Sibanda merely cocked an eyebrow. The sergeant had mistaken grass for a leaf. Ncube had a quaint way of expressing himself. Besides which crocodile tears and excuses weren't his strength. 'What are you here for, Sergeant?'

'The Santana, I am off duty this weekend. I thought I might tow Miss Daisy to my house and work on her. I don't want her sold for scrap. Constable Khumalo tells me she's been instructed to phone around the used car yards for the best deal.'

'It's a lost cause, a heap of junk, Ncube. Don't waste your effort. Let them take it. There'll be a replacement. We can't function with only one vehicle. The Province knows that.'

Heap of junk indeed, Ncube seethed, but swallowed his indignation; he didn't want to tread on a snake's tail, he needed to keep the detective in a good mood and on his side. 'We cannot be ungrateful, sir, *the axe might forget, but the tree never does,*' he had saved up this Ndebele saying because it was about trees. He knew the detective would appreciate it. 'Miss Daisy caught that stinking body-snatching murderer for us,' he said, referring to her brave chase through the bush after the *muthi* murderer. 'She deserves a second chance.'

Sibanda shook his head; he thought Sergeant Ncube was over his love affair with the diesel wreck outside; obviously not. To him, the leaky old tank was a person. Ah well, perhaps he had nothing better to do. If he got out of the office now, he might avoid Stalin Mfumu's wrath. The detective took a second glance at the tedious paperwork now clinging by friction alone to the corner of the desk, grabbed the keys and stood up. 'Right then, I'll give you a tow.'

'Better I give you a tow, sir. If you will just sit in Miss Daisy and steer her, I will drive the Santana. I see that leg is still paining you.' Ncube didn't wait for an answer. He had no intention of being towed by detective Sibanda. They would both probably be killed by his recklessness and Miss Daisy would be damaged beyond repair. He would never be able to replace that radiator, faulty as it was, and what would he have to trade for a panel-beaten bonnet? There probably weren't enough fish in the Zambezi. No, he would drive gently, at an even pace, giving the detective no reason to apply the brakes and skid off the road or smash into the back of him.

The trip was uneventful and barely attracted a second glance from the sauntering pedestrians on the bumpy dirt road to Soweto. Broken-down vehicles were regular occurrences in the village. Gubu was the repository for cast-offs and crippled machines, the last resting place for rusty, patched models of indeterminate age. Their tow convoy did stop once to greet an oncoming vehicle, an ancient Datsun whose colour had faded from firebox-red to sunrise-blush over its thirty-year life of African blistering. It sported a human fuel pump who sat on the open passenger window holding a jerry can upside down on the roof. Gravity-fed petrol trickled down a plastic tube leading from the jerry can's cap and under the wedged-open bonnet, to the motor.

'It's working I see, Onias,' said Ncube to the driver, 'you'll never find a replacement fuel pump for that model.'

'Brilliantly, thank you for the idea. It will get us to the Mission. My wife and son will be glad to see me. '

'How is the young man doing?'

'They have taken his appendix. He is doing well, but they are hungry. Food is short at the hospital. They are eating the scabs on their lips.' He frowned a little to underline the penury of the ongoing hospital crisis. 'See, I have some few things to fill their bellies.' He pointed to a cabbage, a bottle of cooking oil, and a mixed bag of onions and tomatoes on the back seat.

'Go well my friend. Give my regards to your wife and a speedy recovery to your son. Be careful you don't flood the carburettor, young man,' he added to the petrol pumper.

'I have pinched the pipe slightly while we are idling. I am now a practised throttle,' said the man on the window seat without a trace of irony. With that, Onias banged on the roof, the petrol flow was restored and the Datsun lurched forward taking each bump and ridge like a seasoned skier on a mogul run. The human fuel pump rode the obstacles with skill, grinning from ear to ear and waving to passing friends when he could afford to release his grip for a few seconds.

Miss Daisy pulled up next to Ncube's home in a soft landing. Ncube scurried out of the lead vehicle and undid the tow rope.

'Thank you, sir. You may take the Santana back now, unless you would like to come in for a moment for some refreshment.'

Sibanda barely hid his irritation. The journey had been impossibly slow and bothersome. It had cut into his game viewing. Either that or he would be late for his meeting with Thandanyoni. Ncube deserved a lecture on roadworthiness and safety, but the Datsun driver was going to the hospital to see his family. There were no buses. Taxis were expensive. He would turn a blind eye himself. Ncube's mechanical resourcefulness never failed to amaze him.

He glanced at his watch. He should be heading into the Park, but as he bounced and swayed on the end of Ncube's rope it had occurred to him that one of the sergeant's trio of wives might very well have the solution to his current problem.

'I'll pop in just a moment, Ncube, to greet your family and then I must leave for my appointment.'

Ncube beamed with pleasure. His wives would be delighted with the honour of a visit from Gubu's own Detective Inspector of criminal wizardry.

Ncube's township house was as far removed from Sibanda's austere dwelling as was possible. Colourful hand-crocheted throws covered the chairs, hiding the wear and tear of a large family. The cement floors gleamed like polished pewter. Large jugs of assorted wild herbs and flowers dotted tables and the window ledge, instilling the rooms with a fresh and unusually calming air. Bits of baby paraphernalia dotted the décor. The babies were asleep or at school. A waft of something delicious drifted in from the kitchen and Sibanda was embarrassed when his stomach rumbled to the stimulus like an elephant in communication with a distant herd. He needn't have been. Hunger was not tolerated in the Ncube household where thrift, ingenuity, the skills of a master fisherman, and an age-old knowledge of the bounty of the bush kept any prowling wolves from the door.

Sibanda was given food for his journey: a bottle of sickly orange fizz and an empty margarine container filled with Suko's prize-winning *inopi,* a deliciously thick porridge made from the *ijodo* melon, a sweet, anaemic cousin of the watermelon. He got up to leave. With all three wives fussing to see him off, now was the right moment to plumb their domestic flair.

'*Omama,* I can see that you have a well-kept home as clean and fresh as rain-washed petals,' he began, and he genuinely meant it. He abhorred Ncube's polygamous ways, but he envied the home comforts that came with it. 'I have a small problem with a blood-stained cloth, can you tell me how to get it clean?'

'Milk,' came Nomatter's reply.

'And, perhaps a little lemon juice after the soaking,' added Blessing, the senior wife, 'not too much. It may bleach away the colour, but let us wash the garment for you. We will get it clean.'

'No, it's fine, thank you, I'll manage.'

'Are you hurt?' asked Blessing with the knowing look of a four-time mother, 'is that how the blood got on your clothes?'

'Er ... yes, a slight cut,' he said indicating his limping leg. This was the easiest answer, and it was partly true.

'Then wait a little longer,' said Blessing, as she hurried back into the house. She reappeared with a small bottle of clear liquid stopped with a cork, and a jar of salve. The latter was dark brown and smelled pungently offensive from the minute the lid was unscrewed.

'Take three drops of the liquid each morning in your tea and apply a little of the balm to the wound each night. It will stop infection and ease any pain.' The eyes in her serious face pierced with foresight, 'I have made it myself from the boiled bark of the *umnonjwana* and *ugagu* distilled and mixed with healing summer herbs and flowers. Use it,' she urged. 'It will help.'

Sibanda left the Ncube household in a cloud of dust as he revved away from the front yard. The disturbed motes never settled on the tabletops and sills. They didn't dare.

Once in the Park, Sibanda slowed the Santana. The springs groaned with relief and the engine ticked with displeasure as he pulled up outside National Park's HQ.

'One tusk only?' asked Edison Bango, the Park Warden.

'Yes, and currently being examined for blood stains. It was found in the belongings of a murder victim.'

'We haven't seen much elephant poaching in the Park recently, a couple of loners maybe, the odd elephant taken. No big gangs at the moment. We're on top of it. The land we have to cover is bigger than Belgium, much of it just wilderness without roads and water points. At this time of the year the bush is thick and overgrown, making it harder to hunt, but standing rainwater lures the game away to remoter areas. Poachers know that,' the warden sighed as though the weight of the world was on his shoulders; the weight of Belgium at least.

'Do you think this elephant could have been shot in the Park by a local?'

'I can't say. I could do with more scouts, some men who have grown up in the bush. This current crop is all city born, here for the job, not the love of the wild. Most of them come from Chitungwiza,' he said, referring to an overcrowded suburb of the capital some 600 kilometres away. 'They passed their O levels so they qualify. They can rote learn the Wildlife Act and the gestation period of a duiker, but they have no instinct or observation skills, no gift for tracking. You can't teach that. I could do with local boys. Anyway, Detective,' he said, glancing at his watch, 'I have another meeting in a few minutes. Elephants aren't the problem right now; just don't ask me about rhino, you'd weep. That's what my next meeting is about. We're darting as many as we can, removing their horns before the poacher's get to them. Perhaps we'll keep some alive that way,' his tone indicated defeat already.

'I'll turn the tusk over to you when we've finished with it.' Sibanda left the office having taken on the warden's depression, and walked straight into a one-armed, ginger-headed man.

'Sorry,' Sibanda apologised for the collision, 'are you the next meeting?'

The man's blue eyes stared unblinking, his face inscrutable.

'About the rhino?' he coaxed.

The man passed him without answering, a slight upward curve of a pale eyebrow the only nod to Sibanda's presence.

The detective looked back at the disappearing figure and shrugged off the slight. He didn't waste time on judgement. The man had eyes the colour of a vervet's balls, lips that swallowed his own nose and issues too deep and complex for his own good.

Sibanda tried to shake off the tentacles of doom that had reached his gut. What future for elephants and rhino? How were they ever going to hold back the tide of deforestation and habitat destruction that was sweeping through his homeland? A magnificent natural wealth pilfered by the cunningly hopeless from a destitute future. The image was bleak. He stabbed his foot harshly on the accelerator. The Santana lurched and growled. It would suffer by proxy for Sibanda's impotent anger. He was too preoccupied to notice a frantic moth beating against the windscreen in an attempt to escape the glare of a safari sun. If he'd have listened he would have heard a rare squeak from the moth's proboscis. It bore stripes and the distinctive white marking of a skull and crossbones.

By the time he reached Thunduluka Lodge, his mood had changed, lightened by several minutes spent with a sable bull, a shining, jet-black example of radiating health and strutting, virile arrogance – a king of his anthill castle. Scimitar horns swept sinuously back in a curve that almost reached his withers. The twin rapiers supported by an impressively muscled neck had probably seen off many lions and leopards and lived long to tell the tale. He was in his prime and his progeny would be the future. The sable ambled to the pan, dipped his head and began drinking, his masked face reflected in water crazed by the sipping whirlpool. Sibanda felt his clenched jaw slacken and his shoulders relax. The bush was his Valium, but he was more alone than he had been in a long time. Why wasn't Berry sitting beside him to share the joy? He knew the answer. It was a given.

The sable baulked, spooked by a lone fish-eagle that launched itself from a nearby mopani. The moment and the reflection were lost in the lingering cry of the raptor's melancholy. He drove off.

As he pulled into the Lodge car park and squeezed the Santana in between two carelessly immaculate game-viewing vehicles, memories of Miss Daisy and her misbehaviour in this very spot came to mind. Sergeant Ncube's heart would have sung if he could have witnessed the rare and rueful smile that fleetingly crossed the detective's face.

Thandanyoni Barton stood to greet him, despite his own stiff leg. 'Welcome. Come and have a drink.'

'Thank you, sir.'

'Call me Buff, everyone does. My African name is Thandanyoni, bird-lover. That's followed me around for a while.'

'Jabu,' Sibanda responded.

'Short for Jabulani, meaning happiness, always found that to be a wholesome name.'

Sibanda wondered if Thandanyoni could begin to understand how unhappy he was, and would be until he had sorted out his relationship with Berry. 'Sometimes hard to live up to,' was all he said.

'We all have our black dogs at times,' Thandanyoni put his binoculars up and scanned the waterhole in front of the camp. 'Quiet for the moment, the afternoon drinkers should arrive shortly. Talking about dogs, they tell me there's a pack of wild dogs in the area, probably keeping everything on their toes and a bit wary of the waterhole.'

The conversation wandered to the behaviour of insectivorous raptors with the swooping dive of a steppe eagle at the pan.

'Is it the same species as a tawny eagle? Some people think so. They are easily mistaken,' said Sibanda.

'No, definitely not, it's darker, larger and the yellow gape extends past the eye, look.'

'Against the light, I need binoculars.'

'Did you know they follow the weather fronts?'

'After flying ants?'

'Yes, someone somewhere did an analysis of the crop of a mixed flock of insectivorous raptors. Each one had between 1 500 and 2 000 termites inside.'

'Impressive, where do they go in the southern winter?'

'The steppes, I suppose, Kazakhstan or somewhere in that Euro-Asian corridor.'

'Latin name: *Aquila nipalensis?*'

'My old brain could never dig that up. It sounds right. I do know that they battle to cross the Mediterranean, with very little updrafts to soar on. That restricts them to a corridor around Gibraltar, the narrowest crossing. Bit of a bottleneck and the Spaniards love their hunting. They fly during the day to catch the currents, navigate by mountains and rivers. Use that panoramic eye sight. Scientists now believe some migrant birds have chemicals that react with the earth's magnetic fields. Sort of dodgem cars on a pre-set flyway. Imagine that.'

Sibanda settled into a pleasant afternoon of bird banter and discussion. A herd of kudu had come to drink at the pan, sharing guard duty with a bachelor group of impala. A troop of noisy baboons were irritating the still afternoon with their squealing play. Suddenly, Thandanyoni changed tack. 'Jabu, have you seen Berry recently?'

The detective was caught off guard, but at least he could answer honestly. 'No, not since last term and the trip to Khami Ruins, why?' He tensed for a warning lecture – father to unwanted suitor.

'She talks about you such a lot,' Thandanyoni turned his attention from the waterhole and looked straight at Sibanda, 'I just thought ...' His eyes, a masculine version of Berry's sparkling blue lights, clouded with stress.

Sibanda was alarmed. He would savour those words later when he was alone. 'Is something wrong?'

'She's missing.'

'Missing?'

'Well, she's been gone and out of contact for about a week. I'm worried. She does normally phone.'

'Have you contacted Barney?'

'Barney Jones?'

'Yes, Isn't she ... aren't they engaged?' Sibanda swallowed his envy every time he thought of the good-looking ranger. He had desperately wanted him to be the *muthi* murderer.

'No, no, what makes you think that? They had a relationship when they were much younger, at school, but she hasn't seen him since she came back from the UK.'

Another bit of information that Sibanda filed away for later reflection. 'Is there anyone else?' he steeled himself.

'Not that I know of. Look, she has done this sort of thing before. She was always running away and hiding as a child, just never for this long. I'm not too concerned. I just thought that you, as a friend and a policeman, could keep an eye out for her. She's my only child and ...'

'Of course.'

'Berry can be obstinate and defensive. She had a very difficult childhood. Her mother died in childbirth, an unnecessary tragedy. If only I could have taken the short cut, I could have got her to the District Hospital in time. Parks wouldn't allow it. Kept the gate locked. I went the long way around, Lucy died and Berry lived.'

'I'm sorry.' The man was visibly moved and Sibanda couldn't help but feel his loss. 'But why wouldn't they let you through the gate?'

'Times were different back then, tougher, everyone was scrambling for business. So much jealousy existed. Thunduluka was doing well. There was resentment. Lucy used to say we lived in the knitting-and-pickles belt – petty-minded officers married to small-minded housewives.'

'Surely, for a medical emergency ...?'

Thandanyoni shrugged, 'The young warden was particularly hostile. He lost an arm as a child. It twisted him. Lucy said he was born warped. She was very astute at character analysis.'

'Red-headed guy?'

'Yes, Garfield Murphy, he's still around. He doesn't work for National Parks anymore. Now he's a wildlife consultant.'

'Aren't you bitter?'

'He's got to live with himself. After the incident at Thunduluka, when the dissidents came and I was shot in the leg, I realised it was no place to bring up a child. I moved to Kestrel Vale. Left the inbreeds to stew in their swamp of spite. It was a good move. Berry's been happy.'

'Why has she disappeared now?'

'Someone shot her dog, Luka IV. He was bred from Luka I, her mother's dog. The name is short for Thunduluka, of course. You've got to understand, my daughter was a lonely child. She grew up with animals as her friends and playmates. Berry probably just needs space to grieve and work off her anger.'

'Who would do something like that?' Sibanda's heart ached to think of Berry's pain.

'It doesn't matter, the bottom-feeding pond scum is off to Australia or New Zealand. No guts to stay and face the music. There are some sick, misguided people out there, Jabu, as you surely know.'

CHAPTER 6

Andries continued to skirt the paths, even the narrow elephant trails that had been tamped and cleared over the years by the dogged footfall of ancient herds as they made their inherited way to water. He stayed on the short grass where he could, and swept any tracks on bare earth with a leafy branch. A pocketful of dead leaves and a handful of dirt sprinkled over the brush marks would deceive even the best of trackers. Sometimes he circled; sometimes he made false trails in the long grass. No one could follow his spoor back to Mpindo line. Even if they did they would never associate the tracks with him. Beneath his boots he had nailed inch-thick rubber soles narrower and much shorter than his own size nine's. They looked like a woman's footprints. He had schooled himself to take small steps. He was careful. He never took risks. This was Andries's world and he was master of it.

The moon was high. The African night chorus was in full swing. Insects sang in tinnitus stereo. They would only be silenced by movement. The boisterous cacophony meant he was the largest mammal for a hundred metres or so. It gave him comfort. To his left a solitary black-backed jackal barked, a sharp yelp followed by several shorter ones. Beyond the lone dog, some kilometres further on, a spotted hyena whooped to the empty sky. She was calling her clan together. They would be out hunting on this perfect night of silver light, calm winds and lingering scents. Andries could translate all the hyena calls, the grunts and squeals, the growls and yells, the groans and the ethereal high-pitched giggles of nervous excitement when carrion was sighted or a kill made. He understood better than most they weren't the cowards their cringing shape made them out to be. In this park at least, lions scavenged more from hyena kills than the other way around. Someday the book writers and researchers would catch up.

Two eyes stared down from high in an acacia, round, red and unblinking like traffic lights in a moon-washed city. It was *impukunyoni*, a night ape, an insect-eating, bushbaby relative as loveable as a child's stuffed toy. Oversized ears stuck on a baby-monkey face caught the sound of even the stealthiest spider and commando-skilled beetles. They were perfectly adapted to their environment. As a child, Andries had raided their leaf-lined nests, snuggled in deserted barbet or woodpecker holes or convenient hollows, and taken the babies. He had sold the tiny fluff balls to eager passengers on the Bulawayo–Victoria Falls line and made money enough to help his family. Five shillings went a long way. They made good pets. He had kept one for a while, but as soon as it began to piss on its hands and leap around the hut landing on scoured pots, eating utensils and even his mother, in an accomplished display of distance and accuracy, the little creature's days were numbered. It was taken to the station like the rest of them.

The wide, startled eyes and the chattering alarm call haunted him as he strode beneath the camel-thorn acacia. They transported him again to the duck hunt, the blood-red, pain-filled eyes of the injured boy and the clattering of his teeth as he shivered in shock.

He would never be sure what made him run back to the rude, unlikeable white boy – an instinct that he could put things right? It wasn't just his father's signal. He was the only other child around in this group of hard hunting men. Boy Murphy's father was already yelling at his son.

'Get up, you stupid boy. Stop that noise right now.'

'Hang on a minute, Colonel, your son is badly wounded. He should stay where he is. We should try to stop the bleeding.' Those kind words from H.H. were the only ones Andries heard that day. There was a soothing tone in his voice.

All the hunters were now gathering now. 'What's happened here, Colonel?'

'Just a misfire, Sir Bingham. The boy's making a terrible fuss. It's his mother, she molly coddles him too much. Backbone boy! Don't embarrass me,' he barked.

'Doesn't look too dapper, old man. Bit of a mess. Is that bone or muscle hanging out there? Who's got the first-aid kit?' Sir Bingham looked around for a willing helper. He didn't want to be involved with all the gore. He could slaughter birds with no compunction and just last month he had gut shot a pregnant kudu and failed to follow up, but human blood made him weak in the knees.

'I will look for it, sir,' offered Andries's father. Before he turned and ran for the camp, he gave Andries a glance that commanded compassion and action. Not a word passed between father and son, but Andries understood what he had to do. He walked to the boy's uninjured side, took a soft white hand in his own pump-calloused palm and began to sing. He had a sweet voice, reedy and tuneful in the high range, but with warm lower tones which prefigured the tenor he would become. He sang an age-old lullaby, a simple repetitive refrain that his mother had sung to him, and her mother had sung to her. Its composer was unknown. It wasn't written on any stave or played on any instrument, but it had passed through the lips of millions of mamas. Its perpetuity was assured: '*Thula, baba, thula, umama uyezwa* ... Hush little one, hush; your mother is coming ...'

Andries snapped back to the shadowy clearing. He could not afford to lull himself into complacency. Memory had its place. He no longer recognised that child, life and all its cruelties had intervened like a stinging bee hidden in the honey, and anyway, the African bush at night was no spot to be reminiscing. He had work to do.

With the farm work at Hunter's Rest and money from the researchers, life had been going well of late, better than the ageing diesel locomotives that ran with no reference to any timetable on the line he just crossed, and then his brother was no longer at the lodge. Now, he had no place to keep the tusks until they were traded. The one already delivered was lost to him unless he could get it back somehow. Shadrek had queried the delivery of a single tusk only. Andries lied that the elephant had only had one. He had traded the partner for a supply of alcohol, but Mkandhla had not kept his side of the bargain.

Shadrek, the eldest of the Nyathi brothers, had left home while Andries was still a herd boy. He had gone to work in a Lodge kitchen. Andries looked up to the man who came home once a month with his pockets fat with money and his bag stuffed with blankets, sheets and towels of unthinkable quality. Sometimes he brought exotic treats like butter and bacon, tins of peaches and condensed milk. Once he brought a leg of pork and the family feasted for several days on the soft, sweet meat.

Thunduluka Lodge where Shadrek worked was the perfect staging post for Andries's poaching activities. His brother stored the ivory there until it was collected by a third party. Payment came on the nail. Andries's mission this night was to find out where Shadrek had cached the last tusk before he was arrested.

He walked steadily, alert to every faint noise, any trace of scent. The night held many dangers, even for a man like Andries. His ears picked up a herd of buffalo, grunting and snuffling in the long vlei grass that ran towards the lodge. He was wary of these bovine beasts and never shot them, they were his totem, *Inyathi*. Their cow-like appearance belied a vicious streak. They had deceptive speed. Wounded, they lay in ambush, circling the back-tracking hunter, waylaying him, often successfully. If the herd was big enough, they would have their own attendant pride of lion ready to pick off the lame and the lazy or anything else upwind that took their fancy. Buffalo herds at night, on foot, were best avoided.

Andries could see the lodge lights in the distance. He had always delivered his booty at night so he knew the dark corners and unlit stretches. He was familiar with the layout of the buildings and where the security guard liked to snooze in the small hours. He was heading for Shadrek's room. He had to find his secret cavity.

'How do you get away with all this stuff,' the young Andries had asked his eldest brother, frantically licking the last drops from a tin of condensed milk.

'Be careful you don't lick the paint off the tin,' his brother had laughed.

'But how do you do it under the eyes of the *mukiwas*?'

'Ha, they are stupid. The blanket you sleep in comes from the storeroom at Thunduluka. It is thick and rich and keeps you warm on those blistering nights when the air crackles with cold and the earth sucks the warmth from your bones for her own use.'

'But how?' Andries persisted.

'When I come on leave, my bags are always checked, "what have you got in your bag?" they ask. "My blankets and my clothes," I reply. I have always travelled with blankets so they aren't suspicious. Wrapped up in a threadbare old sheet they look like mine. They never check my bags when I return. Of course, there are no blankets in there, just the smelly old sheet.'

'And how do you get the tins out? I want another one of these when you come again,' young Andries threw the empty milk tin in the air, high on the sugar rush.

'Ah, *umnawami*, my brother, the first lesson in life is to find your own *insitha*, your hidey hole. This is where you will store the precious things that come into your world. Never reveal its location to anyone. I take a tin here and there, a few bottles of hot stuff, never too much and never on the same day. Greed is the sell-out, the betrayer. I keep them in my *insitha* until I come on leave.' Andries remembered the hot stuff – vodka, brandy and particularly cane spirit. He had tasted Shadrek's bounty at a young age. It had grabbed him even then.

'How do you get them past the bag checks?'

'There's a false bottom in my bag. It's a simple table that fits across the bag, leaving a cavity beneath.'

'You are very clever and very careful, I will be like you one day,' Andries boasted. And he was. He took those lessons and learned them well. Shadrek had been pilfering for thirty years. He was never caught. Andries had been poaching undetected for twenty. He was as meticulous in his preparation as Shadrek had been. He had his own *insitha*. In it he kept the weapon that walked with him now and all the *kathundu* associated with a muzzle loader, the flints, the black powder, the patches and the lead balls that he made himself.

He reached the electric fence surrounding the Lodge, put there to keep out prowlers of all species. To the front and side of the buildings the fence was dug into a deep ditch so the seamless camera view of the waterhole was not impaired. He searched around until he found his ladder, a fallen tree camouflaged by bush and leaves. In its life it had grown knots, gnarls and branches; in death these were convenient footholds. Andries had used it before. Leaned against an upright tree just inside the boundary, it cleared the live wires and made the perfect entry point.

Andries kept to the shadows and headed straight for Shadrek's room. He knew his brother well and knew the path of his thoughts. He would find his stash. Edging around the camp he came to the car park. It was easy to use the cover of the vehicles to move quickly towards the staff accommodation which lay on the other side. Shadrek's room was the fourth one from the car park. It stood alone, detached, with one window on the back wall and a batten door at the front. Andries circled warily. It was two in the morning, all the staff would be deeply asleep, but natural caution and stealth were his legacy. He turned Shadrek's door handle on the off chance, but it was locked as expected. With the edge of his axe blade he prised the door until the lock splintered. He never pushed it open and was grateful it hadn't swung open. A commotion from inside the room sent him haring in the direction of his nature-made ladder.

'*Ngubane lo*? Who's that, what are you up to? Help! Thieves! Guard!' a male voice screamed into the darkness.

The night guard would take time to respond. He was fast asleep in the laundry accessed via a faulty window catch, dreaming of wealth, power and fawning women, on a cushion of unwashed sheets and towels. Andries ran hard nonetheless. The occupant's yelling would wake someone; he sounded like a warthog squealing with the pain of a leopard claw to the rump. Andries was over the fence in a flash. His cantilevered tree was thrown hastily back into the bush. He distanced himself from the Lodge. The fading self-righteousness of the victim relating his shock and indignation to anyone who would listen, followed him.

This had been an unguarded mistake. Andries was shaking and angry as he moved quickly across the valley to the safety of the tree line. How could he have broken his own rules? He was no better than Shadrek. They would both end up in Khami prison at this rate. He had been careless, assuming that Shadrek's post had not yet been filled and the room still empty. Why? Simple, funds were short. The country was being squeezed by a toxic mix of dizzy inflation and the introduction of the US dollar as the official currency. He had waived his usual risk assessment as desperation eroded his caution and his savings.

All was not lost. The tusk would still be safe and no one could track him. He trudged towards home. The long walk without the following wind of success loomed like the dark shapes cast by the moon-shadowed branches.

Andries followed the vlei line to the west, tiring as the small hours sapped his stamina. Owls hooted and screeched, a goat sucker sang its melancholy lilt to the waning moon. It hopped and fluttered along in front of him, pennant wings flowing like the practised arms of a prima ballerina. In the distance he picked up the faint low moan of a lioness martialling the troops for an ambush. The eager, panting response made him glad he had left the buffalo some kilometres behind. The herd were in for a rough night.

He was just about to leave the valley margins and strike south to Mpindo line when a grunt reached his ears. It wasn't a lion or a buffalo or even a warthog or bush pig, the other well-known bush grunters. This snort was an unusual expression of contentment. Andries was almost certain of what was calling even though he had rarely heard the sound before. His excitement level began to rise. He shrugged off the disappointment of the last hours and stealthily made his way down through the tree line to the open valley, crawling the final few metres on his belly. He took cover behind a low growing shrub. It wouldn't have mattered because the creature he expected to see had very poor eyesight. Its strength lay in hearing and smell.

Andries had come out upwind of the small wallow. Fifty metres from him, the last of the moonlight outlined two honeymooning white rhinos. The female was taking a mud bath in a shallow scrape in the middle of the valley. The male was standing over her, waiting for her to be receptive. He would fight all comers for the privilege. His horn rose majestically from a huge head and massive neck. He snorted again as if to encourage his bride while she continued to roll languidly like a whore on silken sheets.

The night may not be wasted after all. Andries slithered backwards until he was another twenty metres away. Those two were going nowhere. Now was his chance. Rhino horn was first prize.

'Can't you get a rhino horn?' Shadrek had asked.

'Why rhino horn? What's wrong with tusks?'

'Nothing, it's just that we can get ten, perhaps twenty times the money for horn.'

Andries noted the 'we', he suspected his brother took a cut. This confirmed it.

'I hardly see rhinos anymore. There have been many hunting them in the last few years. Some say it's the army, others blame greedy politicians. The official line is it's the Zambians. Best to blame a foreigner when things go wrong. Why are they so valuable?'

'Our contact tells me it's the East. Asian *muthi,* you know it makes them …' Shadrek gestured a universal sign for manhood '… bigger for longer. Some of them want it for a dagger handle. Same problems, of course,' he made a gesture of impotence with a crooked little finger.

'They can't have much going for them down there to pay all that money. Maybe their wives want a good African man. We could make a fortune servicing Chinese ladies,' Andries laughed, 'we Nyathis have never had that problem have we? Anyway I'll keep my eyes open, but there's little chance.'

'Well, if you see one, take the horn. They are much less dangerous than elephants anyway.'

'Only the white rhino, the blacks live alone and are very threatening. Both can run fast, probably fifty kilometres an hour. Two thousand kilograms of angry rhino would be a fearsome foe.'

'But they're stupid. They've got a tiny brain.'

Andries looked at his brother. It was not like him to be interested in the wild. He lived in the bush, but his eyes were elsewhere. 'Where did you learn that?'

'I used to listen to the tourist questions and the answers Thandanyoni gave. Rhinos must be *isitutha* because their brains are smaller than their nasal passages. In fact,' Shadrek continued, proud for once he knew more than his brother, 'their nostrils are set the widest apart of any mammal in the world.'

'They have a powerful sense of smell, my brother. They know of everything in the air. It is their defence.'

Andries had already taken that fact into his planning as he lay now out of sight of the quarry. He was well upwind of his target. He unslung his weapon, checking it from his prone position. The flint was still firmly embedded, waiting to shower sparks into the flashpan. He rummaged around in the bag at his waist and pulled out a small bottle of black powder. His father had shown him exactly how much to dispense. He could do it blindfold. He crouched and poured the powder down the upright barrel, tapping the weapon with his hand to make sure the black dust settled at the bottom. From his bag he took one of several pre-cut squares of well-oiled cloth and placed it across the muzzle. The ball came next, a perfectly rounded shot of lead lovingly rasped smooth, whittled away on a long winter's night around a fire. He rammed the ball down the barrel until, wrapped in its patch, the leaden sphere nestled firmly on the powder. Next, he tapped powder into the flashpan, carefully levelling it off.

Andries was ready. He snaked his way back to the edge of the valley, negotiating the leaf litter and fallen twigs as smoothly as a python. The closer he got the better. His muzzle loader was an ancient weapon handed down from Nyathi father to Nyathi son for generations. It had been cherished like a baby, but it was no match for the high-powered, high-calibre hunting weapons of today, ones that gave the safety of multiple firings and the optical sights of accuracy from a comfortable distance. Hunting nowadays was still a duck shoot. The prey had no chance.

The female rhino stood. Midnight rivers of silvered water from her bath trickled down her body. Beneath her feet she puddled moon-tinted whorls of mud as she danced in a circle to detect the threat. She moved her ears independently, swivelling each one in a different direction to pick up faint sounds; backlit, the hairs on the tips stood out. Her suitor was also alert. He joined the pas de deux, lightness of foot belying his massive, chunky body. His snorts were no longer of love but of alarm.

Andries's opportunity was slipping. He stood using a mopani tree to hide his shape and steady his aim. He cocked the weapon, pulled it firmly into his shoulder and took a bead. He squeezed the trigger. The flint showered sparks onto the first powder. It flashed and ignited the main charge. The ball left the muzzle, accelerated down the barrel by a tangle of expanding gases. It shot out in an impressive mix of gas, flame and billows of white smoke, blinding Andries temporarily. When the fog cleared he would know if his night had been totally wasted. He would know if the male rhino was dead.

CHAPTER 7

Sibanda's phone rang to the ring tone of the fiery-necked nightjar. 'At least it's a bird,' he thought, but it broke the spell of quiet contentment as the two men continued their bird watching and wildlife observations overlooking Thunduluka's waterhole. 'You have the call of the Mapostoli bird as a ring tone, fantastic!'

Sibanda looked confused. 'Isn't it commonly called the litany bird with its *good Lord deliver us?*'

'Mapostoli bird is just a name we used in this lodge years ago. Can't change it now. It's been too long.'

'Sorry ... Buff,' the unfamiliar name was spoken with some difficulty, 'I'm embarrassed. I should have turned it off, but I'm still technically on duty, I'll have to take this.'

'I understand, don't mind me,' said the older man, 'I've just spotted a racket-tailed roller,' he said, pointing to an exquisitely plumaged bird that flashed turquoise and pink against the summer palate of bush green. 'Not normally their range out here, might keep an eye on him for a few minutes and see what he's up to.'

Sibanda walked out of earshot. 'Hello, who's that?' he barked with some acerbity, irritated by the interruption.

'It's me, sir, Chaliss.'

'Charles?' Sibanda was confused for a moment. He didn't know any Charles.

'I'm the cook from Hunter's Rest. Do you remember me? You recommended me for a job here at Thunduluka.'

'Yes, right, Charles. I hadn't realised you got the job. You helped with the last case. It's the least I could do. You don't have to thank me.'

'I'm phoning about something else. I'm in the lodge car park. Could you meet me there?'

Sibanda glanced back to Buff Barton. He was engrossed in his sighting. The detective could probably spare a few minutes. 'I'll be there now.'

Charles stood in the car park looking little changed from their last encounter except that his uniform was immaculate. Gone were the patched knees and well-worn apron, replaced by chef's whites. His sad, drooping eyes still reminded Sibanda of a bloodhound.

'How can I help, Charles?'

'My room was broken into last night.'

'Anything taken?'

'No.'

'I'm not sure I can help. What has the management done?'

'Laughed at me.'

'Laughed? Why?'

'It was an *umfazi*, a female who broke in. They are making a joke, saying I must be a magnet for ladies, that they can't resist me. This is an embarrassment. I am a good Christian man, a member of the Brethren of the Lord's Blood. Your Officer-in-Charge Stalin Mfumu can vouch for me. I have been married to the same woman for over thirty years.'

'Did you see the thief?'

'No, she never entered the room. She must have got a shock when she heard my shouts. She ran away very fast and climbed over the fence. The trail had gone cold by the time I could convince anybody to take a look.'

'Show me your room, Charles. Let me see what I can make of it.'

Sibanda examined the spoor surrounding Charles' room, 'she circled for a while before she broke in. I see she splintered the lock. She must be a big, strong girl.' He refrained from unseemly jokes. Charles was genuinely sensitive and upset. He looked again at the tracks. They were small and neat but without any tread or sole markings. That was not unusual. Shoes in and around Gubu were used until the rubber was worn smooth, often with a few holes earned from miles of walking. Transport was sparse. But there was something odd about these prints, the edges were still sharp and the sole was unmarked by use. They were deep tracks too, indicating that the wearer was overweight for a woman of that shoe size and yet the spoor was straight. Big woman were noted for their toe-out walk, and for uneven rolling footprints.

Sibanda followed further. The robber had begun to run hard towards the fence and the interval between the steps increased as she sped up. He measured it against his own stride. This woman was exceedingly tall. Here and there parallel to the footprints were strange scuff marks in the sand as though the wearer had gone over on her ankle. It was too regular to be that.

'I heard a shot along the valley about an hour later.' Sibanda had forgotten Charles behind him. He was engrossed in the mystery.

'Did anyone else hear it?'

'I doubt it. No one has mentioned it. They were all snoring in their beds by then. I was too jumpy to go back to sleep.'

'Well, she's gone now, Charles. Get the lock fixed. I doubt she'll be back, particularly to the room of a God-fearing man. I'll look into it though. I might just drive down the valley for a while. See if I can pick up the tracks. I'll let you know if I find anything.'

'Thank you, sir. I must go now. We are preparing dinner for the guests. There's an important tour operator staying this evening. There will be a fuss in the kitchen. The manager wants a special menu. I must start preparing early.'

Sibanda strolled back to Buff Barton, still intrigued by the tracks he had seen.

'Ah, you have returned just in time, look what's pitched up in your absence.' Barton pointed to two rhinos at the waterhole, not drinking, heads held high, snorting and sniffing in some distress, turning this way and that.

'They aren't happy,' Sibanda commented, 'something has put the wind up them.'

'Take a look, see what you think, Jabu,' he passed his binoculars to Sibanda.

'Blood on the male, down his flank.'

'Yes, that's what I saw too. From a rival's horn? They look like a mating couple.'

'Probably, although if it had been a black rhino you could say that with certainty given their aggressive nature. They have the highest mortal combat rate of any mammal, even humans … and that's saying something. Something like fifty per cent of males and thirty per cent of females die from combat-related injuries …' Sibanda stood and moved closer. He refocused the binoculars, 'but this is a white rhino. It could be a gunshot that's glanced across the flank.'

'Bastards,' exclaimed Barton. 'Must be heavy calibre if it is, that's a nasty, wide gash. When I ran this lodge we guaranteed rhino sightings. I remember seeing a crash of seventeen before breakfast on one safari. Now there's less than a handful and they're threatened. They'll be gone soon.'

'Crash?'

'It's the collective noun for rhinos. More descriptive than "herd". We must have had a population of between fifty and seventy around these parts. They disappeared over three months and we never even knew they were going.'

They both turned their attention back to the agitated pair, weighing up their chances of survival against the odds.

'They can't swim,' Sibanda offered, 'one of the few mammals that can't, their hump necks would drown them,' he wanted to break away from his own depressing thoughts of their inevitable extinction.

'Hadn't thought about that,' Barton was grateful too.

Half an hour later Sibanda was driving down the valley away from Gubu and in the direction of the shot. It was an unlikely coincidence, but maybe the break in, the shot and the wounded rhino were related. Sibanda didn't like coincidences. Normally, he couldn't interfere in poaching cases, that would be treading on National Parks' toes, but with a break-in involved he had the perfect excuse.

As Sibanda was driving slowly down Thunduluka valley looking for spoor or anything unusual, Sergeant Ncube was close to pulling into his fishing camp on the Zambezi for the night. Miss Daisy had made the hour-long journey with ease. She had huffed and puffed a bit and gasped for air climbing the steep hills to the Zambezi valley, but on the leeward side she showed her mettle and ran smoothly down to the river. Ncube had coaxed the old lady over the basalt-strewn road with care. No springs would be loosened, no nuts or bolts rattled loose, no tyres punctured and most of all, the radiator, something of a weakness if he were honest, had remained mostly cool and calm. If Detective Jabulani

Sibanda had been behind the wheel, Miss Daisy would have been a quivering wreck by now.

'This is a beautiful vehicle, Ncube. I cannot imagine why the police do not need it.'

'Made more beautiful by your handiwork my friend,' said the sergeant to his fishing companion Phiri. It had been the tailor's upholstery of the seats with a robust candy-striped canvas that had saved Ncube's bacon when he had been sent to find a working vehicle in Bulawayo and not to return without one or to pay the price. He had made it back to Gubu with Miss Daisy minus any seats. Phiri had come to the rescue. Chief Inspector Stalin Mfumu, Officer-in-Charge, Gubu, was not to be messed with.

'This is a test run,' he added, in the interests of some shred of truth, 'she has been off the road for a while and I offered to patch her up and get her running again,' Ncube coughed a little to hide his stretching of the truth. He didn't feel comfortable with a bare-faced lie. 'Besides which when the mamba is away, the mongoose is happy. It's the weekend, Phiri, and the chief inspector is already preparing his sermon for Sunday. What does he care about vehicles?'

'Where is this special fishing hole of yours Ncube?'

'We are staying at the police fishing camp at Deka. It's not far,' replied the sergeant. 'It's no good fishing near there though. It's been fished out by many official rods before us. I know the very spot, up river, hard to get to, even with a boat, and never visited. There's a little backwater shaded by a big tree with an eddy beneath and a flat rock sitting out of the water's edge like a maiden's rump just waiting for our fishing stools.' He felt guilty not knowing the name of the tree. Detective Sibanda would have given him a lecture on its uses, why it grew just where it grew and why it attracted the juiciest fish to its shade. Perhaps the detective's madness was rubbing off on him.

Phiri squirmed on his seat and looked uncomfortable. Ncube remembered his friend was a devout Muslim and perhaps it was best not to refer to female body parts in his presence.

'We will settle in tonight, Phiri, enjoy our beef ribs slow roasted over the coals, an early night and then we will be up at first light to challenge the fish. They are waiting for us. They are sharpening their cunning, but we shall be like the jackal that found a land snail without even trying. I have *Amatumbu Webhejane* to lure them.'

'Rhinoceros intestines? Is that legal?' asked the alarmed tailor.

'Ha! Not real innards, just the biggest, fattest, liveliest worms this side of the Limpopo. They won't fail us.'

As Sergeant Ncube gently closed Miss Daisy's door and carried the box of wriggling 'rhino guts' to his chalet on the banks of the Zambezi, so Detective Sibanda slammed the driver's door on the Santana. He was angry. He had seen and found enough evidence to know that the male rhino at the Thunduluka waterhole had been shot at. It had been easy to pick up running rhino tracks along the valley. The female thief's tracks had been harder. She had obviously been careful, avoiding the road and paths. At one crossing point in the valley, Sibanda suspected she had used anti-tracking techniques, but if she had, she was exceedingly clever. He dismissed the idea. Women didn't behave that way. They rarely came into the bush alone, not big game territory. They left that to the men, or did they?

He found the rhino wallow easily. He saw where the female rhino had rolled and left her wrinkled imprint in the drying mud. There was trampling and puddling in parts as the pair milled in vigilance. He could see the picture clearly, read nervousness in their tracks, heard the snorts and alarm calls and then the sudden take off, leaving the deep prints of fear in the mud. It didn't take long for him to find traces of blood.

Sibanda walked around the muddy scrape in ever-increasing circles, stooping every now and again to inspect signs in the short grass. The poacher would have come back to the scene to check for a lung shot or a disabling wound, the colour, quantity and texture of the blood alerting him to the flesh-wound nature of the injury. The killer had not pursued his prey. And it was a 'he'. Sibanda was certain of that. Was the woman thief his accomplice in some way? What was going on here?

Twenty metres from the wallow, Sibanda squatted over a partial footprint and yelled in pain. He had forgotten his leg. The steady ache as he crouched increased to an intolerable stab. Curses flowed freely, but he had found his poacher; it was the 'woman' who had broken into Charles's room. He tracked back, limping, to a mopani tree on the valley's edge and from there it was an easy track through leaf litter carved apart by a slithering body to another large tree. The story was plain for all to see. The poacher had rested his rifle perpendicular, butt-side down as he made his plans. Unusual, he thought. Most shooters rested their rifles parallel to the ground in the safety position. The shoe prints were the small, neat, female-sized spoor from Thunduluka. This was either a gun-toting Amazonian woman, a man with very small feet or a very cunning man who had disguised his footprints to look like a woman's. That made sense of the parallel scuff marks. They were the edges of the man's boots that dug in. Sibanda was impressed despite his disgust. This man was a worthy adversary.

The sun was low on the horizon. There was too little light to make tracking feasible. His aching leg underlined the impossibility. He took one last look at the scene, scanning carefully for anything he might have missed. At that moment a gentle breath of evening air rustled a few leaves and unearthed two cut squares of white material, clinging to one another like shipwreck survivors in a brown sea of rotting compost. Sibanda picked them up. Odd, he thought, someone as canny as our poacher would never wear white in the bush. They aren't torn. Probably cut from an old sheet and steeped in oil of some kind. He sniffed them. The white cotton had been lubricated with gun oil. He rubbed his chin. He rubbed harder. No answers came, just more questions.

He opened his phone battery cover and popped the two white squares safely in the cavity. The bloodstained fragment from Mkandhla's skull still lay glued to the phone screen. Sibanda was certain the pieces were linked, plus poaching was involved in both incidents. He was wary of the obvious.

Sibanda hobbled back to the Santana. His leg was becoming a real problem. He should call in at the clinic. Tomorrow morning would have to do. Leaning against the seat with the door open, he faced west. The sun was plunging recklessly towards the horizon and into the wilderness, bravely traversing an unknown land of thorns and claws, of poison, fangs and dark terrors, to greet his dawn mistress on the other side of the world. Sibanda sighed, did he wish for such certainty of solar purpose and long-term commitment? He sat in reflection for a few moments more before opening Blessing's brown paste and smearing it on his hot, throbbing thigh. The textured sweetness of Suko's *inopi* added to his enjoyment of the approaching dusk as did the final frantic chatter of birds settling, finding their perches, hawking their last meal for the day before darkness fell.

In a sudden flurry, a rare bat hawk stooped and banked over the valley in synchrony with its prey. Bats were about, emerging from their roosts and starting to search for insects over the muddy wallow. The hawk flew two or three passes, large eyes piercing the fading light for a likely target. Sibanda battled to keep the speedy raptor in sight. He tracked it intently as it swooped on a bat from behind with long, sharp talons, grabbing the flying mouse and stuffing the whole creature into its enormous gape in one movement before racing away to new hunting grounds. Its window of opportunity was narrow and night was falling swiftly.

The detective realised that he too needed to move on, the window of opportunity for the Mkandhla murder was closing. He suspected the outcome would not be as easy as picking off a witless bat. And, what had this poaching incident got to do with it, if anything? He drove back along the valley trying to sort out what clues he had and what he knew of the victim. Much as he tried to keep his mental investigation going, the thought of Berry missing and distraught sent grinding waves through his stomach. He would like to get the low life that shot her dog, skin him alive, slow roast him over hot coals and throw him on a nest of flesh-eating Matabele ants. The torture of the mind-numbing monotony of life in the first world with its concrete office culture, grey sameness and lack of elephants would have to do.

Constable Khumalo was about to knock off duty when he returned to the station.

'Anything from Forensics, Zee?'

'Yes,' she smiled triumphantly as she walked back behind the desk to retrieve her notes. 'Our victim is, as we suspected, most likely named Mkandhla. They managed to restore enough of the name on his identity card. The number is beyond recognition though, so we don't know where he came from.'

'Bulawayo.'

'How do you know that, sir?' she asked, although like everyone at the station in Gubu she believed Detective Inspector Sibanda had powers beyond the earthly.

'Not sure, but I'm convinced that's where he's from. I've just got to work out why.'

'The good news is they finally agree he was shot. There is no internal organ damage typical of a lightning victim.'

The detective shook his head in exasperation as Forensics confirmed what he knew all along. 'Any autopsy results? I'd like to find out what his liver was like. There were several crates of empties in his room.'

'You also found a tusk, didn't you? A poaching ring gone sour?'

'He might be a middle man, but hardly a poacher. He didn't fit the bill.'

'Why?'

'Just a hunch, but he was too slightly built. He didn't have the weathered features of a hunter. Too soft, like a desk man from what I saw of him. We found no weapons at the house. Has anyone come forward who knew him?'

'No one; it's as if he has been shunned.'

'Look, Zee, could you get hold of young Patel Barghee and ask him everything he knows about muzzle loaders. He might have picked something up from his great-grandfather.'

'Another hunch, sir? I'm off duty tomorrow. Will Monday be okay?'

'Yes and yes,' the detective replied, 'and one last thing, Zee, why would anyone break into a cook's room when a camp full of foreign tourists with expensive cameras, binoculars and fat wallets were metres away behind flimsy canvas?'

PC Khumalo didn't have an answer. She shrugged. Sibanda walked down the corridor to his office. He could have done with Sergeant Ncube around. He was always a good sounding post and he knew more about the goings on in Gubu than anyone. His wives kept him up to speed on all the gossip. Behind all that genial blubber, gaseous emissions and obsession for engines, he was a shrewd man.

By the time he reached home, Sibanda was tired, irritable and aching. It had started with a note on his desk from Stalin Mfumu demanding that the keys to the Santana be returned, and that he be in his office first thing Monday morning with explanations and paperwork. His throbbing leg was becoming a drain and a liability. He was pretty certain it was infected. He slathered on more of Blessing's smelly brown mixture, swigged a few drops of her potion and sank into a deep sleep, free for the first few hours at least from the anxious dreams that had plagued him.

Just before he dozed off, he remembered to peel the bloodied shred of fabric from his phone screen and pop it in a saucer of milk. He hoped it didn't matter that it was sour. He hadn't stocked up on fresh food for some days.

CHAPTER 8

T he fiery-necked nightjar was calling in the distance, mood music as Detective Inspector Sibanda sat at the pan's edge at dusk with a large herd of elephants splashing and bathing in the cooling muddy waters. It was a hot night. He was burning. He desperately wanted to join them and cool off. Berry sat to his left, her back to him; at least he thought it was Berry, ethereal, like a ghost. He tried to reach her. She was just beyond his grasp and a playful bull elephant had pinned his leg to the ground. He shouted to the shadowy figure to turn and help. She never moved. The nightjar became louder and more persistent until it broke through his dream and woke him. He sat up, bathed in sweat. It was his mobile phone singing the song of the moonlight flyer. He gave himself a few moments to reorientate and then flipped the phone's cover open.

'Sir, thank goodness you've answered.'

'Sergeant, it's barely dawn. What are you doing calling at this hour in the morning?' Sibanda tried to sound irritable although he was glad to be woken from his nightmare.

'Sorry, sir, but there's a body.'

He was alert now. 'Whereabouts, Ncube, in Soweto?'

'No, sir, on the Zambezi.'

'Where?' Sibanda was confused. Maybe his brain hadn't cleared from the dream. Ncube was supposed to be at home fixing the wreck of a Land Rover called Miss Daisy.

'Near the police fishing camp at Deka. I, er ... brought Miss Daisy for a run. She is better, now, sir, almost perfect, I would ...'

'Is it a drowning?' Sibanda interrupted what would surely be a longwinded description of the engine's virtues.

'I can't say what the cause of death is, but it's a white woman. She's close to the riverbank.'

'How long has she been there?'

'Some hours, at least since last night. The rats have been at the body.'

'Hair colour, eyes, age?' Sibanda snapped a staccato list. His heart was beating so hard he thought it would burst through his ribs.

'A young, blonde woman, I haven't checked the eyes,' the sergeant heard a groan on the other end of the phone, followed by silence. After a few moments he asked, 'sir, are you alright?'

Sibanda took some deep breaths and controlled his panic, Berry's hair was ash blonde. 'Yes, fine, Sergeant. Can you secure the site and meet me at the fishing camp?'

'I have left tailor Phiri with the body. I had to travel some way to get a phone signal.'

'Right, I'll be with you in forty-five minutes.'

'That's not possible, sir, the road is very bad in parts ...'

'Be there waiting in forty-five minutes, Ncube,' he slammed the phone shut.

The detective leapt off his bed and immediately regretted it. His leg almost collapsed under him, the ache had now reached his groin. His glands were up. He knew it spelt trouble. He took another swig of Blessing's liquid and smeared the paste on the red, oozing wound. There would be no time for a clinic visit now.

Sergeant Ncube paced backwards and forwards along the riverbank at the fishing camp. His weekend had been ruined. He couldn't blame the poor dead girl. She hadn't met a good end, he was sure of that; there was no peace on her face. His eye was telling his heart this was an uncomfortable death. How had she found his secret fishing hole, and what was a white woman doing alone on the banks of the Zambezi? Why did she look familiar? He wasn't going to waste time trying to work it out, trying to grab the head of a flying ant hoping the rest of the body would be a deliciously nutty treat. Some of them were vile. He would leave all the speculation to Detective Inspector Sibanda. The detective would turn every bean out of every pod in his search for the truth.

The talk of flying ants and beans was making the sergeant hungry. His stomach was rumbling, but he was glad it was still empty when he and Phiri came across the body. His stomach was a delicate organ and behaved badly, particularly in the presence of smells, gore and the exuding fluids of decomposing bodies. His digestive tract produced gases from nowhere that had to be evacuated. It could never be silent and caused Ncube considerable embarrassment and inventive subterfuge. Coughing was a well-honed, synchronous skill.

With the first hint of dawn the eager fishermen had had the singing Zambezi in their sights, bubbling with blue foam and summer ginger fizz fed from rain-washed clay upstream. Ncube had even mentally thrown his first catch of the day on the small sizzling griddle he used for such breakfasts along with Nomatter's fried mealie cakes and Blessing's wild loquat chutney made from the fruits of the mahobohobo tree. The fantasy dissolved rapidly when the body came into view.

As he paced, Ncube wondered if he had time to find some of Suko's goat's cheese and maize balls, rolled in egg and breadcrumbs and deep fried. She always tucked a few of those away for an emergency. Truth was there were many emergencies in Ncube's life and he remembered he had munched most of them for a midnight snack. Sleeping could be a hungry business.

The Santana with Sibanda behind the wheel made it to the fishing camp in forty-eight minutes flat. It bounced into the camp like a springhare avoiding a jackal. Ncube wasn't certain it would make it back to Gubu. Was that the first hint of steam from under the bonnet?

The detective leaned out of the window. 'Take me to the body, Ncube.'

'Sir, we only need one vehicle. Miss Daisy will get us to the spot.' He didn't mention the Santana could do with a rest. There was something strained about the detective's face. He looked about to launch into one of his sarcastic tirades. The poor man was stressed about something. He was normally as cool as the winter sun when it came to crime scenes.

The tension in Miss Daisy's cab could cut through the hind legs of an impala. Every muscle in Sibanda's jaw was taut, every muscle in Ncube's gut was in spasm.

'Can't this old crock go any faster, Ncube?'

'Sir, the bush is thick and the road is rocky, the springs …'

'Damn the springs, Ncube, the body will be a rotted skeleton by the time we get to her.'

'At least we will get to her,' the sergeant muttered, but the words were lost as the vehicle accelerated over the rocks and stream beds of the valley's tortured geology.

'Is this the only way in by road?'

'Yes, sir, as far as I know.'

'Did you see any tracks ahead of yours?'

'I wasn't really looking. I was chatting to Phiri, talking about how to bait our hooks and what weight line to use.'

'There have been a few vehicles this way recently, look ahead of us, can you see those marks?'

Ncube didn't know how to answer. If he was honest and said 'no', he would appear stupid, if he said 'yes', he would be asked some difficult questions about them. Memories of the blue Toyota's Desert Duellers still haunted him. He chose silence. He thought this fishing spot was his secret alone. He was disappointed.

Sibanda didn't notice the lack of an answer. He was willing the Land Rover forward. Normally he would have stopped to have a closer look at the tracks, but he had to get to the girl and find out if it was Berry. From the moving vehicle he could make out several sets of recent treads. If he excluded Miss Daisy's well-worn tyres then there were at least three more – two in and one out and possibly some older ones as well. Had she come here to end it all, devastated by the loss of her dog, Luka, her link to the mother she never knew?

The body lay on her side facing the river, one leg across the other, one arm reaching out to the water she would never touch again. Blonde locks fanned out in a tangle of gold. A few leaves and twigs had woven themselves into her hair almost like a crown of laurels. In death, she was an earth goddess. Sibanda was out of the Land Rover before it had come to a halt. He raced to the corpse. He didn't register the stabbing pain in his thigh. He could barely breathe.

It wasn't Berry. Sibanda knew it before he got close and he almost collapsed with relief. The body was too heavy in build and the clothes too skimpy; a low-cut top and a tiny skirt. Berry would never have dressed like that. Still, he peered hard at the face to make sure. Brown eyes and nicotine-stained fingers were certain confirmation. She'd been dead a couple of days. The ants and flies told him that. Forensics would be more precise.

Suddenly he was overcome with a wave of nausea. He just made it to the nearest tree. He was about to throw up the remains of Suko's *inopi* on the roots when something caught his eye. He turned away at the last moment, vomiting violently in the surrounding bush.

Ncube stood at a polite distance with Phiri.

'Has seeing the body made the detective ill?' the tailor asked.

'I do not think so, my friend. He has seen much worse without flinching.'

'Perhaps he is not used to woman in this state.' Phiri helped the local Imam prepare bodies for funerals. He has been a good man to leave at the scene.

Ncube shook his head. 'No, there is something not right with him. He would normally be barking instructions and prowling around the scene by now like *umangoyi,* an alley cat around a tin of sardines. He is sick. Blessing told me I must look out for him. She said he had a sickness in his body and a longing in his mind. She can tell these things.'

The sergeant walked towards the detective. In his hand, he had a can of fizzy orange. From experience he knew it settled even the most churning of stomachs.

'Drink this, sir. It will help.'

Sibanda took the can. 'Look, Ncube,' he said, pointing to cigarette butts on the ground. 'Our victim spent some hours behind this tree. Why? Was she hiding? She certainly wasn't waiting for two ugly old fishermen like you.'

Ncube hid his indignation. The detective was back to his usual self. 'She smoked a lot of cigarettes.'

'Bag a few of those stubs, then let's go back to the body and see if we can pick up any clues on how she died,' Sibanda swigged a mouthful of the orange fizz, 'thanks,' he added.

Sibanda looked carefully at the young woman. A pair of binoculars hung around her neck. A well-respected make. She had no marks on her body other than deep punctures on her lower legs. They hadn't come from Ncube's rats; the marks were too deep and far apart and there was bleeding. She had still been alive when she had been grabbed. It didn't take him long to work out the perpetrator. Thick snaking tracks led from the body to the river.

'Take a look at this, Sergeant.'

'What made those marks, sir? They look like a snake, but don't tell me a snake can be that thick and fat, unless ...'

'Unless what?'

'It's ... it's an *Umgobo*,' Ncube shuddered; he could hardly say the name of the terrifying creature with the body of a snake monster. It crowed like a rooster, had the head of a vicious dog, feathers like a chief's headdress, fangs that could chew rocks and a mouth that could swallow a person whole. Did one of those frightening creatures live here in his precious fishing spot? Had it been watching him as he wiled away many pleasant hours with a line in the river?

Sibanda shook his head, '*Umgobos* don't exist, Ncube, they are a figment of the Ndebele imagination, something dreamed up by our ancestors to explain mysterious disappearance and death. This creature is far worse, and it's real.'

'Worse? What can be worse?' Ncube began to swallow back a bubbling of burps. Their need to escape was something he understood. He would rather not be here in this dangerous place any longer either.

'These marks are made by a crocodile, a youngish one. It probably lives in this backwater and has its larder deep below the bank over there.'

Ncube turned pale at the thought and began to sweat. His stomach, which had been churning with hunger, now bellowed with anxiety. An *mberezwa* of gently popping intestinal air like a misfiring engine broke the silence. He patted his trousers to disguise the noise and disperse the gases. Sibanda feigned ignorance. He was learning to deal with the vagaries of Ncube's gut. He passed the barely touched can of fizzy drink back to him. His need was greater.

'The croc dragged the body from over there,' Sibanda pointed to a large *Kigelia*, a sausage tree, a few metres away. The pair walked back towards it.

'This is odd, Ncube. The victim didn't struggle, even though she was still alive. Look at that blood trail. Her heart was pumping, but her limbs were motionless. It's as if she was paralysed.'

Both men took a moment to absorb the horror of the girl's death, trapped in reptilian jaws and entombed in a strait jacket of immobility unable even to struggle or scream. Ncube hoped she had died quickly in little pain. Sibanda knew she hadn't. She was still bleeding when the crocodile finally gave up his prey.

'Why didn't the crocodile pull her all the way into the river and down to his … larder?' Ncube broke the silence.

'She was a dead weight and quite far from the water. Crocs can't hunt on land, they like their muscled tails in the water. When they thrash, it gives them better purchase and fiercer ripping power. He still had some way to drag her. He was too small, gave up and went back to fishing for those prize bream you are always boasting about. A fully grown adult might have done it.'

'Maybe one of those big things fell on the girl's head and knocked her out?' suggested Ncube, pointing to the heavy grey sausage-shaped fruit that hung down from the *Kigelia* tree on long stems. 'One of those falling could be deadly.'

'I can't see any on the ground. She may have collapsed from natural causes.' But Sibanda didn't believe that even as he was saying it. A young, dead white woman on a remote bank of the Zambezi spelled murder. 'Let's take another look at the body.'

'No bruising or wounds to her head.' Ncube commented, 'just those rips on her lower limbs.'

Sibanda didn't reply. He was looking at a small puncture mark below the level of her rucked-up mini skirt. It was too small to have been made by a croc tooth.

'Ncube, help me pull her skirt back down.'

'We wanted to do that earlier, sir. Phiri was most insistent that her legs should be covered, but I knew we shouldn't move her.'

'This is not about modesty, Sergeant,' Sibanda snapped, 'the girl is dead. She'll be stripped naked and turned inside out by the pathologists in a few short hours. I want to check where her skirt would have lined up to the small wound on the top of her thigh,' Sibanda was irritable, his own thigh no longer numbed by the terror that this might have been Berry.

Ncube took the reprimand with good grace. He was learning to deal with the detective's mood swings and strange requests. Together they manipulated the body until the skirt was back in place. As they did, a set of keys fell from the mini-skirt pocket.

'Her car keys,' stated Ncube.

'Yes, but where's her car?' They both looked around as if expecting it to be neatly parked under a tree. 'It's got to be here somewhere, Ncube. She didn't fly here. One set of treads never made it back along the track. Scout around, see if you can find it. I want to have a closer look at this mark on her thigh.'

'Sir, I'll take Phiri along. Two sets of eyes are better than one.'

'It can't be that hard to spot a vehicle in the bush,' Sibanda looked into Ncube's round and fearful eyes. 'Okay, but tell him not to touch anything.' Ncube nodded gratefully. He no longer wanted to be alone in this place with prowling *umgobos* and deadly crocodiles.

Sibanda had seen all he needed. Whatever had made the pointed mark in her skin had done so through the back of her skirt. She had been upright. He wandered around the area in his usual fashion of concentric circles. There was nothing to note. He reached the riverbank and Ncube's fishing rock on a small cliff high enough to discourage crocs. It was a perfect spot, idyllic. Overhead the branches of a large ebony reached its cover over the river. Fish enjoy that – no current to fight and a shady spot to pick out the insects that fell from the tree or lived in it and dipped in for a drink. The fish could hide in the cool water from any overhead menace – hamerkops and kingfishers for the fingerlings, fish-eagles for the adults. The shade camouflaged their outline and it was hard to stoop at killing speed with low hanging branches in the way. To his left a narrow inlet, murky and deep, had eroded into the bank, to his right a small sandy beach lured like a seaside poster. Ahead of him across the wide Zambezi lay Zambia, the vista interrupted by a series of small sand islands embroidered with trapped flotsam and grass. On the Zambian side he could just make out a fishing village. Thatched roofs, a few curls of smoke and the occasional clump of feathering reeds softened the thick tree line with tones of grey.

Sibanda's hand went instinctively to his chin and stroked his hard-edged jaw line. What was a young woman doing here alone? The binos indicated she might be a bird watcher, but why this spot? Had she heard of something rare in this area, maybe the endangered Lilian's lovebird, the smallest parrot on the African continent. There were very few around. He would love to see one himself. Was this girl twitching, looking at wildlife or watching something else? Sibanda had noted a few impala tracks, the odd kudu and some old elephant spoor. Unless she was keen on crocs and hippos there was better viewing elsewhere. The detective was disturbed by the returning bulk and heavy steps of his sergeant. 'Sir, we have found the vehicle. I recognise it and I know the victim.' Ncube was breathing hard with a mixture of excitement and effort.

'What have you got, Ncube?'

'It's a Nissan Patrol, sir, quite old and battered. It's had a life of terrible hardship and neglect and ...'

'Sergeant, who is the woman?' Sibanda cut him short. 'I don't give a toss about what vehicle she was driving.' A purple-crested turaco in the sausage tree clock-clocked in mutual agreement before launching itself away from the potential conflict zone in a flash of red, purple and green iridescence.

'She's a wildlife researcher, sir, lives near Gubu and drives her vehicle around the village. I have always thought ...' Ncube halted further comment on the four-wheel drive that lacked upkeep, '... there are often complaints about her and her research, and she has lodged a few herself. She's an American national.'

'Researching what?'

'Not sure. Rhinos?'

'Name?'

'I just know her as Malini.'

'Malini means *how much*? Where did she get that from?'

'It's something to do with her surname and money. She's always quibbling about paying for things.'

Sibanda thought for a moment, unlikely to be Moneypenny. She was certainly no Bond girl. Worth or Stirling could be possibilities, 'Price?' he suggested.

'Yes, that is it!'

'So, Ms Price, rhino researcher, is here on the Zambezi. Not untoward, this is black rhino habitat, thick bush with plenty of browse, but there hasn't been a rhino here for a while.'

'How can you tell, sir?'

'No dung, no middens, no trails through the bush, no spoor. Was she studying black or white rhino?'

'I thought they were all the same colour – grey?' as he said it, the sergeant could have bitten off his tongue. He had wandered right into the middle of one of the detectives minefields. He sensed a lecture in the making.

Sibanda bit his own tongue. The adrenalin rush from discovering Berry wasn't lying dead at his feet gave him an unusual surge of patience. His explanation was mild.

'White is a corruption of the Afrikaans word *wyd,* for the wide mouth the rhino has developed for grazing, but it's no more white than you or I. They called the other one black to differentiate it.'

'So are they two different animals?' Ncube tried to appear interested to placate the detective, but the information would be in one ear and out the other. If it had legs and couldn't be eaten or was dangerous, he wanted nothing to do with it.

'Yes, white rhinos are bigger, calmer, more sociable and they eat grass, but they aren't white. Black rhinos are angry loners and smaller. They eat leaves and they aren't black. The two species don't even live in the same places. In fact one of the few similarities they share is the colour of their hides – grey, as you said. It's unlikely that a researcher would include both. The study would be too wide ...' he looked across at Ncube. Did he realise how closely he had summarised their different personalities? Ncube was certainly placid, bigger and more sociable, even with his own family 'crash'. Was he, Sibanda, the angry loner?

'What sort do we have around Gubu and in the park, sir?' Ncube stifled a yawn. He had read nothing into the comparison.

'Mostly white, so we have to wonder what she was doing here. I want to take a look at her vehicle.'

The car had been parked in thick bush and was not visible from the track. It gave up nothing obvious, no signs of struggle. The glove box had an empty gum wrapper and a pen. On the seat sat a half-drunk bottle of water. The car was in a filthy state. It hadn't been cleaned out in months. The driver's foot well was awash in sand, grass and dirt. A few crumpled grocery receipts from Barghees littered the passenger side. The dash was covered in dust and marks from a coffee mug. Ms Price and cleanliness were obviously strangers. She had hidden her vehicle in impenetrable bushwillow, Jesse bush. Why didn't she want anyone to know she was here? Behind the sunshade, attached with an elastic band and amidst other papers came confirmation of her identity, a driver's licence in the name of Tiffany Price. The smiling white-toothed photo matched the dead woman. She was a picture of tanned good health.

Sibanda, deep in thought, walked back to the sausage tree and leaned against its smooth bole. One or two showy flowers still clung to the high branches, large enough to accept the pollinating attentions of a bat. A few lay rotting among the roots, blood-red cups streaked with yellow veins fading to rusted brown. Death now owned this place.

'Sir, if we have finished here, we should get back to the police fishing camp. Forensics will be coming from Detaba with a body box. I called them at the same time as I called you. We will need to guide them to this spot.'

'I'll take the Land Rover and head back to Gubu. I'll direct the follow-up team here. You stay and keep an eye on Ms Price. Get a lift back to the police camp with them and bring the Santana back to the station.' He threw the keys to the sergeant.

'But, sir ...' Ncube stammered, panicking at the thought of the detective ploughing his precious Miss Daisy over the stubbly terrain.

Sibanda ignored the plea. He strode back past the sausage tree. His leg was throbbing viciously and now there were two murders on his patch. Overhead in the last of the *Kigelia* blossoms a large moth sucked greedily on the nectar.

CHAPTER 9

S ibanda's trip back from the river had been uneventful, although had his sergeant been with him there might have been some sighing and hand wrenching. While the detective focused on the murders, he failed to avoid several tyre-shredding rocks. His technique for negotiating eroded gullies was to take them head-on like an ocean-going breaker in Arctic pack ice. He rarely troubled his brakes or gear shift, his mind was engaged elsewhere. Above all he was relieved he hadn't found Berry dead in gruesome fashion on the banks of the river. Tiffany Price had paid highly for being in the wrong place at the wrong time. She had been murdered, he was sure of that, and once they investigated her contacts a list of suspects would emerge.

And what was going on with Mkandhla's murder? He began mentally scrutinising Mkandhla's room. Had he overlooked something? Half way back to Gubu the missing piece slotted into place like Ncube's key in the dead man's lock. And that's exactly what he needed, Ncube's key. He wanted to get back into that room again. He checked phone signal. There were no bars.

Ncube, meanwhile having guided the police team to the girl's body, decided that his weekend would not be completely ruined.

'Come Phiri, not all the fish in the Zambezi have swum away. We will find another spot and we shall have a competition, three skubhus of Chibuku to the winner.'

'Have you forgotten I do not drink?'

'Ah yes,' Ncube sighed with resignation, 'then three buns and three cans of orange.'

When Ncube finally drove the Santana back to Gubu village on Sunday evening, he was totally unaware that detective Sibanda had been phoning him. His focus had been the competition and he was dejected at losing. Phiri had pulled in a barbel, a monster, whiskery catfish just before they reeled in for the last time. It was bordering on cheating. They had been fishing for bream. Phiri, behind by three, must have baited his hook with leftover beef rib. The barbel weighed more than Ncube's entire catch. Still, his wives would make a delicious supper from his personal efforts, perhaps his favourite – mealie fishcakes with a hint of chilli and wild garlic, served with tomato and choux mollier relish. He slapped his lips, gathered his rod and hauled his keep net into the house.

Sibanda, in contrast, had spent a frustrating day. When he couldn't get hold of Ncube, he had gone to the station. It was a good place to be on a Sunday. Petty crime and minor complaints vaporised, Stalin Mfumu was occupied with his congregation, assistant detective inspector Chanza was in religious tow and even grizzly road accidents avoided the day of rest.

Once in his office he reflected on the happenings of the previous few days – a murder in the township, a robbery at Barghees, a break-in and poaching incident at Thunduluka, a suspicious death on the Zambezi and Berry missing. Mfumu would have a field day at their Monday morning meeting.

He walked back to the desk. Constable Tshuma, the new man, was on duty.

'Good afternoon. Sir, how's the leg?'

'I'm sorry you reminded me, Tshuma, it's burning like a brazier filled with red hot coals.'

'My gogo would recommend a poultice of hot green soap. Can I make you one?'

'No, thanks, I have some *muthi* that's working.' Hot green soap was the last thing he wanted glued on the fiery wound, although he appreciated the constable's concern. 'Just leave this note for Constable Khumalo. She'll be on duty in the morning. Sergeant Ncube has found a body on the river ...'

'Another body, sir. Any clues?'

Tshuma was an eager young recruit. It was all speculation at this stage and not to be shared, plus Sibanda didn't know where the new constable's loyalties lay. 'Nothing much to go on yet,' he replied casually. 'I want Constable Khumalo to liaise with the pathologist. Get him to check for traces of this,' he handed Tshuma the note.

'$C_{25}H_{33}NO_4$ what's that?'

'Just a hunch, Tshuma, and get the US Embassy on the phone.' Ms Tiffany Price was going to be a hot potato. There would be fallout from this unexplained death, diplomatic repercussions. The spotlight would land on Gubu like sun trained through a magnifying glass on a hapless ant.

'Is the victim American, sir?'

'Yes, and a research scientist. Have you heard of Mark and Delia Owens or Dian Fossey?'

'Are they involved somehow?'

'No, just conservationists who fell foul of Africa. Get the embassy on the line, Tshuma; I haven't got all day to chat.' Sibanda ended the conversation. He had probably said too much and Tshuma was too inquisitive.

There was a pattern of researchers overstepping the mark and ending up on the wrong end of wild Africa's temper. The Owens had simply come across a newly and silently erected foot-and-mouth fence protecting cattle and preventing the wildebeest migration. They protested too loudly with graphic photography that made world news. Cattle were more valuable than starving, dehydrated game piling up in suffering layers against a diamond mesh barrier. Politicians were embarrassed, permits were cancelled. Dian Fossey highlighted the plight of Rwandan gorillas, slaughtered for gruesome memorabilia; ashtrays made from their hands, other tasteless body parts fashioned into trinkets. In the end she lost her equilibrium, focusing more on revenge against poachers than scientific data. She crossed too many lines, ruffled one too many feathers and ended up poached herself. Was Tiffany Price another victim of local anger? It sounded as though she had had one or two run-ins if Ncube was correct. He would leave Constable Khumalo to delve into that. She had been on the front desk for some years and had a memory to rival an elephant.

The phone connection to Harare was obviously causing problems. As soon as the area code was punched in, a series of irritating beeps indicated failure to connect and a ghoulish, robotic voice came on the line declaiming: "announ-cement 23, announ-cement 23." Initially only "cement 23" was broadcast. This had caused great consternation and rumours among landline users, some believing it was a code for phone-tapping, others some devious listening device. His personal favourite was as a subliminal marketing tool for a brand of local building materials owned by the Minister for Telecommunications. Who knows what 'announcement 23' was supposed to announce, at least Sibanda didn't have to listen to it. He didn't have the patience, and a series of office phones had suffered desk-slamming damage, some had even gone through the window. He delegated nowadays.

The detective used the wait to strategise. His Monday morning meeting with Mfumu would be tricky. He had a murder and a dead American woman to report on. The Officer-in-Charge would latch onto the foreign death. He would want to be the liaison point with the US Embassy, polish his marble, make important contacts and get a promotion out of Gubu. Everyone knew he was biding his time until he could slither back to Mashonaland and a station of some importance. He would find any excuse to put his nephew Chanza on the case, get his name talked about in terms of promotion.

What he had was a murdered villager in possession of illegal ivory, a dead rhino researcher and a thieving rhino poacher; was there a link? If he could find one between now and tomorrow morning he could keep all the cases under his wing. He would work on the wildlife aspect. With rhinos and elephants in the mix, Mfumu could be confused with an overload of environmental data. It might buy him some time. If they got one over National Parks, Stalin Mfumu would be doubly happy. Sibanda knew the Officer-in-Charge resented the rival civil service branch that had access to endless hunting revenue and tourist cash. The police could only milk the roadblocks. These times of inflation and subsistence salaries spawned jealousy.

He put the phone down to the embassy as the Santana rattled into the station car park. Ncube was back. What had kept him so long? He intercepted the sergeant just as he was dropping the keys at the front desk and making a rapid exit.

'Sir, you are still working?' The detective's presence spelt trouble. The man had no understanding of working hours. Ncube's fish supper was already a fading memory.

'I've got an idea about the Mkandhla case. Give me your front door keys, Ncube. Do you have them?'

'Back to Mandlovu's then, sir?'

'Yes, in Miss Daisy. She's driving quite well. You did a good job on her Ncube.'

'Thank you, sir,' Ncube sighed. His secret was out and the genteel, old Land Rover would once more be at the mercy of unfeeling, wooden feet and grabbing hands.

Once in the cab with Ncube by his side, Sibanda experienced a certain feeling of rightness. The ridiculous colours of the upholstery plus Ncube's weighty presence were surprisingly good. 'Any thoughts as to what happened to that girl on the Zambezi?' he asked. Ncube was startled. He looked sideways in disbelief. This was an unusual turn of events. The detective was like a snake twisting its own intestines, gripping firm to his own point of view. He rarely asked for anyone else's opinion. Ncube knew from experience that it was dangerous to comment. It wasn't only intestines that got twisted. The sergeant's words were often the victim of the detective's devious theories and clever thoughts. He wanted to hint that an *umgobo* had caught the researcher behind the tree and crushed the life out of her, but he stuck to what he had heard, the detective's ridicule could be stinging.

'I don't know how or why she died, sir, but I do know something of her life. I was chatting to Phiri on the way back.'

'Did he know her?'

'Knew of her. There are plenty of rumours in the village.'

'Like?'

'This is a delicate matter, sir, a woman's reputation. I am passing on hearsay and a wild cat shouldn't be skinned in public.'

Sibanda rolled his eyes. 'Ncube,' he snapped, 'it's just you, me and Miss Daisy and unless this ancient crock has developed ears and a wagging tongue what you say will go no further.'

'It's from Phiri's daughter, she cleans for the researchers. They live in the old farmhouse on the railway farm next to the park.'

'On the way to Thunduluka?'

'Yes, apparently Malini used to visit often and spend the night. She would be there in the morning when Gladys arrived.'

'So, she doesn't live with the rest of the research community?'

'No, she lives alone in one of the old staff rooms at Thunduluka Lodge.'

'She obviously visits the house to discuss her research.'

Now it was the sergeant's turn to roll his eyes; was the man so naïve? Research? 'The word is, sir, that she is a rat among pumpkin seeds, nibbling a bit of each.'

'Ah, so she is free with her services?'

'I don't know anything about *free services*, sir. There is talk of money for favours. It may be how she came by the name Malini.'

The Land Rover drew up in front of Mandlovu's house. Sibanda's thoughts turned to Mkandhla's room.

'Mandlovu is not here, sir,' Ncube had already called out to alert her of their arrival with no response. Three small, barefoot children were playing under the lemon tree, pushing homemade cars and trucks fashioned from old wire and flattened cool drink cans. The steering wheels in their hands were attached to an extended piece of wire that worked the front wheels. They were racing their vehicles around obstacles – rusty tins, boxes and piled earth. The boys trilled the sound effects of revving engines and screaming gear changes through vibrating lips. Frequent crashes brought throaty explosions.

Sibanda and Ncube picked their way carefully across the dirt speedway demarcated with pebbles and spoke to the eldest boy.

'Where is your grandmother?' asked Ncube.

The racetrack fell silent. The two smaller boys scuttled behind the eldest. 'She is still at church.'

'A good woman, let us hope the cub of a lion is a lion, eh boys? We are going into the house now to examine the room of the lodger who is missing. Can you tell *ugogo* that when she comes home?'

The children nodded, round eyes widening at their sudden importance as messengers of the police.

'You didn't make these, boys, did you?' asked Sibanda, who had been taking a closer look at the wire cars. They were skilfully fashioned and not the usual township cobbled-together toys.

The boys' wary heads shook from side to side in unison like mongooses scanning their territory.

'Did the lodger, Mkandhla, make them for you?' The three mongooses nodded up and down in agreement, checking the skies for predatory hawks and then the ground for tasty scorpions.

'Were they a gift?' The little heads stared at each other as if at a loss what to say. It was the youngest who chirped up.

'No, we earned them.'

'Earned them, how?'

More confused head turning followed before the middle boy made his contribution. 'We had to collect twenty bottles each …'

'… Not just any old bottles,' the eldest interrupted, 'they had to be glass, not plastic. He said he preferred wine or spirit bottles.'

African beer came in plastic that could be re-filled, or waxed cartons. Milk came in plastic bags and although cans were beginning to replace bottled fizzy drinks, deposited returns were still in place, so those bottles were rarely discarded. Gubu's tastes didn't run to wine and expensive spirits. He wondered if whisky bottles had been pilfered from his own bin.

'Do you know what he wanted the bottles for?' The mongooses shook their heads. Ncube could relate to their confusion. He couldn't imagine where the detective was going with this or how he knew the lodger had made the toys in the first place. The detective had some sort of warped second sight.

Inside Mandlovu's small mud house, Sibanda turned to Ncube. 'You haven't replaced those keys yet then, Ncube?'

Ncube produced them sheepishly from his pocket, 'I'm waiting until payday.'

Within seconds Sibanda was back in Mkandhla's room. 'Wait outside, Ncube. I'm going to grab one of the calendars, but I need a lemon, can you try and get one off that tree in the yard?'

'A lemon, sir? Are you perhaps cooking up something special tonight? Blessing makes a delicious lemon and wild honey pudding from ground sorghum boiled in a little milk. The *abantwana* go mad for it.'

Sibanda gave the sergeant a look that extinguished any culinary thoughts. 'Just get me a lemon, Sergeant.'

The detective gave the room a second going over. There was nothing he had missed. Taking the paper calendar off the wall, he rolled it up, locked the room and took the sergeant's keys back to him. In the yard, he was greeted by the extraordinary sight of a human pyramid with Sergeant Ncube on his hands and knees at the base. The two eldest boys stood on his back while the youngest shimmied up the makeshift scaffold to reach a solitary, wrinkled fruit clinging on the highest branch like a baby baboon to its mother.

'It's the only one on the tree,' gasped Ncube, 'we tried throwing rocks, but nothing was going to move it. It's survived many an assault, so the boys tell me, but we have persevered, sir, even an elephant can be killed if enough ants get together. The boys are learning a good lesson in cooperation and I am learning that my back is not what it used to be.'

Sibanda manoeuvred himself away from Ncube's overstretched rump – he doubted its retentive ability, it was permanently short of skin.'Come on, Ncube, let's go, there's no time for playing in the dirt.' Sibanda limped towards Miss Daisy.

Playing indeed! The sergeant hauled himself upright, dusted off his hands and knees and grabbed the lemon before hurrying after the detective. He wanted to get to the driver's side before Sibanda. He failed, even given the detectives' handicapped leg, he was already behind the wheel.

'Should I drive, sir? Your leg …'

'… Is feeling better, thank you. I'll drop you at home, but be ready early tomorrow morning. I want all Tiffany Price's contacts on my desk as soon as you can. We need to check out how she lived, where she lived and who might have had a reason to murder her.'

'It may be a crime of passion, sir. That one never had to make do with wet firewood. She always lit her fires with handsome, dry kindling.'

'She was a good-looking woman, then, Ncube.' Sibanda realised he hadn't really taken note of her appearance. She wasn't Berry and that had consumed his thoughts. Had he missed something else, some important clues while he was distracted?

'Yes, with plenty of flesh in the right places.'

With that they pulled up next to Ncube's house. A waft of fried fish reached Miss Daisy's windows. Ncube smiled with anticipation, 'I'll be ready tomorrow morning, sir.'

Sibanda drove away before the aroma could torment his tastebuds. His pantry was still bare. He picked up the lemon from the seat and tossed it up as he drove. He must remember to check on the bloodied cloth.

It would be a long night as he planned his strategy for Stalin Mfumu.

The only good thing about the Monday morning meetings was that Mfumu was still floating on the adrenalin of his Sunday performances. He would be full of the milk of his growing congregation and the honey of his wordy oratory. Sibanda had to find the right approach to sustain all that creamy sweetness.

CHAPTER 10

The clinic was locked despite its advertised Monday opening of 7:00am. A message was stuck to the door advising the sister had been called out.

'Where is Sister Engelbertha?' Sibanda asked a group women, sitting, backs to the clinic wall, legs forward on the dirt, chatting idly, enjoying the early morning sun, and patiently waiting for the clinic to open. The few men in the queue were sitting on a wall some distance away. Sibanda pronounced the name, *Angel Better*, in the Ndebele fashion, and thought how appropriate the vernacular usage was.

'She has gone to attend a birth.'

'Far away?'

'On the road to Mambanje. A young woman was walking from there to the clinic, but the baby started to come before she could get here. She only gave birth to the arm. She struggled on through the night until she could walk no longer. Sister Angel Better has gone to try to turn the baby so that it can be born. The poor woman has been in labour for a long time.'

Sibanda knew his own injury was chicken feed compared to the trials of the deeply rural pregnant. The options were to give birth in a hut with little in the way of sterile instruments and expertise to cater for complications, or to walk or catch a lift to the clinic and to time it perfectly. There would be no spare money available to pay for accommodation in Gubu while awaiting delivery. A wife and mother could not afford to be away from home for long.

Sibanda didn't have the patience for a queue. He strode away favouring his injured leg and hoped Sister Angel Better would be back later in the day. The wound was beginning to suppurate. It didn't look healthy despite Blessing's potions. He glanced back at the queue that would linger all day without comment or anger. Stoicism was the curse of Africa. It allowed inefficiencies, understaffing, poor service and a pace of life that, while gentle and kindly, undermined economic progress. Twenty or more working days would be lost in this queue alone, expand that by every village and every city and then multiply the queues for every aspect of life: vehicle licences, passports, electricity vouchers, birth certificates, queues for the communal village pump, queues to cross the border. Some of them went on for days. Sibanda flicked his mind away from the boggling mental arithmetic. He had more pressing issues than cultural resignation and passive fortitude.

Constable Khumalo's cheery face greeted him as he entered the station. 'Patel Barghee will come in later this morning, sir. He says he doesn't know much about the muzzle loaders, but his grandfather did teach him a few things and he might be able to help.'

'Thanks, Zee. Now I need another favour. Do you know anything about Tiffany Price?'

'The American researcher?'

'The very one.'

Constable Khumalo rolled her eyes. 'What don't I know?'

'A regular customer?'

'You could say that. If I'm not receiving complaints about her, then she's making them against someone else.'

'Does anyone stand out?'

'Mark Rhodes, Amanda Carlisle, Thomas Siziba …'

'Whoa, that's enough to be going on with, are there more?'

'I can make a list if you like. Why are you so interested in Tiffany Price? What's she been up to now?'

'She's dead, most likely murdered. Sergeant Ncube found her yesterday on the banks of the Zambezi.'

'Oh, poor woman, was she drowned? She may have been difficult, but she didn't deserve to die.'

'No, she didn't drown, it's more complex. Didn't Tshuma give you a note to phone Forensics?'

'No, not yet.'

Sibanda copied the formula again and gave it to the constable. 'Tell them to check for traces of that substance. I'll be in my office if anything breaks.'

The detective settled his rangy, well-muscled frame into the inadequately sized office chair, sighed and picked up his phone. It had better work. Everyone in the station was up to their eyes. He dialled the Bulawayo chemical lab himself. He was lucky with the connection and the phone remained placidly on his desk. He was put through to the personnel officer, Pretty Mataruse.

'Yes, we did employ David Mkandhla, but he left us six months ago.'

'What was his position?'

'He was one of our chemists.'

'Why did he leave?'

'I am not at liberty to disclose that information over the phone.'

'Miss Mataruse, I am sorry to tell you that David Mkandhla has been murdered. I can subpoena your records, but it would be quicker, easier and more helpful to the investigation of his death and the capture of his murderer if you can let me have that information now.'

There was a pause on the other end of the phone, followed by a gasp, 'oh, he ... he was dismissed.'

'Fired?'

She hesitated, 'Er ... yes.'

'Why?'

A long silence ensued. 'Theft of raw alcohol.'

'How much? A few bottles?'

'No, much more than that – industrial quantities. The theft was affecting our production.'

Sibanda put down the phone gently. The cradle that had steeled itself against the usual brutal slam clicked with relief. The detective unconsciously rubbed his chin. So, Mkandhla was a bootlegger, which explained the bottles. How was he getting his stock in Gubu or was he brewing his own? How was the tusk involved in all this?

Chief Inspector Stalin Mfumu was sitting at his desk when Sibanda entered. Without lifting his head from the task in front of him he held out his hand. Sibanda deposited the keys to the Santana into the waiting palm. A deal was a deal. He didn't bother to protest.

'What have we got on our plate this week, Detective?' the inspector's face rose slowly from the papers in front of him.

'The investigation into the Mkandhla murder is still ongoing although we have some leads. We also have a suspicious death, a white woman, found on the banks of the Zambezi near the police fishing camp, with crocodile bites. We also have a break-in, and all the signs of a poaching ring.' He wouldn't reveal his suspicions yet about the researcher. He was certain she was murdered, but Mfumu would definitely take a second murder off him and give it to his nephew Chanza, particularly since a foreign national was involved. A speedy outcome might induce a reward from the rich Americans, and Mfumu was all for wrapping cases up with no concern for accuracy. Which was odd since everything else he did required regimentation.

'Can you handle all this? Assistant Detective Chanza is already investigating the shop break-in at Barghees, electrical goods stolen. Quite a few fans and the like, and now there is an outbreak of domestic violence and drunk and disorderly behaviour in the village. Do we know who the white woman is? '

'An American rhino researcher based at Thunduluka Lodge.'

'An American national? I must inform the ambassador immediately.'

'I have already done that and told them we'll release the body as soon as we can.' The detective steeled himself for the inevitable tongue lashing at having stolen Mfumu's thunder with the ambassador. He rode the ensuing, bumpy tirade with all the Velcro skill of a rodeo star.

'… you must hand this investigation to Assistant Detective Chanza with immediate effect,' Mfumu spluttered to a spitting halt.

Sibanda knew this was coming. He was prepared, 'the cases are probably linked …'

'…. linked, how, what are you saying?'

'Mkandhla, our man found under the tree struck by lightning, was killed by a low-velocity weapon, something old with slow, but very destructive power, and we found an elephant tusk under his bed. Two days ago, near Thunduluka, I witnessed a wounded rhino. The wound was wide and raking, along the flank; the sort of gouge made by a similar weapon. Tiffany Price, the American researcher, was studying rhino. Rhinos and poaching involved, similar weapon, there has to be a connection.'

'So the researcher was eaten by a crocodile but is somehow involved with this Mkandhla?'

Sibanda didn't reply he just nodded an acknowledgement. That wasn't the scenario at all, but if it kept Mfumu in his office and out of his hair then it would do.

Stalin Mfumu began to straighten the papers on his desk. First he tapped them vertically and then horizontally. They were squared to within a paper cut of their resistance. Sibanda recognised he had won the skirmish. This was Mfumu's white flag. Further argument would be unnecessary.

'Keep me informed. You will have to include Detective Chanza. You won't get far without a vehicle and he has first call on the Santana this week.'

'We don't need to bother Chanza. He's busy. Sergeant Ncube has finally got the old Land Rover running again. He drove it to the Zambezi where Tiffany Price's body was found,' Sibanda never thought he would be so grateful to the ancient, rattletrap, *skoroskoro*. 'We will manage,' he finished. It gave him enormous pleasure to watch Mfumu's deflated face as he left his office.

He limped back to his own office, realising Mfumu had unwittingly given him a clue. If there was a greater than usual incidence of drunkenness in the village, could it have come from illegal booze produced locally, undercutting the market? Had Mkandhla hauled his stolen alcohol up to Gubu, producing *ithothotho,* a highly potent, home-brewed spirit that could blow the brains out of a sensible man, let alone an addled one?

'Sir, should I bring Mr Barghee through to your office?' Constable Khumalo had intercepted him on his way down the corridor. She held a file in her hand, 'I have pulled all the relevant complaints on Miss Price.'

'Thanks, Zee, give it to Sergeant Ncube, he can start sorting through the names; and send Mr Barghee in.'

Sibanda knew that Ncube would have plenty of information on Tiffany Price's contacts by the time this interview was over. The man was a walking, social encyclopaedia on the villagers, surrounding denizens and their habits. His knowledge of people was insightful, his superstitious belief in local myths lamentable and his instinctive understanding of the workings of diesel engines remarkable, if only his knowledge of bushcraft, signs in the wild, tracks, animal behaviour and local trees could equal that, but he had no interest. Sibanda found that hard to understand.

The detective had been expecting young Patel to enter his office, but it was his father who came in. 'I hope you'll accept me in exchange for my son,' he said. 'I wanted to thank you for getting me out of jail, and I know more about my father's weapon than Patel. I may be of greater help.'

'Your father's weapon was disabled?'

'Yes, but it actually belonged to my great-grandfather and has always been a source of pride in our family.'

'Go on,' Sibanda encouraged. He suspected he would have to listen to the weapon's revered history before the technical details were spilled.

'My great-grandfather, Aabheer Barghee, was employed as a *shikar* by a grand Maharajah.'

'A *shikar*?'

'Yes, he was master of the hunt,' the older man settled into his story like Kipling with his pen poised. 'It hadn't been easy for him to reach such an elevated position. He was just a rural boy, but he worked his way up from *shikaree*, a beater to *jilander*, a groom. One day the hunting party was chasing a ferocious tiger. It had just settled on a bait, a live goat that had been tied to a tree. The tiger was beginning to feed, the goat's crazed struggle and bleating had ended. Just as the Maharajah and his party were taking aim, the *shikar*, the hunt master, coughed. He tried his best to stifle it, but it was not possible, then two of the beaters began to giggle with embarrassment.' Barghee leant into the story as though he had been present, a witness to the events.

'The tiger,' he continued in a stealthy tone, 'a cunning, mature male that the Maharajah had been after, took off in a cloud of khaki dust,' the old man interrupted his story, 'that's where the word comes from you know. Khaki actually means dust-coloured. The colonial British got carried away and borrowed the Hindustani word for their dyed military uniforms. Dust-coloured dust!' the old Indian laughed at his own joke.

Sibanda remained straight faced; his reaction to humour was rare. 'Carry on, please, Mr Barghee. Can you explain something of the working of the weapon?'

Mr Barghee coughed to hide his embarrassment at the lack of reaction, even a polite one would have sufficed, but he wasn't going to be hurried in his tale of family legend. 'The great Mogul,' he continued, 'was so put out at missing the kill that he had the *shikar* shot on the spot and the two beaters hamstrung, tied to donkeys and paraded through the city streets. Being in a Maharajah's employ was a dangerous thing.'

'Personally, I would have rewarded the *shikar* and hamstrung the Maharajah,' Sibanda was on the hunt, in the jungle, on an elephant's back. Mr Barghee's excitement was becoming infectious, the shopkeeper told a good tale, but he was glad the tiger escaped.

'You have to understand that times were different. Tigers were everywhere and they were man eaters. They roamed in among the rural villages. It was not unusual for a man visiting the bath house to be eaten on the way, or for a woman washing in a stream to be carried off. The tiger was hated and feared in rural India. People revered the hunters.'

'What about the muzzle loader?' Sibanda tried again to get to the crux of the conversation, but Mr Barghee was not ready to relinquish centre stage. This was his family's history passed down through the generations. He could recite it line for line like a memorised poem, 'Aabheer was promoted to *shikar* after the event. He didn't want the position. It could be a death sentence, as he had seen, but he had no choice.

'One day the Maharajah was out hunting accompanied by the Maharani. She was in a *howdah* on an elephant's back. One of the *shikarees* ran back to the main party to tell them that a tiger had been spotted ahead, feeding on a kill. It was common palace gossip that the Maharani was keen to shoot one to prove herself in the eyes of her people and her husband. She primed three guns, and the party, including my great-grandfather approached stealthily. No one dared make a noise. They had all witnessed the consequences. The Maharajah astride his magnificent steed stayed back in the thick growth giving his wife the hunting ground.

'The Maharani's party came on the tiger tearing at the flesh of a red antelope. It was a site Aabheer described as terrifying. He said the power of the beast was awesome. He hoped he was never dispatched to Naraka, Hindu hell, in case Lord Yama, the lord of justice, had him eaten by a tiger for his punishment. He didn't know in those early moments that he was about to visit hell on earth.

'The tiger continued to fang away the flesh as a knife through ghee, snuffling and grunting its pleasure with each greedy rip, but the Maharani was cooler than a sapphire in the snow-fed torrents of the

Himalayas,' Mr Barghee was warming to his subject, 'she pulled the first muzzle loader into her shoulder and fired. The shot hit the tiger in the belly. It fell back at first, stunned. She fired again quickly with the second weapon and hit the beast in the rump. It started as though stung by a hive of hornets. The great cat was very angry and before the smoke had cleared, the beast summoned all its strength and took a leap towards the *howdah*, its eyes red, its claws unsheathed. Aabheer watched as the Maharani tried to get the third weapon up to her shoulder. She was trembling, her delicate fingers fumbled with the gun and it fell to the ground. Aabheer hesitated briefly, but what choice did he have? It was between certain death at the hands of the Maharajah, or a terrible death in the jaws of the hell-like creature with sinews of flesh still dangling from its bloody fangs. He chose the tiger. He shot it, but again the wound was not fatal. There was no time to reload so he threw himself forward slashing with his sword. The creature was still not without fire. With blood streaming from its wounds it leapt upon Aabheer and began to tear at his arms. He thought he was done for, but the tiger, weakened by the loss of blood, slackened its grip briefly. In the lull, Aabheer freed one of his arms, grabbed his dagger and stabbed the tiger in the eye. It fell away and began to stagger to the bushes. The Maharajah rode up and dispatched the creature with a shot to the head.'

'And the muzzle loader?' Sibanda was getting anxious. He had a long day ahead of him and much as the tale had been fascinating, it wasn't adding to his knowledge of the weapon.

'Ah, the muzzle loader, as the beaters were carrying Aabheer away to medical attention. The Maharajah rode up. Aabheer thought his days were ended, that the punishment would be death, but instead the Maharaja said, "Aabheer, you are a brave man and you have saved the Maharani. Here take this weapon that failed her," and he laid the third muzzle loader on the stretcher with my ancestor. "It is now yours and from this day your name will no longer be Aabheer, herder of cattle, but Gajbaahir, strength of an elephant", and that is the name I, his great-grandson, carry today, but you can call me Gaj,' he ended prosaically.

'Right, Gaj, the muzzle loader, how does it work?'

'What a magnificent piece it is with an extra big bore to take a big projectile. They needed knock-down power in those days to kill a tiger. It compensated for the low velocity. The muzzle loader was a weapon of great craftsmanship made in the mid-1800s when gunsmiths attended to every detail by hand. The hammer, the lock, the jaws, the plate are all engraved silver. The stock is polished mahogany. It was modelled on the Brown Bess, but made bespoke by James Purdey and Sons of London, gunmakers to the British Royal Family. Even today it is a wonder to behold, I …

'Gaj, can you just tell me about the workings?' Anyone who knew Detective Sibanda well would have recognised the ominous tones and the twitch of irritation. He had had enough of Barghee family history.

'Yes, of course, my father showed me as his father had shown him. Firstly, to check the gun is not already loaded you put the ramrod down the barrel …'

'You can dispense with the safety instructions, thanks Gaj. How does it fire?'

Gaj's party piece was being edited by this brusque man, standing over him like a belligerent palace guard, still he had to remember the detective had saved him from some nights behind bars. 'Right,' he hurried along, 'first you make sure there is a flint in place, usually held with a piece of leather to ensure a tight grip. The sharp end of the flint should face the flashpan. Then you put the black powder in the flashpan and it is important to make sure it's the right amount. Too little and there won't be enough to ignite the charge of powder in the barrel, too much and, well, you could lose an eye.'

Gaj Barghee pushed back his chair and stood to give a visual demonstration of the next process. 'Then you lift the muzzle of the gun so that the barrel is perpendicular to the ground …

'So the stock would be resting on the ground?' Sibanda was beginning to form a picture.

'Yes, this is so you can pour the powder down the barrel. You tap the barrel to make all the powder fall to the bottom. Of course, you have to cut some patches first.'

'Patches?'

'Pieces of material lubricated with a bit of gun oil and put over the muzzle. That way when you ram the ball down it's wrapped in the patch and doesn't sink into the powder. It also speeds the ball down the barrel. Once the gun is horizontal again, open the frizzen and keep the gun steady until you fire.'

'What's a frizzen?' the explanation was becoming too technical for Sibanda even though he had undergone fairly extensive firearm training, but the patches were something of a revelation.

'The frizzen is the striking plate, a bit like the sandpaper glued to a matchbox. Once the hammer is released and the flint strikes and scrapes along the surface, sparks shower onto the flashpan which sends flames down the touch hole which ...'

'... What is the firing distance?' Sibanda interrupted, he had heard enough about frizzens and flashpans.

'The closer the better, but they say a good marksman can kill at eighty metres. Look, Detective, is there any chance we will get our weapon back? It is of great sentimental value.'

'You've been very helpful, Gaj, and we are doing all we can to retrieve the gun. On another issue, can I suggest you get in a new range of locks? Every door in Gubu can be opened with the same key,' with that Sibanda ushered the elderly shopkeeper out of his office.

CHAPTER 11

'So who are Mark Rhodes and Amanda Carlisle?' Sibanda shifted uneasily on the Land Rover seat. Sergeant Ncube was driving, avoiding unnecessary bumps. The detective was irritated by the slow progress despite any jolt sending a spasm through his aching thigh. Sibanda and Sergeant Ncube were on their way to visit two of Tiffany Price's list of litigants.

'Researchers, and the most recent of Miss Price's complainants.'

'What does the file say, Ncube?'

'Well, sir, firstly, Amanda Carlisle sued Tiffany Price for … for… alien … alien … nation of affection,' Ncube stuttered through the unfamiliar word.

'You make it sound like a Martian invasion, Ncube.'

'A what, sir?'

'Never mind, whose affections did she steal?'

'Mark Rhodes is Amanda Carlisle's fiancé; Tiffany Price got in between them when Amanda was back in the UK. She entered the heartsore absence like a maggot and wormed her way into his bed.'

'And why is Mark Rhodes on the list?'

'Tiffany Price sued him for breach of promise. She said he had promised to marry her …'

'And had he?'

'It was her word against his. Amanda had returned and now he was millet seed between the *imbokodo* and the *ilitshe*, the grinding stones. You see now, sir, why it is important to have a marriage arranged. These misunderstandings are rare when the elders take care of matters. Miss

Price is like a caterpillar that moves on when the mopani leaves are finished. She found someone else.'

'In my experience, Ncube, most men will say anything to attract a woman. I won't say they lie but they can be creative with the truth. '

'Sir,' spluttered the sergeant, indignation defining every muscle in his fulsome cheeks, 'I have never spoken an untruth to my wives.'

'But maybe you have been a bit sparing with it,' Sibanda didn't mean to goad his sergeant but the man could be a self-righteous prig when it came to women and vehicles.

'What do you mean, sir?' the sergeant's spine stiffened and his hands gripped Miss Daisy's steering wheel as though she were a life jacket in a shipwreck.

'Have you told them how your eyes never leave the fetching *izibunu* of Constable Khumalo when she is bending over the filing cabinet?'

Ncube fell silent. He could think of no reply. Didn't this stupid man understand that attraction to womanly flesh was a given and nothing to do with lies. The detective was snaking words again. Ncube would not fall into his trap. He was learning. After a few stony minutes he changed the topic back to the safer ground of Tiffany Price. 'The thorn has eventually come out with the pus,' he added.

'So, she got what was coming to her?' With that, Sibanda dropped the subject. It was time to get back to work. Miss Daisy's striped cab was, as usual, helping him focus his thoughts, but Berry Barton's disappearance was disrupting them. 'Have there been any reports of dead white women anywhere else in Matabeleland, Ncube?'

'Are you suggesting we have a killer on the loose, sir?' The sergeant sounded alarmed.

'No, no, I am certain Tiffany Price's murder was not random or predatory, a friend is missing his daughter. I said I would keep an eye out.'

'Nothing I've heard of, but have you tried the hospitals? Maybe she was in an accident.'

That had occurred to Sibanda, but until Buff Barton put in a missing person's report, he couldn't go throwing his weight around. He had dialled Berry's number at least ten times, but either she was out of range or had switched it off.

'I'll keep that in mind,' he said, although he actually wanted to rid his mind of the niggling worry. It was affecting his concentration. 'What do you know about *ithothotho*, illegally brewed spirit, Ncube?'

'Not much, sir, but seeing once is seeing twice.'

'So you have tried it?'

'Not exactly, but I have taken *umligazigoni* when I was a child. I was put off it for life.'

'The sleeping herb?'

'Yes, the one you put in *ithothotho* to make it powerful like the kick of a giraffe.'

'How did you get hold of it as a child?'

'It was my grandfather's. He didn't put it in any homemade drink, at least not that I saw, but he did sprinkle it, like seasoning, on his chicken. One day all the family was out in the fields, planting the mealies. I was sent back to the hut to fill the water bottles. It was a hot day. The rain was building. The planting was going well. I was a hungry boy ...' Ncube glanced sideways at the detective, expecting some sarcasm or comment on his eating needs, but the difficult man next to him stayed silent, so he continued. 'I knew *ubabamkhulu* kept his chicken in the rafters, just for himself. I thought I could get away with nibbling some. That's the last thing I remember until I felt the sting of my grandfather's calloused hand across my ear. I had fallen into a dead sleep, my head on the table, and the remains of the snack still in my hand. I could not deny the crime. *Umligazigoni* is very strong stuff and my advice is to stay away from it. Let me tell you, sir, the plump, juicy fig is rotten with worms.'

Miss Daisy turned off the tar onto the dirt track leading to the farmhouse. Despite Ncube's careful driving, the path threw up stones and rattled anything loose or worn about Miss Daisy's person, and she was an old campaigner. Her joints were arthritic and ill-fitting and her exhaust rattled ominously. Conversation became difficult, so both men settled to their thoughts. Ncube's went back to his childhood days of plenty when his well-covered frame was much admired and pinched by other mothers whose children resembled stick figures. Sibanda's went back to his boyhood at Marula Tree School.

It was the middle of the new school term. Sibanda and his friends had reached fourth form. They had grown up and they wanted to flex muscles cramped in the highly disciplined environment. Sam Pickford and Roland Moyo were up to something. They were the acknowledged bad boys of the dorm. Whatever they were doing required frequent visits to the attic. Nearly all the boys had grown enough in strength during the summer break to hoist themselves through the ceiling access and into the dusty space below the tin roof. It was a haven for the smokers and the gamblers. Sam had even tried growing *imbanje,* but that needed more moisture, light and heat than the dry rotting rafters and the rising breath of fifteen growing boys could provide. The green spiky plant germinated, but only managed to produce one leaf before shrivelling and dying in a welter of disappointment.

Roland had a new plan. His uncle, an *isgebenga* like himself, had a thriving *ithothotho* business going in Gwanda. Roland had assisted him in the holidays with production. He knew exactly how to get a brew going.

'Listen guys, I've seen my uncle do this, it's easy, we just need mealie pips. We soak them in water so they swell. Then we spread them out under sacking until they germinate with just a hint of a white shoot. Next, they have to be drained off and left to dry thoroughly. We can spread them out up in the roof. We know it's as dry as the Kalahari up there. Petros, the groundsman, can get us an *ingiga* and an *umgigo* to grind the germinated seeds to powder. I've seen his wife pounding her own mealies. She's a good woman, she'll let us borrow her mortar and pestle.'

'What next?' Sam had asked.

'We add water and sugar to the powder, so, everyone fill your pockets with sugar at morning tea time. Then we leave it to ferment for a night or two. After that, the liquid has to be distilled. We might have to borrow some equipment from the science lab. Leave that to me.'

True to his word, Roland got the brew started. Mandla Tshabalala donated his sock-washing bucket. He had found a cleaner, more lucrative supply from a first-former anyway. The young men all grabbed handfuls of sugar and took turns to pound the dried, germinated grain in the large wooden mortar. The physical labour gave them plenty of opportunity to work off frustrated steam. A bucket of promising liquid covered with plastic was soon bubbling away contentedly in the rafters with remarkable similarity to a witch's cauldron.

It continued to gurgle for some days with no sign of any distillation equipment. Scrounging tubes and pipes from the chemistry lab was proving more difficult than first thought. 'Don't worry,' Roland reassured them, 'the longer it brews up there, the more potent it will be. We are in for some fun times, guys.'

After a week, fumes started to penetrate through the ceiling; after ten days the asthmatics began to wheeze. It wasn't Jason Stein's fault that his glowing cigarette butt ignited the alcoholic vapours in an explosion that blew a significant hole in the ceiling and set fire to the roof. He was lucky to escape with singed eyebrows. Roland was expelled on the spot and Sam followed him a few days later. The rest of the fourth-formers were variously gated, suspended, and/or beaten.

Sibanda tried hard to remember some of the heated discussions and blame that followed the disaster. He particularly remembered his friend Moses Banda, from Blantyre, the son of a Malawian politician, offering some overdue advice on how *ithothotho*, or *kachasu* as it was known in Malawi, was traditionally brewed. Moses had said they used the ripe berries of the buffalo-thorn boiling away in a pot to get the infusion going, but it was something significant about distillation he was trying to dredge up when Ncube hit a large antbear hole in the road causing Miss Daisy to bounce violently on her ancient and flaccid springs.

'What the ...' Sibanda didn't finish the expletive. He was too busy grabbing his swollen thigh, beads of sweat broke out on his forehead. 'You're driving like a lunatic, Ncube. Take more care.'

Ncube had nursed Miss Daisy with great caution over the poorly maintained road. How could that man even suggest he was driving carelessly? Hadn't he witnessed the detective's own abuse of the fragile Land Rover on numerous occasions? He muttered under his breath, 'and you're just a baboon laughing at another baboon's forehead.'

Sibanda heard enough of the mumble to understand he was being called a black pot insulting a kettle. He was honest enough to recognise the truth of the insult.

The Land Rover rattled to a halt in the driveway of an old homestead. No one was in sight. On the veranda, thick leaves of peeling red polish bore witness to long-vanished knees and backache. No one had applied Cardinal Red for some years. A chair of unravelling cane supported a mish-mash of discarded clothing, old towels and a lonely sock. Ncube scarcely took in the lack of domestic care. His eyes were drawn to a cardboard box further down the veranda bursting with rusty, discarded spare parts. He edged towards it. On top of the box sat a lately discarded reel of fishing line and various lures. Beneath that, under a windblown blanket of dust, leaves and what appeared to be the companion sock with an impressive hole, he could see a radiator cap joyously similar to Miss Daisy's troublesome equivalent, and it had a seal that was black and firm and in perfect condition. He turned to the detective, but Sibanda had disappeared into the house during Ncube's covetous exploration. The sergeant hesitated, looked around, whistled the tuneless distraction of the opportunist thief, pocketed the cap, glanced regretfully at the fishing equipment and went in search of the detective.

He found him deep in conversation with Mark Rhodes. The talk was not of Tiffany Price.

'… no two are alike. The background colour, the spots and rosettes all vary. That's how we recognise them. Look, this is Ophelia. Her ground colour is very pale and buff and her spots very dense around the chest. Compare it to Poppy and her cubs Paw Paw and Polenta, they are more golden in colour. It's fascinating. A bit like fingerprints I expect.' The tall researcher was flicking through leopard images on his computer. Sibanda was looking on over his shoulder.

'Did you know fossilised leopard bones were unearthed to the north-east of London?' Sibanda had desperately tried to recreate Africa in the UK during his time there. He devoured any snippet of wildlife-related detail.

'Amazing.'

'London has the leopard's head as its silver hallmark. In fact London had a lot to do with the spotted cat. King John, the English king, kept a menagerie of leopards at the Tower of London. Henry III even sent some to the Holy Roman Emperor Frederick II.'

Mark Rhodes looked at Sibanda. There was more to this rural policeman than met the eye, and he was enviously easy on the eye. 'I wonder if they were snow leopards …'

'So what are the populations like in this area?' Sibanda asked.

'Diminishing, the IUCN has leopards on the near endangered list due to habitat destruction. We visit all the park boundary communities, Tsholotsho, Mpindo, Lupane, right down as far as the Botswana border. Try to educate them not to trap or shoot leopards killing their stock.

We've set up a compensation scheme.'

'Good results?'

'We think so. There are some excellent men living on the boundary. They know the land. We've befriended a few. We're working with one guy in particular to patrol ... um ...' the researcher faltered and then changed tack, 'Yes, definitely making progress.'

'And the populations in protected areas like the Park?' Sibanda noted the hesitation.

'Even there, the home range is growing,' Mark Rhodes was back on stride. 'In the seventies and eighties the territory for males in the Park was around 32 square kilometres, fourteen for females; now we are seeing fifty kilometre ranges due to heavy hunting pressure. Natural prey like impala, reedbuck, duiker, warthog were decimated to feed hungry park staff during those inflationary days and now, even though salaries have improved, it's very hard to give up a butchery on your doorstep.'

'But aren't leopards resilient, eat anything, including rodents and jackals? I know they love domestic dogs.'

'That's true, but when the food chain is sent spinning out of balance by unrestrained hunting ...'

'What about the farming areas?' Sibanda knew the answer would be grimmer. Poor farmers given land they could barely grub a living from would see a leopard as a big pay day.

'The range is much bigger, maybe even up to one hundred square kilometres in a harsh landscape. In the more rocky areas the populations are better. The Matobo Hills, for instance, reputedly has the densest populations of leopards anywhere in the world, although with the increase in the trapping of dassies, rock rabbits, their main prey in the area, it's bound to have declined. I'm hoping to get down there soon to have a look. It's a beautiful spot, Detective. Do you know it?'

Sibanda had visited with his brother Xholisani and been amazed at the theatre of ancient mountains and tumbling rocks just outside Bulawayo. He remembered well the heart-stopping views, from the soaring grandeur of Mount Efifi to a glorious tangle of unnamed hills and koppies. And then there were the painted caves and the history of the Matabele and their wars and rebellions. But the black eagles had been his main reason for visiting. He and his brother found a nesting pair high up on a cliff ledge. They had scrambled and climbed to a good viewing spot high on one of the round *dwalas* that broke out like smooth breasts among the crenulations and sculptured contortions of the weathered landscape. He and Xholi watched as one jet-black beauty marked with a white V on its back cruised along the sheer face, wing tips surely brushing the rock wall. Suddenly the eagle stooped, folding in his spoon-handle wings, blurring against the ochred stone as he lunged on a sunning dassie who knew little of his fate.

It had been a good day. It stirred another memory. Hadn't Berry said something once about the Matobo Hills, caves and running away – a hidey hole? 'If ever I'm missing, you'll find me among the bald heads, in a cave like this, licking my wounds,' she had said. They had met up for a beer in the oldest pub in Britain, The Trip to Jerusalem, a dark grotto-like tavern and a Nottingham tourist icon. It was mid-winter in England, cold and grey and both were homesick and wanting to flee the urban rat race, although Sibanda had known he would be perfectly happy in any environment if he could sit opposite Berry and watch the flecks in those remarkable eyes dance and dazzle like fireflies. Was she now in Matobo Hills? The Park was named for the bald-headed, smooth-domed rocks. Berry had hardly been out of his thoughts since the meeting with Buff and the discovery she wasn't in a relationship with Barney Jones, but he couldn't focus on Buff's comment that she *talked about him a lot,* or indulge his fantasies here.

'… dogs, are the problem now,' the researcher was well into his topic, he hadn't realised that Sibanda had been in the Matobo Hills with eagles and his mystery love. 'Leopards are notoriously hard to hunt, secretive, solitary, nocturnal. They've always been baited, but many of them are wily and skilled. They know how to avoid a bullet. We've imported the American laziness of hunting with trained dogs, and it's legal. There's no skill left in a leopard hunt – baited waterholes, tripwires, microphones, cameras and lights that come on slowly to imitate the rising of the moon. If the animal is wary enough to avoid all that, they set a pack of dogs on him, hunt him down until he's exhausted and climbs a tree. The hunter waddles, or just drives up and takes a pot shot as though he's in a shooting gallery, it's …'

Ncube had been in the room for several minutes. He could see the detective's jaw beginning to stiffen. This conversation would have put him in a mood and Ncube knew exactly who would be on the receiving end of anger building up about the leopards' plight. He didn't know there was a missing love in the mix as well. It didn't bode well for the rest of the day. He coughed and slid his shoes over the tiles producing a disruptive squeal.

The researcher took the cue, 'Sorry, Detective, unethical leopard hunting is one of my hobby horses, but I'm sure that's not why you are here.'

'No you are right, but it's been educational.' Sibanda focused. 'Do you dart the leopards?'

'Yes, we put collars on and track them with radio telemetry.'

'Who has the licence?'

'I do, but I'm training one of the other researchers. It helps to have two of us able to use the dart gun and handle the drugs.'

'Who is that?'

'Amanda Carlisle, she's a colleague studying baboons.'

'Is your log of darts and chemicals up to date?'

'We're very careful. It's a requirement of the licence. Look, Detective, what's all this about?'

'When did you last hear from Tiffany Price?'

'Oh, no, not again! What's she been accusing me of now?'

'Nothing, I'm afraid, Mark, she's dead.'

The young researcher collapsed back in his chair. 'Dead? Did a rhino finally get her?' he looked shocked, but Sibanda had seen this before from murderers – the practised reaction, the clever comeback line.

'No, we're unsure of the cause of death. She was found on the banks of the Zambezi. Do you know why she might have been up there?'

'No ... no, are you certain it's Tiff?' he had removed his glasses and was rubbing his eyes.

Sergeant Ncube stepped in. He was beginning to understand that there was more to this love triangle than the police file indicated. 'When did you last see Ms Price?' he asked.

'Not for some time ...' he glanced over his shoulder at a closed door behind him. 'We weren't on good terms.'

'We see from our files that she sued you,' the sergeant continued.

'Yes, but it was all a misunderstanding, and in the end she had to drop the charges. I never meant to hurt her. You don't know how sorry

I am about the whole crazy situation. You see I ...'

Mark Rhodes's apology was interrupted by the door behind him opening with the wind of officiousness. A young woman entered. Her stride indicated a no-nonsense sort of person, solid in build and solid in temperament. Her cruelly cropped auburn hair was cut for comfort rather than style. It made her nose longer and her cheeks chubbier.

'Who are these people, Mark? What are they doing here? You're supposed to be entering data. Haven't you got a deadline?'

Sibanda recognised a well-educated voice to send shivers down the spine of an English duchess and fathomless brown eyes to scare the cucumber out of a thinly cut sandwich. Formidable was the adjective that sprang to his mind. He was beginning to feel some sympathy for Tiffany Price. 'Difficult,' was the judgement of Sergeant Ncube, who liked his women soft and understanding.

'It's the police, darling ...' this last word stuck in his throat like dung to a blanket. Ncube took note.

'The police, oh God! Not that bitch again. What has she been up to now?' The words tripped off her tongue with practised ease.

'She's dead, Miss Carlisle, Tiffany Price won't be troubling you any further,' Sibanda watched the reaction. Her eyes flicked momentarily to her boyfriend's. A look passed between them – Guilt? Relief? Triumph? He couldn't read it. Ncube might be able to interpret the glance later.

'Oh, did she kiss one too many rhinos? They were never going to turn into a handsome prince,' there was no compassion in the voice whose volume spoke to an audience well beyond the confines of the room.

'They don't know how she died, Amanda. She was on the Zambezi.' Was there a warning note in Mark Rhodes's voice, as if to say, be careful, show some respect? Sibanda sensed an undercurrent.

Amanda picked up on the cue, the next time she spoke her voice was buttered in smarm. It fooled no one. 'Well, I'm sorry she's been kill ... she's ... er dead, of course, I am ...'

'Miss Carlisle, can you help with any details of Ms Price's recent movements?' Sibanda cut short the insincerity.

'No, we hadn't had any contact with her in a long while, not since the court case a few months ago. She got off, I expect you know that, and I had to pay costs. Tiffany produced a letter from Mark that indicated he initiated the relationship, but that wasn't true, was it Mark?'

Mark Rhodes looked at his feet and shook his head. Was his silence a hint of shame or an inability to lie in the face of the death of his ex-lover? Sibanda hoped Ncube was observing all this. When it came to relationships and the subtle nuances between couples, he was a complete failure. At thirty-three there was still no one significant in his life, just a string of lost loves, while Ncube was well settled with three wives.

'You think Tiffany Price was murdered?'

'It wouldn't surprise me. We weren't the only ones who ran afoul of her,' Amanda's voice was beginning to crescendo. It put Sibanda's teeth on edge. 'She had plenty of enemies.'

'Like who?'

'Well, that new manager at Hunter's Rest, Thomas Siziba, the governor's nephew, and his horrible sidekick, Marx Gumbo, I believe they had a real run in, and there are plenty of game guides around who would like to see the back of her.'

Sibanda sensed rather than heard Ncube's reaction. Constable Khumalo had mentioned Thomas Siziba and now it was confirmed he was in the governor's employ and related to him. They had tangled with the governor before and it had cost them both dearly. Ncube had only just recovered from all the witchcraft and harvesting of body parts in the last case they were involved in. Sibanda's highly superstitious sergeant had suffered nightmares for weeks, fearing the governor's powers both temporal and supernatural. The rest of the day was going to be a trial.

'Where were you both this weekend?'

'Here,' Mark Rhodes replied for them both.

'Is there anyone who can confirm that?'

'No, we didn't see anyone. Some of the other researchers headed into Bulawayo on Friday for the weekend and a couple are still away, overseas on their Christmas break.'

'We did pop into Thunduluka for a drink, Mark, remember?' Amanda prompted.

'Yes, of course. Stupid of me to forget.'

'Do you visit the lodge often?' Sibanda asked.

'No, not all that often.'

'When was the last time you were there?'

Mark and Amanda looked at one another. They had no answer.

'Before the problems with Tiffany Price, too uncomfortable to visit while she was still alive?' offered Sibanda. 'I suggest you don't leave the district until we have confirmation of how Tiffany died. I'll take your darting log. It could be useful to our investigations.'

'Darting log?' Amanda Carlisle's voice rose in a very fair imitation of Lady Bracknell and her *handbag* line. Sibanda had been to very few plays, but Berry, with free tickets, had dragged him off to a production of Oscar Wilde's *The Importance of Being Ernest* at the Nottingham Playhouse. He would never have gone but for the thought of Berry sitting right next to him for three hours. They had both laughed until they cried at the ridiculous plot and stilted mannerisms of Middle-Class England. He smiled now. He couldn't help himself.

'What's so funny?' Amanda Carlisle asked.

He shook his head and ignored the question. 'Just the log book, please.'

They were leaving the house, log book in hand, when Sibanda spotted a glass-topped case on a side table. It was full of moths pinned to white kyalite.

'Who's the collector?' Sibanda asked.

'We all are, it's a tradition that if you come to this research station then you can't leave until you've added and identified ten new moths not already in the collection,' Mark offered.

Sibanda knew that Ncube was impatient to be on his way. Even from a distance he could hear the gurgling of a worried gut and see the perspiration gathering. Ncube was going to fret for days until the Thomas Siziba interview was concluded. He should go and give him space to expel whatever bomb was accumulating in his system, but he couldn't help asking the researcher, 'Have you ever seen a moth with a skull and crossbones on its back?'

'Ah,' said Mark, 'the death's head moth, quite a famous fellow with lots of creepy myths and superstitions attached to him, a bit of a wolf in sheep's clothing.'

Sibanda glanced across at Ncube whose eyes and ears were primed to take in the ghoulish horror of another irrational belief.

'It's one of the hawk moth family, an interesting bunch, they have particularly long proboscises to reach deep into the nectaries of long-trumpeted flowers. In fact, an early botanist, Alfred Russell Wallace, discovered a Madagascan orchid with its nectar at the end of a ten-inch tube. He predicted that eventually a pollinator, probably a hawk moth with an equally long tongue, would be found, otherwise how could it be cross-pollinated? Twelve years later, in 1903, a moth with a ten-inch proboscis was discovered. They stuck *predicta* on the end of its Latin name. Our literary star, the death's head moth, on the other hand, has a shorter proboscis because he goes about his feeding in a completely underhand manner, robs bee hives of their honey under the cover of the clever disguise ...'

'Literary star?'

'Oh yes, the death's head moth features in a few books and is widespread, occurring as far afield as Transylvania,' the researcher added drama to the last word. He enjoyed telling a good story.

'Where's that?' Ncube asked, 'it's not somewhere near the old Transvaal is it?

'No,' Sibanda interrupted, 'and you don't want to know where it is, Ncube'. The detective was sorry he had brought up the topic.

Mark Rhodes was undeterred, he was warming to his topic, 'Count Dracula the vampire sent specimens of the death's head moth to Renfield, a zoophageous maniac in a lunatic asylum. He ate them, of course.'

'What's a vampire and a zooph ... whatever ... lunatic, and why did he eat moths?' Ncube was becoming alarmed and he liked to be forewarned of possible danger. This death's head moth and associates sounded terrifying.

Sibanda ignored the question, but Mark Rhodes ploughed on. 'It is said the moth first appeared in England at the beheading of Charles I, but the winged devil had to wait a further century after Bram Stoker's *Dracula* to get another literary mention,' the ghoulish voice was hammy but effective.

Sibanda decided to spare his sergeant further nightmares, although he was intrigued by the literary reference. 'Much as I would like to hear the details, we have to be elsewhere. Perhaps another time?'

Chapter 12

Miss Daisy was squeaking, rattling and grumbling along the valley road towards Thunduluka Lodge. Overhead rain clouds were gathering and a navy gloom smothered the sun. Neither Sibanda nor Ncube were concerned. This had been happening every day for the last couple of weeks without a drop of precious liquid squeezing out of the clouds – all debilitating heat with no rain. Sibanda did check the windscreen wipers. He had previously been caught out in a particularly vicious rainstorm in pursuit of the *muthi* murderer, without wipers. He was pleased to see new rubbers fixed to the blades, so new that little extrusions from the moulding were still in place.

'Have you ever stolen anything, sir?'

'What?' the detective looked askance at his sergeant.

'Sorry, sir, I wasn't accusing you of anything. It's just …'

'… No, and yes. I suppose I have walked away with several police-issue pens and not bothered to return them, and as a child I took food without asking. And you and I collaborated to steal Mandlovu's last shrivelled-up lemon, but if you mean actual theft, then no. What have you been up to, Ncube?'

'Er, nothing. I have heard stories about stolen goods being useless, that's all.' The purloined radiator cap was burning a hole in his pocket.

Sibanda mentally rolled his eyes. What would this man, filled with fable and fancy, come up with next? 'What have you heard, Ncube?'

'My sister's friend stole nappies in Botswana …' he glanced across to the passenger seat and the unforgiving man next to him, '… not many, but you will remember when times were very hard here, and there was nothing on the shelves. Anyway, when she got them home, she washed them, and they never dried. Then there was my cousin who "borrowed" a few mealies from a neighbour's field one night. He boiled them for hours, but they remained as hard as pebbles.'

Sibanda snorted, 'Rubbish! *Ulamanga!* The nappies would have been hung out on a day like this when the air is saturated, and the mealies weren't ripe. That's how superstitions start.'

'Sir! I never lie! I may have st …' he swallowed the rest of the sentence.

The detective recognised his sergeant's discomfort. There was something troubling him and it wasn't just the governor's manager, but they had more to discuss than enchanted theft. 'Did you hear Amanda Carlisle almost let "killed" slip out. We never mentioned how she died.'

Ncube gulped, he had almost let 'stolen' slip out, perhaps he could find a way to return the radiator cap, but Miss Daisy was hissing again, she really needed the help. 'I did, sir, but are we sure Tiffany Price was murdered and if so, how?'

'I have my theories, Ncube. Let's assume for now it was definitely murder.'

'Miss Carlisle looked very capable of assault. I would need to swallow a stone to meet up with her when the moon crosses the sun.'

'Yes, she's a tough nut alright, Ncube. What about the relationship with Mark Rhodes?'

Ncube was on more comfortable ground, this was his forte. He settled his buttocks into the deck chair upholstery. 'Did you see how upset Mark Rhodes was when you told him about Tiffany Price's death? He is still in love with her. It is written in his eyes. And did you watch his face as Amanda Carlisle walked in? He is scared of her. She is like the bone of the snake, full of poison. If Tiffany Price was murdered, then she would be top of my list.'

'It's interesting that they are studying leopards and baboons.'

'Why?' The sergeant could not imagine anything remotely interesting in either of the creatures, one was dangerous and the other a crop-raiding, chicken-eating pest.

'They are sworn enemies. Did you see the look that passed between them, Ncube? Could he be an accomplice?'

'Burnt soot is common to most pots, sir, but I doubt it on this one.

If I'm not wrong then the rhino researcher was the love of Mr Rhodes's life. He wouldn't have helped in her death, but he may have some knowledge of it now.'

'An accomplice after the fact? That makes sense, there was certainly some discomfort in that room. Mark Rhodes was quite cagey when talking about people they were dealing with on the Park boundaries. Could they have roped someone in to do their dirty work? Mind you, neither of them has an alibi for the weekend … and is it a coincidence that the first time they visit Thunduluka since the conflict with Tiffany Price she's already dead and they feel relaxed because they know she's not likely to appear?'

Sibanda's musings were cut short when three rhinos boiled out of the bush in front of them and crossed the road into the valley, a family grouping of a huge male with a horn so long it rivalled an elephant tusk, a smaller female and a baby. They flung themselves around light-footed, as though on springs, snorting and stamping and eventually settling in star formation, backs to the centre. The big horned male was staring right at Ncube.

Miss Daisy came to a shuddering halt, 'Sir?' Ncube wailed. 'They look angry, what should I do?'

'Keep your head, Ncube. They're certainly agitated, something has upset them, just don't panic.'

The sergeant took no notice of the advice and proceeded to go to pieces. 'They are too close and enormous, and now they are on my side. We are going to be killed,' he wailed, 'that one has a spear on its nose that could pierce the outhouse wall at Detaba Secondary.'

'Relax, Ncube, stay calm and hang back for a while. They'll settle. White rhino aren't normally aggressive.'

'But, sir, they look extremely angry … Ayi! I am a ground bean stuck in the millet. I shouldn't be here, this is not my place …' He covered his eyes with his hands to make them disappear, his bulk shivering with fright.

Sibanda was getting irritated. He ought to have been driving, he cursed his wounded leg. Ncube was a buffoon with wild animals. 'Sergeant, open your eyes now, before I open them for you.'

'I can't, sir, this bird has had its tail plucked out, ayi! Misfortune is upon me.'

'Pull yourself together this instant,' Sibanda threatened, in a voice Ncube could not mistake. 'Look, the male rhino has moved some distance away. We should be able to get going. We can't sit here all day.' Sibanda could have watched the rhinos for some hours, but not with this fool of a man next to him.

The sergeant's hands were quivering as he reached for the ignition. He sent up a prayer to the patron saint of diesel motors to assist Miss Daisy in this her hour of need. His whole body was wobbling like a jelly. Miss Daisy started, but only in slow motion, burping gases and belching smoke in an alarming fashion. Keen to get moving, Sibanda hadn't factored in the behaviour of the calf; curiosity and fearlessness made the little explorer run into the road in front of the vehicle and then veer away back towards his mother.

'We are in trouble now, Sergeant.' Sibanda knew an anxious rhino mother, black or white, was not to be tangled with.

Ncube nearly fainted, 'What, sir? Are they coming for us, are we going to be killed?'

'Get your foot flat, Ncube, we need to move quickly,' there was unusual anxiety in Sibanda's voice. He glanced across to the sergeant who was refusing to look in the direction of the oncoming grey bulldozer pounding down on him. His eyes were firmly fixed on the road ahead, his lips tightly shut and he was leaning into the steering wheel as though his prodigious weight could add propulsion to Miss Daisy's teasing attempts at a quick start.

'Get going, Ncube,' Sibanda was shouting, but despite Ncube's heavily soled police regulation boots slamming hard on the accelerator, Miss Daisy was having none of it. She had never competed in a 0–60 second race in her life, even in her youth, and she wasn't about to start now. Gently she puttered away from her standing start like an old-fashioned inboard, and even more sedately, she gathered what little speed was at her ageing disposal, wheezing at the indignity of the treatment. Her best efforts were far from enough. Sibanda, whose eyes had never left the charging beast, head lowered and horn to the fore, braced himself for impact.

The rhino slammed into Miss Daisy, making contact on the door frame just behind Ncube's head. She hit with such force that Miss Daisy teetered sideways on two wheels. Sibanda thought later how fortunate it was that Ncube was in the driver's seat. If the sergeant had been the passenger, his great weight would have tipped Miss Daisy onto her side and exposed her underbelly to an extremely angry and hugely powerful mama. As it was, he balanced the fulcrum and the Land Rover continued to career down the road like a drunken cyclist. After several heart-stopping seconds of eternity, Miss Daisy slammed back down to earth, wobbled wildly from spring to spring and finally gained enough speed to distance her shaken cargo from the threat.

Ncube, normally a slow and measured driver, was now speeding like a teenage loon over corrugations and potholes with little concern for his beloved mechanical mistress.

'It's okay, Sergeant, you can slow down now. Are you alright?'

'*Mai babo*, I will never be alright again,' he squeaked, his nose still over the top of the steering wheel urging Miss Daisy on. 'I could have been skewered like a kebab by that wicked horn. I could be mortally wounded. I daren't look behind me. Is that thing still coming? Is Miss Daisy wrecked?'

'No to both, Ncube, the rhino is way behind us. She's given up the chase and Miss Daisy appears to have suffered no damage, but for a moment there I thought we might tip over.' Sergeant Ncube's large bulk falling across the seat onto him would have caused him greater injury than the rhino. 'This vehicle needs seatbelts, Ncube, get onto it.'

'We will need more than seatbelts if we are to travel in this Park often,' he shuddered, 'we will need armour plating.' Ncube eased back from the wheel, still shaking, and imagined the story he would tell later to his wives and children of his heroism in saving the detective from a charging rhino. The tale was taking shape, growing in stature and becoming legend even as he continued to tremble and sweat from the shock.

Sibanda, unaware he been saved from certain death, was considering the likelihood of a link between the wounded rhino at the Thunduluka waterhole and this clearly stressed family. Perhaps there would be an opportunity after examining Tiffany Price's room to check on the poacher's tracks, although they would be old by now and difficult to follow and if the threatening rain arrived it would wash away any spoor.

Miss Daisy processed along the road, woken from lethargy by her recent astonishment. For once she was running like water down a hill.

Everyone, including her, knew it wouldn't last. In the valley a group of zebra were grazing, accompanied by a lone wildebeest martialling his territory and taking advantage of the watchful extra eyes in his patch to eat the shorter sweeter grasses he preferred after the zebras had conveniently cropped the longer stems. Against the laden clouds, jealously guarding their cargo, a squadron of kites, buzzards and insectivorous eagles were hawking flying ants drifting skywards like wisps of smoke from the mounds dotted across the valley. Sibanda spent a few pleasing moments identifying what he could. Was that a cuckoo hawk? A pale grey striped bird rested from its efforts and full crop in a buffalo-thorn at the edge of the valley. Beneath him lay the rotting, red-brown fermenting fruit of the tree. What was it Moses Banda had said about distilling those berries?

'A gun barrel!'

'What, sir?' Ncube jumped, he was startled by the sudden outburst. He had been mentally parading the edible laurels awarded by his wives for his quick thinking, bravery and skilled driving.

'That's it, Ncube. I knew there was something I was missing. Our man, Mkandhla, was fired for stealing raw alcohol. We know he was in the business of selling illegal spirits and that's why all those bottles were in his wardrobe and why he sent the children off in search of more. What I couldn't work out was the link between his death from a low velocity weapon and the theft of the muzzle loader from Barghees.'

'But wasn't he killed before the theft occurred?'

'Yes, and that's the bit I can't understand. What I do know is, traditionally in Africa, particularly Malawi, an old gun barrel is used to distil the fermented spirits. A good wide bore is preferred for the job, like Gaj Barghee's muzzle loader. It's easier to cool and condense the steam as it rises from the brew.'

'But why did he have a tusk under his bed?'

'That's another bit of the puzzle I can't work out. Maybe it was payment. If we find the distillery then we will have our murderer. I'm sure of that. Sounds like Mkandhla crossed the Al Capone of Gubu.'

Ncube stayed silent. He knew of no Al Capone in the village and he knew almost the entire population. It wasn't an Ndebele name, perhaps he was a recent immigrant from the north.

Miss Daisy rattled into the Lodge car park. Ncube parked her as far from the safari fleet as possible. He didn't want her overshadowed by the gleaming bodywork of the fleet.

Sibanda was out of the vehicle in a flash despite his leg. 'Let's find John Berger, the manager, and check on Tiffany Price's room, Ncube.'

If you don't mind, sir, I'll just give Miss Daisy the once over. It's not every day you get hit by a rhino.' Ncube rolled out of the vehicle, legs still unstable from the fright. He wanted to make sure all his own parts were in working order before he faced the *mukiwa* manager and perhaps he could secretly slip the new cap onto Miss Daisy's radiator. She was threatening to explode. All the chasing and racing had left her huffing and puffing. He had also spotted the silver Toyota from the roadblock in the car park and the last thing he needed to run into after the rhino encounter was a smug white man with blood-coloured hair and a metal arm, nor his companion with the mean, squashed face.

Sibanda hobbled off in the direction of the office. There was something disturbing the sergeant and from all indications it didn't appear to be his ridiculous digestive tract. He found John Berger at his desk. The manager stood and greeted him. 'Detective, you're back. I saw you chatting to Buff Barton on Saturday, but then you disappeared before I could say hello.'

'Your new cook Charles asked me to have a look at what happened at his room.'

'Ah yes, some randy female on the prowl. I'm afraid we all had a good laugh at his expense. Shadrek never had that problem, try as he might with all the female staff. He never managed to lure one of them. Just as well, I suppose. Charles is a great employee, by the way, thanks for recommending him.'

'I'm glad he fits. So, is he occupying Shadrek's old room?'

'Yes, we cleaned it up of course, gave it a lick of paint, new bedding, after what happened ...'

'Of course. Is Buff still here?' Perhaps he would share the Matobo Hills idea with him.

'No, he left yesterday afternoon. School term starts in a few days.'

Sibanda wondered if Berry had been in touch. Buff would have had no reason to phone and let him know. It hadn't been a formal missing person's report. The old safari guide had no idea how he felt about his daughter, how he had spent most of the weekend fretting that she was distressed and then perhaps dead on the bank of the Zambezi. He couldn't ever remember feeling as anxious as he did when Ncube's call came in. Mostly, he couldn't bear to imagine that wide smile withered and those sparkling eyes dull and crying. But he had to focus on the present.

'I'm actually here about Tiffany Price. When did you last see her?'

'Tiffy? Not for a while, but that's not unusual. She lives in a staff room at the back, looks after herself, and often we don't see her for days. She spends most of her time with the rhinos. They're collared and she follows them. Why?'

'She has been found dead on the banks of the Zambezi.'

'Tiffy? No! Are you sure, Detective?'

'Positive, I'm afraid. I'd like to take a look at her room and my sergeant will be in shortly to talk to you and the staff about her recent movements.'

'Tiffy? But … She and my wife were close friends. This is going to come as a blow. How did she die?'

'We don't know yet, but we have to investigate any unexplained death.' And, I'm certain you didn't have anything to do with it, he added silently. That reaction had been genuine.

'Can we be discrete? I have an important tour operator staying at the Lodge. We're hoping he will bring in large groups next year. Tourism has taken a bit of a knock recently and we need to put on a good face. Show the world that Zimbabwe is still a great place to visit.'

'How could anyone think otherwise?' The detective was genuine. 'Can you point me in the direction of her room?'

Tiffany Price's room was like her car, messy. The bed was unmade. Dirty coffee cups and a plate of curled food sat on a side table. A cockroach scuttled away from the light offered by the open door. A column of ants had pioneered a trail from the ill-fitting corner of a window, down the wall, across the floor and up the table leg. The unappealing plate of stale food was a heaving mass of formic marauders.

'Sorry, Detective, she hasn't been here for a few days. Do you want me to get it cleaned up before you have a look?'

'No, I can handle the disorder, thanks,' he didn't like to admit that his own room was little better. He hoped the ants hadn't found the patch of bloodied fabric now swimming in a bath of lemon juice. He had taken the precaution to sit the saucer in a shallow dish of water. He absorbed that trick while growing up. African houses had no protection against the indefatigable and overwhelming habits of many different ant species. No sooner had his mother managed to rid the house of one tribe than another would find a new invasion route. He learned early to put the legs of his bed on tin lids full of water and he was as diligent as his mother in keeping a thick trail of ash around the hut. Powder of any sort discouraged their explorations, and ash was cheap and readily available.

'I'll leave you Detective. I should go and tell my wife the news.'

Sibanda just nodded and set about his own exploration. The room was quite small and fusty, reeking of stale bedclothes and the sickly smell of cheap scent mingled with cigarette smoke. On a desk sat a laptop amidst a scattering of printouts, discarded papers and overflowing ash trays. Above it a shelf displayed a lone file leaning drunkenly against the wall. It had been there so long that its cover had collapsed under the weight of its own pointlessness; even the lever was out of alignment. A quick flick through the contents showed little more than ageing pages on rhino sightings. There was no analysis or scientific explanation. Where were the field notes, the jottings? A laptop battery could only last so long out in the bush. He opened it, but it was password protected. He typed in *rhino*, it was rejected. He typed in *white rhino* and the screen popped up. The screen saver was a picture of Big Horn.

Ncube had used the detective's absence to gather his wits, replace the radiator cap with the pilfered replacement and to check Miss Daisy's wounds. She had a large knot hole in the door frame where the horn had penetrated, bigger and uglier than the jealousy bullet holes in the driver's door. Ncube had clucked and clicked but there was nothing he could do, Miss Daisy would carry the scar for the rest of her life. He had given the silver Toyota a wide berth as though it could infect by association. He wanted nothing to do with Spots and Stripes Safaris, although he did notice a triple intertwined 'S' blazoned on the door. Ncube's stomach was beginning to gurgle. He longed for a can of fizzy orange and perhaps one of Blessing's decoctions to settle the seismic rumblings. If only he could remember the name of the tree whose bark she gave him to chew, the detective would surely recognise it, but no name surfaced. He would suffer in silence. He joined the detective.

'Have you found anything yet, sir?' he asked, announcing his arrival.

'Not yet Ncube, but I'm into her computer. So far, nothing, not even any papers on rhinos, but her life will probably be on this screen in some social media site. Forensics will have to trawl through it. I'll check for anything obvious and then I'll give the rest of the room the once over. You find the manager's wife, Mrs Berger; she was close to Tiffany Price. She may have confided in her.'

Ncube headed off, relieved he didn't have to share a confined space with the detective. Suko had prepared him a sauce for his maize meal of *umfushwa*, gently poached pumpkin leaves, spread out to dry to a crisp in the sun and then cooked, mixed with peanut butter and a spoonful of cream, risen overnight to the top of the milk. It was rich. It played havoc with his innards, but it was irresistible. Ncube had wolfed it down before leaving the station. With all the digestive hampering drama of the rhino charge, he was paying the price.

Sibanda wasn't sure if the sergeant had left his usual calling card or if Miss Price's foetid clutter was becoming overpowering. He drew the curtains of a small window in front of him and pushed it open. Behind, if he clambered over the bed was another. Together they might create a through draft. He argued with the second window for a while, but it was stuck, a wooden lintel above the frame had come loose and was jamming the pane, preventing it from opening. He tried to manoeuvre the support back into the brickwork, but it wouldn't fit. The plaster was loose. A chunk had probably fallen behind the wood. If he removed the rafter, would the wall come down? Ncube would certainly witter if present, but to concentrate in the stale atmosphere was impossible. He wrenched the lintel out and immediately saw the reason for the misfit; a notebook was wedged behind the timber beam, Tiffany Price's diary ...

'Can you say Miss Price had many friends, Mrs Berger?'

In front of the sergeant, a large lady with a head of black, rapunzeline hair sat dabbing her nose with a tissue. 'Oh, laddie, she was a misunderstood wee girlie, wi' a bag full of windy sorrows that would keep a piper blowing a long lament on a lonely battlement.'

Ncube cocked his head towards John Berger, seeking translation, he wasn't sure even the smoothly, multilingual detective would understand this speech.

'Tiffany Price had issues, sergeant, and she wasn't the woman everyone painted her. She was insecure and lonely. Why on earth would a single woman come to Africa to chase rhinos? Her funding ran out a couple of years ago. She was hiding, but I'm not sure from who or what.'

'Noo, John, dinee blather, the lass was just a wee bit lost, in the crags maybe, or a hill lamb in the heather in the first snows, but she was doing great, she was finally on her way to safety.'

Ncube looked towards the manager again, but he just shook his head.

'Did she have any enemies, Mrs Berger?' Ncube sensed he was getting nowhere. So far he hadn't picked up one word, let alone any information that might be of use.

'Oh aye, she had enemies alright, more than a whole clan o' Campbells, but she was like the MacDonald's, she took friends into her confidence and got the massacre of Glen Coe for her troubles. Sergeant,' she looked up at him, eyes brimming with tears. 'Remember, it's not always your enemies that are treacherous.' She dabbed her nose again. Ncube was fascinated by the red glow it was producing. He understood her distress if not her meaning.

John Berger finally came to his rescue. 'Dear, do you know the names of anyone who might want to harm her?'

'Amanda Carlisle, she is such a spiteful, jealous madam, and then there's Bigboy Dube, and that wife of his, as nasty a piece of work as you'll meet since Flodden. I've told John not to employ him again. The clients don't like him much anyway.'

The manager interpreted, 'Bigboy Dube is a freelance professional hunter, he guides for us when we're busy at the lodge. Tiffy took it upon herself to champion the cause of all animals, Sergeant, not just rhinos. She accused him of unethical hunting, overstepping his quota. His wife is very defensive, a bit of a tiger. You wouldn't want to tangle with her. Tiffy could be high-handed. She also had a run in with Thomas Siziba, there was plenty of bad blood there, but he has high connections ...'

'... Right, Mr Berger, thank you.' Ncube didn't want to hear anything about 'high connections', but he was grateful he had names and something to report to the unforgiving detective.

Detective Sibanda, unperturbed by his implacable status, was flicking through Tiffany Price's diary. Much of it was coded, with initials and strange, disconnected words written at the top of each page. He would need time and space to read through the dense yet distinctively curly American handwriting that sprawled across the line like a series of fat ladies on a bench. One name did stand out, underlined and in capitals, Thadeus Ncube. Why had this book been hidden, and how had his sergeant come to feature in the diary of a murdered American girl? Ncube was behaving oddly. There was something going on and, until he found out what it was, the less he shared with him the better.

CHAPTER 13

Night was falling and a slew of early stars were cannoning off the scudding clouds like pin balls. Andries made his way to his *isiphala*, his grain-storage bin. He had built it many years ago, and it now wore the multi-coloured mud surface of numerous repairs. Each year the rains ate away at the plaster, dislodging chunks here and there which he patched, but so far the main construction had weathered the storm. The frame was of smooth, hard leadwood, designed to discourage the marauding jaws of ants and the climbing skills of rats and other voracious nibblers. Seated on the platform was the mud-rendered bin into which he tipped his maize ears. As an insecticide and repellent he had pulverised the pods of *umketsheketshe*, the snake bean tree and lined his *isiphala* with the powder, very effective against termites and weevils. There was nothing in the bin now. Last year's crop had been consumed and this year's was barely growing. Unless the rain came with some consistency even he, Andries, the master farmer, would be struggling. He made his way to the *isiphala* despite its lack of mealie cobs, because it wasn't completely empty.

Andries had taken Shadrek's advice and built an *insitha*, a hidey hole, a false bottom in his maize store. The small wooden access door underneath the bin was plastered with mud. It fitted seamlessly. Here he stashed his illegal booze and the tusks until he could deliver them by night to Shadrek for onward collection, and in it he also kept his weapon wrapped in oil cloth along with powder, patches, flints and lead balls ...

'Andries, come here my son.' His father had summoned him again.

He was sitting on his stool, the muzzle loader across his knees, caressing it with an oiled cloth. The flintlock intrigued with silver scroll work that chased down the barrel until it came to an abrupt end where a previous owner had chopped it shorter as firearm technology deemed such a long, unwieldy barrel unnecessary. The stock radiated a patina polished with the clammy adrenaline of many a hand that had stroked the wood. It spoke of excitement and terror over the long years of its hunting use.

'Take a closer look at what is written here,' his father said, pointing to the stock.

Andries strained to read the letters. After a few years in school, he had learned them, but he was never to be a scholar, any joy in learning was beaten out of him early on, 'Mjr Sir WCH', Andries was disappointed. It meant nothing.

'No, not on the end of the butt, here, look again.'

Andries followed his father's pointing finger and then clapped his hands in excitement. On the stock carved in uneven letters was his name. 'Did you do this, Baba?'

'No, this was carved many years ago by one of our ancestors and one day this weapon will be yours.'

'But what about my brothers?'

'They show no interest in the land. They want easy money and a city life. I can see that you, Andries, have a natural gift with animals and wild things. Anyway, it is written that it should be yours.'

Andries traced the bumpy relief with his fingers, feeling the letters as though he was blind and it was written in Braille. He felt a warm and spiritual connection to the weapon with his name carved in the stock. From the first moment he touched the precious inheritance it spoke to him instantly of danger, excitement and great adventure. He smelled the blood and the fear. He could taste the risk and it tasted sweeter than Shadrek's treats. He didn't sleep for days imagining his finger on the trigger choosing a duck for his supper, an impala for a family feast and the brave challenges that would assert his manhood.

He wouldn't sleep this night either. There was much to achieve. With Shadrek out of the picture he had phoned his contact, something he had vowed never to do, but he needed money. The Land of a Thousand Lakes was in danger of becoming the Land of a Thousand Dust Bowls. A couple of tusks would do the trick. He could collect some cash, and hunt again at leisure and set up a new trade route. This once he didn't mind dealing directly, it was repetition and habit that led to carelessness. But it wasn't his contact he was worried about. It was the partner he resented, loud mouthed and loose tongued. The eyes spelled betrayal and worse ... cruelty. He could never trust those eyes. Somehow, he would have to see his connection alone. It wouldn't be easy, but the cover of darkness would help.

His path would once again be through the Park. He pulled on his walking shoes with the false soles. They lay hidden with the rifle. He tapped them first to expel scorpions and millipedes. He had suffered the punishments of both. The neurotoxins of the former lead to nerve endings screaming with pins and needles of indescribable malevolence, the latter relying on a cyanide injection. Both tiny creatures had laid him low for some days. He never blamed the poisonous crawlers, he knew they didn't want to sting him, accumulating all that venom takes massive amounts of energy, but it was a case of expend big or have your exoskeleton crunched. He shook his boots again, vigorously, using them to flick away the growing collection of empty bottles.

The clouds were clearing as he left his hut, and the stars exhausted from all their early hyperactivity now lolled in stylish splendour on a throw of black-and-navy tie-dyed velvet. The moon would appear later, still full, but a little less proud and a couple of hours lazier. The bush was dark and would remain so until the moon got her head off the pillow. Andries didn't mind. He knew the path, his ears were trained and the rest of his senses worked their shifts equally.

He was after elephant. They were plentiful, but scattered. Even the pitiful amount of rain received so far meant that a few pools would have gathered in dryer areas. The herds would be moving on, bored with their winter dependence on larger waterholes. They wanted fresh browse, the excitement of new territory and travel. The rains had extended their range. This didn't bother Andries. He knew the young bulls would linger. They took their cue from the old bulls who could reach for choice pickings on the higher branches and rattle a few trees to dislodge and hoover up stubborn, late-forming pods still full of protein. He never shot the big tuskers, they were the seed for the next generation, the gene pool of future giants, and anyway he could never manage those heavy, ivory curves on his own. Some he had seen weighed almost fifty kilograms a tusk. It was instant riches and he had been tempted, but the lessons learned in childhood served him well: enough was enough; the duck hunters had taught him that; greed was the enemy – Shadrek's lesson; and partnerships, no matter how solid, brought bickering and betrayal; the wife of his youth was the perfect example of duplicity. Andries had been a careful and considered loner for many years until it became obvious that if he wanted some kind of sustainable wealth then he needed to meet and cultivate a few people in and around Gubu, people who could serve his financial ends, not his social needs. He began by trading smoked fish for biltong from the fat sergeant and the wife with those wide-set, wary, cow eyes. He certainly had a trader's head on his shoulders, who would ever have thought a policeman could become so useful?

He stepped out carefully on his doctored boots until he loosened into the rhythm of his stride and then he was away, eating up the terrain effortlessly. He was three kilometres into the Park before he saw his first creatures, a herd of bachelor impala grazing earnestly on a patch of green. Their noses each carried a gleaming gold star from the moon's first daub. Their pale cream-and-rust coats were curried and sleeked with summer vitality. He could have shot one with ease, skinned it, buried the evidence, carried the carcass home and had it hanging, out of sight, from the roof of his maize store within the hour, but that was not his mission tonight. He left the unloved teenagers to their supper. They had been chased from the herds by fathers jealous of their youthful prowess and mothers focused on their newborn lambs. The boys were careless and still unpractised in the ways of the wild; they had gathered together for security but, if *he* had been able to approach undetected, Heaven help them if a leopard pitched up.

Overhead a scops owl syncopated his steps with its reedy, repetitive whistle and in the distance from a lofty perch a giant eagle-owl hooted the bass riff of a village drum. Andries was once again in his element. The worries of lost tusks, undelivered alcohol, little money, and a failing crop left him as he immersed himself in the environment he knew best. The weight of anxieties fell away, his shoulders relaxed and his wiry frame melted into the forge of belonging, soldering him to the bush and the ancient sands in a silver bead of contentment.

He smelled the elephants long before he heard them. First came the warm musky scent of elephant skin spattered with the fermenting mud of churned water, and then the rich, acidic odour of fresh, wet summer dung scoured through winter guts habituated to dry leaves, dry pods and stringy bark. The distinctive thud of dung balls dropping on the still-hard ground confirmed the species, and the same dull echo helped him locate the herd. As he drew closer, the rip of grass and abdominal rumblings pinpointed the distance. He was upwind on a breathless night and his footfall was as silent as a civet's.

It was as he expected, a gathering of young bulls, five in all. He saw traces of a larger herd of cows and calves, but they had moved off, always relocating, always wary. The boys were lingering, enjoying a particularly lush patch of early growth. A couple of older bulls were with them. Andries discarded the adults from his plan immediately. One had a missing tusk, but the other was magnificent; his trunk reached for a branch of newly minted leaves, eyelashes brushing long, fine lines against the rising moon. A golden shaft rested along the parabola of his ivory. Andries knew he would have to tread carefully. Both mature bulls would be wily campaigners. They might seem relaxed and unconcerned, but they hadn't lasted to this age, raiding mealie crops in bordering villages, avoiding hunters who waited and baited with water on the park boundaries, and park rangers who slaughtered them in the massive culls of the '80s and '90s, without acquiring supreme survival skills.

He withdrew fifty metres into denser bush. The grey gathering wasn't going anywhere in a hurry and if they moved off, he could follow them at leisure. He had already chosen his victim, a young adult with tusks he could manage and would bring enough reward to fund his drinking and occasional whoring.

He primed his weapon, glad of the first moonbeams although he could have done it in the dark, the routine was second nature. He had started young, at his father's side, watching, fearful his father might make a mistake and ruin the weapon before it became his. Eventually he took over the task, carrying the flints and powder, cutting the patches and rounding the balls, until one day his father finally passed him the muzzle loader and he took his first shot. He laughed silently at the memory of landing firmly on his backside, humiliated and bruised. That had been another of his father's lessons: 'Every bull was once a calf, remember that, son,' he had said. 'It takes practice and a lot of head-butting to become the bull, and in your case, backside butting!'

Andries was now master of all he surveyed, superior to the massive beasts that grazed metres away, superior to the Headman whose crops withered and whose cattle died, better than his brothers who had wasted their lives and made bad choices, and unofficial king of Mpindo line. A wry smile reached his lips. It was still curling at the edges as he moved stealthily towards the targeted bull. The youngster had conveniently grazed further from the main group. Andries wanted to get as close as he could. Distance is the enemy of accuracy. He honed in on an *umnonjwana*, a Scotsman's rattle, a large canopied tree about twenty metres away. It still sported several 'rattles' of long, brown pods full of seeds. He had to avoid them on the ground. The crunch underfoot of the rotting husks would give him away. Once there, he could brace himself on the bole, have a bulwark to steady his aim and a retreat from the other bulls that might be confused and charge in his direction in their panic to escape.

He took to his toes and stalked to the tree like a leopard, landing each foot with care, every muscle taut, every movement minimal and judged. He took aim, a bead on the ear vent and then adjusted to a couple of centimetres below. An elephant's brain is small for the size of the head, a honeycomb of passageways crammed into the top of the skull. Andries would kill the young bull with the first bullet. A lung shot behind the shoulder would be easier, offering a bigger target, felling the massive beast within a hundred metres as he drowned in his own blood, but there would be suffering and shock. He preferred a head shot, if he could take one, for anything he killed. It was a clean, soundless end. He didn't kill for sport, for the hunter's thrill of conquering a wary opponent in an unpredictable environment, for the macho competition of measuring horns and mounting trophies, he hunted for necessity; it was his job.

Once at the tree, Andries stilled his breathing. With practised control he inched his trusty muzzle loader to the upward angle required and squeezed, easing back the silver trigger with a touch of the love he could never show his wife. There was only one chance with the weapon he carried, no second attempt, no double barrel. He didn't wait for the smoke and gas to clear. He knew the shot had hit the target. The dull thud of lead penetrating flesh and bone was his music and Andries knew every note, he was the maestro of bullets in flesh, pinpointing the position of the entry wound from the symphony it played on the night air. A tympanic thump of the leviathan body as it dropped was confirmation.

The crashing and screaming that followed the shot was predictable. Confusion reigned among the herd before sense prevailed and they ran headlong into the night, felling saplings and snapping branches in a blind haste to exit the killing field. Andries left his makeshift gun rest and walked towards the downed elephant. He was cautious, but the animal was dead, the eye already fixed and glazing.

He lost no time hacking out the tusks. They were much smaller than he had gauged, barely worth the effort. He was furious with himself; all that exertion for little reward. The bulls must have changed places in the dark. This one was barely in his teens. He chopped away with precision, chipping the tusk socket carefully and axing his anger. His contact didn't like damaged goods. Within the hour of death, the bull was minus the curves that marked his progression to manhood and Andries had stripped a *msasa* of its bark and fashioned rope slings for the tusks. He walked off with them draped over each shoulder, their weight a very disappointing cross to bear.

He headed towards his rendezvous. 2am was deep sleep hour. No one else would be about and the ivory could be carried to a safe place in stealth and security. How it moved onwards from there he didn't know or care to know. He just wanted the cash.

The night was near perfect, cool, and the rising moon, albeit with a nibbled edge, was illuminating his path. He took care with his tracks, particularly in the vicinity of the kill. A sharp-eyed ranger on patrol might spot vultures in the morning, enough of them to set alarm bells ringing. He stayed away from padded elephant trails that could reveal his spoor and destination, and he backtracked from time to time.

Andries's mind wandered as he walked while his ears, eyes and nose kept watch for danger. Perhaps it was the slightly lopsided moon or the following breeze of blood and death that brought back the memories. It was definitely the configuration of a pair of Zimbabwe teak trees that leaned into each other, encouraged unnaturally sideways as saplings by an eland head butting and marking his territory with pheromones from glands situated near his horns. It sharpened the recollection …

'Bigboy, are you coming with me tonight?' Andries had sprinted to the home of his best friend in the neighbouring village, bursting with excitement.

'Where to?'

'Hunting.'

'Hunting?' Bigboy spluttered loudly.

'Ssshhh, keep your voice down. No one must know. Baba said I must go alone, but I knew you would be desperate to come. Of course, I'll carry the weapon and do the shooting. Can you get away unseen?'

'Yes, my father is in Bulawayo and Mama knows we roam together. Should I bring my slingshot along?'

'If you want, but we are after something bigger than birds.'

'How come your father is letting you use the weapon?'

'He is serious sick. He has flu and is very weak these days. We need food to build him up. Mama has been begging him to let me go and find something.'

'I'll come if you promise to teach me how to use it.'

They met that shaggily moonlit night under a huge camel-thorn acacia, one that often served as their rendezvous point for exploration when they could escape their home duties of herding or ploughing and tilling. The fields were fallow now. It was winter. The night air crackled with raw cold, dying grass crunched beneath their feet, leaves curled like potato chips, but their bodies were immune to the chill. Excitement and anticipation warmed them like a tot of hot stuff. They walked steadily into the Park. It was no use hugging the edges; they would find nothing to shoot. The villagers saw it as their territory and snare lines abounded. Rangers dismantled them or ambushed at a kill waiting for the owner to pitch up and claim his bounty, but it was all a game. Magistrates only got excited if the wire was copper and the Copper Act was breached, then a custodial sentence might be passed, but by and large the guardians of the law agreed with the villagers that it was their right to harvest the game and the miscreants rarely got more than a slap-on-the-wrist fine. Slowly the boundaries were pushed further and further in as the animals nearer to the villages became sparse. But snares didn't always target edible meat, and that night as they approached a pair of leaning teak trees, the boys came across a truly dreadful sight.

'What's that?' Andries was the first to spot the strange apparition.

'I don't know, but it looks spooky, let's get out of here.' Bigboy set off in the opposite direction.

'Come back, it's dead whatever it is.'

'Are you sure? Look at those eyes, they are ...'

'They are telling a terrible story, but the thing is dead.'

The boys approached warily on sprung feet ready to flee if the horror in front of them came to life. Closer, it was easy to work out the series of events that had brought about the tragedy. Andries was first at the site.

'It's an *impisi* in a snare.'

'A hyena? It can't be, the eyes ...' Bigboy was transfixed by the round black orbs. 'Are you sure it isn't a witch?' He was still tentative in his approach.

'It's just a hyena, but it has suffered a terrible death, that's what you can see in the eyes. They are speaking with the voice of the damned.' A great sorrow descended on Andries's shoulders. He was cursed with empathy.

Bigboy was close now. 'Ayi, this is a horrible thing that has happened. See, the hyena was guided into the snare. The noose was set between these trees. Either side has been bushed in so the creature had no choice but to travel this way.

'He was trapped for some days before he died, maybe a week. The poachers were after kudu. They tied the line high and the noose low and then never checked their snares. The hyena must have struggled for days to get out, weaving the wire around the trees in his panic, tightening the noose and shortening his leash. See, you can read his desperation in the churned earth.'

The rotting carcass was strung up like a hanging man, forefeet straining to reach the ground. Bigboy took a closer look. 'He tried to bite his way out. The snare has worn through the flesh and cut across the corners of his mouth.' The wire had sawn into the jawbone with the barbs of a devil's snaffle. The boys stared at the dangling creature. The hyena stared back with black eyes that spoke of unimaginable agony, of slow self-strangulation and of a lingering thirst that only the hot, dry winter sun could provide.

Andries took a vow that day. 'This has been done by our neighbours. They are not real men who take on the wild with wire, anonymity and safe distance and are too lazy to even check. They are cowards. I will never do this, are you with me Bigboy?'

Bigboy hesitated. This could be the handiwork of his father or his uncles. 'But we have already sworn to be hunters and to make our living from this wilderness.'

'Not like this, never! Swear it, swear it now.' With that, an agitated Andries sliced a sinew of dried hyena skin, nicked his forearm until a drop of blood formed, and bound it with the riempie of fur. Everyone knew that hyenas were the familiars of witches who rode them through the night. Their body parts carried special powers.

Bigboy followed his friend, 'I swear it too,' he said as he bound his own flesh. He lived up to the promise, they both did. They made their money from wildlife and not always in ways the conservationists would approve of, but they never set a snare. Bigboy, despite marrying a difficult, sly woman with a dangerous habit, remained his closest friend. He liked a drink himself, enjoyed the oblivion of a good session with the bottle, but she was in its grip. Alcohol had her on a rope like a bull with a ring through its nose, one pull and she trotted after the hot stuff unable to resist until she collapsed.

Andries was jolted back to the present by a familiar grunting sound that no longer took him by surprise. He crawled up towards the valley margins. White rhino liked open spaces. The wide grassy depression was perfect territory. Their black cousins retreated to thick bush. Andries unloaded his tusks, careful that they didn't touch and clink with the shrill echo of bone china. He watched undetected as the three rhino moved along the grassed valley. When he got a good view of the trio he could see they were a family. The big male had a horn the likes of which he had never seen before. It curved, a scimitar into the night sky, hooking the stars and piercing the moon. In that instant Andries made the decision that the magnificent horn would be his and his money worries would be over for this growing season and the next.

The rhino were travelling steadily and his window of opportunity was narrow. If he followed them much further he would be too near to Thunduluka, radio communications and nosy rangers with vehicles. He needed a closer shot, having missed before from this distance. He stalked towards them, trying to stay parallel and undetected. Keeping them in sight, he reached for his patches and powder, excitement mounting with every step. His adrenalin breath came in short, sharp bursts, puncturing the dark with silver-tinted vapour. Andries had never loaded on the move before, but the prize was too big to ignore. The trio hadn't picked up his presence; the big male would never know what hit him. This was going to be like shooting ducks on the lakes. Andries hesitated briefly to ram home the ball and then he was off again, the family in sight, riches on his mind. The male stuttered. Maybe he had smelled a hint of danger, maybe he was chivvying his wife and youngster to get a move on; it gave Andries the moment he needed. The rhino turned in his direction. The hunter raised the ancient muzzle loader, took aim between the eyes and pulled the trigger. As the flint scraped the frizzen and showered sparks on the flashpan in preparation for igniting the powder in the barrel, Andries already sensed something was terribly wrong.

CHAPTER 14

Sibanda left Tiffany Price's room, her diary tucked away in his shirt. His jacket that normally hugged broad muscled shoulders and a slender waste was unbuttoned. The profile of the diary would be undetected. Until he had examined it at length he wasn't going to share it with anyone.

'Detective Sibanda,' he looked up to see he had almost bumped into John Berger heading for a shady outdoor table with a couple of men in tow. He recognised the sour, red-haired, one-armed man from the warden's office. 'Please join us.' The invitation was less than hearty. Sibanda knew the manager wanted to keep the unexplained death under wraps. He hesitated and then ambled over, disguising his limp, news of the rhino dehorning would interest him and perhaps the ex-warden knew something of Tiffany Price, but he didn't have any desire to explain his injury to a one-armed man. 'Let me introduce Garfield Murphy and Jim Slocum,' Berger continued. 'Garfield is a local wildlife consultant.'

'I believe we have met,' Sibanda offered his hand as he addressed Murphy. The pale man stood. The enthusiastic handshake was different from the insipid eyebrow of dismissive arrogance he had received at their first meeting, but the man now understood he was a detective and there was nothing like a police badge to instil civility where rudeness was the norm.

'And Jim here is a tour operator from Nottingham,' Berger said. 'We are hoping for big things from him later this year.'

The handshake, in contrast, was limp, the face flaccid, the stature unimpressive. 'Nottingham?' queried Sibanda, 'I spent a year there on secondment, interesting city,' he couldn't think of anything else to say. Nottingham had only been tolerable because Berry was close. He mustn't start thinking of her now, but cold tentacles of anxiety were reaching into his gut. He hoped she was safe wherever she was.

'I don't spend much time there,' replied Slocum, 'I travel a lot, Africa, the Far East, the Americas.' The flat nasal whine sent Sibanda straight back to the city more effectively than any photograph. He was remembering the attempts he and Berry had made to copy the accent in order to fit in. They had both been hopeless at it, but it had kept them laughing much to the bemusement of barmaids and shopkeepers. She had hugged him once during a laughing fit, a tingling embrace where her body melted into his like ice in a shot of warm whiskey. It was brief and tantalising. He had convinced himself that she was merely keeping her balance as she chortled uncontrollably and wrestled with the vowels. Sometimes he imagined otherwise … He dragged himself back to the present and offered a practised conversation starter:

'There's always the controversy about Robin Hood. Was he a terrorist, a rebel with a cause, a common criminal, or just a romantic myth?' Sibanda had been well and truly exposed to the legend during a college debate about the boundary of criminality versus civil liberties.

'Keep your 'ands of our Robin, 'e's good for tourism, you've got your elephants, we've got our rural crusader.'

'And Mr Murphy, how's the rhino dehorning going?' Sibanda focused on the gleaming hook resting on the table. It took his mind off Berry.

'Some success, four done so far.'

'Have you seen the rhino with the massive horn? His lady friend gave us a bit of scare earlier on today, she was obviously distressed and with a calf. Perhaps she has been in your sights.'

'We know the grouping and we'll reach them in due course.'

'If the poachers don't get there first. It's something of a race, I imagine.'

'I was booked to escort Jim around long before the rhino dehorning strategy began,' Murphy bristled.

Why was this man so touchy and uncomfortable?

'No criticism intended at all. It's just that I suspect there are poachers active. In the last couple of days I've seen a rhino that's been shot at and a very agitated rhino family under some threat.'

'Well, we've seen no evidence of recent poaching.' The tone was defensive from the man with the whey face.

'Did you find what you were looking for, Detective?' John Berger interrupted a conversation that was getting hostile.

Sibanda knew this was a PR sacrifice. The lodge manager didn't want this tourism operator knowing there had been a suspicious death, even if it was on the Zambezi and some kilometres away, but it did give him the opening to find out if Garfield Murphy had known Tiffany Price. 'No nothing of interest,' he lied. He turned to the red-haired man. 'You must have run into Tiffany Price, Mr Murphy.'

'Tiffany Price? The rhino researcher?'

'Yes, she died recently.'

'Oh, dear, really. Yes, I knew of her and may have met her on a couple of occasions, but I'm no rhino specialist, detective. I just dehorn them.'

'You haven't seen her lately then, perhaps exchanged data?'

'No, I haven't been to Thunduluka for a while.'

'What sort of a dart gun do you have, Mr Murphy?'

'Unfortunately, I don't own one, too expensive.' The man's eyes held his in an expressionless, white-lashed gaze. Sibanda couldn't read them.

'So how do you dart the rhino to saw off the horns?'

'I borrow a weapon from National Parks. They have a couple.'

In his peripheral vision the detective saw his sergeant hovering like a pied kingfisher, steadying itself, hovering above water, waiting for the right moment to stoop on an unsuspecting dragonfly. What was holding him back? He normally relished interruption.

Sibanda excused himself from the trio. John Berger was agitated, Garfield Murphy was hostile and Jim Slocum, the pasty Englishman, had begun sweating in the African sun like a bachelor in a brothel. Berger followed Sibanda for a few paces until they were out of earshot. 'Sorry that didn't go too well, Detective, I've been on edge myself. Thanks for not mentioning our problems here, and now Tiffany. This isn't going to be good for business.' He turned and walked back to his guests.

'Are you alright, Ncube? You seem distracted,' Sibanda reached the sergeant.

'Just a little indigestion, sir,' he hesitated, rubbed his stomach, which, to his delight, had settled, and smiled. 'Perhaps hunger. It is long past lunch. I will be fine when we get back to the station – I have something there to ease the pangs. My youngest wife, Suko, has prepared her sweet potato and rapoko pancakes. With tomato jam they are …'

'… Don't you ever think about anything but food, Ncube?'

'Water can never give up its path, sir. Was there anything in Ms Price's room?'

'No, er, nothing at all. Did you get any information out of Mrs Berger?'

'It was very difficult, she swallowed words like a chameleon with a long tongue.'

'Didn't she offer anything of interest?'

Ncube hesitated, there were names, but he wished there weren't. He did not want to go near Hunter's Rest and Thomas Siziba. Bigboy Dube was part of his problem or rather Blessing's. He didn't want to go near him either.

'Ms Price was not much liked, *eyemzini ziyayihlaba*,' he hedged, 'she was a strange beast in the herd, that's why she got gored.'

'I need names, Ncube, not metaphors,' the detective's impatience was beginning to thin. Ncube recognised the signs, if not the words. He took out his notebook. 'We know about Amanda Carlisle, and, er, Thomas Siziba,' he swallowed the name and quickly moved on, 'but there was also Bigboy Dube.'

'What was the problem there?'

'Tiffany Price thought he was hunting too much and he has a fierce wife. He's also a safari guide who sometimes works at Thunduluka.'

'Hunting too much? How and where? Spit it out, man.'

Ncube flipped open his notebook again and read what he had written down. It didn't sound too incriminating, 'exceeding his quota at, at … Flodden.' Maybe he hadn't put the complex words in the right order. It had been a difficult interview. Flodden? Sibanda shook his head in despair, 'For God's sake, Ncube, we have enough leads in this country without venturing into the Scottish Highlands. Let's get going, I'll drive.'

The sergeant scratched his head, perplexed by the geography and distressed by the detective's mood and more so, his decision to drive,

'Sir, are you sure, your leg ...' but his words were lost in the wake of a determined limp.

No one was driving anywhere as it turned out. Miss Daisy had endured enough excitement for one day and she would need cosseting to move a metre further.

'What's wrong with this heap of junk now, Ncube? I thought you'd sorted the starting problems. Don't tell me we have to push.' Sibanda was pumping the accelerator and turning the key on and off violently. Miss Daisy was winding up like a cawing crow.

'Stop, stop, sir, you are doing the starter a grave injury and pushing will not help. Miss Daisy will die for a few crumbs like a rat in a trap if you continue to wrench on the key. She is being starved of fuel. There must be a blockage in her insides.'

Sibanda could feel the tension rising. He had been here before in this very car park shamed by the antics of this ancient British crock. The row of gleaming Japanese safari vehicles still looked on, and to add insult to injury there appeared to be a newcomer, a brand new silver Toyota with a triple 'S' logo cleverly superimposed over an elephant emblazoned on the side. 'How long to get this constipated rattletrap on the road, Sergeant? We haven't got all day,' he snapped. It didn't help that as he looked down the valley a black cloud disgorged its watery burden in a localised squall over the very area of the poacher's activity. There would be little point in checking the tracks now. A few wayward drops reached the car park before petering out in a sizzle of dust.

The sergeant swallowed his distress. The detective was very lucky to have any vehicle to use at all. Couldn't he understand that? This difficult man obviously slept on a bed of nails. He knew no peace. Maybe if he found a woman who would stay with him it would soften his edges and make him less irritable. He should go to the clinic and get his leg fixed, it was obviously still paining him. The sergeant offered none of this advice, he merely said, 'Perhaps half an hour.'

Ncube cast around for a stick to prop open the bonnet. He still hadn't found a replacement support arm. Sibanda hobbled off, muttering. His phone was showing bars so he could contact the station and see if anything had come back from Forensics. He could also phone Berry.

He walked to find shade and to improve his phone signal. He didn't want to return to the front of the lodge with all the explanations of vehicle failure, again. He headed towards the kitchen. He ought to catch up with Charles anyway and find out if there had been developments regarding his prowler. The intruder was a male running around on false shoes, and a poacher, if the wound on the rhino tied in. Why was he trying to break into Charles's room? Maybe if he told the cook his Peeping Jim was a male, Charles might have some idea.

'Hey, Mdala,' he called through the kitchen window. The old man was spooning a sweet-looking mixture into a dish, 'that smells good.'

'Salibonani, Detective. This is banoffee,' he replied, 'caramel, bananas and cream. Those two important *mukiwas* have requested it, Shadrek, the last cook, made it for them every visit.'

'I've got some news on your burglar, she was a he.'

'What do you mean?' The old man walked out into the sunshine.

'I'm pretty certain the prowler was a male wearing lady's soles nailed under his own as a disguise. Why would anyone want to break into your room? Have you got anything of value in there, or enemies that might want to harm you?'

Charles thought for a moment and shook his head. 'No, I'm broke as ever and I haven't quarrelled with anyone. I am a peaceful man, Detective.'

'Could he have mistaken your room for someone else's?'

'It's possible; all staff rooms look the same, like a flock of guineafowl, the same spots, the same red-tipped wattle, the same yellow helmet. Picking out the young, tasty one is a decision made in an instant before the knobkerrie flies.'

'So, you're an old poacher as well as a cook?' the detective laughed.

'In my youth, when herding the cattle if I saw a flock and my aim was straight.'

'Keep your eyes open Charles and let me know if anything unusual is going on?'

'Yebo, Detective.'

Sibanda walked further, past the houses and into the bush behind the lodge. It was thick and crowded, typical of valley sides. Each species knew its water table tolerance and never ventured further, but they massed at the edge of their range. He found a fallen log that arched conveniently beneath a shady canopy and sat down. His thigh was beginning to throb. He swallowed a few drops of Blessing's clear liquid for the pain and took a moment to absorb the life around him. At his feet, ants were busying clearing the ground, carrying tiny multi-pinnate acacia leaves to their nest openings and piling them up in what looked like a garden makeover. There were several of these piles, one for each colony and the earth around them was swept as bare as a village yard. Why did they do this? What was the point? He had no idea. The bush was a constant source of mystery and his life sadly too busy to investigate. He rang the station, but no one answered the phone, probably a shift change or an overload of crime on the desk. He scrolled down to Berry's number and dialled, there was no response. His heart sank. Perhaps he should contact Buff, see if there had been any progress, but a noise overhead distracted him, a frantic chitter-chattering, an insistent call to the hunt.

Sibanda, checking the branches, found the noisy culprit, a honey guide, luring him to a sweet, shared feast. He stood. The innocuous brown bird fluttered away to another branch and called again in an age-old ritual that bonded man and bird. Sibanda followed and then lost sight of the chatterer. He knew what to do to call the honeyguide back. It was part of his childhood. Picking up a stick, he banged hard on a trunk and whistled. The canny flyer swooped back to a nearby branch and made himself obvious with his babbling call before flying off again. Sibanda followed. The pair repeated the performance several times, Sibanda banging the stick, the honeyguide flying back to collect his lagging assistant before he hopped on a branch and refused to move. The treasure was in sight. Sibanda didn't spot the hive straight away, but it had to be nearby.

The bird had led him a couple of hundred metres into thick bush. Fallen trees tangled with vicious undergrowth and the hooked thorns of a wait-a-bit bush. Wading into the labyrinth without a panga or an axe was not an option, he was never going to rob the hive anyway, but the bird was insistent and it would be satisfying to spot the bees and to know that he and the honeyguide had fulfilled nature's intent. Perhaps he could find a better entry from the other direction. He circled until a partial clearing gave him a less-strewn path. Wading forward, he spotted a knot hole in a *msasa* with a hovering of bees advertising the hive's location. Job done, he smiled and saluted the honeyguide, 'Thank you, friend,' he said, 'but you will get no tasty bee grubs for your efforts today.' Unknown to Sibanda, inside the hive, doing the raiding for them was a death's head moth, hoovering up the bees' hard-earned honey with his proboscis, squeaking occasionally, perhaps in a buzzing frequency to pacify suspicions as he went about his theft. The bees left him to it, despite his size. His orange-striped thorax meant they thought him one of their own.

Sibanda backed away from the find satisfied that his skills hadn't left him. He picked his way over fallen branches, favouring his injured thigh and halting to unhook thorns from his jeans and jacket. During a particularly delaying unpicking session he noticed a curious tree, an acacia, cruelly twisted and gnarled, a straggler from the grove in which the lodge had been built. Arthritic boughs and a leaning trunk spoke of great age, but it hadn't chosen a favoured site and had never reached grandiose tent-sheltering potential. It had been shunned by Thandanyoni and his design plans. The tree's roots had pulled away from the ground and a large chunk of quartz had become wedged between the exposed roots. Even though the rock was strewn with dead wood and leaves, Sibanda was convinced it had been rolled into place by forces other than nature. The camouflage was just a bit too artful. He checked the area for signs of human activity. There might have been a path, but it hadn't been accessed for some weeks. Given his wound it took more effort than he thought to clear the woodland debris and roll the stone away. It was like opening a treasure chest, behind the quartz lay someone's cache of tinned fruit, beans, condensed milk and a solitary tusk, twin to the one found under Mkandhla's bed. Someone had excavated a substantial hole beneath the tree, deep enough for the tusk to sit upright, wide enough for twenty tusks. It was a clever hiding place. No one would ever find it. He had the honeyguide to thank for this.

This second tusk threw up more questions than answers. Was the poacher based at the Lodge? Was Tiffany Price somehow involved or, given her crusading nature, was she a menace and disposed of? Was Mkandhla supplying the lodge with illegal alcohol and being paid in ivory? Did he threaten to expose the whole bag of tricks? And who owned the muzzle loader? These were queries that buzzed around his head like the bees he'd just left. He rolled the rock back and left the contents in place. He couldn't pitch up at the vehicle with a tusk, certainly not with his sergeant around who was somehow caught up in all this.

In the car park Ncube was finishing reassembling the fuel filter. It should have been changed many kilometres since, but CMED had no spares and the station had no budget for servicing. He didn't want to think what the oil looked like, probably a sump pit of thick sludge and grime. It was a serious worry. He shook his head and tried to concentrate on the matter in hand. Tracing the blockage had not been difficult. The fuel filter had been the culprit. Making a plan to clean it had stretched his ingenuity to the limit. He could have bypassed it altogether, but that would be too temporary. Diesel these days was full of sediment and more water than was healthy for an engine. Once again he had been obliged to steal, but the length of hosepipe he cut from a coil conveniently placed for washing the lodge vehicles would not be missed. He kept a pen knife in his back pocket to slice off slivers of biltong, his favourite snack. He used the same knife to cut through a discarded cooking oil container to form a bucket and hoped it wouldn't leak. It didn't, but it had been a frustrating and lengthy operation given the size of the blade. He then had to fill his homemade bucket with diesel. Miss Daisy was always short, always running on vapours, could she spare her life blood? He looked across enviously at the fleet of Toyotas. They would be brim full.

The sergeant sighed. 'Sorry Miss Daisy, I have to raid your tank. I hope you will be able to get us home.'

He didn't want to risk running empty in case the detective chose that moment to insert them into the middle of a herd of elephants or a pride of lion, or in case another rhino attacked. His knees almost buckled at the thought, but he was more afraid of the detective's sharp verbal quills and ridicule of Miss Daisy than wild animals.

It took exactly thirty minutes to drain the filter, remove it, clean it as best he could in his makeshift bucket and using the hose, suck diesel from Miss Daisy's tank to prime the fuel line so there wouldn't be an air block. The irritating detective wouldn't understand any of this. He just wanted a vehicle that went without any concern for the workings.

The detective chose that moment to reappear. Ncube watched his envy as he walked past the safari vehicles. The man would never understand the challenge of the engineering under Miss Daisy's bonnet; never know the joy and satisfaction of keeping her on the road. He didn't have a trace of mechanical compassion in his blood.

'All done, Sergeant?'

'I hope so, sir,' replied Ncube with grubby fingers crossed behind his back and a whispering exhortation to Miss Daisy on his lips, 'I should drive though, just in case.'

There was no dispute from Sibanda. He had a lot to mull over.

'I know that vehicle, sir, the one you were looking at, she is handsome indeed.'

'Personal friend, is she? As close as a milk hedge and a locust, are you?' Sibanda's leg was throbbing. He was touchy and the thought of another anthropomorphic addition to Ncube's family was more than he could tolerate. Sarcasm was his pressure valve.

'What, sir? Who are you talking about?' Ncube was confused again. First the manager's wife, and now Sibanda was speaking in tongues. It had been a long day and he was hungry.

'The silver Toyota.'

'Oh, yes, I see,' but he didn't see at all. The safest thing was to ignore the confusing words and continue as planned. 'It arrived at the roadblock with a pair of grumpy *mukiwas* in it. I didn't want to bump into those two at the lodge. The man with the hook arm has a face as ugly as a box of baboon's backsides and not to be looked at twice, and the eyes of his friend are too small and piercing. How he sees anything out of them, I don't know. That face could cast an evil spell.' Miss Daisy began coughing with promise. The sergeant's spirits were lifting. The Land Rover spoke a language he understood without effort.

'Which way did they come?' Sibanda relaxed and smiled at the apt description.

'From the north,' the sergeant nodded, 'they said they'd been visiting the Victoria Falls.' Miss Daisy spluttered, hoiked in a most unladylike manner and agreed with some reluctance to begin the journey back to Gubu. 'You disappeared, sir, did you find anything else?'

'I followed a honeyguide, Ncube. It passed the time Miss Daisy wasted.'

'But you have brought no honey back.'

'No, I didn't rob the hive. It takes a lot of work to accumulate all that honey. Bees are industrious. Anyway, a chopped tree lets in water; it can rot and become diseased.'

'You mean the bird took you to the hive, yet you did not reward it?

Ah, sir, that is a terrible mistake. Next time, do not follow the *insedlu*. He will lead you to a snake or a leopard instead. The bird will never trust you again, you have betrayed it.' And all for the sake of a tree, he thought. It confirmed his opinion of the detective as a mad ox.

Sibanda looked across to his sergeant. Could he trust him or was Ncube taking him on some path that didn't lead to honey? Police corruption was rampant. He had always thought the sergeant was clean, but he was beginning to doubt his own judgement.

That night at home, Sibanda drained the last of the cheap scotch and chinked his glass against the bottle, hoping for news of Berry, better days in Zimbabwe and the miraculous arrival of a single malt or at least something that wasn't whiskey essence in a vat of cane spirit. He eased his leg onto the bed, slathered Blessing's evil-smelling paste over the wound and drank more of her drops. He hoped it wouldn't fight with the fire water in his stomach; he had much to think about, mostly he tried to imagine who had hidden the tusk in the base of the tree. He had a feeling the old acacia was key to the murders.

Earlier, he had cooked himself a steak, he hadn't eaten red meat for a while and the beef tasted good. He settled down with Tiffany Price's diary and tried to decipher what she had written. Her code was not complex but it was uniquely personal. Who was CJ? He or she made numerous appearances as did Snail Spunk, often just rendered as S.S., Fe fi fo fum, sometimes reduced to Fx4, File and The Cat. There were other oddities, some might have been places, and names written in full including his sergeant, Thadeus Ncube and Edison Bango, the Park warden. Was her killer's name among them?

As he cleared up the dishes he noticed the saucer with the fragment of cloth. He hadn't checked on the frayed scrap. The lemon juice had done the trick. The weedy light from the overhead bulb was enough to illuminate the bleached fabric. There was no doubt, given the tiny sliver of pastel stripe emerging, that the material came from Miss Daisy's upholstery, he would recognise it anywhere. This was Ncube's territory. What was he up to? Murder? Did he need extra money to feed all those wives and children? Was he involved in ivory and alcohol, swapping one for the other? He was doing a roaring trade in fish. Had he expanded his business into more lucrative deals? He hadn't wanted to leave the roadblock and had been obstructive and resistant to breaking into Mkandhla's room where the tusk was found. Sibanda didn't like it, everything was pointing to his sergeant, being up to his eyes in whatever was going on.

CHAPTER 15

A miserable, steady drizzle greeted the early attendees at Gubu Police Station. The summer morning was already hot and the *guti* barely enough to dampen the hard ground, but Gubu's babies were nonetheless bundled in blankets and swaddled in towels. Adult fleeces and knitted hats were out and about as if a hint of rain and damp might bestow unimaginable disease on the unwrapped. The waiting bench in front of the desk steamed with soggy woollen vapours. Dripping umbrellas, some of golfing proportions, with furled, cheerful colours brought a festive feel to the gloomy interior. One woman with a weave that patterned her head like an intricate corn circle wore a plastic bag over it as protection for the expensive hairdo. No one gave her a second look; grocery carriers were de rigeur as rainwear in Gubu, or perhaps it was the sight of her purple eye and cut lip they were trying to avoid.

Sibanda strode into the station with purpose. His leg was beginning to heal. His glands were still a bit tender, but he barely noticed the ache now. Beads of diamond rain shimmered on his head and shoulders crowning him chief, but he didn't need jewels to reinforce his leadership, it was there for all to see in the width of his shoulders and the set of his lips. He leaned forward as he passed the desk and muttered something into Constable Khumalo's ear. She shut her charge book. The man who was currently detailing his complaint was waived back to the bench where he squashed in between a lady whose buttocks resembled two shovels and a man nursing a bucketful of dead chickens. The constable hurried down the corridor in Sibanda's wake.

'Right, Zee, has any information come in from Forensics on either case?'

'Yes, but only to confirm that Mkandhla's liver was not diseased and that a large object smashed through his skull. He had probably been dead about 36 hours when you found him.' The constable was standing in front of Sibanda's desk. 'Is that all, sir?

'No, sit for a moment.'

PC Khumalo looked startled. She had never been invited to sit before. The detective was legendary for his abrupt dealings and, anyway, the chair in his office rarely offered sedentary opportunities. Sibanda never indulged in idle chatter or passed the time of day over a coffee. He was on another plain and didn't need earthly comforts. His only failure was girlfriends, but who was ever going to match his glorious perfection. PC Khumalo fantasised about the detective, those troubled, bottomless eyes with long curling lashes, a ripped torso, barely disguised under his shirt and long-fingered hands that sent a tingle to her very core, but she was wise enough to know that his prickly, demanding personality would drive her mad like a plague of ticks on a donkey. Still, a fling would be an attractive option. In truth, most of the idle chatter over the coffee was speculation about Detective Sibanda and his love life. Just as well he didn't join in.

'Have I done something wrong, sir?' she asked, drawing her eyes reluctantly from hands that caressed a very lucky pen; what else could be the reason for the invitation?

'Any missing person reports or any other unusual deaths in the region?'

'Yes, plenty, Detaba have a whole list of crimes and dead bodies. Their updated bulletin came in this morning.'

'Is there a white woman among them?' Sibanda held his breath, looked down, daren't hold her eyes in case they read his concern.

'No, but there is a report of a Zambian national dead at Kenmaur.'

'Outside our jurisdiction,' he replied, inwardly relieved. He changed tack now that Berry was still technically alive. 'What do you know about the old Land Rover?'

'Only that it's the bane of the Officer-in-Charge's existence, to Chief Inspector Mfumu it's like an ant bear constantly looking at him, bringing him misery. Until it's beyond repair, the station will never get a replacement.'

'I know the feeling, that's one topic Mfumu and I agree on at least,' Sibanda muttered, more to himself than the constable.

'Sir?' PC Khumalo looked confused.

'Never mind,' he brushed aside the distraction, 'where did the Land Rover come from?'

'You should ask Sergeant Ncube that. He was the one who brought it up from Bulawayo.'

'I'm asking you, Zee, Sergeant Ncube is not in yet.'

'The sergeant has a brother at the CMED. Together they found the vehicle in the yard, almost scrap I gather, and got it going and that's all I know except it's a trouble-causer and Ncube spends hours fixing it. He's even given it a name.'

'Yes, I know.' He cut her short; he didn't want to admit he had christened Miss Daisy in an effort to keep Sergeant Ncube placated; he must be going soft.

He hesitated for a moment, caressing his chin. 'How has Ncube been lately? He seems preoccupied.'

'Same as usual, cheery, hungry, chatty, although …'

'… although what?'

'He was a bit scratchy a couple of days ago.'

'When exactly?' another staccato question from the detective.

Constable Khumalo took a few moments to reflect. 'The morning he went on roadblock duty, the morning you discovered Mkandhla's body. He came in early, mumbling and a bit irritable, not his annoyingly flirty self. Does he have a problem?'

'Perhaps, Zee. Let's not overburden him with information on the current investigations. You know how sensitive he is. He obviously has other issues on his plate. What do you know about the case of Bigboy Dube and Tiffany Price?'

'Only what's on the file. He's a hunter, freelance, on some of the newly acquired farms. They've all got quotas now. Tiffany Price thought that Bigboy Dube was shooting more than he has licences for. She reported him.'

'And was he?'

'We couldn't find any evidence and we don't have the resources to police every hunt. They had a big bust up over at Thunduluka Lodge. He was drinking, she threw a beer all over him. Said he was a killer, claimed he had shot an elephant off quota.'

'An elephant? Where?'

'Not sure, and that was the problem. It was all hearsay, rumour, stories of trucks running around at night, no hard evidence.'

'Any ivory?'

'Not that anyone saw. It can't be exported without a permit, but the border …'

'… is worse than a vagrant's socks, full of holes and stinking of rot.'

'What can we do?' PC Khumalo shrugged helplessly. 'Can I go now, sir, there's the usual queue outside plus Mfumu is chasing all the filing and paperwork, and it's no use boiling that pot of water until the maize is ground to meal. I should get back.'

'Yes, go Zee, but don't mention I asked about Ncube. He won't like us prying into any troubles he has.'

'This river won't make a sound, sir.' PC Khumalo stood. At the door, she turned, 'Have you heard the news, sir, Mandebele Giants are in the final.' Sibanda didn't react, 'and I should tell you that Stalin Mfumu is hopping around like a one-legged stork.'

Sibanda looked up, 'What's Cold War's problem now?'

'A phone call from the American Embassy, and he's after your blood like a whining mosquito.' She closed the door and set off back to her queue of clamourants. She thought of the bench with maternal propriety. She would calm their anger, receive their fines, solve their arguments where she could, and advise them of their position with regard to the law if necessary. Mostly, she got neighbours talking to one another about the minor disputes that didn't warrant a trip to the local Chief's Court for arbitration. She knew, Nelson, the man with the bucket of dead chickens, was there to complain about his neighbour's dogs. She had already decided how it would be solved. The dog owner would buy new chickens for his neighbour who would be instructed in turn to erect a better dog-proof chicken coop. They would both mutter for a few days before getting back to the easy-going harmony of Matabele neighbours.

While Constable Khumalo planned village concord, Sibanda pondered station discord. What bee did Mfumu have in his bonnet now? What had the American ambassador called about? It could only relate to Tiffany Price. He was no closer to an arrest in either her case or that of Mkandhla. What suspects did he even have? Mark Rhodes and Amanda Carlisle were front runners. If he was right, the wound in Tiffany Price's upper thigh was caused by a needle from a dart gun, and the researchers had access to one, but so did Garfield Murphy. Did any of them have a muzzle loader? Could a conservationist be an ivory trader? Unlikely. Edison Bango, the warden, also had access to a dart gun and he was mentioned in the diary. Parks was another of the public services strapped for cash and on derisory wages needing a top up from a lucrative sideline. Was he up to his armpits in this? There was a poacher out there with a weapon that could have shot Mkandhla, did he have a connection to the suspects and what role did the illegal alcohol play? Was there a still at work in the village and an argument over profits that led to murder? But then how did the ivory fit in and the stash at the base of the tree and who were the coded individuals in Tiffany Price's diary? Most disturbing of all was the fragment of fabric found in Mkandhla's brain. It had come straight from Miss Daisy's upholstery and that led to Sergeant Ncube. There was no clear thread in these cases. He was going to have to fudge it with Mfumu, a scenario he didn't relish.

Officer-in-Charge, Chief Inspector Stalin Mfumu, was agitated. That man Jabulani Sibanda was an irritation, a misplaced file in the cabinet of Mfumu's neat office, a filthy infidel in the unsullied pews of his beliefs. He had to be reined in or saved from his own apostasy. Last Sunday at the Brethren of the Lord's Blood congregation he had preached from Ephesians Chapter 4, Verse 14. The verse spoke of infants being tossed back and forth by the waves, and blown here and there by the cunning and craftiness of people in their deceitful scheming. Mfumu had exhorted his followers to watch carefully who their children mixed with, and to monitor the teachers who held their minds. There were schemers in the population goading their children to turn from the Lord, to follow the God of Mammon, to taste the demon drink and to fall into the miry pit of promiscuity. But that was the simplistic interpretation. What the verse really spoke of was all the peoples of the Earth, the children of God, led into dissipation by false prophets or, on a strictly personal level, members of his own police station in the grip of Sibanda's warped and unhealthy leadership. Their heads had been turned. They looked on him in awe, thought he had special powers. There was no doubt he was oddly popular and a pleasure to look upon, but the devil came in many guises. Sibanda's uncanny ability to solve crime was a pointer to a relationship with the supernatural. Mfumu had put matters in place to monitor his moves, but right now, it was his withholding of all the facts causing a headache. Exorcism would have to wait.

Unsettled and restless, the Officer-in-Charge stood and patrolled his office in search of disorder. He walked *inside* his clothes, not *with* them. His regulation khaki trousers pressed with an impossibly sharp crease moved independently like an exoskeleton, not touching skin, never wrinkling. His grey police shirt starched to the point of self-governance lived a life completely detached from human contact. The station staff also called their boss, *Ufudu,* Tortoise, as a variant to Cold War because he lived in a shell of clothing that he carried on his back. They speculated that he didn't hang his uniform at night, or drape it on a chair, but stepped out of it and left it standing like The Invisible Man, a movie that recently played to great popularity on the old video machine in the Gubu Railway Club.

Mfumu's diminutive size did not allow him to give detailed attention to the top shelves, which was as well because PC Khumalo had not dusted them of late. His eyes marched in a disciplined line along the lower shelves straightening police manuals and assorted files that ranged in size rather than topic. Content mattered less than conformity.

Sibanda wanted to get out of the office and check on the other suspects, but Mfumu was waiting.

'Ah, Detective Sibanda.' Mfumu looked through thick-rimmed glasses that gave him a presidential edge. 'I'm glad you have arrived. I've had a call from the American ambassador, he is not happy,' he hovered without crease back to his desk. He could not compete with Sibanda's physical presence and the desk gave him status and a barrier against … against what he didn't really know. The man had an unmistakable aura and he didn't want the power force interfering with the way he liked to run things.

'What's his problem? Tiffany Price?'

'Precisely, her parents would like to take her back to the States for burial but Forensics are not releasing her body because you have asked for more tests.'

'There are some concerns with the way she died.'

'She was killed by a crocodile. The American ambassador is happy with that, her parents agree and I want this case wrapped up now before it becomes an international incident. What is this ...' he glanced down at a piece of paper in his hands, '... $C_{25}H_{33}NO_4$?'

'A chemical formula.' Sibanda was being deliberately obstructive.

'What has that got to do with Ms Price's unfortunate death?' Mfumu was beginning to splutter. Foam was gathering at the edges of his mouth like snake spit on morning grass.

'It may have caused her death.'

'How? Did the crocodile give her a drink before she died, poison her?' Theatricality was creeping in. Mfumu's voice had taken on his preaching tones, the same singing, American Baptist-belt evangelist oratory he used when asking rhetorical questions of his congregation. He stretched his arms wide as if to gather an equally spurious answer.

'It's just a theory at this stage until Forensics confirms its presence.' Sibanda kept his cool, his voice remained professional.

'A theory?' Mfumu spat, 'we can't experiment on dead bodies, they are to be respected. Ms Price should be sent home for burial and her onward journey to her Heavenly glory.'

'Amen,' said Sibanda, without a trace of irony. He hoped it would get Mfumu off his pulpit.

Mfumu was startled into a temporary silence by this affirmation. Was he being ridiculed? He couldn't be sure. His anger increased. 'Why am I only learning of this now? Where is the paperwork? I can't tolerate this slipshod way of working.' He began to dust imaginary crumbs from his desk, fiddling and rearranging pens and folders, raising his voice. Amen indeed, the detective was definitely mocking him. He was a menace, why had he been cursed with a stubborn heretic at his station?

Sibanda knew the drill, it was well practised. He held his ground and waited for the outburst to subside, the compulsive desk tidying to reach perfection and verbal exhaustion to set in. But, as Mfumu's tirade fizzled, Sibanda's stress levels flourished. 'Tiffany Price deserves the truth,' he said in a low voice edged with steel, 'and the capture of her murderer. If that means delaying her meeting with the Lord and the choir of cherubim then so be it.'

Sibanda turned on his heels, slamming the door as he left. Mfumu leaned back in his chair, tense and drained. Why did he have the feeling he had been put in his place rather than the other way around? He started to fiddle with his pens and pencils again, leap frogging one over the other, rolling them until they sat tight, level and motionless like a log-lashed raft on a millpond, an inky sea of calm before a storm of diverting paperwork.

Sibanda steamed down the corridor and back to his own office, wrenched open the desk drawer and grabbed Tiffany Price's diary. Sergeant Ncube was nowhere to be seen and neither were the keys to the Land Rover; there would be no quick start to check on Bigboy Dube, his next port of call. He leafed through the pages, reading and jotting down every acronym and code name he could find. She was on to something, but what?

November 16ᵗʰ The ivory is coming through regularly now. Are we the staging post, but how is it getting here and from where? Fx4 flexing his muscles and adding his own booty to the pot? Vehicle is backwards and forwards with links to ship the goods on. Burn has the perfect contacts. Easy for them to dispose of the goods. Clever pair. Cover their tracks. (CJ)

November 27ᵗʰ (CJ here, Pit Bull snarling) The Cat is hovering. That means Snail Spunk won't be far behind. It's a strange coupling. They don't fit. Something is keeping them together and it isn't love!

November 28ᵗʰ Thaddeus Ncube. What is he up to? Where does he fit into all this? Local facilitator? Keeping watch? The third man? The insider?

December 10ᵗʰ Jefferson and File have been here. I don't trust either of them. (CJ)

A recognisable cough brought his head out of the pages. He slammed the journal shut. It was covered in a colourful scrapbooking of pink hearts, flying angels and wide-eyed puppies. Tiffany Price was schmaltzy if nothing else. Sergeant Ncube had reached his desk and was staring down at the girly cover.

'Sorry to disturb you, sir, but you're needed.' The sergeant's face was inscrutable, but who knew what he thought of the flowery decoration. The diary could just be Sibanda's police notebook. Gubu Police Station threw up some rum items: pastel envelopes with butterflies, bought hurriedly from Barghees when the Government-issue brown ones ran out, they gave a cheery welcome to the fine or summons inside; a chipped mug in the canteen with a curvaceous bare backside attached by a wire that swung provocatively when the drinker raised it to his lips, but his personal favourite was a vase with a faded and rubbed seaside scene emblazoned on the front. It was full of pink and purple feather flowers of indeterminate provenance. It sat, feathers fading, on the counter, trying to instil seaside enthusiasm into a populace harried by drought and niggled by penury, a population that could never dream of the vast oceans of water that lay a couple of days' journey away – plumed optimism and irony in a jar.

'So you've finally got here. What's the matter? What do I need to sort out?' Sibanda was on edge.

'Sorry, sir, a little difficulty I had to attend to, it delayed me. You know a fly never jumps over milk.'

'The immediate problem, Ncube?' he snapped, knowing Ncube's 'fly' would have indulged in some hearty breakfast cooked up by his wives.

'Assistant Detective Chanza has arrested someone for the break-in at Barghees. He's got him in the interview room.'

'Where did he pick him up?'

'I know nothing. Chanza is very secretive. He wouldn't even invite a shivering dog to share his fire.'

Finally, a possible break in the Mkandlha case. He palmed the diary back into the drawer. 'Right, Sergeant, find the keys to the Land Rover, get it fuelled and running. I'll check out the suspect, see if he's got anything to say about the muzzle loader and homemade booze.'

'Miss Daisy?' the sergeant queried.

'Yes, Ncube, is there another one? Make sure the crock isn't going to seize up, and don't take the keys home with you again or I'll turn you over to Cold War for misappropriation of police property,' Sibanda focused on a key-like bulge on the sergeant's left hip. His trousers were stretched to their tolerance against the well-padded frame leaving little slack for anything to slip unremarked into the pockets.

'The keys? *Mai babo!* I must have forgotten them in my trousers last night,' he slapped the protrusion at his side feigning surprise; ingenuousness was not Ncube's forte.

'And pigs might fly, Sergeant,' said Sibanda as he brushed past him on the way to the interview room. Ncube followed him, flummoxed by the idea of porcine flight.

'A word please, Chanza,' Sibanda summoned the assistant detective from the room where he was prowling around a seated young man, head in hands with an electric fan by his side.

Assistant Detective Chanza, Mfumu's nephew, his sister's only child and from the same pint-sized gene pool as his uncle, followed Sibanda into the corridor. His politician lookalike glasses had slid down his impressively wide nostrils and were perched like a crow on a drainpipe.

'Who is he? What have you got out of him so far, Chanza? Did he do it alone? What led you to him?' Sibanda wanted information, and fast.

'Lazarus Maphosa. He's denying theft, of course, but we found him walking down the road with the fan under his arm and it's the same make as those reported stolen from Barghees.'

Sibanda pushed past Chanza and into the interview room. The young man looked up, both eyes were blood shot, but the right one was beginning to close. Chanza's interview techniques were robust.

'So Lazarus, where were you last Wednesday night?'

The young man looked up with a glimmer of hope in his good eye. 'That's what I've been trying to tell the other detective, I only arrived in Gubu yesterday morning.'

'And Wednesday night?'

'At home with my family in Bulawayo.'

'Can anyone else confirm your alibi?' Sibanda was beginning to see the solution to Mkandhla's murder slipping.

'Yes, many people, my parents were entertaining. The Minister for Transport was there. He will remember me.' Sibanda knew with clarity that Lazarus Maphosa was telling the truth.

'Ah, he is talking rubbish,' Chanza broke in, screaming, 'come clean, you snivelling maggot on a dog turd!' He punched Maphosa's head with more clout than a man of his size should pack, consigning the right eye to the same outcome as the left.

Sibanda tried to intercept the blow, but he was on the wrong side. He leapt around the table, grabbed Chanza by the scruff of the neck, lifted him like a child swinging a rag doll and threw him out of the room. The resounding thump of buttocks on cement went a long way to neutralising Sibanda's anger. He slammed the door, excluding the little bully, and sat opposite the cowering suspect.

'Right, young man, tell me when you arrived and how the fan came into your possession,' Sibanda's voice was encouraging and mellow, it flowed over Lazarus Maphosa like an anaesthetic balm soothing the pain. Later, he was sure he had been hypnotised.

'I arrived by overnight train from Bulawayo in the early hours of yesterday morning. My friend was at the station to meet me.'

'What friend?'

'Praisemore Ndlovu, we went to school together. Yesterday we mucked around and then had a few beers at the Blue Gnu. The night I arrived was so hot and the mozzies were eating me alive so I asked Praisemore for a net or a fan. He didn't have either to spare, but said he was sure I'd find one for sale in the village. I asked around and bought this one.'

'Name of the seller?'

'I didn't ask for a name. I bumped into a few people, asked if they had a fan or a mozzie net for sale. Someone ran down the street and offered to sell me the fan. The sale was over pretty quickly. I paid twenty dollars and was on my way back to Praisemore's when a vehicle passed me, did a u-turn and that man ...' he pointed to the corridor, 'and another police officer leaped out, threw me onto the ground and arrested me.'

'Can you give me any sort of a description of the seller?'

'Medium height; short, shaved hair; maybe my age; baggy jeans, well-washed T-shirt.'

There must be a hundred young men who would fit that description in the village. 'Nothing else that would make him stand out?'

Lazarus took a moment. 'He had a nasty wound on his right cheek.'

CHAPTER 16

Miss Daisy was chuffing and chugging on the road to Dingane, Sibanda at the wheel. Sergeant Ncube had done as he was asked and then settled himself firmly in the driver's seat. When Detective Sibanda opened the door he could read thunder in his face. Ncube meekly handed him the keys. He knew that jawline as well as he knew his fishing rod. He could read when it had too much tension, when a line was in danger of becoming snarled, when the weight was too light or too heavy and the reel needed a bead of oil. That jaw, right now, spoke of a snapped rod beyond repair. News had reached Ncube of the manhandling of Chanza while he was checking Miss Daisy's water. Chanza's humiliation had raced through the offices and corridors of the police station like a herd of stampeding wildebeest. The sergeant didn't know what to think. He didn't like the little weasel, Chanza, any more than the next man, but he held Mfumu's ear and Mfumu was king. Absolute power was terrifying. Detective Sibanda wouldn't be at Gubu for much longer, he'd probably end up at some remote two-man outpost east of nowhere and Ncube would be the other man on station. He shuddered and cursed himself for being sucked back into the detective's ways. At the very least, a long stint of roadblock duty loomed. He determined not to say a word and to try to distance himself from the incident. After all, no one ever had to mourn at the home of a coward.

'You heard, Ncube?'

'Heard what, sir?'

Sibanda turned sharply; no one was a bigger gossip and scandalmonger than the sergeant. It was his strategy to fit in, to share a secret that would bring him friends and allow him into his circle of the chosen. Why was he pretending? The whole station was abuzz, 'about Chanza,' he said.

'Chanza, sir?'

This was getting ridiculous; the man was repeating his questions. 'Yes, he arrested the wrong man. I've sent him off in search of the right one.' Ncube would surely have known of a man with a deep cut on his cheek in the village, but on second thoughts, given his possible involvement, he might just keep that to himself. Chanza should be on his way to the clinic now. Sister Angel Better would anoint his bruising and point him in the right direction of the thief.

Sibanda changed tack, he patted the middle seat. 'I've got used to Miss Daisy's interior, Ncube, interesting choice of fabric.'

Now it was the sergeant's turn to stare, the detective was definitely out of sorts today. Saying something that wasn't rude about Miss Daisy was unheard of. Had he got a worm in his brain? I must be careful, he thought, a stone trap for catching birds is, after all, only supported by a very thin stick. 'Yes, it has become familiar like an old blanket,' the sergeant replied, and then he thought about snakes and other creatures slipping under blankets unnoticed. Ncube was wary.

'Did you choose it, Ncube?'

'Choose what, sir?'

'Damn it, Sergeant, are you going to repeat all my questions? You sound like a parrot. Mimicry doesn't suit you. The upholstery, did you choose it?'

Ncube was at home with the detective's irritability, but he knew to be concise and not offer detail. His answers often brought on mockery. 'No, I did not choose it.'

'If you did not choose it, who did?' the detective spoke the words one by one as if to a child.

'Why would anyone *choose* it, sir?' the conversation was becoming as pointless as a polled cow. When had the detective become interested in furnishings?

Sibanda reined in his frustration. The sergeant was cagey. He was skirting the issue of the candy-striped upholstery like a mongoose circling a cobra. Sibanda knew from Tiffany's diary that she was onto an ivory poaching ring and Mkandhla had ivory under his bed. Who was moving it and where? The two murders weren't similar and maybe not even by the same hand, but they were linked and one of them was linked closely to the fabric he was sitting on now. At that moment the radio crackled into life, 'Gubu base to Gubu mobile, can you read me?'

Sibanda grabbed the handset. 'Only just, Zee, you are breaking up.'

'Chief Inspector Mfumu has ordered you back to the station.'

'Sorry, Constable Khumalo, I'm not reading you at all, too much static.' The detective pressed and released the speak button, breaking up his reply.

She repeated the message. Sibanda toggled the wires to the handset, interrupting reception and distorting his speech even more, and then he switched the radio off altogether.

There was silence in the cab, broken only by a gurgling rumble in Sergeant Ncube's gut. He was too distressed to disguise the noise. This latest turn of events spelled catastrophe. The calf had finally kicked the medicine over, all was lost.

'We should turn around, sir, yesterday is not yet buried, maybe you can patch things up with Cold War,' although he didn't believe there was any way back and he wished he'd somehow insisted on driving.

'No, we'll keep going, Ncube, I'm only interested in now. How far are we from Bigboy Dube's place?'

'Not far, Dingane Camp is about five kilometres after we turn off the tar.'

'So Bigboy Dube lives at Dingane Camp?'

'He's just the caretaker. It's not open any more. There are no customers.'

'Do you know him?'

Ncube seemed a little uncomfortable as he answered. 'Not well, but I have met him,' and he didn't want to think about this next meeting, particularly if his evil wife was around. There had been words between her and Blessing over how best to treat the bush boils on little Godsend Mpofu. He had been obliged to get involved and he hated confrontation. His stomach was now roaring like the rapids below Victoria Falls. He wished he had brought his lunch box with him, a snack might just settle the turbulence, but it was back at Gubu station. He knew the contents, having peeked in before getting Miss Daisy ready – a beautifully smoked bream, gloriously golden on the outside, the skin shiny and crisp, the flesh inside all soft and creamy, accompanied by Suko's special bread. She had brought the yeasty starter for the bread with her from home after the lobolo had been fully paid and her parents were happy to let her go. It had been a prized gift from her gogo who had been given it by her mother. Who knows how long the mixture had been going before that, maybe to the very beginnings of the Ndebele nation. Suko, his third wife, said there were natural yeasts in the air and it was just a case of using the right grains and leaving them for a few days to ferment and gather the magic. As well as shop-bought flour, his third wife ground many traditional grains into the mixture and the resulting bread was hearty and filling. White slices were unknown in the Ncube household. He could almost taste the rustic treat and his stomach was pleading loudly for it.

'What's he like, this hunter?'

Ncube tore himself away from his feast. 'He's okay, keeps himself to himself, but his wife … turn off here, sir.' The turn off had come upon them suddenly. Sibanda wrenched the steering wheel and turned onto a dirt track. It led away from the Park into Forestry's own wildlife estate. Sibanda could feel himself relax long before the first animal came into view. The drizzle had disappeared, having gently rinsed the leaves and perked up the shrubs. Tall grasses lined the track, a fork-tailed drongo swooped and lunged in typical wave-like flight, hawking for the insects Miss Daisy disturbed with her passing. Ahead, on the damp road a pair of hoopoes stalked like roosters on disproportionately short legs, their crests proud in a furl of rust, cream and black, probing the soft earth with a long sharp beak for hidden morsels. They flew off like butterflies as the Land Rover approached, fluttering and floating, then landing again further down the road to mine a new seam of damp ground with their pick axes. A small herd of impala sipped from a rain-fed dip. Long slender legs and impossibly dainty feet negotiated the muddy margins with some distaste, their sleek and glossy fastidiousness broken only by two long black streaks that striped down their buttocks. Here and there a grove of teak trees broke up the grassland so it looked for all the world like an English country park. If only he knew that Berry was safe, today would be near perfect, even Mfumu's wrath didn't worry him, but Berry's absence niggled like a toothache. Where was she? Why hadn't she been in touch with anyone? Sibanda tried to wipe his thoughts of the worry. The day was otherwise perfect because he was back in the bush and out of the office. He enjoyed a challenge and the two murders were a jigsaw without a picture. He couldn't find the corner pieces, but he had a feeling that Bigboy Dube might just offer up a few straight edges.

'What were you saying about Dube's wife, Ncube?'

'She's a tiger.'

'Very aggressive?'

'She's Chinese and has claws that could hook the eyes out of a buffalo. I don't like her. She scares me.'

'You are frightened of your own shadow so that doesn't count. Chinese, you say?'

Ncube disguised his hurt, his wives, at least, thought he was brave. 'Yes, the story is she came over with her first husband. He was helping to build the Gwaai/Shangani Dam and got buried in the quick-setting cement. The gossips say she pushed him in. Anyway, she didn't want to go back to China so she married Bigboy in a hurry.'

Sibanda didn't want to think about the Gwaai/Shangani Dam. It had been over twenty years in the making and promised the luxury of an end to water rationing for Bulawayo and the provision of irrigation schemes for the rural poor of drought-prone Matabeleland north. The dam remained a coffered shell after all these years while less-needed water supplies were being built in Mashonaland. He wanted to weep for his neglected people, doomed forever to suck the hindmost teat of the fat political pig, but there was no time to dwell on regional injustice. He was interested though in the nationality of Bigboy's wife, a Far East link would make a very tidy connection to ivory smuggling.

Miss Daisy struggled along the sticky track until Dingane Camp came into view. What must once have been a thriving tourist mecca was now a sad relic. A half-moon of treehouses hugged the waterhole. The thatched houses sported a range of hairstyles, nit-picking baboons and the weather had seen to that – comb-overs, ragged fringes, badly cut bobs and backcombed beehives spoke of hirsute neglect. A couple of verandas lurching this way and that would, if occupied, have spilled their residents into the oncoming path of anything on its way to the waterhole. Weeds grew up through paving stones and walls tilted and discarded plaster chunks. An empty swimming pool was faded to a shade of mottled duck egg. A tannic soup of foetid water had collected in the bottom. Rotting leaves, dead and dying lizards and beetles were the only things that had swum in it for some time.

Miss Daisy pulled up at the arched entrance. She had saved up her displeasure at the mud-splattered ride and displayed it now by emitting a carbon-belching roar from her exhaust pipe as her engine was turned off.

'That should get someone here,' snapped Sibanda, already out of the vehicle and having a look in the building that had served as reception, bar and dining room. There were several doors that led off the main room, probably storerooms. The detective wanted to get into those, but they were locked.

'They are cooking, sir, I can smell *mathumbu*, and maybe *ulude*,' Sergeant Ncube's discerning nostrils were quivering. His stomach would rumble in sympathy shortly.

'Lead on Ncube, you have the nose.'

The sergeant set off down a narrow corridor and pushed on a swing door; beyond it, a man stood before a pot on the stove.

'I heard you arrive, but I didn't want to burn lunch.' A tall thin man turned and spoke to them, '*salibonani*, Ncube.'

'Greetings, Bigboy, this is Detective Inspector Sibanda. We have a few questions about Miss Tiffany Price.'

Bigboy Dube turned back to the stove and his pot of bubbling tripe, guts and wild spinach. 'What about her?' he spoke into the ripe-smelling brew.

'She's dead,' Sibanda delivered the shock wave, 'murdered,' he added.

Dube stopped his stirring. 'So, why are you here?'

'It's known you didn't get on. There were arguments and witnesses.'

Bigboy shrugged his shoulders, 'she threw beer on me, I didn't retaliate.'

'But you didn't like her ...'

'... Like her? No one liked her. She was an interfering foreigner. She came here to tell us how to run our affairs.' He turned then and faced Sibanda. 'These white people are ruining our lives, they take our land, have businesses that should be ours, came here and enslaved us, put us under the yoke and herded us into barren land, made laws to keep us there, made laws to restrict our cattle numbers and impoverished us. Tiffany Price is just a neo-colonialist, creeping in under the cover of research and telling us what we can and cannot shoot. The western world has slaughtered its own wild herds and eradicated predators and now they come here to tell us what to do with ours. She hasn't even put out one scientific paper. Where's the point in that?'

Sibanda understood the bitterness and recognised a grain of truth in the argument, but it wasn't that simple. Cultures, values and economic realities often clashed, and conservation was always the big loser, but he wasn't here to be drawn into an argument. 'Where were you at the weekend?'

'Here and there, I can't really remember.'

'Did you leave the district?'

'No, I'm getting ready for a hunting safari starting next week. I've been checking my equipment and servicing the vehicle,' he nodded towards a Land Cruiser beyond the open kitchen door. Sibanda noted the beige-painted vehicle, an older model, still in good order. On the back were the bench seats and gun racks that marked it as a hunting vehicle. He itched to get a closer look. What he had also seen in the back courtyard were bottles, some lying on their sides, some upright, a variety of shapes and sizes, but enough to keep a distillery in business for a couple of months.

'Starting a brewery?' he asked.

Bigboy was taken off guard by the change in questioning; he turned from his pot. 'What?'

'You have a large collection of bottles out there.'

'Oh, those,' he turned back to his stirring, 'my wife drinks a bit, Detective.'

'Is she here?'

'Yes, somewhere, Li, we have visitors,' he shouted through the doorway towards a brick-built cottage. A small-boned woman shuffled towards them. Sibanda recognised her Asian features, amber skin, high cheeks and long, impossibly straight, blue-black hair. As she neared the doorway, it was obvious from her crumpled face that she had barely woken up. Grey bags hung under a remarkable pair of eyes, no wonder Ncube called her a tiger, her eyes were almost fluorescent yellow; they shone out of her pasty skin like headlights in a Nottingham pea souper.

'Li, this is Detective Inspector Sibanda, and you know Sergeant Ncube.'

'Yes, greetings, Ncube,' she spoke with an accented, choppy drawl that missed out the Rs and swallowed the ends of her words. 'How is Blessing? Has she stopped bad-mouthing me yet? Tell her my potions are more powerful than hers and she had better watch out.' As she spoke, her eyes flashed in alarming fashion and she poked the sergeant in the chest with a long fingernail curved like a claw.

'Er …' the sergeant stumbled, beads of sweat had broken out on his brow and there was an ominous squelching noise from his innards.

Sibanda stepped in as much in the interests of olfactory wellbeing as anything else, although he did feel a certain chivalry towards Blessing. She was a strangely comforting figure and had healed his wound. It still twinged, but the worst was surely behind him.

'MaDube, Li,' he interrupted, 'can we talk instead about those bottles outside?'

Her eyes narrowed to slits, irises grew and her pupils shrank to the pin pricks of a cat on the hunt, but something completely unexpected happened as she focused on the detective, and Sergeant Ncube, when telling the tale later, swore he had never seen anything like it before. Those dangerous eyes retreated into their sockets and like a chameleon on a muddy branch they changed from the colour of dyed margarine to the lifeless brown of over-boiled beef. It confirmed what Ncube had known all along – Sibanda had strange powers.

The detective walked through the door towards the pile of glass, the tigress following meekly.

'These are just bottles,' she said, 'it's not illegal to own bottles, is it?'

'Not at all, but it might be illegal to purchase the contents. Do you know a man called Mkandhla from the village?'

She looked through the open door to her husband, now smoothing the mealie porridge against the side of the pot with vigorous strokes. He looked up and nodded his head imperceptibly, one of those husband-and-wife signals that often go unnoticed by anyone outside the pairing, 'Yes,' she said.

'Did you buy alcohol from him?'

She glanced again for guidance, the extra-sensory message was not forthcoming, she hesitated, 'Yes,' there was more reluctance in the answer.

'When was the last time you saw Mkandhla?'

'I can't remember.'

'This week, last week? And, Li, I suggest you think carefully, Mkandhla has been murdered and you are now a known associate.'

The pot clattered on the stove, the twizzling stick used to hunt out the lumps of mealie meal flew, splattering red hot droplets of the white porridge across the wall. Sergeant Ncube ducked and missed the worst of it. Bigboy Dube stormed outside, 'you said you were here about the murder of Tiffany Price, how have my wife and Mkandhla got mixed up in all this?'

'I don't know, Bigboy, you tell me, I have two murders on my patch within days of one another, Tiffany Price with whom you openly fought and your wife's personal brewer, Mkandhla. That puts the pair of you right in the mix.'

Li looked up at her husband, willing him to stay calm and offered, 'Early last week, yes, Monday, I went into Gubu to buy food and I got a couple of litres of his stuff. Mkandhla asked me to return his bottles and I said I would take them back when I next went into the village. I was going in tomorrow.'

'My wife drinks and I didn't like Tiffany Price, but that doesn't make us murderers,' Bigboy was agitated, he was hiding something and Sibanda wished he had a warrant to search all those storerooms. He was certain there would be signs of ivory or illegal hunting in them.

'Bigboy, I want to inspect your weapons and licences, where do you keep them?'

Sibanda instructed Ncube to stay with Li and question her about Mkandhla. He could see the sergeant's reluctance, but he was the best man for the job and the tigress had been tamed.

Bigboy lead him to the cottage and a gun box bolted to the wall. Inside were two rifles and an assortment of ammunition. The heavy-calibre .458 hunting weapon didn't interest him but the other weapon did. 'Is this a dart gun?

'Yes, I used to tranquilise animals for some of the researchers around here. Tiffany Price isn't the only one who thought we couldn't look after our own wildlife.'

'Used to?'

'They've all got their own licenses and weapons now. It's cheaper for them to do it. Can't even profit from the bastards.'

'So, you haven't used it for a while?'

'Maybe a couple of weeks ago. I did a job for the lion research team. We collared a big male. Their licence holder was on holiday.'

'We'll be checking that. Have you ever used a muzzle loader?' Sibanda wasn't sure why he asked the question except there was a third space in the gun box that lay empty.

He hesitated, and in that moment Sibanda knew for certain he had, but the hunter denied it. 'Um … no, never owned one. It's a really old-fashioned weapon, isn't it? No call for them here, still use them for hunting in the USA though.'

Bigboy locked the case and walked back towards the main building; Sibanda followed. As he walked past the Land Cruiser, the detective glanced in the back. People were careless, and items of interest often sieved their way into corners of the pick-up unnoticed, particularly a pick-up with a big hunting rig bolted on the top. He scanned the tray for squares of cloth or a discarded dart, anything to tie Bigboy to the murders, but no such luck. He was about to give up, knowing he couldn't dawdle much longer when he spotted it. He pocketed the trophy seamlessly and followed Bigboy into the kitchen.

They had needed Bigboy's Land Cruiser to get Miss Daisy started. The hunter had towed them up and down the muddy road for a good half hour before she agreed to cough and splutter into life. They had tried pushing at first, but the stubborn madam had her heels dug in like a mule with attitude. Sibanda was furious and as soon as she was chugging along back to Gubu, he spewed out his anger.

'Sergeant, get this *skoroskoro* fixed by tomorrow or it'll be your guts boiling in a pot.'

'It was just a little air bubble. I am sure she will be fine now, sir.'

'How does it look to be rescued by our prime suspects?'

'Prime suspects, sir?'

'Yes, take a look at this,' Sibanda pulled a mangled plant from his pocket and threw it across to Ncube. He didn't mention the hidden tusk at Thunduluka or link it to Bigboy's guiding stints there. He would keep that to himself until he knew where Ncube stood, but with all the other leads it definitely put the hunter and his wife at the top of the list and the man had a short fuse.

The sergeant caught the limp red flower and was none the wiser. What should he say, how should he handle this? It meant nothing to him. There were no flowers in the cases they were investigating. 'Interesting,' he replied. Nomatter had told him this was a vague word that might help in these circumstances.

'Isn't it just? I found it in the back of the Land Cruiser and Bigboy denied having been out of the District, but he has been to the Zambezi and there's the proof. The flower hasn't dried out. It may be wilted but it's only a few days old at most.' Ncube turned the blood velvet *Kigelia* blossom in his hand and tried to look knowing.

'So, Bigboy has been up at the Zambezi?' answer a question with a question when in doubt, that had been a nugget of advice from tailor Phiri, his Malawian friend.

'Yes, the sausage tree only grows up there, like the one we found Tiffany Price under. We don't get it on the Kalahari sands, but Bigboy's denying having been there and his wife has a link to Mkandhla. Did she tell you anything?'

'Only that she didn't know Mkandhla's alcohol was illegal.'

'And you believed her?'

'I don't know about the drink, but she does eat unusual things.'

'What do you mean?'

'Well, if there is anything dead on the side of the road, a dog, a donkey, anything at all, the locals call it MaDube's Chinese Takeaway.' Somehow, this didn't improve the detective's mood as he thought it might, so he tried again. 'Li said Mkandhla had warned her against buying home brew from anyone else in the village. He had a rival. She didn't know his name. Al Capone meant nothing to her, so it must be someone else.' This last piece of information didn't improve the detective's mood either; in fact, he was now rolling his eyes and shaking his head.

Sibanda drew up a couple of kilometres from the outskirts of the village. He pulled off the road into the bush and drove for some metres until he reached open grassland where they couldn't be seen and no prying eyes could tell Mfumu he was in the area. He wasn't in the mood for more confrontation. He got out of the Land Rover and walked some way to check for phone signal. Constable Khumalo would tell him the lie of the land. He dialled the station. PC Khumalo's reply was drowned out by a bloodthirsty yell from Sergeant Ncube who was jumping up and down and throwing his arms about. The rolls of his vast stomach followed the upward and downward leaping motion seconds later in a full body wave. Sibanda yelled to Constable Khumalo that he would call her back later. He sprinted towards his sergeant.

'Ncube, are you alright?' the shrieks were coming thick and fast and louder at each calling.

'Agh, save Miss Daisy, save her, look, sir, there,' Ncube was pointing to a long tube glistening pearlesence in the afternoon light and heading rapidly in Miss Daisy's direction.

'Grab it by the tail, Ncube, if it reaches the Land Rover we're in trouble.'

The sergeant took a moment out from his cries of distress to digest the ridiculous instruction from the detective. He dismissed it instantly as the suggestion of a lunatic, and continued his wails. Sibanda raced to the scene, but was too late to prevent the snake from reaching the Land Rover, wrapping itself around the engine and extending its extraordinary length down the prop shaft.

'Shoot it, sir, shoot it, quickly, it's eating Miss Daisy, crushing her to death.'

'For God's sake, calm down, Ncube, there's nothing we can do. You know I don't carry a weapon and we can't kill the python – it's a protected species.'

'Surely, when life is in danger ... do something, sir!'

'Why didn't you grab it? Let's take a look at how it has got itself wound up. Open the bonnet, Ncube.'

Ncube was speechless. Did the detective seriously believe he was going anywhere near that monster relative of the *umgobo*?

'Come, open the bonnet, the snake can't hurt you, it has no venom. It kills its prey by squeezing it to death. Stay away from the head because it can give a bit of a bite. I've never seen one this long before, what do you think, four to five metres? Magnificent specimen.' The detective rattled the bonnet trying to open it.

'There's a catch, sir, Miss Daisy doesn't like to be shaken like that.'

'There's always a catch, Ncube ...' Sibanda shared his philosophy with the afternoon breeze, he knew it would fly over his sergeant's head. 'Now are you going to open this bonnet or am I going to wrench it open?'

The sergeant edged towards the Land Rover, sideways, like a suicidal man on a ledge, having changed his decision, one shuffling step at a time, unsure if life was, after all, worth the living given the terrifying drop below. 'Pull that bit of wire sticking out of the radiator grill, sir. It will release the catch, and you will need this,' he threw a stick towards Sibanda.

'I won't need to defend myself, Ncube.'

'No, sir, it's to hold up the bonnet. I haven't fixed the support arm yet.'

Sibanda followed instructions and surveyed the engine. Ncube's curiosity eventually overcame his fear and he shuffled closer to Miss Daisy. He peered into the engine well and couldn't believe his eyes. Coils and coils of large thick-patterned snake were wrapped around the engine like a thick scarf around a winter throat. He couldn't even see the head. He began to imagine all the electrical connections and hydraulic pipes that would be damaged, cracked, snapped under pressure. They were irreplaceable. As he stared at the intricate blotches and chevrons that ran along the python's body, they began to move, shivering like a conveyor belt of diamonds. The sergeant's head slammed upwards against the hood in blind panic. The makeshift stick holding the hood in place dislodged and the bonnet slammed down on Ncube's head trapping him in the engine well with the python.

CHAPTER 17

Sibanda turned Miss Daisy left onto the tar road instead of right and back to Gubu station.

'Where are we going now, sir?' questioned a limp and wrung-out Ncube who felt as though he had been through his nextdoor neighbour Mamoyo's mangle, a great wooden affair with two rollers that she cranked with gusto and which pulverised every last drop out of the Moyo family sheets on wash day.

'I would take you back to the station to recover but Cold War will be waiting in a foul mood and that might be worse than a close encounter with a python.'

Ncube couldn't imagine anything worse than what he had just been through. The Officer-in-Charge's dark moods now seemed like a kitten mewling over a lost teat. When his grandchildren were at his knee this is the tale he would tell them and they would beg to hear it again and again. It was so horrible they would shriek and run away in terror and then come back to have it repeated.

The detective had eventually come to his rescue, he was assured, in seconds, but Ncube knew that he had been trapped in that hell pit for hours. He could still feel the smooth cold skin slithering against his lips. He had eyeballed the detailed pattern of the overlapping scales. He registered that the pulsating body wasn't slimy to the touch and then thankfully he fainted. When he came to, he was on the ground, Sibanda kneeling over him dribbling Miss Daisy's bottle of spare water over his face.

'It's okay, Ncube, you're safe,' the detective was laughing. Ncube didn't know when he had seen such mirth in Sibanda's eyes. His terrible experience had been worth it to see this man's face crease with laughter. It was a long time since they shared such a relaxed moment even though the detective's good moods were as notoriously rare as hyena gravy. In that instant Ncube understood something had changed in their relationship. Their bond had never been hearty or as close as a mopani worm and a mopani leaf, but there was always trust and respect. What had gone wrong?

'We're heading for Hunter's Rest, Tiffany Price had a big bust up with Thomas Siziba, didn't she? Right now, I'm putting my money on Bigboy Dube and his wife, they have the motive, the anger, the humiliation, and the greed. Plus, they may have found a way to move the ivory to the Far East. Li Dube will still have family there. The Chinese are born merchants, can't resist it and she openly admitted the connection with Mkandhla. Tiffany Price had a big argument with Bigboy about some elephant she suspected he had shot illegally. Maybe he killed it to pay off his wife's bar bill. Mkandhla had a tusk under his bed. Bigboy may have done away with Mkandhla as well. But we need to exclude Thomas Siziba and it's probably better I don't make an appearance at the station right now.'

The sergeant digested the words Hunter's Rest and began to gurgle from deep within. More stress, he didn't want to go there for all the bream in the Zambezi. The farm belonged to the governor and they had tangled with him before. Couldn't the detective understand that it would be career suicide to go there again? It was leaving one snake behind to visit another. The governor still owned the farm. He ruled the district and he might well have a grudge against them. It hadn't gone well for him last time they were there.

'Sir …?'

'It's okay Ncube; this is just a routine visit. We will be polite, get an alibi and move on. You will be home soon.'

Ncube sat back against the pastel-striped seat and willed himself to relax. It didn't work; no amount of deep breathing could sooth the internal terror that was building up, layering against his already battered day. It was hopeless, he felt as doomed as a chicken upside down with its legs trussed. He decided to take his mind off the impending visit.

'What about Mark Rhodes or Amanda Carlisle, there's more there than meets the eye? She hated Tiffany Price. I can tell you now, sir, that a jealous woman is more dangerous than a cage full of green mambas.'

'Women, like elephants, never forget, do they?'

'Do elephants not forget? What have they got to remember?'

'You forget I ever said it, Ncube,' Sibanda didn't want to get caught up in a discussion about elephant memory. 'What else did you learn about the researchers?'

'Mark Rhodes was in love with Tiffany Price – that is as plain as the coat on a goat – and scared of Amanda. I can't say I blame him. He looked as though he had been struck by a whole army of dung beetles. '

'So you think he is depressed? Could that be caused by his guilt?'

'Maybe, or his undying love for Ms Price and now she is dead. Neither of them had an alibi. Amanda may have known the affair was still on the path, that it wasn't over, I could tell that. She has a heart that grinds rotten things. Tears of sorrow never left those eyes; they cried inside her and turned to the bile that eats her up. She is jealous.'

'Always a good motive for murder, Sergeant, but we can't place them at the Zambezi and they don't have a connection to Mkandhla.'

'We might be able to find a connection to the Zambezi.'

'What do you know, Ncube?'

'Well, sir, when you were talking about leopards and that mysterious moth creature. I was … er … I was looking around on the veranda and I saw a box. It had fishing stuff in it.'

'That doesn't mean they were fishing up at the Zambezi. There are a few dams around here with fish in them.'

'The line was heavy and the lures and spinners were for tiger fish. Tiger are only caught in the Zambezi.' Ncube never went for the fighting fish himself. They were too much effort to catch, all that reeling and playing exhausted him and the ugly mouthful of razor-sharp teeth was off-putting. Mostly though it was because they were not good eating, with too many bones, but if he did snaffle one then Blessing had a wonderful roll-mop fish recipe that dissolved the pesky needles and it involved Coca-cola, that much he knew. Oh for that wonderful, soothing taste now, his insides were jelly.

'Had the equipment been used recently?' Sibanda didn't know he had interrupted the sergeant's favourite reverie.

'It was on top of the box. Everything else was covered in dust and leaves.'

'Well done, Ncube,' Sibanda was over hearty with his congratulations, aware of the sergeant's shock. Perhaps it hadn't been kind that he laughed at Ncube's plight but it had been the funniest thing he had seen in years; legs and arms flailing and noises he had never heard from a human body exiting every orifice. He smiled now at the memory, and then his detective's brain questioned how well the sergeant had done. Was he covering his own tracks and perhaps some involvement with Bigboy Dube by implicating the researchers? There were more threads in this case than a Persian carpet. And thinking of threads, he would have to confront Ncube about Miss Daisy's upholstery soon, but he would pick his moment. Ncube was still in shock

'So the researchers are definite suspects,' he continued, 'let's hope we can exclude the governor's nephew and narrow it down a bit.'

'I'm sure the governor's nephew is an upstanding man, sir.'

'Is that based on fact, fancy or perhaps sycophancy, Ncube?'

Ncube knew *interesting* would answer the detective's question about *sick fancy;* he was struggling to think straight, his mind was still tangled with twists of writhing snake so he stuck to answering with a question of his own, 'What do you think, sir?'

'From the case file, he was within his rights to chase Tiffany Price off his land, but he slammed into her vehicle, definitely not within his rights, pretty aggressive.'

'He claimed it was an accident, the only witness, Marx Gumbo, agreed with him.'

'How does Gumbo fit into this?' Sibanda had only skimmed through the file. The surname Gumbo rang a bell. It was common enough, but had he read something in the newspapers or heard stories?

'He's a friend of Thomas Siziba, spends time at Hunter's Rest. There is a rumour that their fathers are close, both high-ranking Civil Servants.'

'What was Tiffany doing at Hunter's Rest anyway?'

'A small section of the north-west boundary of the ranch touches the Park. One of the rhinos wanders between the two areas. Tiffany Price followed him onto Hunter's Rest. Thomas Siziba said she was trespassing. She maintained her research permit gave her permission to go wherever she liked. They clashed like two buffalos butting heads.'

'Who came off worst?'

'Siziba was fined for reckless driving. Ms Price came away without charge.'

'She won all her cases, Ncube. Was she clever or blameless?'

'Definitely not clever, sir, because she failed to see that what she pushed behind her, in the end, came to the front.'

'Revenge? Is that what the motive is?'

'Yes, you cannot feud forever like a pit full of scorpions without someone getting stung.'

'So where does Mkandhla's murder fit into your scenario?'

'Maybe Al Capone is their friend ...'

Sibanda was almost pleased to see the turn off to Hunter's Rest. His tolerance of Ncube in consideration of the snake incident was coming to an end.

Miss Daisy negotiated the grand old farm gates that had sunk further into embarrassment since her last visit. One of the wrought-iron barricades, unable to bear the shame of its rapid descent from rococo splendour to rusted fraud, had fallen to the ground and hidden beneath a covering of weeds. The other still lurched on corroded hinges, ashamed, envying the escape of its companion.

If Sibanda noted the continuing deterioration, he didn't comment. He had seen too many *cellphone* farms, run at a distance by fat cats who wanted to answer their cultural call to the bush with a readymade weekend retreat. Actual farming and the production of food was never in their acquisitive mix. He had thought for a while that sharing with the original owners might work, but that had been naïve. Berry's childhood sweetheart, Barney, hadn't lasted long back here at Hunter's Rest; he'd taken off for easier climes.

As the gracious farmhouse came into view, Sibanda was pleased to note some farming activity had been taking place. Rows of mealies were pushing through the ground, not in complete uniformity, but a crop would be harvested.

'Perhaps I'll just have a little look at Miss Daisy's pipes while you talk to the governor's nephew, sir, just to make sure ...'

'Actually, Ncube, you had better step away from Miss Daisy and not check her pipes at all.'

'Why not, sir?'

'Just sit on that rock over there and wait until I come out. Gather yourself, you've had a nasty shock.'

'But, sir, I am feeling a bit better,' Ncube was startled at the detective's concern, perhaps their relationship was growing closer at last, not as close as a colony of dassies on a rock, but a return to the respect that had previously shared.

'I am sure you are, Ncube, but you won't be quite so chipper when you know that the python is still wrapped around Miss Daisy's engine ...'

Sibanda moved away toward the farmhouse. He looked back to check that his sergeant was still upright and then blocked his ears to the shrieks of surprise and distress. He knew that Ncube would assume the python had left the vehicle and moved into the bush during his fainting fit, but it hadn't. The snake would probably only leave tonight in the quiet of darkness. Until then they would have to put up with the uninvited passenger.

Unlike his sergeant he wasn't worried about Siziba's political untouchability, but he didn't relish reliving some of the memories the farmhouse threw up, particularly those of Khanyi, his ex-fiancé. He heard she was doing well in South Africa, had found herself, grown up and taken responsibility for her actions, and there was talk she would be coming home soon. The wounds she inflicted were still healing, returning to Hunter's Rest had picked the scabs off them. He didn't want to examine his emotions closely; they were in enough turmoil with the unknown whereabouts of Berry.

The detective walked towards the back of the building. In the lands beyond he saw a tractor heading toward the house. It struggled along the dusty track, pulling a substantial four-wheeled trailer piled high with labourers, shovels, mattocks and picks. As the convoy neared, the noise grew to a cacophony – a mixture of twanging metal jolted out by the ruts and bumps in the road, a chugging, syncopated engine laying down the back track and the high shouting of male voices adding lyrics to the agricultural beat. This was a uniquely African CD. Sibanda closed his eyes and let the familiar rural music of his childhood wash over him. It was a symphony of hard work and companionship, of sweat and aching backs, of hope for a good harvest and the satisfaction of a job well done.

The tractor drew up by the outbuildings and the army of the young and not so young leapt out of the trailer with the same enviable spring of muscle and lean, work-hardened flesh. The driver instructed them to go off for a few hours; he would not call on them again until the sun dipped. He walked towards the house and straight to the detective.

'You are here about Tiffany Price,' he stated, 'I've been expecting you.'

'Thomas Siziba?'

'Yes, that's me. That woman has been murdered, and I must be one of your suspects?'

'The jungle drums have been working overtime, I see.'

Siziba scowled, 'the messenger with the note carried in a forked stick is a thing of the past. Do you know those white colonialists used a stick because they deemed it less tainted than African hands?' he brandished a smart phone. 'No one is going to keep us down. Our footprint is all over this country and the bleating westerners must get used to it. This is the future,' he waved the phone again, 'and anyone who thinks we are staying in the dark ages had better watch out.'

A hot-headed young rebel, thought Sibanda, and confrontational, but trying to wrong-foot the police wasn't going to work as an alibi. 'You're right, I am here about her murder. Can we talk about the car incident?'

'Sure, come through to the house.'

For the second time in as many months, Sibanda stepped over the threshold of the farmhouse at Hunter's Rest. Little had changed in the kitchen except a few more tiles had cracked and the tap dripped without hindrance or old inner tube rekin. The living room was tidy. Sibanda sat in an overstuffed armchair. He was glad to take the weight off his leg. The wound had closed but it still ached. Siziba settled opposite, after a morning on the hard tractor seat his rump deserved the peace and quiet of a soft chair. He eased his smart phone onto the coffee table.

'The accident wasn't deliberate; I was trying to block her way. I've got nothing against rhinos or her research, but she never asked permission to be on this land. Tiffany Price thinks she can go anywhere like the marauding invader she is, well, the tables have turned. When I found her at the boundary waterhole we had an argument. I told her to leave, she insisted she had the right to follow rhinos where she pleased. Even then I wouldn't have minded as long as she let me know when she was on the farm. We could have sorted out some kind of arrangement but she was so arrogant and … and … so white. The *mukiwas* should all go home. What more do we have to do to make them understand they are not wanted?'

'So you rammed her vehicle.'

'No, although I wish I'd done a better job. I parked side-on across the track, she rode up the side of the path to try to pass. I nudged forward to cut her off, her vehicle slid sideways into my Land Cruiser – the road is steep sided and sandy at that point – I couldn't reverse.'

'She lodged a complaint …'

'… And I got fined, when she should have been charged with trespass.'

'You've made it plain you had a grudge against her.'

Siziba looked down at the coffee table and then up at Sibanda. 'Can I get you a drink, Detective? I am as dry as a grass basket. It's hot out in the lands.'

Sibanda was beginning to feel hot and thirsty himself. He would have done with a glass of water but if he could tie Siziba up in the kitchen then he could examine the smart phone that lay tantalisingly close. His request for a cup of tea was countered by the offer of an ice-cold beer. He stuck to the tea and the delay it would offer.

As soon as Siziba left the room, Sibanda grabbed the phone. He scrolled through recent calls, there were plenty to Marx Gumbo, some to Governor Ngwenya and a recent one from Bigboy Dube no doubt alerting him to Tiffany Price's murder. The message bank had nothing of note, recent football scores, jokey comments and a list of groceries sent probably to his mother. He listened for Siziba's return but the kettle was still boiling and he could hear cupboard doors and the chink of cups. He opened the camera and flicked through the photo albums. There were hundreds of shots, mostly of scantily clad girls, some of a family wedding and then, there it was, a selfie taken at a river with a male friend. Sibanda tapped the screen and enlarged the shot. He could tell from the vegetation that it was the Zambezi and even if there hadn't been a tell-tale tangle of location-specific spiny *Combretum* with its show of silvery-white leaves, then the very width of the river was a giveaway; only the Zambezi or Africa in rare flood hinted at such plenitude. It was recent, one of the last shots on the camera roll. The dreadlocked friend was staring into the camera, or trying to; he was squint, his eyes were set at quarter to four. Sibanda managed to slide the phone back on the table before Siziba stomped into the room slopping a mug of what looked like Limpopo mud.

'Sorry, Detective, I'm running out of milk but I've spooned in four sugars.'

Sibanda took a sip of the syrupy tea. He was polite enough not to wince at the sickly sweet mixture and continued his interrogation. 'We were talking about your grudge?'

'Yes, I admit I hated the arrogant bitch, but I didn't murder her.'

'Do you ever visit Thunduluka Lodge?' The detective knew he had to establish the triangle of the river, the lodge and the ivory; somehow, that was the key to this murder.

'Only a couple of visits since that white woman went to live there. She spoiled a good beer with her whining voice and colonial attitude.'

'She was found dead on the banks of the Zambezi.'

'So I heard.'

'Have you been up there recently?' The hesitation was shorter than the beak of a seedeater but Sibanda knew a lie was coming.

'No, haven't been to the river in ages, too busy here.'

Sibanda wouldn't reveal his knowledge of the lie until he had more to go on. 'Any weapons at the farm?'

'Was she shot? I thought …'

'What did you think, Siziba?'

'I imagined she'd been … er … strangled, that's what I would have liked to have done.'

Sibanda recognised the quick recovery. Thomas Siziba knew far more about this murder than he was letting on, 'do you have any weapons?'

'Just a .308 for taking a kudu or an impala for ration meat, or if we need to put down an injured *mombi*.'

It would be a brave man that took on an elephant with a .308. 'Where were you last Saturday?'

'Here, at Hunter's Rest.' Siziba shifted in his chair.

'Can anyone vouch for that, your staff?'

'They were all at the match. I sent them to watch Mandebele Giants. Maybe you didn't hear, they've made the finals. The staff worked Sunday instead with a few sore heads.'

'So, no alibi for Saturday?'

'I didn't say that,' his tone was becoming hostile; 'a friend was here, Marx Gumbo. He'll confirm we were together.'

'Where is Gumbo, now? He'll need to give a statement.'

'He's gone overseas, to university, left a couple of days ago.' Was there a smirk in that voice, a self-satisfied gloat?

'Where and how can we contact him?'

'He's gone to Beijing. His father's the ambassador.'

Sibanda thought the name Gumbo rang a bell. There had been a big fuss over the appointment. Several people had queried the choice of ambassadorial candidate. The liberated coterie of the press blazoned headlines about Gumbo having no diplomatic training and no track record in the Civil Service. Where had he come from? It was eventually assumed by those in the know that like all governmental anomalies, a favour had been pulled, a relative leant on, or a large amount of money had changed hands. The news was all too familiar, pointless to pursue and not worth more than a couple of headlines. The story died the death of public apathy and private fear.

The detective didn't like the way this interview was shaping up. He had wanted to exclude Thomas Siziba from the murder, not to find reasons to complicate the investigation. Now he was unearthing circumstantial links. Marx Gumbo's sudden disappearance to the Far East was definitely suspicious.

'Get your friend to corroborate your alibi, Siziba. This investigation might not go well for you given your past history with Tiffany Price. I suggest you contact Gumbo.'

'Don't threaten me, Detective, I have friends in high places. You might find yourself out of a job.'

Sibanda stood with some difficulty and moved towards the door, although Thomas Siziba would never know that the detective was slightly dizzy and in renewed pain from his leg. He turned to the governor's nephew with deliberation, 'that's what your cousin thought, Siziba,' he snapped, 'and look what happened to him ...'

Ncube was hovering at the Land Rover surrounded by a group of farmworkers, equally fascinated by the peripatetic reptile. From time to time he bent down to look under the vehicle as if he needed to check the coils and coils of snake were still there. He reported the state of play to the audience. He couldn't understand how Miss Daisy had managed to keep going burdened as she was with this ... this rapist. He couldn't believe the detective had made her travel with the evil creature wrapped around her innards. He was a cruel man with no thought for Miss Daisy's suffering. The onlookers listened, nodded and gasped as was appropriate.

'Still there, Ncube?'

The sergeant jumped. He hadn't heard the detective approach or seen the spectators melt away, 'yes, sir. And what are we going to do? Miss Daisy can't travel on with this creature as a passenger.'

'Well, she got here fine and she will get back to Gubu in the same way.'

'I cannot possibly travel with a monster snake. It is not natural; you cannot rear a jackal with lambs.'

'Either you travel with the snake or you stay here with the jackals,' Sibanda eased his throbbing leg into the vehicle and slammed the door.

The atmosphere in Miss Daisy's colourful cab was stony. Ncube chose the lesser of two evils and reluctantly got in. He was sitting with his feet off the ground and his backside squeezed as tightly as his well-practised, retentive muscles could achieve. The snake wasn't entering his body.

Miss Daisy had been just as eager to beat a hasty retreat. She had started with a purr. The python didn't faze her at all. She had experienced worse.

Sibanda was the first to break the silence. 'Did you find out anything interesting from the labourers, Ncube?'

'Not much, sir.' He found it hard to talk with all his muscles tensed. Keeping his feet from the floor required bracing his stomach. The flab was beginning to ache and the questions were distracting him from keeping every sense alert for a cab invasion. 'The farmhands tell me they have been busy. Thomas Siziba has called in a farming expert from the Mpindo line on the edge of the Park. The crops are in and the cattle are dipped.'

'I can see that. It's good news.'

'Not for the farmhands.'

'Why?'

'They say the farmer, Andries Nyathi, is a poacher and they are worried that now he knows the lay of the land he will return at night and they will get the blame for lost animals.' Ncube was nervous and shamefaced. Would the detective notice? He had been trading smoked fish for biltong with Nyathi. It didn't take long to work out that the dried meat had been illegally obtained, but he had tucked the niggling guilt away in a corner of his mind, one that didn't long for the delicious salty sticks that could be sliced and eaten as a snack or converted by his wives into an evening meal of unimaginable delight.

'Ha!' Sibanda snorted, 'that lot have probably set the snares already and Nyathi will be the fall guy for their activities.'

Ncube relaxed, the detective hadn't noticed his discomfort. He vowed there and then never to approach Nyathi again. 'They say he has a weapon, a big old thing. He doesn't use wires. Anyway, the workers seem very happy on the farm, like mice in a maize field. Thomas Siziba is a good boss. He even insisted they take the day off to watch Mandebele Giants. Did you know they are …'

'… in the final? Yes!' There was irritability in the tone and Ncube knew to keep further football news to himself. The whole village was abuzz with excitement, why couldn't this man show some joy, he only laughed at the misfortune of others.

Sibanda was more concerned with the increasing suspects in the case than football success. Nyathi was a common enough name, still, it wouldn't harm to check the records, see if he had any previous form. Check the firearm licences. He didn't know how much of this he could share with his sergeant. It was a worry. His thigh was aching again, why hadn't he brought Blessing's drops?

He pulled off the road once again and into the bush.

'Sir, is it wise to stop? The snake might be angry now. It could undo its knots and attack us. I saw how fast it can travel. I wouldn't be able to get away.'

'We'll leave Miss Daisy here for the night. When it gets cool the python will slip away. We can't take the snake into the village.'

'No, you are right, sir.' Ncube peeled himself out of Miss Daisy like an orange segment. He had squashed himself into the upholstery to appear smaller and less of a target so much so that he thought he was glued in for life. His legs, once on the ground, were shaking and he hung onto Miss Daisy's door for support.

'Ncube, who do you know who can run an errand from the station?'

'Tshuma's on duty. Can't he do it, sir?'

'No, he can't, I don't trust him.' Sibanda had taken a good look at the piece of paper Mfumu had waived in his face. The formula was the one he wrote out for PC Khumalo to check on. It had gone straight from Tshuma's hand to the Officer-in-Charge.

'I thought you said he was a good man, sir.'

'First impressions aren't always correct; he's a mole, Ncube, an *imvukuzane*.'

'You mean he burrows underground?' Ncube was confused.

'He burrows all right, but he's not a real mole,' Sibanda was getting exasperated. 'He operates undercover and he's working for Mfumu. To put it simply, he's a frog eating the cream left in the back of the hut, *ixoxo lidla amasi emsamo*.'

'Ah,' Ncube's penny dropped, 'I see, we smell a rat.' He was not unhappy with this judgement, he rather liked being the detective's favourite even if it always led to trouble. He sensed Tshuma could have overshadowed him in Sibanda's estimation, particularly after this recent humiliation with the snake. 'I'll call my son; Sampson can run the errand.'

Sibanda wandered from the vehicle and phoned the station. PC Khumalo answered.

'Can you talk freely?'

'No.'

'Then, Zee, just pretend you're talking to your boyfriend. Don't let anyone know you're talking to me.'

This was going to be easy, she thought. 'Hello, baby, I'm missing yuh honey, what yuh been doin'? What's goin' down?' The soft canoodling tone suggested the language of flirtation was something she was familiar with.

Sibanda shuffled uncomfortably, he scuffed the sand beneath his feet, unearthing a startled millipede that high-tailed it to a nearby fallen log, it was far too hot in the late afternoon sun to be out and about; Sibanda would have liked to have followed him and found his own dark place. 'Er, right, Constable Khumalo, could you go to my desk. In the left-hand drawer is a book covered in pink pictures. Disguise it in a bag and find someone to bring it to me here. No one must see it. I'm about three kilometres south of the village, not far from the cattle grid.'

'Anythin' foh you my big bowl of hot, brown sugar,' she continued and then her tone changed to Sibanda's relief, 'Sir, no one can hear me now,' she whispered, 'who should I send? Constable Tshuma is on duty.'

'No, Zee, don't send him, make sure he knows nothing. Ncube's son Sampson is coming to collect it.'

Sibanda wandered further away and continued the conversation with PC Khumalo. She told him that Mfumu was in one of his worst tempers ever, stalking around, dispensing havoc. The whole station was steering clear of him and the longer Sibanda stayed away the better. Chanza had returned from the clinic with no news of anyone with a damaged cheek and had given up the search, declaring it a complete waste. 'Sir,' she continued, 'he is saying he had the right suspect and that you let him go. We've all been forced to agree with him,' she hesitated for a moment, 'I am on your side, just thought I'd let you know that the vultures are hovering.'

'Thanks, Zee, say what you must to keep the peace. Anything from Forensics?'

'Yes, the result on that chemical formula has come through and there was no trace of it in Ms Price.

'$C_{25}H_{33}NO_4$ – nothing at all, are they sure?'

'Yes, there are no traces of any chemicals, so how did she die … er … my hot bite of chilli chocolate?

Sibanda never replied. He was for once lost for words. He returned to the Land Rover and hoisted himself back into the seat. Tiffany Price had been darted, he was sure of that. M99 or $C_{25}H_{33}NO_4$. The drug used to immobilise animals was the obvious culprit. She hadn't died from shock or the small puncture wounds inflicted by the crocodile, but if there were no chemicals in her body, had he got it wrong? The ache in his leg was increasing and he probably had a temperature. Ncube stayed some distance away and lay on the ground to check if the bulging coils were still clamped to Miss Daisy's person.

Sibanda took his mind off the pain and this new complication with the murder and concentrated on an emerald-spotted wood-dove that rummaged in the undergrowth at the edge of the clearing. It was a drab sort of bird with a pale cinnamon breast and chestnut wings. In shade it appeared dull grey until brilliant emerald wing spots flashed in the sunlight like exotic jewels. The ornithological classifiers had recently changed the bird's name back from green-spotted dove and, with the addition of a single prosaic adjective, the bird had reclaimed its rich and regal heritage. He wondered what Buff made of all the renaming of birds; his childhood discovery and excitement gone to appease the scientific tidy-uppers. He didn't want to think about Buff because that brought his thoughts to Berry. The ache in his thigh was only now rivalling the turmoil in his heart. He was grateful when seven-year-old Sampson came into view riding a big old black bicycle. The boy was as lean as his father was large and he rode the machine with great skill. This was not easy because his head barely reached the handle bars and the seat was a distant luxury. To depress each pedal meant standing hard and guiding the frame to the side so that the little leg on the other side could accommodate the pedal's high arc. Sampson bobbed up and down on the bicycle as steady as a piston while the frame lunged alarmingly from side to side at an angle that defied the laws of physics. There was no question that the boy was in complete and practised control.

Ncube went to greet his son with the face of a proud father. A hug and a brown paper package were exchanged. Ncube brought the latter to the detective.

'You wanted this, sir?'

'Thanks Ncube, you can go home now. We'll leave Miss Daisy parked here for the night.'

'Will she be safe?'

'You can put a notice on her if you like – *beware of the snake*. Who would want to steal this old heap of junk anyway?'

Ncube huffed with hurt; the detective's words could cut him like a panga through mealie stalks.

'Aren't you going to show your son the python?' Sibanda continued. 'It's a rare thing to see one so close up.'

'It will give him nightmares for the rest of his life. This is a tale better told than lived.'

'You can go home then, Ncube.'

'I can give you a lift if you like, sir. Sampson can fit in the basket and there is room for you on the carrier.'

'I'll walk thanks. It's not far through the bush.' Sibanda didn't feel much like walking but he felt even less like balancing on the back of a bicycle with his arms clamped to Ncube's expanses.

He watched the tandem duo set off for the main road. Sergeant Ncube on a bicycle might be a vision that revisited often. Large dollops of buttock drooped over the seat and his stomach barely fitted in the space behind the handlebars, knees protruded at right angles to the pedals to accommodate the sergeant's pumping thighs. Sibanda shook his head in disbelief. It was a picture of the impossibly large riding the improbably robust but somehow the whole worked with a carefree happiness he envied. The fading giggles and laughter echoed as he set off.

There was still plenty of daylight and it wasn't a long walk. He trudged on a forager's path twisting through the woodland. It had been scoured clean of every burnable item. Soweto awaited the much-promised arrival of electricity, but since the supply to the cities was rationed and intermittent, it was unlikely this rural suburb of Gubu in the heart of opposition territory would ever see a charged particle this side of the apocalypse. Twenty minutes in, he stopped to gather his strength. He was sweating abnormally and felt as weak as Gubu Station's chicory coffee. He pushed on with the promise of Blessing's drops and soothing paste as his reward. When his phone rang it took several rings of the fiery-necked nightjar to waken him from his dogged stupor.

'Jabu, it's me, Berry. I'm sorry, my dad has been pestering you. I've just got back. I had some issues to sort that's all. Jabu? Jabu are you there?'

Sibanda never answered, he had fallen unconscious into a snowberry bush ignored by the villagers for its unpleasant-tasting fruit and spindly, incombustible branches.

CHAPTER 18

S ibanda hadn't been here before. He struggled to make sense of the vivisectional animals, the zebra with a leopard's head, a four-legged martial eagle running for take-off and the bizarre landscape. When had Salvador Dali painted Africa? He was being pushed by a crowd of unknown people towards a railway line anchored on ivory sleepers that stretched like piano keys into the distance. Miss Daisy was riding the rails, bearing down on him, a steamtrain driven by a giant fire-snorting snake. Across the line he could see Berry, her hand outstretched. Could he reach her before Miss Daisy ran him down? The effort was superhuman but he made it and was rewarded with a hug and a cool hand on his brow.

'Jabu, Jabu, are you awake? It's Berry, you're going to be okay.'

Sibanda didn't think he was asleep, why was she trying to wake him? They were together; he didn't want to change that.

'He's coming around. Sergeant Ncube, go and call the nurse. Jabu, wake up.'

The landscape dissolved as he opened his eyes. He was hooked up to tubes and an oxygen mask, surrounded by green curtains and Berry was leaning over him. He lifted the mask. 'Where am I? What's going on?' The scene might be less threatening but Sibanda was still confused.

'You're in Detaba Hospital, Jabu, you collapsed, don't you remember?'

Sibanda was having difficulty even remembering his name with those large, blue eyes so close to him and a curtain of white-gold hair falling across her cheeks as she leaned forward. 'Yes, I was walking home through the bush, you phoned.'

'I had a devil of a time trying to find you. I knew something had to be wrong. You answered the phone and all I heard was a groan and the heavy thud of you falling. I called Gubu Police Station and a very nice officer, PC Khumalo, put me in touch with Sergeant Ncube. I picked him up from his home. He took me to the Land Rover, Miss Daisy ...' her cheeks dimpled in amusement at the name, '... and together we tracked you. It was already getting dark, but we were able to follow the path.'

'How did I get to hospital?'

'Sergeant Ncube is as strong as an ox. He picked you up, slung you over his shoulder and got you into my car. I drove you here and the sergeant followed in Miss Daisy. He said something about her being okay, that the unpaid passenger had gone.' She had not understood the significance.

Sibanda's head was clearing and he was beginning to remember the events of the day, 'How long have I been here?'

'A day and a half. They had to operate on your leg. It had a splinter of wood lodged in it, a real mess. You're lucky,' Berry had taken his hand in hers and was stroking the back of it with her thumb. His skin, including drips and drains, only felt her touch. It was all he could focus on. In the background he was aware of lesser sensations – a tightness in his thigh, a raging thirst and the beginnings of a headache.

'Lucky? Why?' He did feel lucky but it had nothing to do with his leg and more to do with the caress. He concentrated for a few moments on the tenderness before reality intruded. A day and a half in hospital meant he'd just wasted a couple of days on his back when he should have been closing in on the murderers.

'You could have lost your leg, it was badly infected. The doctor didn't understand why gangrene hadn't set in, or why you had put up with such pain for so long.'

Silently, Sibanda thanked Blessing. Her bush remedies had probably saved him.

'I'm glad you're back, Berry, you gave us all a scare for a while.'

'I know and I'm sorry. It was childish, but I was pretty cut up about Luka, and Dad ... well, he doesn't really understand.'

'What about your friends?'

'There's no one left, Jabu. Most of the kids I went to school with have gone overseas. Zimbabwe is hard on my generation. There are no jobs, and no future. Anyone who can has gone. I'm one of the few who have come back. Precious is a doctor in New Zealand, Kelly is temping in London, Thandi and Rose are mucking out stables in Newmarket, I could go on.'

There was need in those remarkable eyes and something more … Sibanda wanted to wrap her in his arms and tell her she had him and he would always be here, he wasn't leaving for greener pastures, but the thought came out as a lame and emotionless suggestion, 'You could have come to me. I would have chatted it through with you.' He couldn't be sure, but he interpreted her look to say that talk what not what she wanted right now.

'I'm fine now, Jabu, so don't worry anymore,' she said, breezily.

He recognised that he had chickened out again and the moment had passed, what was wrong with him? Why was he holding back? Was he scared that making a move would be opening a wound that could hurt much more than a dagger in the thigh? He changed tack, 'I have to get out of here, Berry, today …'

'… Oh no, I don't think so, young man,' an elderly nurse drew back the curtain followed by Sergeant Ncube. 'You will need several days' rest. That was a nasty wound you had.' She picked up his wrist to take a pulse and stuck a thermometer in his mouth.

'Ah, sir,' Sergeant Ncube's impossible smile dissolved a faceful of anxiety. There were so many of his perfectly matched teeth on show it could have been a dental convention. 'I am so happy to see you awake. Blessing, Nomatter, Suko and I have been very concerned. My wives have sent gifts for your recovery,' the sergeant pointed to a pile of various containers at the side of the detective's bed which appeared to contain enough food for the entire ward.

Sibanda grunted his thanks through clamped lips before the nurse removed the thermometer, studied it and wrote on the chart at the bottom of the bed. 'Now rest, young man, you've been very lucky, God's morning dew has fallen on you.' She left the ward.

'I believe I have you to thank for rescuing me, Ncube.'

'It was nothing, sir, without Miss Barton, no one would have known that you were sick, and without her vehicle we would never have found you. You are very lucky, sir, born on an eating mat, and by the way,' he leaned in closer to the bed and lowered his voice, 'Blessing sent this. She said it will make you heal faster,' the sergeant placed a bottle of thick, murky green liquid next to the detective's bed. It would probably taste terrible but Sibanda knew he would drink it, as prescribed, until the bottle was empty.

With the triple affirmation of his luck Sibanda understood he had somehow dodged an unpleasant fate. There were no one-legged policemen. He would have been pensioned off with a pittance and sent home to moulder. He managed to hoist himself up in the bed, woozy as he was. He had to get out of hospital and back on the case before Mfumu gave it to his derelict nephew Chanza.

'What's happening at the station, Sergeant, any news?'

'There's good news, sir, excellent news, the Officer-in-Charge has forgiven you for the assault on his nephew. He says you must have been delirious. But there's bad news too. He's angry again because a report has come in from Forensics to say there were no traces of drugs in Tiffany Price's body,' he took out a carefully folded piece of paper from his top pocket and started to read the details. 'No sign of …'

'M99.'

'Yes, that's it and Chief Inspector Mfumu says you have delayed the return of the body unnecessarily. What's M99?'

'It's a drug used in immobilising animals. I was certain our victim had been darted. What else?'

'They are chasing Lazarus Maphosa; he hurried back to Bulawayo once he was released.'

'And the man with the cut on his cheek, the one who sold him the stolen fan?'

'What man, what cut? I know nothing of this.' Ncube was confused.

Sibanda remembered he had kept that information from his sergeant. He looked across to Berry seated on the other side of his bed. Was now the moment to find out how Ncube was involved in all this? Somewhere during the conversation she had released his hand and was flipping through a book – a book with a pink cover.

'Berry, where did you get that?' He tried to grab it but was too weak to lean far.

She appeared to examine the cover for an answer and then looked up. 'It fell out of your jacket when Sergeant Ncube picked you up. It's the diary of someone called Tiffany Price. Ncube said it could be useful in your current murder investigation. He and I have been going through it together, sitting here waiting for you to wake up. I could get hooked on this investigation stuff, very cloak and dagger with all these codes.'

'Berry, you shouldn't ...'

'... I know, but when have I ever done anything anyone expected of me?' She stared at him for the briefest questioning moment, a hint of flirtatious defiance and then it passed. 'The sergeant and I have managed to work a few things out.'

'Sir, you aren't going to believe it, but my name is in Tiffany Price's diary. I am married; I have never met her other than at the station. How can she include me with all the other men she has written down in her book?'

'Maybe you were to be a future conquest Ncube.' The sergeant spluttered and shook his weighty head and accompanying jowls in discomfort.

'Don't be such a tease, Jabu, that's not fair and you know it,' Berry piped up.

Now the sergeant was shocked. He had never heard anyone speak to the detective with familiarity, and to reprimand him. He waited for the stinging tirade that would follow as surely as a pack of village dogs after a bitch on heat, but there was only a wry smile and a mild question from the enigmatic detective.

'So what have you two come up with?'

'Tiffany Price was onto an ivory poaching ring. There are a whole load of coded references to people that may be involved. Sergeant Ncube says you have suspects but he won't give me any names. I could help match the suspects to her code. Jabu, you know I love cryptic crosswords ...'

'... What else?"

Sergeant Ncube butted in, 'Miss Barton says ...'

'... Call me Berry, please, Sergeant, everyone does.'

Ncube didn't like this one bit, it felt too intimate. Next thing she would be wanting to call him Thadeus, even his wives didn't use that. 'Miss Barton says that Tiffany Price visited my fishing spot on the Zambezi before. She names it in her diary as ...' He looked at Berry.

'... Well, it's what she calls *Styx Crossing,* look here at this entry for

January 4th this year: *Back to Styx Crossing. Who is Charon?* And then her last entry: *Styx, and this time I'm sure who'll be there. With photographic evidence, they won't be able to deny it.'*

'We didn't find a camera near the body or in her car, sir, and Miss Barton says Charon is a ferryman somewhere.'

'In the underworld, working the Hades trip, but don't bother yourself with that Ncube. You're right, though, we didn't find a camera and no researcher worth her salt would be without one. They, whoever *they* are, probably pitched it into the river after they murdered her. It's floated to Mozambique by now.'

'Tiffany Price obviously saw Sergeant Ncube at the fishing spot, which is why she has his name in the diary. You made a trip to the river about then didn't you, Sergeant?' Berry wanted to make it plain that the sergeant was an innocent bystander. She had grown fond of the rotund policeman during their watch together and she could see the respect he had for Jabu.

'Yes, I went fishing. Our stocks were pretty low after Christmas and New Year. Nomatter had made a big feast of pickled fish, mealie dumplings and bean relish for our extended family get-together over the festive season. Twenty-six of us there were, including all the little ones. It was followed by Blessing's stewed wild plums with herbs and Cape gooseberry jam and Suko's sweet buns.' The sergeant smacked his lips, trying to relive the memory. It encouraged an appreciative burp which he disguised with a following throat clearance.

'So the fishing spot is the Styx mentioned in the diary and that's where the ivory is being shipped across?'

'Yes, if we've interpreted Tiffany's diary references correctly,' Berry said.

Sibanda ripped off the plaster holding the cannula in place and disconnected himself from the drip.

'Sir, what are you doing?' Ncube was alarmed.

'Jabu, you can't do that, you need to stay in bed,' Berry tried to push him back as he lifted himself from the pillows.

'Ncube, get my clothes, I'm out of here. This case is closing in.'

'Don't you dare get the clothes, Sergeant Ncube, Jabu has to stay in hospital.'

Ncube hesitated, looked from Berry to the detective whose jaw was set in a familiar clenched line and collected Sibanda's clothes from a chair in the corner. 'Sorry Miss Barton.'

'Berry could you leave us for a minute, but don't go away, we might need your help with the diary.' Sibanda didn't want Berry caught up in crime. He could probably interpret the code alone but he wasn't quite ready to give up on her presence. She made him feel alive just being there. He didn't know if the relief he felt was her being okay or his leg still being attached to his body. A stream of complex emotions were running through his head, he had to clear them and get back to the murders.

Berry hesitated, arguing the ill-advised decision. Sibanda threw back the covers, she stood, accepted defeat and left the curtained-in area.

'This is not right, sir, you shouldn't be out of bed,' Ncube huffed as he helped Sibanda dress.

'Are you trying to keep me off this case, Sergeant?'

'No, why would I do that? You are the only man for the job. You will be the one to find out who committed these crimes, but you are not well. My wives won't forgive me if anything happens to you.'

'You and I have a lot of talking to do, Ncube, and mostly, you have a lot of questions to answer, but right now, give me a shoulder and help me out of this place. I take it Miss Daisy is waiting outside.'

'She is, and she will be happy to see you on your feet.' Sibanda leant on his sergeant and grabbed the green bottle. Ncube collected the food, there were some very tasty morsels in those packets and he wasn't about to waste them. He could smell the curried *ulude*, garlic and goat's cheese samoosas, a rich, stinky waft that had been tormenting him for some hours, but it wouldn't be right to raid the supplies of a sick man.

'Jabu, this is crazy,' Berry joined them in the corridor.

'It's alright, Miss Barton, *wamfaka ekhwapheni*, I have him under my wing.'

'Then I suppose I'll take the other one,' she sighed and leant into the detective, allowing him to take the weight off his bad leg. Sibanda slowed his progress, leant into Berry, soaked up her touch. He wrapped his arm around her shoulder and hung on more tightly than needed, moving his hand against the bare flesh of her upper arm, a fleeting moment of intimacy that left him weaker at the knees than was advisable. He had to get back to full strength and back to work.

There was considerable protest at the reception desk, the old nurse spluttered and threatened dire consequences, but as Ncube predicted, she caved in when Sibanda's charm got to work and he fixed her with his hypnotic gaze.

'I will sign you out as long as you promise to see Sister Angel Better at the Gubu clinic daily to dress the wound, and keep taking these pills.' She gave him antibiotics, and as he hobbled off between his two human crutches, wondered why she had agreed to the discharge. She had never released a patient early before. The detective was a very persuasive man.

Berry chatted all the way to the car park, mostly about the diary. 'Taking into account that Tiffany Price was American, some of these references are quite obvious, I mean *Jefferson* brings to mind *Airplane* from the sixties group. Do you have a pilot as a suspect?'

'No, no one with a licence that we know of,' Sibanda said.

'What about a drug user or dealer or someone who smokes marijuana?'

'What's the link?'

'Well, the name Jefferson Airplane is American slang for a match used to hold the nub end of a reefer so you can smoke it right to the end.' Berry caught Sibanda's glance. 'It's okay, Jabu, I don't smoke the stuff. I just follow sixties folk rock.'

'Ncube tells me there's not much pot around in the village at the moment so it's not relevant.' Sibanda winced as his leg took the weight.

'Then there's the American president, Thomas Jefferson, do you have a Thomas on your list?' Sibanda and Ncube looked across to one another. 'I take it you do,' she noticed the glance. 'The other easy reference is Fe fi fo fum; maybe you have an English-eating giant among the suspects?'

'Thomas is something of a racist, I suspect he'd like to chomp on a few colonials but he's no giant.'

'An *isiqhwaka*?' Ncube chipped in, 'not an *isiqhwaka*, or maybe *izimu*, an ogre ... ayi. Did Tiffany Price see an ogre?

'Enough, Ncube, Fe fi fo fum is just a quote from a fairy story. There are no giants or ogres on this case.'

'Maybe someone who plays for the Mandebele Giants?' Berry suggested. 'How exciting they have made the final.'

Ncube held his breath expecting the detective to explode at the mention of the local football team and their success, but all he said was,

'Unlikely, although I know who Fe fi fo fum might be.'

They reached the vehicles in the car park. Since it was getting late and the light was fading, it was decided that Ncube would drive Sibanda back to Gubu in Miss Daisy and that Berry would return to Kestrel Vale. School had started. History lessons couldn't wait.

The sergeant moved away to start Miss Daisy, understanding that these two people might want a moment together. So this was the missing friend the detective was so concerned about. Sergeant Ncube understood the attraction. The young woman was lovely in any colour, a little skinny for his tastes perhaps, but there was a warm inner beauty that surpassed the physical, although it was hard to go beyond the ash-white hair and the eyes of … what was that colour? Ah yes, Mediterranean sapphire – the perfect description, such a pity that he would always associate the colour with a brutal murder. He looked back at the couple; they were standing close and chatting. There was familiarity and attraction, but if it was some kind of a relationship, it was doomed. This thing they called multiculturalism was a total failure. There was a reason tribes had traditionally stuck together and not intermarried, it was taboo. But then this didn't include tribal raids and the capture of women who were carted home as slaves and wives. Maybe new blood was needed. The whole topic was too confusing. He would discuss it with his wives.

'Berry, I'm truly grateful for your help and for rescuing me, but I have work to do. I promise I'll phone you …'

'… Like last time?' She tilted held her head in a way that sent a thousand butterflies brushing and hovering around Sibanda's heart like a rabble of dancing dotted borders, a corps de ballet at an elephant puddle.

'No, I will phone, just let me get this case sorted.'

'If I can help with some more of the clues …' she stared at him, her eyes flickering disappointment. Sibanda dragged his gaze away, wondering what he could read into her insistence, and hobbled towards Ncube and the Land Rover. With the sight of Miss Daisy, her paint-battered body, bullet-holed door and lopsided springs, his butterflies along with his anxiety settled like a lily floating on a waterhole and he refocused on the task at hand. Now he knew Berry was safe it was one less distraction. He turned at the Land Rover door and shouted back to her, 'You were in the Matobo Hills weren't you?'

She nodded her head and smiled.

'I knew it,' he smiled back and waved. Ncube, who witnessed the rare show of happiness on his boss's face, was struck by the beauty of the man. It was true, he had the face and body of a Matabele hero, a legend from the past when tribal kings ruled the land, when *indunas* lead their battle-hardened men across the country, running for days without rest to reach the enemy and confuse them with their speed and endurance. That was the age of supreme warriors, of toned athletes who would leave today's marathon runners in the dust, a proud nation, a united people. Ncube patted his stomach rolls, pondered his nation's decline into subjugation and acceptance, and sighed.

'No python aboard, I hope, Ncube,' Sibanda quipped as he swung his bad leg into the cab.

'You were right, sir, it made off as dusk came and the engine cooled down.' The girl had put the detective in a good mood. This might be a pleasant journey for once.

'And no damage I see,' Miss Daisy was ticking over with as much regularity as she was ever likely to achieve.

'Er … no, sir.' Ncube lied. Initially, he had been amazed that the great crushing serpent had left most of Miss Daisy without a scratch, but the assessment had been too good to be true and Miss Daisy was soon up to her old tricks, boiling and steaming like an old battered kettle on a roaring fire. There was damage to the new radiator cap. The python had squashed and mangled it beyond repair. Ncube hadn't been surprised. It was true what everyone said, stolen goods never fulfilled their promise. Once Miss Barton had sped off with the detective, he had followed with Miss Daisy, calling in at home to retrieve the old cap and a pile of old inner tube rekin to cut and replace the gasket when needed.

'I have tried to have this conversation before, Ncube, but where did this upholstery come from?' He pointed to Miss Daisy's delicate, pastel-striped interior. 'I don't believe the CMED came up with this.'

Ncube's heart sank; maybe this journey would be less than comfortable after all. Why was the detective pestering him about this, making him eat wild herbs from a stick? Somehow Miss Daisy's seat covers had become involved in murder and he was worried for his friend Phiri. 'I can't remember exactly, my memory isn't like your elephants.'

'Either you remember right now or I'll arrest you for collusion in these murders.' Sibanda's tone was serious, hissed and deadly. Ncube could not mistake the intent.

'Ayi, ayi, how can you believe I am part of this,' Sibanda's words had wounded before but this accusation was like a jealous lover's boiling oil on a sleeping face. It shocked, pained terribly and would scar him for life.

'What else am I supposed to believe, Sergeant? You didn't want to leave the roadblock to assist in this investigation; you have been dragging your heels whenever we visited any suspects and now you don't want to tell me about these seats.'

'And you kept Tiffany Price's diary from me,' Ncube accused, 'perhaps you are the one with something to hide.' The sergeant immediately regretted the words. He had never been so bold before, but he had to use his mouth as a tail to drive away these flies of accusation. Now, he would end up in handcuffs, he would be consigned to the cells and starved on a diet of dry, hard mealie meal and water. His wives would be widowed, his children orphaned. It didn't bear thinking about.

'Okay, Ncube, maybe there's been a breakdown of trust between us but just tell me where the fabric came from,' Sibanda's tone was intentionally mild. Peace-making might work better than his temper, which was hanging by the thinnest thread.

Sergeant Ncube reassessed his future. The detective's words were no longer poking him in the eye so he would not plan his funeral yet, but he was still wary. 'Can I ask why you want to know, sir, this is important.'

'Mkandhla, our illegal alcohol producer, was killed by a low velocity weapon, probably a muzzle loader. These old weapons tend to be around, hung onto, unlicensed and mostly rusting relics. Even my family had an old WWI Martini-Henry. We used it to chase elephants from the lands. I've no idea where it is now. Thrown into a dam when owning a weapon became a dangerous declaration of independence, I expect. Anyway, when I found Mkandhla's body there was a fragment of cloth in his brain. The lead shot used in muzzle loaders, as I learned from Gaj Patel, is wrapped in fabric patches, something to do with making the ball pass more easily and swiftly down the barrel. The scrap I found in Mkandhla's skull matches this rattletrap's upholstery, so where did it come from? If we can track that down we'll find our murderer.'

'You kept the discovery of that evidence from me too?' Ncube felt like the provider of a feast to which no one came, shunned and distrusted.

'You were the one who had access to the fabric on these seats, Ncube, no one else at the station knows anything about the upholstery. It puts you right in the frame along with the diary references.'

The sergeant recognised the facts and the path along which they might lead a dogged stone-turner like the detective. He turned to Sibanda and looked him in the eyes, willing his innocence to be transmitted, iris to iris. 'I've got nothing to do with poaching and murder, sir, but I know where I got Miss Daisy's canvas and I know someone in the village with a large plaster on his face. It pains me to say this but there is a connection between the two.'

CHAPTER 19

The detective, the sergeant and the Land Rover were heading for Gubu township, night was falling fast and Ncube was hoping it would slow down a bit. The moon was well over its early rising effort and Miss Daisy's headlights were feeble. Illumination was one of her many weaknesses. The atmosphere between the two men had calmed, each accepting the misunderstanding. There was no need for apologies, they returned without further fuss to their normal working relationship and began to discuss the investigation.

'So it was tailor Phiri who re-covered the seats and used his material.'

'Yes, sir, you may remember Chief Inspector Mfumu had threatened me with all manner of evil if I didn't get some sort of a working vehicle from CMED. I found Miss Daisy abandoned in a corner under a heap of discarded exhaust pipes, but she had no seats. Phiri helped me out.'

'And you say his nephew had damage to his cheek?'

'Yes, a bad one. When he arrived at the roadblock in his mini bus, I thought he had been in a fight. You know what young men are like, a bit sheepish and embarrassed. He'd been drinking. Phiri is a good Muslim, he would have been shocked by his nephew's behaviour. Children are supposed to resemble their relatives as pumpkin juice comes out of a pumpkin, but in this case perhaps the nephew, Banda Phiri, is less juice and more like the grass seed that pricks before it has ripened. Sometimes children are not what you expect.'

'There's another connection too, Ncube.'

'What?'

'Phiri is a Malawian name, isn't it? The family must have moved to Zimbabwe.'

'Yes, Phiri told me the story of his father who in the 1930s walked from Blantyre all the way to Johannesburg to work on the gold mines. That's about 1 500 kilometres. It took him five months to get there.'

'How did he land up in Gubu?'

'After a couple of years working underground, he was walking home. He got as far as Gubu and met his wife. He ended up settling here, buying a sewing machine with his earnings and setting up a business. Why is being Malawian important?'

'It's just a hunch but Malawians, particularly those from the south, were known for brewing *ithothotho* or *kachasu* as they call it. They used fermented berries; picked them ripe once they had fallen and boiled them up in a big pot. An old gun barrel was fixed to the pot and sealed so all the vapour steamed through the barrel. That was cooled off with water so the vapour condensed and dripped as *kachasu* into containers. It could blow your brains out at 70% proof.'

'That doesn't sound healthy, sir.'

'It isn't, but surprisingly few people die from drinking it unless the brew is cut with battery acid or fertiliser.'

'Ugh, why would they add that?'

'To add punch, it's the modern equivalent of *umligasgoni*. There's even talk of antiretrovirals being added as a catalyst to speed up the process.'

'Those drugs are a lifeline for many HIV-positive unfortunates. There aren't enough to go around as it is. Who would steal from the dying?'

Sibanda didn't reply, theft was always ugly, Robin Hood was a myth, philanthropic crime didn't exist, his sergeant was naïve. 'All this modernisation of the process makes me wonder if the stolen fans from Barghees aren't being used to further speed up the distillation process and cool off the potent vapour.'

'If Banda Phiri with the cut on his face was the one who sold the stolen fan to Lazarus Maphosa then he might be the one brewing *ithothotho, kachasu*?'

'Yes, and if his uncle supplied the striped fabric for the muzzle loader, then maybe together they murdered David Mkandhla to get rid of the opposition whose raw alcohol was undermining their local distillery.

The Phiris have probably been running the traditional business for years.'

'No, not Phiri, he is a good man.'

'Africa is littered with men who say they want to help people, uplift the poor, bring us democracy ...'

'... What are you saying, sir?'

'People can disguise themselves as pillars of society, fool us all, like a hyena in a kraal, hiding in a goat's skin and creeping up on the tasty young kids, or like the death's head moth you've been worried about. With its yellow markings, it looks like a bee so it can enter a hive unnoticed and steal the honey, the heard-earned wealth of the colony. The harder the bees toil, the more for the parasites.'

Ncube didn't like this talk one bit. How could the detective compare a moth, with a dead man's bones painted on its back, to his friend Phiri? 'We are nearly here, sir, Phiri's house is on the next corner. How are we going to handle this, sir?'

'Don't alarm him. Let him think we need a bit more of that canvas for Miss Daisy until we know what we are dealing with.'

'What? What fabric?' The old tailor pushed back his embroidered Muslim kufi, an intricate and skilled testament to his beliefs, and scratched his head.

'Don't you remember, Phiri, you re-upholstered Miss Daisy in the striped canvas? We talked about it on our fishing trip.'

'Did we? I can only remember that I beat you and caught more fish. I won't forget that in a hurry.'

Ncube swallowed his response about cheating with rib bones and stuck to the matter in hand. 'You saved my hide by re-covering Miss Daisy's seats over a weekend when she was naked and exposed. You must remember.'

'Ah, yes, the pastel-striped deckchair canvas, I have some of it here somewhere. Left over from a job I did for the nuns. I always thought it wasn't a very sober fabric for such quiet and religious ladies.'

'From the nuns?' Sibanda was feeling woozy and less than steady on his feet, but his brain was working as well as ever and he knew he could tick off the inhabitants of the convent of St Monica as innocent. They were selfless workers in the Gubu community. One less category of suspects for his list.

'Yes, they wanted to brighten up the sitting room at the old-age home. Not a practical choice, maybe they got the fabric cheap.' Phiri had been rummaging among a pile of off-cuts stacked in a corner, 'I'm sure I had a bit of it left. Do you need it to patch the seats?'

'Does anyone but you have access to this fabric, Phiri?' Sibanda asked.

Phiri shook his head and scratched it again, looking across to his machine for answers. 'Many people, I am a busy man. There are always customers in and out wanting repairs or new uniforms and I have a very healthy clientele for African attire.' He fingered a piece of busily patterned navy and ochre Java print that he'd fashioned into a stylish outfit with a matching and toweringly flamboyant Nigerian turban for Betty Gwabi, the lady who sat in the dust on the corner of the road in all weathers. She had an upturned crate as a counter for selling tomatoes, sweets, loose biscuits and airtime for cellphones. She had not haggled over payment; trade was good, everyone needed to speak these days.

'Like who?' Sibanda asked.

'Several ladies are regular customers, and Thunduluka Lodge, they sent someone in yesterday with all these fly sheets for repair.' He pointed to a heap of green canvas. 'I love the wind. It keeps me in business.'

'I saw your nephew Banda at the roadblock the other day, Phiri.'

'Banda? I haven't seen him for a while. He visits, but he knows I don't approve of his lifestyle.'

'He's just a youngster, maybe a bit hot headed?' Ncube said.

'Old enough to have made a young woman pregnant and he drinks too much.'

'He has an injury on his cheek, I noticed.'

'Yes, silly boy, his mother told me that the axe head flew off when he was chopping, and struck him. He's lucky to have his eye. He'll have a bad scar.'

'How is his taxi business going? Doing well?' Sibanda asked.

'Very well, he has a new licence which allows him to carry goods and passengers all the way from Victoria Falls. He does the run at least once a week. His mother tells me he is saving to buy another kombi, business is so good.'

Sibanda and Ncube glanced at each other. They knew, as did everyone, that the taxi business was a cut-throat affair, particularly in a small village like Gubu. The pickings were lean, fuel costs high, licence fees exorbitant and the fines, both legal and illegal, extracted from roadblocks and toll booths were inventive, endless and crippling, highway robbery under any guise. Taxi driving was a hand-to-mouth occupation. If Banda Phiri was making significant money it was coming from other means. The Vic Falls run rang alarm bells.

'So, do you need me to patch the Land Rover seats with some other fabric?' the tailor asked.

'Er, no thanks, Phiri, we just needed the striped canvas to … er …' Sergeant Ncube stumbled.

'… to make a matching steering wheel cover,' Sibanda came to the rescue.

It satisfied the old tailor, who received similarly odd requests. The police, he gathered, were not immune to eccentricity with their decor.

'What a kind thought, sir, a matching steering wheel cover for Miss Daisy would be excellent,' Ncube commented as they drove away from the tailor's house.

Sibanda merely scowled, he hadn't patience for the sergeant and his infatuation. 'It's obvious that old man Phiri is not involved in this, Ncube, but the remnants of striped fabric are missing and whoever took them pulled the trigger on Mkandhla.'

'Banda lied to me at the roadblock. He said his facial injury had come from a fight. Why lie if the injury was from an axe?'

'And he's come into money from where?'

'Banda Phiri is our next call Ncube, but not tonight. He'll keep. Let's raid his house tomorrow. First though, I want to go through Tiffany Price's diary, see if I can find the links to the ivory ring. Banda Phiri is somehow up to his eyes in this.'

Sibanda was propped up in his bed, which unusually welcoming. An irritating dip and wave in the mattress now provided the perfect support for his injured thigh. He was surrounded by plastic containers of freshly prepared food from Ncube's wives, and Blessing's pharmacopoeia was near at hand. Tiffany Price's diary lay open on his lap. Thanks to Berry he had Thomas Siziba's code name, Jefferson. The diary linked him to File and Ncube's fishing spot, the Styx river crossing. He knew from Siziba's cellphone selfie that he had been up on the Zambezi, but who was File? He went through all the file meanings he could think of – nail file? Could that be a woman with long, cared-for nails, Li Dube had a set of remarkable claws, or something to do with carpentry? Or maybe a different file altogether, the sort found in offices. The only filephile, (was that a word?) he could think of was Cold War and he was obsessed with them, but Sibanda didn't believe he was involved in ivory smuggling. The File clue was a tough one. He had already worked out the Fe fi fo fum reference, the fairytale giant had to be Bigboy Dube. CJ was the most used code in the diary and those initials were familiar, but the harder he concentrated on the monogram, the further away the reference slipped. The codes were proving more difficult than he thought. He needed to get into the mind of the young American woman if he was to have any chance of cracking the secret language.

He lay back against a lumpy pillow, eased his leg and ate some of the Ncube clan offerings followed by antibiotics and Blessing's drops and green sludge. Sounds of Gubu village settling down for the night were comforting. It was an atonal lullaby he had become used to: a gathering of men over the road muttering and grumbling over a shared *skhubu* of African beer, passing the plastic container from mouth to mouth, the drinker silent for a few sips and then passing on the African quaich and re-joining the grousing chorus; Masithole's cooking pots next door clattering in competition with her neighbour's babies screaming for a clean nappy or a change of breast; old man Ndlovu's donkey bells tinkling on the common as the hardworking beasts dipped their heads to the grass, free at last from the harness; a squealing of young children racing home after a last minute errand run to Barghees for a loaf of bread; a territorial spattering of cockerels from each compass point crowing a final *kukurikooo* for the day before roosting on roofs and fences, outhouses and rusting car bodies, milk hedges and rubbish heaps; and in the distance the ubiquitous thud of an axe as a wood poacher stole life from a barely teenage tree to find fuel for the family meal and a companionable fire to sit around.

During the evening serenade Sibanda fell into an easy sleep, the pink diary resting on his chest. He slept for some hours while the medicines, both modern and traditional, worked their magic and the diary's words penetrated his psyche.

He woke with a start and a blinding wave of clarity at 4:30am. 'Work backwards,' he chided himself. Why hadn't he thought of that before? He looked at the list of suspects and tried to match them to the coded names rather than working from no reference at all. By 5:00am he had it cracked, names, dates and locations, except for File, which didn't match anyone. The Cat and Snail Spunk were a mystery too; neither related to Banda Phiri which was a worrying anomaly.

Sibanda edged out of bed and limped to the shower. It had attitude as usual, trickled derisorily on his head and spat with venom in every direction but down. It was difficult to keep the wound-covering dry. He dressed, found some coffee and swallowed his regimen of pills and potions along with the remains of the Ncube clan offerings. By 7:00am he was first in line at Gubu clinic.

'It's healing nicely, but you should try to keep the bandages dry.' Sister Angel Better had cut away the hospital dressing and was carefully reapplying a clean one. She wasn't rushing the job. It wasn't every day she treated a specimen like Sibanda. His damaged thigh muscle was hard and defined. She was fairly sure she could detect similar definition in the stomach muscles beneath his shirt. She glanced up at the smooth-skinned face and brooding eyes. Such perfection was a bonus in the Gubu clinic where a stream of snotty noses, hollow rattling chests, pot-bellied malnutrition and haemorrhoids were the daily fare.

Sibanda, unaware of the effect he was having on the clinic sister, was not averse to the attention he was receiving. Angel Better was tall with model proportions and eyelashes that swept the high bones of her cheeks. There was a kindness in her eyes and a gentle healing touch in her hands. He could understand her popularity as the village medical carer. He would not be averse to reporting daily for his dressing.

'Is there any chance of borrowing a crutch?' he asked when the last of the sticking plaster was firmly in place and his trousers were back around his waist.

'Of course, you must be in a lot of pain.'

'Not really,' he said, and inwardly thanked Blessing once again for her drops, 'but, I can't put too much weight on the leg at the moment.'

'Sorry, we only have one available,' she passed him the support and he stood with her help which lingered just a fraction of a second too long to be strictly medical. 'Here, take my phone number, you can contact me after hours if you have a problem.'

'Thanks,' he grabbed the piece of paper and hobbled out of the clinic and past the growing line of the sickly, the rurally downtrodden and the undernourished.

Sister Angel Better watched him leave. The flush that had risen in her cheeks subsided reluctantly, and with a sigh she turned away and called in Loneliness Dhlamini and her fluctuating blood pressure.

Sibanda soon mastered a speedy one-legged gait and was at Gubu Station in under five minutes.

'Sir, aren't you supposed to be resting?' PC Khumalo was a picture of concern.

'I'm fine, Zee, where's Ncube.'

'Here, sir,' the sergeant appeared from down the corridor, 'but why have you come in? You are sick, you cannot heal walking around like this, even your foot can stumble.'

'It certainly would without this crutch, Ncube,' he said, deliberately twisting the Ndebele proverb of infallibility, 'and right now we need to get onto the trail of Banda Phiri. I take it Miss Daisy is fuelled up and ready to go and you know Banda Phiri's house?' The detective turned and hopped towards the station car park. Sergeant Ncube gave PC Khumalo a knowing look.

'Can you keep Cold War happy for a little while? He'll be as rabid as a foaming jackal when he knows the detective is here and hasn't checked in with him.'

'I'll try,' she said, as she picked up the station Bible. The constable flicked through, looking for a dense, inexplicable text and stabbed her serendipitous pencil into a likely verse. She hoped the detective appreciated the time she would waste having the Book of Job Chapter 25, Verse 6 explained to her: *Man is a worm.* Actually, she thought she might quite enjoy this lecture.

In Miss Daisy's cab, Sibanda began to pick apart the case. The sergeant was a good sounding board. 'So, Ncube, we still have several suspects in the mix. Tiffany Price had her eyes on several people she thought might be involved in an ivory-smuggling ring. I've worked out some of her codes. Thanks to Miss Barton we have Thomas Siziba as Jefferson, and CJ, who was the most mentioned in her diary, is obviously Mark Rhodes, CJ standing for Cecil John, king of the colonial invasion. Probably most of the CJ references refer to his nightly visits to her. The initials are often coupled with Pit Bull ...'

'... Amanda Carlisle? It suits her.'

'Yes, it does and Mark Rhodes covered his illicit trysts with nightly tracking of his collared leopards.'

'Could he not be The Cat, sir, what with the leopard connection?'

'I don't think so, Ncube, but I haven't worked that one out. I'm also stuck on File and Snail Spunk, Could either of those be Banda Phiri or the possible poacher Andries Nyathi?'

'What about Fe fi fo fum, the er ... giant?' Ncube swallowed, not wanting to hear what Tiffany Price had unearthed in the way of monsters or to discuss Andries Nyathi. Everyone he had been in touch with recently was a murder suspect.

'That's Bigboy Dube, the simplest code of the lot and his wife, Li, is Burn.'

'Burn?'

'I puzzled over that. I knew Burn had to be Li Dube because of the connection to Bigboy and then I remembered a young police officer in England twisting the skin on my wrist until it burned like fire, an initiation of sorts. "Enjoy the Chinese Burn," he said, "pass it on to the next new recruit." I'm assuming Tiffany Price was familiar with the childish torture.'

Ncube thought that foreign cultures did have something to offer. Twisting skin to make it burn sounded better than twisting ear lobes, which he had done as a child to his pesky little sisters. 'At least we know that Ms Price suspected the same people of ivory smuggling as we suspect of murdering her, but was she murdered? If Forensics could discover nothing, then maybe she did die of crocodile bites or just plain fright,' or, an *umgobo* that had squeezed the life out of her and been disturbed by the crocodile before it could swallow her whole, he wanted to add, but he kept that last thought to himself.

'She was murdered, Ncube, but by a drug I'm not familiar with. She was paralysed when the croc was dragging her, alive and most likely still conscious. If Forensics can find no trace of Etorphine, M99, then there has to be something they're missing. I can't phone any of the local experts because they are all suspects, but there may be someone who can help ...' Sibanda grabbed his phone and began to dial.

'You're going to have to convince the chief inspector, sir, he believes she was killed by a crocodile, in fact, he's closed the docket. He thinks we're investigating Mkandhla's death.'

The detective barely responded, just a raised eyebrow. He was already deep in conversation with Buff Barton, who was enquiring about his health, chatting about Berry's return, and taking questions on darting drugs.

'I'm not sure, I'm no expert, Jabu, but I've heard of something out there that replicates a chemical naturally in the body, something to do with the nervous system and the synapses. Mammalian systems break this substance down spontaneously, leaving no trace. It's completely metabolised by the body's processes so no residue would be detected in a corpse. In fact, it's the drug of choice for euthanising large wild animals like elephants that will later be consumed, because no trace of the drug remains in the meat of the dead animal.

'I don't like the use of it myself; you can't imagine a worse death than collapsing, being totally unable to use any of your muscles, slowly dying of asphyxiation and yet fully awake and in control of all your senses, able to hear everything going on around you, still able to feel pain and yet unable to do anything about it ... wish I could remember the name – Scoline? Choline? Something like that. Glad to hear you're up and about, by the way, Berry was very worried.'

'It's thanks to her I was even found.'

'She can be a bloodhound when she gets onto tracks, Jabu, doesn't give up easily. Sorry I can't be more help with the dart drug.'

'Thanks, Buff, you've helped a lot.' Sibanda closed his phone and turned to his sergeant, 'sometimes a negative can be a positive, Ncube.'

Ncube didn't reply, once again the detective was not straightforward; he was like a goat rubbing on an outside fence, sniffing around, looking for a gap to get into the kraal to eat the rape. The detective had found the opening and was already munching away on the leafy green vegetable by the look on his face.

'If it wasn't M99 that killed Tiffany Price then it was a drug that leaves no trace. All we have to do now, Ncube, is get hold of everyone's darting logs and check who is familiar with the stuff and who had access to it.'

'I thought all drugs could be found in the body after death. You already have Mark Rhodes's book, sir.'

'Yes, but I wasn't checking for drug types, Ncube. I was convinced it was death from the drug M99.'

'Should we go back to the station and check the log now?'

'No, we have time on our side; whoever killed Tiffany Price believes we will never link her death to a dart drug because this one is natural and all traces of it disappear.'

'It can't have been Banda Phiri, sir, because he is stupid. He wouldn't have that information.'

'No, but he had access to the striped fabric found in Mkandhla's skull. He has a smashed cheek and has been selling stolen fans from Barghees and whoever robbed Barghees stole the muzzle loader. We have a death probably from a different muzzle loader and the victim was in possession of a tusk. Too many coincidences, Ncube.'

'Right, sir then we had better detain him and find out what he's been up to.' Slowly and with great reverence, Ncube depressed Miss Daisy's accelerator and encouraged a modicum of speed from the old duck. Later, she might need all the velocity at her disposal to catch up with a hot-headed taxi driver, in a kombi, used to the hair-raising antics of a youthful foot.

CHAPTER 20

Sibanda, Ncube and Miss Daisy negotiated the winding tracks that lead from Soweto across a patchwork of cultivated fields and into distant shrubland. Here and there a few women were at work hoeing the weeds that grew with more vigour than the mealie crops they competed with. Mothers, with babies slung on their backs and toddlers at their feet, bobbed up and down in deferential worship to the earth and her produce, each stab of the hoe a victory over want, a promise of full bellies for their children and a dream of plenty. In reality, it was all a delusion of hope over patriarchal indolence, inadequate inputs and marginal meteorology, but at least there was hope of sorts.

The sun was already high, the dew on the plants had evaporated, the dew on the brows and in the armpits of the struggling women had proliferated. Glistering skin, the occasional stretched and arched back, the swig from a much-used and scarified plastic bottle were all testament to the hard work of a full-day's labouring compressed into the cooler dawn hours.

'Are you sure Banda Phiri is staying here?' Sibanda asked, surveying a collection of dilapidated mud huts some way east of the village, beyond the fields.

'Yes, Suko was telling me last night that his mother has kicked him out of the family home. This is an abandoned kraal; no one comes near it since the baboon incident. He must be desperate to live here. The place is damned by the *nyanga* and haunted by spirits. I'd rather not go any further, sir, can't we just call him?'

'Drive closer, Ncube, and stop blathering. I can't negotiate these abandoned furrows with a crutch,' he said, surveying the crumbling uneven dirt in front of the kraal, 'and a heap of compacted mud isn't going to bewitch you.' Sibanda could feel his irritation rising. He knew that Ncube's traditional fears would bring on his 'digestive issues' and that any further travel with him would be intolerable.

Once closer, they viewed the collection of huts cautiously. 'Remember the man is armed and possibly dangerous, Ncube.'

'And there could be a mad baboon, a witch's familiar in the cupboard,' the fear in Ncube's voice was palpable.

'What?'

'Don't you know the story, sir? It is famous and terrifying,' his voice wobbled.

'No, and I don't want to hear it.'

'But you must, sir, it is true, many witnessed it. Some years ago, the people living in this kraal and others close by were blighted with poor crops, infertile cattle and the loss of many children before birth. They called in a *nyanga* fearing they had been *loyaed* by an *umthakathi* ...'

'Ncube, I don't want to hear about witches and spells, this is the 21st century.'

'Wait, sir, this is really, really true, not a myth, ask old Manyathi, she saw it herself,' Ncube was not to be deterred; 'the *nyanga* called a meeting of all the inhabitants, then pointed his stick at an old man in the kraal, blaming him for the village woes. The man lived in a hut a little apart – where the rubble is over there. The hut was completely destroyed after the cleansing ceremony and he was chased from the kraal forever.'

'Ncube, enough!' Sibanda's blood was beginning to boil.

'Anyway,' the sergeant continued, oblivious to Sibanda's growing anger, so immersed was he in the telling of his tale, 'when the villagers entered the hut and opened a cupboard door, as instructed by the *nyanga*, a baboon burst out, fangs blazing and running like a demon on fire ...'

Ncube never finished his colourful account, Sibanda used his crutch to poke the sergeant in the back of the knees, causing him to collapse and plant his face in the chunky, abandoned sods.

'It's all trickery, and sleight of hand for which the *nyanga* will have charged a small fortune. He was a con artist preying on superstition and ignorance, and what about the poor baboon? It was lured by a banana into a cage and then stuffed into the cupboard by accomplices when the *nyanga* called his meeting. It must have nearly died of fright. Lesson number one, Ncube, never leave your dwelling unattended during a witch hunt.'

Ncube spluttered to his knees. 'Sir, that was not kind,' he muttered, as he brushed the clinging dirt particles from his face.

'It was the only way to shut you up, now let's concentrate on Banda Phiri. From what I've observed during your diatribe, there's no one home. Let's go and take a look.'

Ncube rocked himself back to upright dignity and wondered how the detective had managed to put tribal doings in the mix. He had never heard of the Dias or their tribe. The man was confused, and as crabby as a cow with a dead calf and a full udder. He had thought the brush with death and hospitals had made the detective more vulnerable, but he was back to his old ways. The sergeant sighed with resignation, knowing all pools of water, however sweet, eventually dry up.

The largest of the huts was the most liveable. The rotting thatched roof had been patched with bits of rusting tin and tattered plastic sheeting. The windows were blocked with cardboard boxes tacked on from the inside. The door was locked with a new Barghees lock.

'Your keys, Ncube, although I doubt we'll be lucky twice.'

They weren't, to Ncube's relief. Sibanda hopped around the perimeter of the house and knocked in a cardboard window by hammering it with the crutch. The interior was dark and gloomy but he saw enough in the room to order Ncube to break the lock.

'A warrant, sir ...?'

'Just smash the lock, Ncube, there's an entire brewery in there.'

It took seconds for the soft Chinese metal of the lock to bend under the lever of a rusted fencing standard. Inside, with the light flooding through the door, they could make out the stolen fans carelessly discarded, plastic tubing and enamel pots, a sackful of fermenting maize starting to shoot and the dismantled parts of Gaj Barghee's muzzle loader, the scrolled silver chasing shining in the gloom like an exotic temple chalice. There was no furniture in the room; a mattress on the floor was the only indication that the hut was occupied. Further rummaging among rumpled bedding and a filthy cardboard box advertising, with not a trace of irony, the fresh, sunshine-dispensing properties of green laundry soap, produced nothing of interest. With his crutch, Sibanda flipped up the yellowing, foam mattress, chunks nibbled from the edges like mouldy cheese in a rat trap. Underneath lay scraps of Miss Daisy's pastel striped upholstery.

'We've got him, Ncube.'

There was no reply from the sergeant, he was lost in the horror of the discovery of Miss Daisy's raiment hidden under the bed of a murderer.

'This weapon hasn't been used, no sign of powder or shot through this barrel in a hundred years.' Sibanda was peering down the muzzle loader.

'So where is the weapon that killed Mkandhla? I don't understand.'

'I was confused too when Barghee's weapon was stolen after the murder, but I've got an idea. No time for explanation, let's get on the road and after Banda Phiri.

Miss Daisy didn't like having the old radiator cap back. She wanted the new one. Every girl enjoys a new bonnet and she wasn't thinking about the hinged metal cover that clothed her engine. She had been proud of her new hat. It fitted snugly and while hardly a jaunty little number, with barely a whisper of difference from the previous incumbent, it was, when all was said and done, new. She was quick to show her displeasure at Ncube's unusual burst of speed. She began to cough and splutter. Steam issuing from her radiator rivalled the steam coming out of Sibanda's ears.

'I thought you had fixed this problem, Ncube.'

'Don't worry, sir, there is nothing so bent it can't be straightened, I will have her sorted in a minute.' Ncube grabbed a freshly cut piece of rekin from under the seat and re-lined the radiator cap, all the while cajoling, 'guga mzimba, kusale inhliziyo, your body may be old, but your heart still beats, so settle down, Miss Daisy, this is an important mission and that man has no patience.'

'Radio the station, tell them to contact the roadblock and detain Banda Phiri and his taxi,' Sibanda barked from the passenger seat, 'we'll never catch up with him at this rate.'

The old girl did her best – cooled down slowly and took a swig from the skhubu while the radiator ticked off the wasted seconds. She started up again on first asking, but it wasn't enough to catch up with Banda

Phiri. He had already cleared the roadblock and was heading north.

'What now, sir?'

'After him, Ncube, he hasn't been gone long.' The rest of Sibanda's speech was a rude tirade against Miss Daisy and her temperamental disposition. Ncube ignored the detective's frustration that ran around like a headless chicken in a mealie patch and whispered encouragement under his breath, '*zidele amathambo*, go for it, Miss Daisy, bones and all!'

Miss Daisy steamed down the road in pursuit of Allah is Great, concentrating fiercely on her task. Sibanda and Ncube both leant forward as if to urge her on.

'What is your theory with the muzzle loaders, sir?'

'We know Banda Phiri stole Gaj Barghee's muzzle loader *after* the murder of Mkandhla, why?' The sergeant hadn't a clue why so he kept quiet, 'because he needed a new barrel to continue with his distillation of *ithothotho*. The old one he was using had probably blown up in his face when he reassembled the weapon to kill Mkandhla, that's how he got the face wound. The fans came in handy as well to cool off the barrel and condense the liquid. Phiri's a Malawian by descent, Ncube, and they have always used old gun barrels to make their moonshine. It's a tradition, along with the use of the fruits of *Ziziphus mucronata* or *umphafa* as you know it. Blessing will know of the buffalo-thorn's properties. Among other remedies, the chewed leaves are an aphrodisiac ...'

'... I know nothing of that, sir.' Ncube's spluttered denial suggested otherwise.

'There are a couple of possible motives – competition for one. Mkandhla moved in on Phiri's turf. He had probably been producing stuff for the shebeens. Mkandhla arrived in the village with his ready-made hooch and took over the trade.'

'What about the ivory?'

'Here's my second theory: Banda is somehow caught up in this ivory gang, maybe he's the transport link, moving the ivory from the river or the border. Somehow Mkandhla found out his rival was involved – remember there was a tusk in his room, so he knew something was going on. He blackmailed Banda, hoping to shut down his still. Banda had to get rid of Mkandhla. The gang couldn't afford anyone knowing about the trade in tusks.'

'Did he get rid of Tiffany Price as well? She was obviously onto the gang.'

'No, she didn't know about his link to the ivory. He doesn't appear in her diary. I've combed through those codes. None appears to refer to him.'

'So who killed Tiffany Price?'

'That's what we're about to find out. Pull over, Ncube; look, there, through the trees. It's a kombi.'

'Right by the turn off to the valley, and my fishing spot, sir.'

'Why would Banda Phiri be hanging about here? This is State land. No settlements, no people. He can't be looking for customers. Let's check it out.'

The vehicle was abandoned, but still warm. Banda hadn't been gone long.

'We'll wait here, Ncube. He'll be back soon. Hide Miss Daisy. We'll ambush him.'

The sergeant inched the old vehicle through the thick bush wary of unseen holes and fallen logs, bridging shrubs and clambering over anthills as delicately as a midwife delivering a first baby. He made the return journey on foot with less concern for himself or the noise of snapping branches, shuffling leaves and snagging thorns. He planted his deceptively small feet as heavily as possible, hoping to chase away any lurking reptiles or other bitey creatures that scuttled and foraged in the rich mulch of the forest floor.

'For God's sake can't you make less noise, Ncube, do you want to advertise our position?' Sibanda hissed. He had hunkered down behind an ant heap housing a shrubby *mangwe* tree divided at the base, each spindly bole rising upwards in a struggling curtain. Despite its poor choice of lodging, it would survive. Foraging termites would leave it alone, the yellow, hard wood too tough for their jaws. The leaves of the *mangwe* had already turned their signature rose pink. The colourful confetti offered perfect intertwined camouflage.

'Sorry, sir,' he whispered.

'Get down, Ncube.' Sibanda lay on his stomach, his head just above the ant heap but behind the leaves. He had a perfect view of the kombi. Ncube viewed his options. They were limited. Agility was not one of his aptitudes. He struggled to his knees and rolled onto his gut. The subsequent displacement of air through the highways and byways of the sergeant's colon took some time to percolate but when it finally exited, the explosion was meteoric. At least it's downwind, he thought.

Sibanda never commented, he had heard a rustling moments before Ncube's resounding *bhuu*. He put a finger to his lips and pointed in the direction of the movement. Banda Phiri emerged from the bush and walked towards his kombi. Sibanda was upright in a flash despite his leg and had Phiri cornered against Allah is Great. Sergeant Ncube levered his bulk off the ant heap as best he could but Phiri was handcuffed before Ncube reached the kombi.

'Who are you? What do you want?'

'Police, you recognise Sergeant Ncube, I'm sure.'

'Yes, but I have all my licences. How much do you want? I've just paid one roadblock five dollars because my wastepaper bin is loose. It only wobbles a bit, I'll fix it tonight. The other lot didn't even tell me what the ten-dollar fine was for, muttered something about my licence crooked on the windscreen. Is there no end to this?'

'We aren't interested in your vehicle, Phiri. We're interested in the distillery in your house.'

'You've been to my house? Don't you need a warrant?'

'Banda,' Ncube counselled, 'you have more to worry about than warrants. It's illegal to produce unlicensed alcohol and you know it.'

'You broke into Barghees, as well, we found the fans. Let's add robbery to the mix.' Sibanda was reeling him in slowly. Once he had an admission of guilt on both crimes they could start on the riddle of the muzzle loaders and the murder.

The culprit stuttered the beginnings of an excuse and then clammed up. 'I have the right to remain silent.'

A diet of too many TV crime dramas, thought Sibanda, all of which were made in democratic Western nations. Zimbabwe didn't work like that. The detective ripped the grubby dressing off Phiri's cheek, uncovering a congealing mess underneath. Raw flesh and exposed bone revealed a devastating wound. The man would be an ugly gargoyle for the rest of his life. Phiri yelped. The injury began to bleed. Ncube winced at the sight, and weakness shot through his legs in a tickling aversion.

'Why did you do that?' Phiri gasped, hanging his head.

'I wanted to see the wound made by the axe head, or was it from a drunken fight?'

'What are you saying?'

'That you have a different story for everyone, but I know the truth Phiri. Your old muzzle loader, the one that had been in your family for years and used for distilling hot stuff through the barrel, blew up in your face.'

Phiri shook his head.

'Look, Phiri, no one knows you're here, we can't be seen from the road and just over there is a nest of carnivorous Matabele ants, piranhas of the leaf litter. I can stir them up, get them angry and then hold your cheek over the entrance. These ants have such powerful jaws, raw flesh will be a nice change from decapitating termites, and it'll be free food on their door step. Our Ndebele ancestors found this a rather effective way of gathering information, didn't they Sergeant?'

Ncube's eyes watered. He knew the large, aggressive species well. The sting brought a pain that couldn't be measured. Having an entire colony munching away at an open wound would be torture in the extreme. 'Er, um, sir,' he wanted to protest.

'And Ncube has just volunteered to sit on your head and keep your cheek firmly in place,' Sibanda added.

Phiri, the blood now streaming down his face, kept his mouth firmly shut.

'Come, Phiri, can you detect that smell of crushed cockroaches and strong tobacco? That's the acid in their stings charging up. The ants are on the move, they're hungry.' He grabbed Phiri's arm and pushed him in the direction of the mound. The taxi driver began to struggle. 'You can't do this, arrest me if you have to, but you can't feed me to ants.'

They reached the mound hole. The major workers were lining up ready for a raid on the nearby termites, the smaller, shinier, minor workers, the camp followers, at their side in a double military file. A few soldiers were scurrying along the line, finding their spot in the battalion, awaiting the command to attack.

'Perfect,' said Sibanda, 'we've saved them a march into battle.' He pushed Phiri's head down until he was on his knees. The pungent smell of the formic troops was almost unbearable.

'No, no, please don't do this, stop, I'll tell you all about my still and the robbery,' Phiri was pleading.

Sibanda released his grip, 'Tell us everything, Phiri. It had better be the truth, the ants are disappointed.'

Ncube, who had been standing back and watching in horror, now breathed more easily, 'Yes, Phiri, tell us everything. My stomach wouldn't be able to stand an ant feast.'

The driver began hesitantly, 'Okay, I … I have been distilling *ithothotho*, but just enough to keep my taxi business going, you know what it's like, the made-up fines, the tolls, the … the … bribes. It's impossible to keep a taxi and pay off a police force.'

'And the muzzle loader?' Sibanda ignored the reference to corruption. It was rampant, unstoppable and lamentable, but if he was honest, economically essential. Police with families and school fees to find could never cope with the variable pay days and slim pay packages, highway robbery was the only alternative. The police required creativity.

'I was using the barrel to produce the drink. My mother's family brought the tradition from home. My grandfather always used to brew his own.'

'But then you turned it back into a weapon, didn't you, and it blew up – your face is witness to that?'

'I put it together to hunt a few guineafowl for the pot. I must have used too much powder, the barrel burst at the end. Shrapnel flew back into my cheek,' he pointed to the deep gouge.

'That's why you broke into Barghees to replace the barrel of the muzzle loader.'

'No, that was a lucky discovery, I wanted the fans.'

'To speed up production?'

Phiri just nodded.

'How many guineafowl did you shoot?' Sibanda continued. Ncube shuffled his feet; he couldn't understand why the number of guineafowl mattered.

'… Er, a few.'

'But you didn't eat them because they would have been smashed to pulp by a ball from a muzzle loader, even if you managed to hit a small, moving target with such an old gun.'

'I don't know what you are saying.'

'That you never used the muzzle loader to shoot gamebirds. You had a bigger mark in mind.'

'I didn't shoot elephants, if that's what you mean, I just ...'

'Ah, yes, the ivory, I was coming to that. What did you *just* do?'

'I carried it. I picked the tusks up in the bush near here and delivered them.'

'Where to?'

'Thunduluka Lodge.'

'Who did you deliver them to?'

'The old cook, Shadrek Nyathi. He would walk out to the back of the lodge at night. I would slide them under the fence. He would pass me my money. That's all I know and all I'm saying.'

'And where does Mkandhla fit into all this?'

'I don't know anyone called Mkandhla,' his eyes were alive now, darting from detective to sergeant, searching their faces for clues.

'I think you do, and that colony of ants certainly thinks you do too. That's why you needed to produce more booze, because he was a rival in the business and a more reliable supplier. He was stealing your customers, wasn't he?'

Phiri looked down and shook his head. Sibanda walked over to the nest and used the end of his crutch to agitate the Matabele soldier ants. Phiri glanced across at the foraging horde swarming now like vultures on carrion and pumping themselves up for battle. He reassessed his options.

'He wasn't a rival,' he offered.

'But he was producing *ithothotho*?'

'We were doing it together. I had the Gubu market, he had the know-how. His method was easy. He just had vats of the raw stuff. He was clever, when the drunkards came back for more, staggering, slurring their speech, he sold them the watered-down version. No one ever noticed, no one ever complained. That way we stretched his supply.'

'Where is Mkandhla now?'

Phiri was quick with the reply, 'I don't know, his booze ran out, I haven't seen him for a couple of weeks, maybe he's gone to find more alcohol.'

Sibanda let silent moments ratchet up the pressure, watching the beads of sweat roll down the driver's cheeks into the wound, the stinging salt a reminder of the pain the ants' bites could inflict. He ignored the tension and listened to a bellyaching of birds tweeting a dirge of doom and destruction – a black-chested cuckoo moaned his hypochondria, 'I'm so sick, I'm so sick', a red-eyed turtle-dove joined in and cooed repetitively, 'hands up I've got you covered' with the cajoling tones of a practised gangster, a ground hornbill grumbled about the cost of living oblivious to dollarisation, 'one pound, one pound, one pound ten' and the emerald-spotted wood-dove not only bleated about the loss of his jewels but the death of his entire family 'my mother's dead, my father's dead, dead, dead'."Sibanda was the only one to hear the bush lament, his ears naturally attuned to every sound, time for him ticked by pleasantly. He broke the silence when it was becoming unbearable. 'He's dead, Phiri, bullet through the brain, a ball from a muzzle-loader, like yours.'

'What! I know nothing of this.' His growing dread said otherwise.

Ncube stepped in, the ants might feature if Phiri didn't come to his senses and start telling the truth. 'It's no good lying Phiri, we have evidence. You used patches in the muzzle loader made from fabric stolen from your uncle's workshop. The detective found a fragment in Mkandhla's brain. We know the fabric well. We sit on it every day.'

'Why would I want to kill Mkandhla? He was my partner.'

'Ivory, Phiri, the illegal distillery is just a hobby, isn't it, a bit of pocket money? We found a tusk under Mkandhla's bed. He knew there was a substantial ivory trade going on in the village and when he found out you were involved with the transport he threatened to expose it. He was blackmailing you.'

Phiri's body sagged. He raised his cuffed hands to wipe away the sweat that had become a torrent. 'I wasn't going to kill him, but …' he hesitated.

'Come on Phiri, the tale is just getting interesting; let me finish it for you. You weren't going to kill him, but you were ordered to by your masters, the ivory smugglers. They were frightened their secret ivory road would be uncovered and they had gone to a lot of trouble to keep it underground.'

The driver looked at the detective with defeat in his eyes, he turned to Ncube, hoping for support, but the sergeant just shrugged his shoulders. He had no idea how Detective Sibanda had worked it all out but he was never wrong.

Sibanda continued. 'You lured Mkandhla out to the edge of the village on the pretext of meeting your contacts for payment and then you shot him.'

'If it hadn't been for the detective finding the body and recognising a gun shot, you might have got away with it Phiri, because Mkandhla's body was burnt by a lightning strike like a bone thrown into hot coals.' It was important to underline the detective's powers. 'And what about Tiffany Price?' he added.

'Who?' Phiri looked confused.

'Never mind,' Sibanda recognised the confusion as genuine. He had never believed Phiri had had anything to do with her murder, 'but I'll find your muzzle loader, Phiri, and prove it's been used even if I have to go over the entire village with a double-sided nit comb. Come clean, it'll go better for you. Give me the names of your contacts.' Sibanda was becoming impatient.

'I can't.'

'Why are you here?' Sibanda ignored the answer, 'there are no passengers for your taxi. You've come to pick up a consignment of ivory, haven't you?'

'Yes,' whispered Phiri.

'Who's pulling the strings? Who told you the ivory would be here? Who told you to get rid of Mkandhla?' Sibanda barked out the questions.

'I can't tell you.'

'I have a nest of ants that says you can,' Sibanda strolled over to the mound and carefully picked up a straggler, 'shall I give this fellow a taste of what's to come?' He placed the ant on Phiri's good cheek, 'he'll find the banquet soon enough.'

'I can't, I can't,' Phiri was screaming now and flicking his head.

'You can, Phiri, that ant looks hungry.'

'I can't tell you because I don't know who they are.'

CHAPTER 21

'Would you have really fed Phiri to the ants, sir?'

Sibanda looked up from his desk and the cellphone he was investigating. 'Matabele ants prefer termites, but the threat worked. Phiri talked in the end.'

'But there was no ivory at the rendezvous spot and we didn't learn anything about the smuggling ring or Tiffany Price's murder and Chief Inspector Mfumu is refusing to keep the docket open on her case.' Ncube was agitated. If Detective Sibanda believed the researcher had been murdered, then he believed it too even if it was difficult to swallow, but Cold War was a blind as a worm when it came to complex cases. He preferred to sweep them out of the kraal yard like unwanted rubbish. Ncube feared the confrontation that would follow.

Sibanda didn't appear in the least concerned. 'Mkandhla's murderer is behind bars, Chanza has his robbery all neatly tied up and Gaj Patel will get his muzzle loader back. It's a good result.'

'But, sir …'

'Can you nip home Ncube?'

'During working hours? I'm on duty.'

'Yes, I'm ordering you to do a thorough search of the village for Banda Phiri's muzzle loader, starting at your house.'

'What? Why …?'

'Banda Phiri received all his instructions by text message. Firstly from Shadrek and when he was no longer available from another unknown number, which is why he hasn't a clue who his contacts are. He was waiting for delivery details. Constable Khumalo has checked with the network for a name but the account was a prepaid one, the details given obviously false.'

'So how will that help us catch the gang?'

'I have all the text messages on his phone, the last one instructs Phiri to head for the drop-off point. There's going to be a delivery of tusks in the next day or so. He was to check every morning.'

Ncube was confused, 'so why am I searching for the muzzle loader?'

'You're not, Chanza is already doing that. I want you to go home and get those wives of yours to rustle up some food. We are heading back to the river, to stake out Styx crossing and we might be there for a while. I don't want you to … er, suffer and, Ncube, don't say a word to anyone in the station. Cold War would stop us going.'

'I won't, and thank you sir, that's very thoughtful,' Ncube looked at his watch, 'but it's Friday, the prayer meeting for rain is coming up. Cold War will notice we're not there.'

Through the window, Sibanda looked at the blue, cloudless skies. 'Pointless, Ncube, today at least, and all the more reason to get a move on and out of here.'

The Zambezi River is a special spot on a mild summer's evening, like Goldilocks's porridge it's not too hot and not too cold, just perfectly delicious. A playful breeze was ruffling the reed beds, tousling their creamy linen tassels and igniting the racing river with sparkling foam. Sibanda and Ncube had parked Miss Daisy behind a bush and camouflaged her with a few branches. They had a clear view of the effervescent river and the crossing.

Ncube had been snoozing on and off. Sibanda would have liked to close his eyes for a few moments, his leg was stiff and a drain on his energy, but his brain wouldn't relax. He was frustrated. He couldn't work out who was going to pitch up, which one of the coded names. Whoever it was would need a four-wheel drive. The trip to this part of the river was rugged. That probably cut out Andries Nyathi, who was firming up as the local poacher in Sibanda's scheme of things; Ncube said the farmer didn't have any transport. Which of the suspects did he favour? Bigboy had a safari vehicle which would suit the terrain. Thomas Siziba had mentioned the vehicle he rammed into Tiffany Price to block her entry to the farm, what was it, a Land Cruiser? So, no problems there. The researchers, Mark Rhodes and Amanda Carlisle would need a robust vehicle to trek around the bush after leopard and baboons. There was no narrowing the suspects down by vehicle. They were all in the mix. Tiffany Price must have had a good idea of who the culprits were, but her diary was not conclusive. She was murdered for interfering and no wonder, a recent report had indicated that the price of ivory had risen four fold. The Far East made all the profits. Banda Phiri and the man who died in Livingstone would have made peanuts, African peanuts at that, just enough to make the risk worthwhile. The Mr Bigs of the illegal trade in wildlife were the facilitators and the end traders. Africa, as usual, was being ripped off in a neo-colonial rape of resources.

As if to underline the injustice of the trade and the meaningless end for the ivory, a herd of elephants chose that moment to cross to the nearby islands like pods of grey whales with periscopes, diving and surfacing in an effortless undulation before clambering baggily up the bank as though their trousers were falling off and melting into the foliage. Sibanda watched them with a deepening sense of futility. Was he the only person who thought ivory looked better on elephants than on the arms and in the display cabinets of the wealthy, tricked up by a dentist's drill to resemble art, or as some kind of wall trophy, a primitive chest-beating assertion of manhood?

Several of the elephant cows hesitated to examine a herd of impala picking at the island's choice grasses. Reassured, they plunged seamlessly into the reeds. Their steady, calm progress and the relaxed grazing of the impala told him that no human scent was about on the river. He stretched back in the seat and tried to get comfortable. It had already been a long wait.

Ncube stirred and reached for one of the many packages and plastic containers provided by his wives, he opened one and offered the contents to Sibanda.

The detective surveyed the green parcels sitting snugly like an army of fat caterpillars. 'What are these, Ncube?'

'Blessing's mealie meal cooked in a tomato and fried onion sauce then lined with homemade cottage cheese and wrapped in wilted spinach leaves.'

Sibanda took a bite, he didn't notice the taste, being more engrossed in the identification of a tawny flanked prinnea, just another in the amorphous pantheon of indistinguishable brown birds. Buff colours made it difficult to pin down in the fading light, but a wagtail flagging up the discovery of its own luscious morsel gave its identity away.

'I am a lucky husband,' Ncube said as he licked his finger and dipped into the container for another pupa, but he could not contemplate his good fortune or the green treat for long. Both men heard the vehicle.

'Where's that, Ncube?' Sibanda wasn't expecting a vehicle now, had he got it wrong?

'Behind us, sir, on the road that runs parallel with the river. It has gone past the turn off. It isn't coming this way.'

'What's further along, any villages?'

'No, the bush gets thicker and the road gets worse.'

Had the smugglers abandoned their crossing point, wary of police activity? Sibanda had wanted to bring a larger detachment of men with him, his leg was a hindrance and Ncube was not a sprinter, but Cold War had closed the docket on Tiffany Price, her death reported as accidental. There would be drama on his return if they didn't catch the gang. He could hear the tirade now – *waste of police resources, wild goose chase, no respect for authority, stain on your record.* It didn't bother him, his record already looked like a much-inked blotting pad, but Ncube had a family to feed. The sergeant had never questioned his theory on Tiffany Price's death, Sibanda was uncomfortable that he had doubted his loyalty.

The breeze was dropping, the evening was settling in and the sun was scarlet and puffed in the face with the effort of trying to drown itself upstream. The red orb was almost submerged, leaving a trail of blood, snot and tears bobbing on the now still waters of the Zambezi. Sibanda took his eyes from the mesmerising struggle, grounding them in the trees or on the stubbly earth for relief from the dying rays before returning to his vigil. He scanned the nocturnal burrowings of spring hares (or was it rooting porcupines?), two-day-old tracks of a big giraffe and the fresh, pointed-heart shapes of impala spoor. A lone warthog trotted past the Land Rover, unaware of the vehicle's presence, tail aloft and antenna-rigid with the assurance of a referee awarding a penalty. He wondered briefly when their stake-out would end, and if Ncube would make the football final tomorrow.

Layered against the bleeding sky, the smudged, charcoal hues of the far bank painted a perfect backdrop for the river's denizens, and as the sun finally dipped below the horizon even the crocs, basking in fearful splendour on the sandy spits, managed to look less menacing.

He nudged his sleeping companion and replaced the lid on the food. 'Ncube,' he whispered, 'wake up. Those green worms can't feed your eyes, open them and take a look at Africa.'

Ncube blinked and reached for the container of food but it had been moved to the back seat. 'Are the gang here, sir, can you see them?'

'No, but look at those hippos.' The sergeant sensed he would get no further peace until the detective had explained the creatures' habits to him. Two prime hippos postured in the channel preparing for a territorial punch-up. Their agitation of the river and the evening light set a series of liquid gold hula hoops spinning around their massive heads.

'Look, Ncube, hippos open their mouths wide when displaying. Those teeth are the most dangerous in Africa,' Sibanda pointed to a row of ivory tusks growing lethally from gums set in a cavernous mouth. 'Even though they are herbivores, they kill more people than any other animal.' Before Ncube could reply, the hippos belched their cacophonous challenge to one another.

'It's only a ritual song-and-dance affair, like a village wedding,' explained Sibanda, as the hippos started up with a boggling range of contrapuntal snorts and chortles, bellows and barks. The operatic duet ended abruptly with a clumsy, dung-dispersing pas de deux, tails whirling and the proverbial hitting the resultant fan. A hadeda ibis syncopated the chorus with his signature 'ha-de-da' as he skimmed the water. Deep in the distance a hyena added a lone, whooping contralto and a troop of cheeky vervets chattered a treble. Africa's orchestra began to tune up. Sibanda was enchanted. Ncube was horrified.

'Most dangerous creature, you say, sir,' Ncube gulped, this sort of knowledge was best left unknown.

'Actually ...' Sibanda's response was halted by a shot reverberating along the river, followed swiftly by a second. 'There's the most dangerous animal in Africa, Ncube – man. Which direction were the shots?'

'Further along the track, probably from that vehicle, what should we do, sir?'

Another shot rang out. Sibanda hesitated for a heartbeat and then replied. 'Take Miss Daisy, Ncube, and follow the tracks, get as close as you can to the shooter without alerting him. Follow on foot if you have to but don't approach, he's armed, and don't use the headlights if you can help it.'

This last instruction was no problem; it hardly made any difference if Miss Daisy's lights were on or off. 'What about you, sir?'

'I'm staying, Ncube, I'm still convinced the ivory is being transferred at this point and the moon is coming up now,' he glanced at the chipped yellow toenail paring that was rising in the eastern sky. Not full, but enough to illuminate a stairway across the river.

'I don't like to leave you here alone with all those wild creatures about and no Miss Daisy to retreat to.'

'Just go, Ncube,' he hissed, 'I can look after myself, and keep the bloody vehicle as quiet as possible.' Sibanda slipped out of the Land Rover and closed the door with not a sound. He waved Ncube on.

'Now listen, Miss Daisy, I don't ask a lot of you, but please start up as quietly as a broody hen, we could be in danger.' Ncube caressed the steering wheel, turned the key and prayed. Miss Daisy, petulant at times, cantankerous at others, understood the gravity of the situation and came to life with a whispering purr. Ncube smiled at the detective to share his pride but Sibanda had already melted into the bush. He leaned across to the back seat and retrieved the plump green parcels. No point in going hungry, he thought.

Sibanda used the crutch to hop silently behind the very tree that Tiffany Price had stood watch from. It was the perfect lookout and gave a panoramic view across the river. He had her binoculars with him, she wouldn't mind if he borrowed them to apprehend her own killer. He listened as Miss Daisy disappeared in the direction of the shots. Had he got it wrong? Had the smugglers moved their site downstream? He hoped to God they hadn't for Ncube's sake. His sergeant could be walking into a colony of mud wasps. He checked the scene, the village on the far bank was glowing with fires and the sand islands were dotted like stepping stones between the two nations. No, this was still his firm choice. He settled against the bole of the tree, taking the weight off his leg.

He put the binoculars up yet again, squinting against the darkness and the shape-shifting shadows that materialised on the islands and far bank, blinking to keep his eyes alert and wide. And then, he was convinced he saw movement. Was it genuine and not a figment of his overworked retinas? A faint wake, rippled near the Zambian bank, a hint of disturbed water edged with silver moon-tipped foam. His eyes never left the spot. He tracked the watery lace until he knew with certainty that whatever was ruffling the river was coming towards him.

It was a dug-out, the narrow shape gliding across stream, paddled by two oars. Sibanda had the binoculars trained on the two paddlers, desperate to see which culprits he was about to arrest, but the outlines in the canoe were still too vague to recognise. The pair made steady and stealthy progress. There was no chatter to echo off the banks and no hitting of paddles on the dug-out sides. He strained in the faint moonlight to pick up a clue. Halfway across and for the briefest of seconds, a moon burst gave Sibanda enough information to identify the ivory smugglers. It was only a hint of a reflection but it was an unmistakable glint. Clues tumbled into place faster than a twig over the upstream rapids. How had he missed the obvious, the coded names he couldn't interpret? Sibanda smiled wryly at Tiffany Price's sense of humour. These adversaries would be more dangerous than he thought. They had more to lose. He was going to need Ncube's help, but the bush was as silent as the river. Miss Daisy was out of earshot.

Miss Daisy was actually stationary, parked a hundred or so metres from an abandoned safari vehicle. Ncube had attempted to follow the driver on foot, but his tracking skills were less than competent during the day and at night he would be as lost as a dog with no nose, besides which the bush at night was no place for a sane man. He recognised the vehicle. He would have known it by touch alone. He prided himself on his sixth sense when it came to anything automotive. Bigboy Dube was up to no good, of that he was sure. He had been right all along, of course, Bigboy was the poacher and the murderer. He never really imagined it could be the researchers. Mark Rhodes was too in love with Tiffany Price to murder her and Amanda Carlisle was just a jealous woman and poison was the chosen murder weapon of the green-eyed monster. A poisonous dart had been used? Was there a difference? Anyway, she was now found innocent, thanks to him. The governor's nephew could not possibly be involved. The family had one maggot-riddled pumpkin in the patch. That was enough. No, it was definitely Bigboy and his evil wife, Li "Chinese Burn" Dube. The shots they had heard earlier were most likely him poaching another elephant. He would deliver the tusks to Banda Phiri's pick up point later. Case solved. The sergeant was rather proud of himself. The detective was wasting his time sitting at the river crossing. He hoped he would be safe, although the man seemed at home in the dark surrounded by lurking bush dangers. Sergeant Ncube had no intention of confronting an armed and cornered Bigboy Dube who might well shoot him with his paralysing darts. He shuddered, not able to imagine a more horrible death. Ncube had thought of a far better and less hazardous solution. It wouldn't take long and Detective Sibanda wouldn't mind the wait, he'd probably be happy idling away the minutes watching some angry creature chomping at the water.

Sibanda was listening hard for the return of Ncube and Miss Daisy. He would have to make his move soon. The dug-out wasn't far from the bank. If he let the murderers reach the shore, they might bombshell into the bush and he would have no hope of finding them. They must be stopped at the shore line. He cursed the hindrance of his stiff leg as he crawled closer to the river's edge, dragging his crutch behind him.

'Careful now, this is a tricky landing, don't wobble the boat. Let me get out first,' came the first whispering through the darkness.

'Well hurry up and get out, we're nearly at the bank,' Sibanda would have recognised the foreign voice anywhere, 'at least that bitch isn't waiting for us.'

'Thanks to you,' the voice spat with disgust, 'I never wanted to be part of a murder.' This was followed by a splash as the rear paddler left the dug-out and shoved the primitive canoe towards the sandy bank. Sibanda watched, ready to pounce. He could see tusks stacked in the boat, almost up to the edge. They had been lucky to make it across without sinking.

There was an unexpected splash, for a second Sibanda thought the dug-out had tipped it's cargo into the river.

'What the … aagh, shit, help, for God's sake help me. It's a croc,' the terrified, screaming voice disappeared under the water. Garfield Murphy emerged seconds later, gasping for breath, his good arm in the croc's jaws, his metal claw waving above his head. The river was running pink with spume whipped up from the thrashing tussle. He sucked in a few precious breaths and yelled as he fought to stay above the water, 'Jim, get here now! It's got me.' But Jim Slocum from Nottingham was frozen to the spot. He hadn't signed up for death in a crocodile's jaws. His part of the bargain was access to the Far Eastern markets. The yellow streak down his spine outshone the moonlight.

The crocodile, a wily and practised hunter, knew his craft. He took Murphy under again in a death roll. He was a Jurassic survivor, a clever stalker that had hovered a whisker below the surface, still as a log, only yellow eyes visible above the tree-shadowed water in the eddies near the bank. He had stared, unblinking, as the canoe approached, and set his trap. Now he would outlast the struggles of his exhausted prey until he could drown him and take him down to his pantry deep in the river bank to rot and ferment until the flesh fell from the bone like prime rib.

'Slocum, help me,' Murphy gasped, as he wrestled with every last sinew of strength to keep his head above the water, hacking at the croc's head with his metal hook. Slocum never answered. He was as paralysed as Tiffany Price after he had put the dart into her. His friend went under again. Large water-logged eyes begged with a scream silenced by suffocation.

Sibanda, still some distance away, took a few seconds to understand the situation. He leapt up.

'I'm coming Murphy, hang on,' he said, as he raced to the bank. He hesitated for a micro second at the water's edge; he knew that the odds of other crocodiles swimming towards the disturbance were high. Crocs were drawn to thrashing and water turbulence like hyenas to blood. It signalled easy meat. With the icy courage of this knowledge, Sibanda jumped into the churning water and reached for the desperate man.

At that moment the croc's worrying jaws broke Murphy's good arm and shredded the flesh. The sound was sickening, the ensuing scream a high-pitched cry of agony sweeping down the river. Sibanda was roaring at the predator and punching hard. He clambered onto its back wrestling the monster reptile. He tried to prise apart the jaws, but the croc rolled with ease, snapped its tail and shook him off. Now the creature had the injured man around the chest. Several layers of shark-like teeth sank into the bones. The croc could easily have latched onto Sibanda; he was as much a target, vulnerable, in deep water, heaving and bleeding from his exertions. Murphy's eyes met Sibanda's fleetingly in understanding of the shared danger before the crocodile renewed his assault, shaking and worrying the already torn flesh. Sibanda trod water, considered the options, assessed the danger and then scrambled aboard the bucking green bronco again. He clung to the bony ridged skin and reached for the eyes, blocking his ears to the shrieks and groans and the ugly sounds of ripping flesh. His fingers gouged desperately into the sockets. The croc thrashed around, trying to dislodge him. Sibanda hugged the corrugated torso with his free arm for all he was worth, the muscles in his forearm straining, but a quick flick of the tail saw him back under the water, swirling, drowning with no idea of where his next breath would come from. His life never flashed as they said it would, just an image of Berry laughing with the joy of life, her wild, white hair sweeping around her face, her eyes full of wonder and amethyst lights. He broke water in a rush and sucked in lungfuls of air. The giant water monster had gone quiet. The prey was no longer struggling. Murphy lay limp in his jaws. With one massive heave the croc threw his meal in the air and changed his bite again, grabbing Murphy's arm with the metal hook.

Sibanda saw an opportunity. He kicked towards Murphy's bloodied arm floating on the water. The croc had made a tactical error in altering his grip. Sibanda grabbed the broken and mangled limb and began to pull.

'Murphy, we can do this,' he urged, as the croc's twisting started up again, aware of the renewed struggle, shaking the man as though he were a dead chicken. The tearing vibrations shivered up through Murphy's arm into his own.

'I can't hang on much longer, I am done for. The pain in my arm is unbearable. Let me go.' The crocodile wrenched Murphy's flesh with renewed vigour.

'Can't do that, I need you to face a murder charge,' he quipped, but this was a deadly game. He could lose his prime suspect and his own life. He was tiring.

A tug of war began, Sibanda versus the crocodile with Murphy as the rope. The only spectators were a couple of cautious, heavily hunted, night-drinking elephant bulls standing at the water's edge scooping up trunkfuls of the Zambezi, their interest held momentarily by the spectacle before they resumed their nervy siphoning. Jim Slocum had legged it.

Sibanda's body beneath the water felt vulnerable. His stiches had burst and his wound was bleeding. The longer the tussle went on the more likely it would be that a second croc would arrive at the scene.

'For God's sake Murphy, try to help me, get your feet on the ground and push towards the bank.'

Murphy just groaned and rolled his eyes, he was beyond comprehension. From somewhere Sibanda found extra strength. This had to be his last effort; there was nothing left in the tank. He gripped harder on Murphy's arm, both hands clasped and every muscle straining. Was he beginning to win? Sibanda's toes touched the firm, tree-anchored mud and then his feet were grounded. He was able to pull harder. The croc, sensing it was losing impetus, whipped its tail with venom. Tremors of more bones breaking and more flesh ripping ran up Sibanda's arm, but he held firm. Briefly, the thrashing stopped. With each lull, Sibanda pulled again. He began shouting for Ncube. Where was he? He had no hope without help. Crocodiles rarely gave up.

As he heaved closer to the shallows, Sibanda had a clear view of the massive head and stinking teeth clamped onto Murphy like vice grips. He concentrated harder on the tug of war. There was blood everywhere, swirling in the churned-up mud like pink feathered icing on a chocolate cake. Despite the cloudy red film Sibanda began to see moving shadows, more sets of deadly jaws beneath the muddy water ready to join the hunt. Every fibre of his being, every survival instinct was telling him to leave the battle and get out of the water while he still could, but he never let go. Was Murphy even still alive? A groan slipped from the wounded man's bloodless lips.

'The pain ... the pain ...' came a feeble cry.

'Not as great as the agony you'll experience when I get you into court,' Sibanda encouraged, and heaved even harder. They had to get free of the river, any minute now he would be grabbed and both of them would be done for. The muscles of Sibanda's back bulged and sweat dripped from every pore. He tugged on the arm until it popped its socket and the whole of Murphy's tortured body emerged from the water, the croc still yanking on the opposite arm. Sibanda's legs almost gave way at the sight of the injuries. Garfield Murphy was a half-eaten man. Ragged wounds and deep punctures pitted his body. Needled clothes dripped blood, draining as if through a sieve. The crocodile fought its hold even on the hostile territory of dry land, but the odds were evening out. Sibanda held firm.

'Ncube,' he shouted, 'where the hell are you? Get here now!' he looked for Miss Daisy's pathetic headlights and knew he would never complain about them again.

Garfield Murphy tried to speak, to pass some last words. Only blood and spittle dribbled. Sibanda was exhausted, he couldn't hold on any longer. 'Hang on Murphy, help is coming; my sergeant is close by, listen.' And he was certain he heard it, Miss Daisy's chugging farts punctuating the night air like popping corn in a pan. Ncube was on his way. Sibanda's shouts had reached the cab as the sergeant was driving back to the crossing. The breeze had turned on a whim and taken the cries for help inland. He had driven Miss Daisy faster than he ever had before. Had he been a jockey with a whip he would have been banned for life.

Ncube raced out of the Land Rover with a deceptive turn of speed that even he didn't know he was capable of. He grabbed hold of Sibanda and added his anchoring weight to the struggle. Sibanda's urge to give up and let Ncube take over the contest was overwhelming but the fight was far from over.

'Grab a log Ncube, quickly, hit the croc, hurry up. I'm losing my grip.' The sergeant scavenged a branch from beneath his fishing tree; one that he had used often to dispatch barbel if he pulled one in. He beat the crocodile on the head, brutally and accurately with the precision of the skilled Ndebele axman he still was. Each blow hammered nails harder into Murphy's flesh, but the alternative was unthinkable.

The crocodile abruptly released his prey and with lightning speed reversed, snake-like, back to the Zambezi, jaws wide open in threat, teeth strung with blood and sinew. He sank like a stone beneath the river, invisible in seconds; a final lashing of his tail propelled him away from danger.

'Are you okay, sir?' Sibanda was sitting with Garfield Murphy's body across his legs.

'I'm fine Ncube,' Sibanda struggled to speak, gasping for air, 'but it was a close run thing. This man is going to need urgent medical attention. His partner, Jim Slocum has run away.'

'He won't get far, I'm sure he was meeting up with Bigboy Dube, that's who was shooting, and he isn't going anywhere. I have disabled his vehicle.' Ncube took a piece of turned metal from his pocket and threw it in the air before catching it. Sibanda had no idea what it was but he trusted his sergeant's mechanical ability. If he said the vehicle was disabled then it was.

We've got The Cat, Ncube. Garfield is a famous American comic strip character, a marmalade *umgodoyi*. I should have got that earlier, and Snail Spunk is on the run.'

'Snail Spunk?'

Ncube wouldn't get the joke or the humour involved, 'I'll explain that one later.'

'The man's metal hand is missing. The crocodile must have swallowed it.' Ncube had been fascinated by the metal limb since first catching sight of it and now the thought of the crocodile making off with it sent a wave of revulsion through his gut. The gurgling was ominous.

'Shades of Captain Hook, Ncube,' Sibanda quipped, still catching his breath, 'but where were Peter Pan and Tinkerbell when I needed them?'

'Interesting,' Ncube answered, believing the exhausted detective was becoming delusional and confused with talk of snails and pans and bells. You could hardly blame him; the struggle had been courageous. Ncube knew he would have left Murphy to his fate. He would never have jumped into the water. He shuddered at the thought and his stomach sloshed. He moved on to other thoughts. The detective was crazy, mad and difficult, but he was a man of steel forged from the bones of his brave Ndebele ancestors. He walked a few metres away to spare the detective his digestive affliction.

'Are you okay, Murphy, can you hear me?' Sibanda was trying to stem the blood flow by applying pressure to the worst of the wounds and wrapping strips of his shirt around others.

Murphy didn't reply, but a hint of a smile puckered his lips and then he gasped, 'but you got it wrong, Detective, I am not the murderer.' His blood was pumping fast and red over Sibanda's arms and knees. Sibanda's bleeding thigh wound joined the stream. Together the life blood of the poacher and the detective dripped along a runnel of mud into the Zambezi, diluting with the current to swirl over rapids, weave through steep-sided gorges, linger in a Mozambican lake, power electricity schemes, and finally, after an epic journey, reach the Indian Ocean more than three thousand kilometres away.

EPILOGUE

Garfield Murphy was in hospital and would be for some months. His injuries were catastrophic. The prognosis for his remaining arm was not good. Jim Slocum had been picked up three days later wandering, lost, terrified and dehydrated near the river. All that water and too frightened to drink. He babbled like a baby, spilling the story of the poaching ring. With his travel experience in the Far East he had set up the market place, got the orders, but he needed the product. He started a tour operation in Zimbabwe and met up with Garfield Murphy. It was the perfect match. Murphy had the contact at Thunduluka Lodge who could direct operations so their names would stay out of the chain. Andries Nyathi, the brother of Shadrek the cook, and Murphy had been boyhood friends since he lost his arm in a shooting accident. They had some kind of blood brother thing going. Shadrek had recruited Banda Phiri as part of the transport link. Andries had got Bigboy Dube involved. It was a clever arrangement because hardly anyone knew who else was part of the gang. Secret drop-off points had been set up. It had all gone wrong when Shadrek had lost his job and Tiffany Price, living at Thunduluka, had got wind of the ivory.

'Yes, I shot her, Murphy was too squeamish,' Jim Slocum was blubbering, 'she'd found us with a load of ivory we'd just brought across the river. I grabbed Murphy's weapon. I didn't know it was a dart gun. I've got no experience with weapons. I aimed for her head, Murphy tried to stop me, he pushed the barrel upwards, but a dart isn't like a bullet, it drops quickly, in an arc. It struck her in the thigh. Murphy said no one would know because the drug was invisible, couldn't be detected. He swept away all our footprints afterwards. I thought it was the perfect murder.'

Ncube offered him a handkerchief, his dribbling nose was an ugly sight in the sly face. 'It would have been if not for Detective Sibanda. He was the only one who thought Tiffany Price had been murdered.'

Sibanda had checked Murphy's darting log. He regularly used acetyl choline, the drug Buff had talked about. Jim Slocum would go down for one murder and inciting another. He had instructed Banda Phiri to dispose of David Mkandhla. Garfield Murphy was charged as an accessory and for concealing a crime. When he was well enough and if they ever found enough spare skin to patch him up, he would stand trial. Who knew when that would be, infections were setting in; croc teeth were a rotting hive of foetid bacteria. Sibanda was lucky; after he was restitched he kept up with Blessing's potions. His wound was clean and healing.

Bigboy had been picked up for transporting ivory and adding a few tusks to the pot. He couldn't give any further information because he didn't know who was involved. This had been his first rendezvous. They hadn't found Andries Nyathi yet. He had disappeared, probably lying low until the heat was off. The names of the poaching ring had been communicated to the Zambian police. The little village on the opposite bank had been raided. Everyone believed the poaching tide had been stemmed for now. Far Eastern names were bandied, but Sibanda knew it was futile to pursue them. They had political cover and not only in Asia.

A week later the news broke of the death of a hundred and fourteen elephants in the park, making the ivory gang's haul look like matchsticks. The herd had been poisoned with cyanide, and found dead at a waterhole. A passing helicopter had reported the slaughter. Every tusk was gone, already smuggled. Sibanda was depressed. Buff's 'black dogs' had attacked. The future for wildlife was bleak. Would they ever be able to stop the poaching? When he got the phone call from Mark Rhodes he was grateful to get out of the office, the suffocating paperwork was killing him and Mfumu's tirades were becoming intolerable. The Officer-in-Charge had received a reprimand from the Minister of Transport for the beating up of his innocent nephew Lazarus Maphosa. He had swung angrily through the station. Ncube had said he was like a bull after a session with the burdizzos. And then the US Embassy had complained to the Minister for Home Affairs that no one told them there was a murder investigation ongoing. Mfumu received a further rap on the knuckles. He was apoplectic, his dreams of escape from the rural Matabele backwater scuttled. His target was Sibanda, the cause of all his troubles. The office tension was ratcheting up again and the compensatory spring cleaning unrestrained. PC Tshuma was whitewashing the rocks around the flagpole and PC Khumalo was down on her hands and knees polishing the floors; a fetching sight, thought Ncube who had conveniently allotted himself the scrubbing of nearby walls with sugar soap. They chatted about how Mandebele Giants had let themselves down in the final, still, there was always next year. Crime took a back seat.

Sibanda jumped into Miss Daisy and set off for the research station. The day was still young and Miss Daisy amenable. His mood lifted with the view of a bachelor herd of zebra grazing placidly on the summer grasses. A troop of baboons lazily picked at seeds and beetles and their own parasites while overhead a pair of blue-grey flycatchers were hawking for insects disturbed by the baboons and the scattering, chattering play of the youngsters.

'I'm sorry to call you, Detective, but you're the best person to deal with this. I know you've been busy with Tiffany's murderers. I'm glad you caught the murdering scumbags.'

'What about Miss Carlisle?'

'She's gone home. The relationship wasn't working,' a wistful expression came over his face with the realisation of what might have been had Tiffany Price lived.

'But that's not why you've called me out. It sounded urgent.'

'It is. I was tracking one of my collared leopards early this morning and I found a body in the bush.'

When Sibanda and Mark Rhodes reached the victim, a hideous sight awaited. The body had been hauled up a tree and partially eaten. A few shreds of clothing clung in rags, and on the dangling feet that hung from chewed and fly-blown legs were a pair of boots with smaller soles tacked on the bottom.

'I don't understand; leopards rarely attack unless they're injured or cornered. Poppy is fit and healthy or at least she was a couple of days ago.' The researcher was distressed.

Sibanda found the drag mark. 'Let's follow this to the site of the attack. We may get a better idea from there.'

The kill site wasn't far away. The earth was scuffled and pools of blood had soaked into the sand. The victim had tried to run leaving a blood trail, but disoriented, he had run straight into a tree. His foot prints had been going around in ragged circles for some time before the leopard pounced. Under the tree was a rifle.

'What on earth is that,' Mark Rhodes asked, 'some kind of antique?'

'Yes, it's an old muzzle loader and, oddly, I've seen a few of them lately.' The weapon had been fired recently. Black powder and heavy burn marks around the flashpan indicated quite a flare up. He turned the ancient polished butt over in his hands. The name Andries was carved into the stock. An even older monogram in formal lettering was on the butt end, but it meant nothing to Sibanda. He might ask Berry about it. 'It's a local poacher, Andries Nyathi. We've been looking for him in connection with the ivory poaching. Irony I suppose, the poacher poached.'

'Andries? I didn't recognise him. He was one of our leopard spotters, the best, but we always suspected he was a bit of a scoundrel. Good in the bush, knew his stuff.'

'He was a supreme bush man. He certainly knew a thing or two about tracking.'

Back at the body, the scene began to make sense. Sibanda climbed the tree and looked at the face of the dead man. There was little doubt that he had been blinded by an explosion of powder from the muzzle loader. Severe burn marks around the eye sockets told a tale. How long had he been wandering alone, sightless and desperate? He might have been able to make some headway to the boundary by feeling the sun on his face, but he would never have found water. He must have been on his last legs when the leopard attacked.

'So Poppy's not a man eater?' Mark Rhodes was relieved.

'No, just following the law of the bush, dispatching the wounded. She's innocent.'

They drove back to the research station with the remains of Andries Nyathi wrapped in a blanket.

'Must be terrible to be blind in the bush. We alerted Parks to a giraffe that had lost its sight. Poor buggar had been hanging about near the waterhole for weeks, just skin and bones. They shot it.'

'Why would a giraffe go blind? A spitting cobra couldn't reach those eyes.'

'No, it was caused by a cattle eye moth, one of the body fluid suckers. They live on eye secretions and spread eye disease. This virus probably came from a cow on the boundary.'

'That doesn't sound healthy.'

'Not as unhealthy as the vampire moth but that's only found in Asia.'

'We have enough of our own parasites here.' Mark Rhodes glanced across at the detective for traces of double entendre, but his expression was bland.

'In Madagascar, there's even a moth that looks for sleeping birds, feeds on their tears. It pokes its harpoon-shaped proboscis in between the eyelids, sucking out the liquid while the bird dozes.'

'Have you added any more moths to the collection?'

'No, I've done my ten, that's enough for me.'

'You said something about the death's head moth and another literary connection last time we met.'

'Don't you remember *The Silence of the Lambs*? It was a pretty creepy book, and a horror movie. The moth was used as the calling card of the serial killer, Buffalo Bill. He stuffed it down his victims' throats.'

Sibanda wouldn't share that bit of information with Ncube. After dropping Mark Rhodes at the research station, he headed back to Gubu with only the remnants of Andries Nyathi for company. Miss Daisy was travelling solemnly and with dignity. Sibanda tried to coax a bit more speed out of the old dear but she refused. She took her hearse duties seriously.

When his phone chirped with the nightjar's song he was ready to pull over and defuse his frustration.

'Hi Jabu,' Berry sounded cheery and exactly the boost he needed, 'just thought I'd catch up. I heard you captured the murderers. Were they among the coded names in Tiffany Price's diary?'

'It was The Cat and Snail Spunk – Garfield and Slocum.' A tinkling laugh travelled through the phone and into his heart, he loved her quick wit and sense of humour, 'I never worked out File though.'

'Any clues?'

'It might be someone called Marx Gumbo, he wasn't involved, although for a time I thought he might be. He had been up on the Zambezi with his mate Jefferson Airplane who had a motive. But it was just unscheduled time off from Hunter's Rest. They had taken a couple of girls on a jaunt. But why File?'

She laughed again, 'I've got it! It's not File, it's Fillet, but it's spelt File. It's from New Orleans – File Gumbo, a spicy fish and chicken dish from the southern states of the USA.'

He wasn't sure he would ever have cracked that one, 'what about Mjr Sir WCH?'

'Why are you asking, was it in the diary?'

'No, it's on an old weapon I found in the bush.'

'Does it have a date?'

I can't see one, but it has the name of the owner, Andries, carved in crude letters on the stock.'

'You might have a real historical piece Jabu. Mjr Sir WCH could be Major Sir William Cornwallis Harris. He was one of the earliest hunters to come here. A famous Hottentot called Andries Africander hunted for him. Cornwallis Harris even gave him a wife, the luscious Truey Davids, passed her on when he'd had his fill. She had been kidnapped by Mzilikazi in one of his raids on the Griqwas and given to Cornwallis Harris as a gift. Shocking the way they treated woman in those days like chattels ...

'Are you listening Jabu, or are you mocking me again?' Sibanda was smiling at her fiery feminism. He loved it that she wasn't a pushover like other girls he'd dated. Maybe that's what attracted him to her so much.

'I'm still here, Berry.'

'We'll, there are plenty of pictures of Cornwallis Harris and Andries Africander with an old weapon. I'll try to find a book. Maybe we can match them up.'

'Okay, Miss History Buff, here's a puzzle for you. Can you find my house this evening and come for a drink and tell me the whole story then? I have a decent bottle of red left over from my brother's last visit. It's in one of the packing boxes. I've moved house,' Sibanda held his breath, had he kept the invitation light enough, flippant?

A sunbird's wing-beat of hesitation followed, 'I'd love to, Jabu. Where are you living now?'

'Buffalo Avenue. I moved in a couple of days ago, last house on the road.'

'I'll be there.'

Lazarus Maphosa's father had turned out to be the Head of Railways and was grateful to Sibanda for releasing his son. 'Is there anything I can do for you?' he had asked. Sibanda was quick off the mark with his request. Once he had the key, Ncube's wives had gathered with pails and mops, polish and dusters and had licked the derelict house into liveable condition. It still needed a heap of work but he would take it slowly. He smiled at the lie; if he was honest he would probably do nothing at all. The veranda with a good scotch and a view of the bush made up for no curtains, chipped tiles, a brown, lime-scaled toilet and a barely functioning shower, cousin to the one he had just left.

As the sun was setting, highlighting the season's grasses with yellow, the distant trees with an orange halo and the tip of the mare's tail clouds with a bubbly pink, as birds flocked to roost and twittered 'goodnight' and ducks flew in V formation, wheeling across the marbled sky, there was a rap on the door.

'Hi, Detective Sibanda, you haven't been to have your wound re-dressed for days,' it was Angel Better, 'Sister Hove from the hospital has been pestering me to check on you. I was in the area so I thought I'd pop in and save you a trip to the clinic.'

'Right, er, will it take long?'

'Ten minutes, at most.'

Once again Sibanda's pants were around his knees and he found himself laughing along with Sister Angel Better as she regaled him with her stories of how local lothario and cool kid, Tembo Chimuka, had sat on a buffalo bean and been stung on the buttocks with thousands of small hairs that itched until he had to visit the clinic and have them individually tweezered out along with his dignity, and how old Mavis Ndanga, stalwart of the church, had got her wide-knuckled hand caught in the narrow opening of her neighbour's maize bin and had to be wheeled to the clinic in a barrow with everyone pointing fingers.

Through the window, Berry watched the merriment of Jabu enjoying an evening with his girlfriend. In her hands was the housewarming present she had searched her house for earlier. It was a small Cape yellowwood and stinkwood table that had made the journey to

Zimbabwe with her mother's family in 1889, a prized possession. She had wanted him to have it and to know how much she thought of him, how much she loved him. There, she'd said it, if only to herself. She had loved him forever, since the first time they met at a Nottingham bus stop in a deluge. He had offered her his umbrella and they had discovered they were both homesick Zimbabweans. She and Jabu had laughed and joked and reminisced, nostalgia threatening to overwhelm them. Now he would never know how she felt and it was probably better, she might have embarrassed them both. Tears welled and ran down her cheeks. She wiped them away harshly; she had to be stronger than this.

As she strode back to her car, she remembered a couple of lines of poetry from school, '*Tis better to have loved and lost/Than never to have loved at all.* She had thought it endlessly romantic at the time. Now she knew it was rot. The poet, Tennyson, can never have known a love like this or what it was like to lose it. Berry wished for all the world she'd never met Jabulani Sibanda, she wished she could run away and hide again or curl up with Luka and let him lick the deep wounds in her heart, but Luka was dead and Jabu might as well be. Instead, she closed the car door softly, gave freedom to her tears and drove off into the colourless African night.

ACKNOWLEDGEMENTS

My thanks to my editor, Megan Southey; to Peter Cook for his memories; to Paul de Montille for his information on darting drugs, although I stress that any errors in this field are mine; to the Bulawayo book club girls who keep me sane; and to my family and friends near and far for their encouraging support.